ADVANCE PRAIS.

"*Grace in the Flames* is a beautiful, heartrending depiction of God's love and grace. The characters' struggles, mistakes and pain were achingly real and God's faithfulness was the path-lighting ember in each of the characters' journeys. This is an emotionally evocative and profoundly moving tale of mistakes redeemed and lives intertwined in a divine tapestry of grace and hope. Highly recommended."

— Cheryl Wyatt, USA TODAY bestselling author
of award-winning *Wings of Refuge* series.

"Michelle Massaro's distinctive voice captivates and enthralls in this outstanding debut novel. *Grace in the Flames* is unforgettable...out of the ordinary...pure literary magic. I look forward to whatever comes next from this talented author."

— Delia Latham, Inspirational Romance Author

"*Grace in the Flames* is a stouthearted story of people who find grace, forgiveness, and hope through their pain, loss, and regrets. Massaro crafts a vivid picture of redemption in her debut novel."

— Jessica R. Patch, author of the Seasons of Hope series, Fatal
Reunion, and Protective Duty.

GRACE *in the* FLAMES

MICHELLE MASSARO

Orange Grove
Press

Published in Corona, California, by Orange Grove Press.

Scriptures taken from the Holy Bible, New International Version®, NIV®. Copyright © 1973, 1978, 1984, 2011 by Biblica, Inc.™ Used by permission of Zondervan. All rights reserved worldwide. www.zondervan.com

Scripture taken from the New King James Version®. Copyright © 1982 by Thomas Nelson. Used by permission. All rights reserved.

Publisher's note: This novel is a work of fiction. Names, characters, places, and incidents are either products of the author's imagination or used fictitiously. All characters are fictional, and any similarity to people living or dead is purely coincidental.

ISBN-13: 978-0997327304 (Trade Paper)
ISBN-10: 0997327308
LCCN: 2016902786

Printed in the United States of America.

For Jehovah-Jireh, my provider.

And for my family, who have stood beside me on the journey.
You are my heart.

"Though he slay me, yet will I trust in him."
JOB 13:15a (NKJ)

Prologue

Blessings are not evidence of faith. Not something to be earned through checking off the tick marks of religiosity. John Douglas understood well enough that God cannot be directed or contained—and the danger of attempting to do so. Whether He gives or takes away, God is still God. And life without Him is no life at all. In everything John had been through, he'd learned this: there is no *why*.

There is only do you love Him still, do you love Him *even if?*

John peered up at the fluffy white clouds drifting across the blue November sky. *Yes, Lord. No matter what happens after today, I will love you.* He rested his elbows on his knees and gazed out across the landscape. From somewhere deep within, an assuring anchor steadied him. He checked the time. She'd be here soon.

Despite what the fairy tales would have people believe, deep and passionate love *was* possible more than once. John knew this firsthand.

He'd met her after the worst of his nightmare was past—when he was full of the exuberance of being newly sober, newly forgiven. Her tenderness strengthened him through those first months of thirst and healing. Her smile blew hope through his dusty heart until it came alive again to love.

John had come alive in a lot of ways these last six months.

After all these years, he was finally beginning to understand what faith meant.

His throat went dry as he watched his shaking hands.

He had no delusions about happily-ever-afters. Doing the right thing did not mean he would get to keep the girl. In fact, it likely meant exactly

1

the opposite. But, it was time to put feet to his faith and act on what he had learned.

No matter the cost.

And so he sat here on the park bench, waiting to do the one thing he never imagined he'd have to do.

Lay his love on the altar.

Chapter One

Two years earlier

Hannah Douglas sang softly as she pressed her fingers into the ground beef, pushing it into the corners of the loaf pan. She moved to the sink to wash her hands then plucked her wedding ring from the window sill. The diamond glittered in the late afternoon sunbeams. She slipped it on with a smile, glad to have it back on her hand rather than the chain around her neck—the only place for it when her fingers had swollen to twice their usual size. Along with her feet and face.

The bundle secured to her chest squirmed.

"Shh." Hannah swayed side to side as she moved about the kitchen, grabbing the pan and sliding it into the oven, then firing on the burner under the potatoes. So far so good on Operation Romantic Dinner.

She padded into the living room and lowered herself into a chair. The bundle squirmed again and emitted a sad, desperate noise.

Hannah offered a sympathetic face. "I know, little one. You want your dinner too."

Snug within the folds of cotton wrapped around Hannah's body, little Katy brought a tiny fist to her cheek. She'd been patient long enough. Hannah smiled and loosened the knot of fabric at her hip. A moment later, the material had been tossed onto the arm of the couch and the infant lay on Hannah's knees, her arms and legs flailing. The tiny face scrunched and reddened and a heartbreaking cry filled the air. A knot formed in Hannah's belly.

The familiar tingling sensation quickened her efforts with her blouse. "Hang on, sweetheart. Mama's hurrying."

The baby wailed again.

"Shh. Shh." Hannah guided the newborn into position and felt a gentle tug as Katy latched on. The rhythmic action caused Hannah's body to release the sole nourishment for her daughter. Once again, the awe of it welled up inside Hannah's heart.

She smiled down at her baby. "Is that better, love?" Hannah brought her fingertips to Katy's soft forehead and smoothed the thin blond wisps on the side of her head.

Katy's greedy gulps melted the tension of Hannah's long day. Heaviness weighted Hannah's eyes but she resisted closing them, instead savoring the sight of her daughter nursing. She hummed as she relished the feel of the warm baby in her arms. *Lord, help me be a good mother. Help me show Katy how much she is loved.*

Katy pressed her fist against Hannah's flesh and blinked up at her. Hannah lifted the tiny fingers and kissed them. "My sweet girl." She leaned her head back against the soft leather of the recliner and yawned.

Twenty minutes later, Hannah carried sleeping Katy to the bassinet in the master bedroom and lowered her into it. "Night night, little one. Sleep a good few hours for me, okay? I miss your daddy." She closed the door softly behind her and crept back out to the living room. John would be home soon.

Her pulse jumped and a smile spread across her face. In short time, she lit the candles on the dining table and cleared the cushions of baby blankets and burp cloths. The potatoes were a bit overdone by the time she drained and mashed them, but they'd do.

The door handle turned.

Hannah hurried to the entry to greet her husband. "Hi." She beamed at the sight of him—blond hair askew, exhausted as she was, and...home.

He stepped in and looked around. "Hi yourself. What smells so good?"

"Meatloaf and mashed potatoes." His favorite. No frozen meal tonight.

John's eyebrows rose.

Hannah grinned and slipped her arms around his neck. "Did you have a good day at work?"

"I did." John tossed his keys on the coffee table and ran his hands up and down Hannah's arms. "What's all this for?"

Hannah shrugged and buried her fingers in the hair on the back of his neck. "Just felt like it."

"You did?"

"Mm hmm." She pulled his head down for a peck. "I missed you today."

"I missed you too." He wrapped her in a hug. "Both of you. Where's my Katy bug?"

"Sleeping. Hopefully, for a couple more hours." Butterflies flitted about in her stomach. Pressing into him, she looked into his eyes. "They say six-week-olds should start sleeping longer stretches at night. I think we're getting there."

John tucked her hair behind her ear, and she leaned into his hand. "Six weeks already?"

She nodded and planted a kiss on his throat. "Yes."

His Adam's apple moved beneath her lips as he swallowed. She felt his pulse throb.

As bone-tired as she was, she missed her husband—missed the way he held her, the way he responded to her touch, the way their souls intertwined when they were together.

John hooked a finger under her chin and tipped her face up. He stared at her with those blue eyes that had stolen her breath for years. Hannah studied the angles of his face, the squareness of his jaw, the whiskers of his five o'clock shadow. Her heart hammered as he leaned in and touched his lips to hers.

The food would get cold. But if he didn't mind, neither did she.

He tipped her head to the side and kissed the soft spot below her ear. "I love you," he whispered.

She closed her eyes. "I love you too." She trailed her fingers across his chest. "What did we do to be so blessed?"

"We did things God's way. We waited."

A flicker of uncertainty passed over her, but at John's kiss, it vanished.

The baby monitor carried the sound that shattered the sacred moment. Hannah dropped her head and groaned. *Come on, Lord, can't we get a break here?* John's chuckle caught her by surprise, and she cut her gaze to him. "What?"

"Looks like we're not done waiting."

She let out a soft laugh despite herself.

When she moved toward the bedroom, John caught her arm. "I'll get her. And don't worry. It'll be worth the wait." A sly smile curved his mouth.

"At least we'll get to eat our dinner while it's still somewhat warm."

"See, there's always a bright side."

She watched her husband disappear down the hall and return a moment later with a fussy Katy.

She reached out for the baby. "She probably needs a fresh diaper."

"I got it." He patted Katy's back.

Hannah followed him into the nursery and watched him gingerly lay her on the changing table. The painted scripture on the wall arched above them: *I will rejoice over you with singing.* "What a beautiful picture you make."

John glanced at her, Katy's raised feet clasped in one hand, a baby wipe in the other, and lifted a brow. "Are you kidding me right now?"

She shook her head in the negative. "I'm absolutely serious. I've never been more attracted to you." A new father caring for his baby's needs, the soft pink room, the Bible verse…

"All right, Katy bug. Is this better?" He finished the task and snapped Katy's onesie back in place, then lifted her to his chest. He bounced her softly but she continued to screech and cry. "Okay, guess not." John looked at Hannah and raised his brows. "Music time?"

Maybe hot meals were over-rated. She sighed. "Looks like it." Microwaves worked wonders, right?

He handed the baby to her and went to wash his hands and retrieve his guitar. Hannah cooed and smiled at the fussing infant, cradling her head in her palm as John sat and began picking notes of a G chord. Eyes locked on Katy's, Hannah began to sing. She sang of God's great love, of wellsprings of life, of rest for the weary. And, sweet Jesus, was she weary. But oh, so happy. Her gaze moved to her husband, his fingers gently plucking the soft melody, adoring eyes resting on his baby girl.

Katy's eyes finally closed, her tiny chest rising and falling in slumber. A tear fell down Hannah's face as the song faded. "Works every time," she whispered.

"Hey, honey...are you okay?" John set down the guitar and squeezed Hannah's shoulder.

Hannah sniffed and wiped a palm across her cheek. "Yes. Don't mind me. It's just...hormones." She produced a wobbly smile, her eyes welling again.

John returned Katy to her bassinet then came and knelt in front of Hannah. He cradled her face in his hands and smiled. "It's overwhelming sometimes, isn't it?" He moved to the couch and patted his knee. "Come here."

Hannah sat on his lap, encircled in his arms, and nuzzled her face into his neck. As his fingers played up and down her back, she registered the spike in his pulse against her cheek, quickening her breath. Running her hand over his chest, she captured his earlobe between her lips then whispered, "No more waiting."

"Thank you, God." He scooped her up and stood, carrying her into the bedroom as she dotted his throat with kisses.

Yes, thank God. From whom *all* blessings flow. And she had so many. But none better than this man right here, holding her tight; caressing her, loving her.

As he lowered her down, she pulled his face close and pressed a kiss to his jaw. "I love you," she murmured over the pulse roaring in her ears.

"Oh, Hannah." His ragged voice elicited gooseflesh. "I love you too. Forever."

He covered her mouth with his and words fell away as he deepened his kiss and sent her body soaring.

Nothing existed beyond this right here. Hannah had everything she could ever imagine wanting. Enough blessings to last a lifetime. Nothing could take that away.

John scanned his list of international suppliers. Saphira International needed a hero—and John needed it to be him.

A miscalculation of square footage had them short on their out-of-stock laminate flooring. If he could swoop in and save the day for such a big client, he'd soar into next week's performance review. Then he'd emerge victorious, and Hannah would bounce and laugh and say he was *the man.*

Visions of the scene flashed through his mind—Hannah's dimpled smile that slammed his heart into overdrive, her delicate hand pulling his head down for a kiss, the warm, newborn bundle cradled in the curve of her neck. She would be thrilled. They could get out of Indiana for that long-awaited beach vacation this summer. And most important, a hefty raise would allow Hannah to stay home with little Katy bug, which surely was God's will. John would give Him all the glory.

But first, he needed seventeen more boxes of Harvest Oak #H327.

Phone lights flashed—suppliers on hold from Germany, India, Belgium—and Japan refused to answer. "Come on, pick up." John's growl blended with the grumble of the copy machine. His leg bounced in time with the pencil he tapped on the desk. *Please, Japan, have what I need.*

The future was so close, on the other end of a phone line.

A rap on the door preceded Misty poking her head through. "Mr. Douglas? Your mother's holding on line one."

John rubbed away the tension headache mounting in his temples. "Tell her I'll call her back in an hour. I'm swamped."

Misty hesitated. "She…says it's urgent."

Pushing down the clipped words forming on his tongue, John drew in a slow breath. "Okay Misty, put it through please."

He glanced at the cell phone on his desk, set to silent, and noted three missed calls and a text.

Germany's light quit flashing. *Great.* Japan still hadn't answered.

What could be urgent? Was Dad okay? Maybe Mom just wanted to know what to bring for dinner tonight. Wonderful grandma that she was, she'd offered to drop off a meal so Hannah could rest. God love her.

Germany's button re-lit with Mom's call. John inhaled lacquer-tainted air and used the pencil eraser to push the call button. "Sorry, Mom, I'm super busy—"

"John, you need to get home!"

He yanked the receiver away a few inches. Straightening in his chair, he tried to decipher her unfamiliar tone. "Mom? You okay?"

"Do you hear me, honey? You need to come home." She'd lowered her voice a notch, but it was still steeped in anxiety.

A sick feeling bubbled in John's stomach. "Yeah, I hear you. Are you all right? Something wrong with Dad? Listen, just let me—"

"No, John. *Now.*"

His breathing stopped. His ears went hot. An eerie knowing settled over him, and he shivered as sweat seeped into his shirt out of nowhere.

What was this? Fear crept into his chest and seized his lungs.

He spooned out his words slow and measured. "Mom, you're freaking me out. What's going on?"

"Listen to me." The last word squeaked to a halt, followed by staccato breath. "There's a fire. You need to come *home.*"

For a second—or an eternity—life froze. Thought spun away. Then he propelled himself from his office chair. He darted around supply boxes, shoved past faceless bodies of customers and coworkers, raced down aisles of paint cans and carpet samples, and somehow emerged through the glass doors into the parking lot. His dead legs barely kept him moving, but he had to get to his family. His breath came in puffs and did little to unwrap the invisible fingers squeezing his insides.

"Oh, Jesus, help." He fumbled with the keys, then forced his hands to stop shaking. From the corner of his eye, he registered Katy's car seat, and his knees buckled. "Father...Oh Jesus, please. Please, please, *please!*" He swallowed back the sour taste as a new surge of panic boiled up from his chest.

Breathe. Just breathe.

He had to calm down. Hannah probably left something on the stove too long. Surely, he'd come home to a kitchen full of white foam and a distraught wife. Nothing more dramatic than that. John mashed buttons on his phone as he slammed the car door shut. The missed text was from Hannah that morning—the Scripture-of-the-day and a note that she was joining the baby for a nap in their room. His muscles relaxed a bit. Still, he floored the gas pedal as he punched in her speed dial.

No answer.

"Argh!" John pitched the worthless phone onto the passenger seat and sped past a stop sign. Even before he turned the corner onto River Birch Drive, the wail of sirens assaulted his ears and billows of black smoke drifted into view. This was no pan on the stove...and it couldn't really be happening.

9

Screeching the car to a halt, he stared out over his steering wheel. The acrid stench of melting plastic and burnt wood wafted through the vents. His heart thudded as he took in the scene. Men shouted to each other outside the car window. Ashes were everywhere—falling down through the air, onto his car, onto the ground, swirling in the breeze.

He shot out of the car, not bothering to close the door.

"Hannah!" Her name dissolved in a cough. The sun disappeared behind smoky clouds. John's throat burned and his eyes watered.

"Hannah, where are you?"

Within two breaths, soot coated his tongue. He covered his mouth and nose with his arm and scanned the scene. A charred maple branch cracked and crashed in his front yard. The shrubs were a blackened tangle.

"Mom, are you here?" Eyes wide, he zeroed in on one insane detail after another.

A fire truck, lights flashing, blocked his driveway. Neighbors dotted the street, staring. Mrs. Anderson held a rag over her mouth and nose as she talked with a firefighter.

His gut seized. Where was Hannah? Brushing past an officer, John charged toward the house. Through the smoke and water spray he made out what was left of it.

It wasn't much. A burnt-out husk.

From inside, a flash of water hit the glass and the front window blew out. John staggered back as glass peppered the splintered porch. He coughed, watching smoke curl up and away from this surreal version of his home.

The image didn't fit. He kept trying to wrap his mind around it like an elastic band that couldn't stretch quite far enough. He searched for something familiar—a face or a scrap of lawn to prove this was his life.

There was Mom, standing at the curb and staring as firefighters buzzed around. John rushed toward her, eyes glued to her tear-stained cheeks. Her graying blonde hair blew away from her face and her hands were clasped under her chin. Her lips moved in familiar, silent prayer. As John approached, she glanced up, pain evident in her puffy eyes.

"Mom, where's Hannah?" He searched her lined face for the answer he so desperately needed.

Her brows pulled together and her mouth hung open, silent. She moved her head from side to side.

"Where *is* she?" He choked on the words, his mind running through the endless possibilities. Was she giving a statement? Was she at the hospital? Had she...been hurt?

"Oh, John, I'm so sorry. I'm so sorry, baby." A fit of sobs overtook her, and she collapsed into his arms.

Baby. Where was *his* baby?

"Mom?" John whispered. "Katy...what about Katy?" He leaned back to see her face. His mother's lips pinched shut and her chin quivered. She clung to the front of his shirt and hung her head. A scratchy moan escaped her throat. An approaching fireman saved John from the urge to rattle her and scream for answers.

"Sir, are you John Douglas?" His raspy voice was much too grave.

John inhaled and straightened, trying to pull himself together. "Yes. What....?" He struggled to form words. "Where's my family? They need me." His eyes raked the crowd, searching for Hannah's blonde hair and slender frame. She was here somewhere.

She had to be.

The man placed a hand on John's arm. "Please come with me—"

John wrenched his arm from the man's grasp. "I'm not going anywhere until I find Hannah and Katy." Mom clutched his shirt tighter as he cupped his hand around his mouth. "Hannah—I'm here, honey!" His ears strained for the sound of Katy's newborn cry. Mom's sobs turned to wails, and she pressed her cheek to his chest, hands gripping his arms as though she'd collapse without holding on.

"Sir."

Unless...maybe this man wanted to bring him to his family. John nodded. He reclaimed his arms from around his mother, who found the strength to stand on her own. She covered her face with her hands and rocked back and forth. When John squeezed her shoulder and stepped back, she made no move to follow. The fireman led him away from the chaos toward an ambulance. The back doors hung open.

John's shoulders relaxed. Hannah must be there. Of course.

She must be a wreck. He ached to pull her close and ease the fear from her. They'd get through this. Insurance would cover the loss, their church family would support them any way they could. Everything would be okay.

He walked faster, imagining her ordeal. They would be giving her oxygen to clear her lungs of smoke. She was probably sitting with a medic blanket around her shoulders, holding a mask to her face—like on TV.

But when they got around to the other side, the ambulance stood empty.

John's breath burst in and out of his lungs. Casting off panic, he clung to white-hot fury. He bit his lower lip, but the words would not be swallowed. He glared at the fireman beside him and heard a high-pitched, maniacal version of his own voice. "Where are Hannah and Katy? Tell me where they are!" He stood, chest heaving, trying not to murder the man who had the answers.

"John, please sit down." The man's patience unnerved John. But he forced himself to obey, sitting on the back of the ambulance—in Hannah's spot.

"The fire was called in by a neighbor. Ramona Anderson. The damage is concentrated on the right side of the structure. Most likely started with the space heater, but it will be several days before we can determine a cause."

John's blood boiled as he squinted at the man. Why was he going over this now? John didn't care about the stupid report. He had to find his wife and baby.

"It spread too fast. We did everything we could, but by the time we got here it was already too late."

A neighbor called in the fire? Not Hannah? John was falling behind.

The man paused.

John scrutinized his grimy face and forced his mind to catch up. The fire spread fast and they were too late...

Too late for what?

"John, I'm so sorry." Vein-streaked eyes grabbed John's gaze. "They didn't make it." His voice was low and steady, and those red eyes, now glistening, darted back and forth between John's, as if urging him to comprehend...*something*.

John stared at a black smudge on the man's forehead and waited for the punch line.

"Hannah and Katy are gone."

Chapter Two

"Hannah! Where are you?"

"John?"

"I'm here, Hannah!" John can't see through the burning smoke, but he stumbles toward the sound of her voice— "John. Help!"

A burst of heat and flame lights the room, and he sees them. Hannah and Katy huddle in the corner, pressing into the wall. "Hannah!"

She stares at him, eyes wild with fear.

Katy's shrill cries grow until she is screaming at the top of her lungs.

"Daddy's coming, angel!"

Her tiny arms flail, and Hannah, choking, curls her body around the baby, shielding her.

"John!" Hannah calls his name again and again, but he can't move. Her face is stricken, her eyes begging to know why he won't help them.

Fire lashes out at his wife, his baby. Piercing screams rip his heart. "Hannah!" But he can't seem to get any closer. They're alone, trapped, terrified, shrieking.

A gravelly voice cuts in— "Hannah and Katy are gone."

"No!" John woke with a gasp, heart pounding. He blinked in the darkness, fighting for his bearings.

A light flipped on in the hall, drawing his attention. He looked around. This wasn't his house. Or his bed. This wasn't right. He should be waking up to Hannah's smile and Katy bug's coos and gurgles.

A knife twisted in his gut. He swallowed the rock closing his airway and raked clammy hands through his hair. He registered the footsteps padding closer.

13

Oh, Hannah.

They were supposed to share their whole lives with each other, raise a family, grow old together. God had brought her to him…hadn't He? They'd done everything right. So how could she be gone?

And their sweet baby girl…dead?

His stomach lurched, firing hot acid up into his throat. Was this actually happening?

"John?" His mother's voice carried from outside the door. "John, are you all right?"

No. He'd never be all right again. "Yeah, I'm okay. You can go back to sleep."

The door creaked open, spilling light into the room. Mom crept over and sat on the edge of his bed, like when he was a child awakened in the night. But these dragons couldn't be slayed. He didn't want her to even try.

She brushed a damp clump of hair from his forehead. Her familiar cherry-almond soap surrounded him. "Oh sweetie, I know this is so hard for you. For all of us."

He worked his jaw. "Yeah."

What did she want him to say? He sat trapped in her presence, straining for composure. She looked at him, head tilted, brows pulled together. Too much reality reflected in her eyes and John escaped by studying the shadowy pattern of the bedspread tangled around his legs.

"Let's pray." She didn't wait for a response. Just grabbed his hands and squeezed. Her sincerity cut off blood to his fingers.

He tried to listen to her words, but they seemed so…distant. Strange. They couldn't be about him.

With a sniff, his mother spilled her heart. John reeled at the sound of their names on her lips. For a moment, he wanted to cling to her and give himself over to grief. But he locked his spine and ground his teeth instead.

Mom's voice fell to a shaky whisper. "Carry us, Lord." She finished with a soft, shuddering "Amen."

A wisp of comfort washed over him but evaporated in a cloud of agony.

John coughed and searched for his voice. "Thanks."

"I love you so much." She placed her hand on his cheek. "I miss them too. I know how hard tomorrow is going to be. Cling to Jesus, Son. Don't let go." She kissed his forehead and left the room.

In the stillness, her cherry-almond fragrance faded, and he sat alone. His hands trembled, his teeth clenched, his tongue burned with questions.

The thirteen shadows cast by the window blinds shifted with the rising sun. John rolled onto his back, stared at the ceiling, and drew in a deep, shuddering breath.

Time to leave one prison cell and prepare to enter another.

He went through the motions of shaving and combing his hair, pulled on a new pair of socks and tied his stiff dress shoes.

"Are you ready then?" His mother's soft question pressed in on him.

He forced his voice out. "Yeah."

They rode down to the church in silence. His dad's absence was palpable, adding to the wrongness of the world. Dad was the lucky one really, unable to understand what had happened. In truth, John couldn't understand it himself.

An unimaginable world lay outside his window. Colorful trees towered along their rolling path. The bright reds and golds looked nothing like the dark world inside of John. He ran his finger inside his collar, straining against the choke hold of his tie. He didn't want to be wearing this crisp suit. He wanted to crawl back in bed and never wake up. Not to this. But he was hopelessly carried along by propriety and the Honda holding him hostage.

God...?

He swallowed hard and pushed the shapeless questions back down. Time enough to search his spirit for answers later.

They pulled into the parking lot and John set his jaw and unbuckled. A biting gust of wind pelted them as they walked arm in arm through the lot. His mother held him close to her side as they walked up the steps, the once-friendly steeple looming above. Menacing. Sniffles and low music hung in the air of the foyer.

"John." The pastor's wife approached, tissue clutched in her fist, and embraced him. "I'm so sorry."

"Thank you." He blinked several times.

"We've been praying for you day and night." Her glistening eyes whispered over his face. "God be with you." She squeezed his hand.

He gave a solid nod. "He is." At least, He was supposed to be. Though John couldn't feel Him now.

Half a dozen pairs of eyes followed John as he pushed forward into the small sanctuary. Wordless condolences poured over him from every somber face in the pews until he could no longer meet anyone's gaze.

He felt a light tap on his elbow. "Right here, Son." His mother motioned to their spots in the front pew and John was grateful to turn and shield himself from the mourners behind him.

Daisies brightened the small stage, one of Hannah's favorite flowers. She'd covered the nursery walls with them. John's gut coiled. He tried to muster appreciation for the gesture, but couldn't. It all felt so hollow— the photos, the bouquets, the colorful programs. He pressed his fingers into his palms. Funerals weren't meant for young mothers and their babies.

As the service began, John stared straight ahead. He clenched his aching jaw and fought the quiver in his chin. *Oh, Lord...*

"Hannah was a light and a joy in this community. Her sweet spirit touched all who knew her..."

John closed his eyes and saw Hannah nuzzling Katy's downy head, pressing her lips into the barely-there hair. Blowing out a shaky breath, he blinked the image away. He didn't dare glance at the two white coffins— one heart-wrenchingly small.

John's attention to the eulogy faded in and out. No doubt it was a beautiful memorial—but he couldn't process it.

At the appointed time, he took the podium and read the words he'd prepared. When he returned to his seat, his mother clutched his arm and wept in silence. The beauty of her gently lined face, in open grief, made John's heart ache all the more.

He kissed her temple. Katy had been her first grandbaby. She'd gone shopping just a few days before the fire and bought several frilly dresses. *It's a grandma's right to spoil her granddaughter rotten,* she'd said. The dresses were still in her trunk.

What would they do with them now?

John wrapped his arm around her as the service went on. Dad should've been there to do that, if only he were well enough. He probably wouldn't know who they were crying over anyway.

Pastor Barry tried to comfort in the usual way. "First Thessalonians four thirteen assures us that we do not mourn as those who have no hope." He seemed to implore the listener not to hurt. "So, Lord, we look to the day we'll be reunited with those who have gone before us. Those waiting to meet us at the gates. And we ask that Your arms be around John and the family in the coming days, comforting and steadying."

John squeezed his eyes tighter, balking. Arms of the Lord? What he wanted was the arms of his *wife* around him. Had he spent years of his life serving God, for this?

Shock exploded in his brain at the rebellious thought. *Forgive me, God.*

As the conclusion of the service, friends and acquaintances lined up to share their condolences.

"Let me know if you need anything—anything at all."

"I will. Thank you." He shook a hand.

"We love you, buddy."

A nod.

"You're in our prayers, John."

"Appreciate it."

"God is with you."

"Yes, He is." *But where?*

Each tried to look past his eyes into his soul to see how he really was. Everyone wanted special access to his innermost thoughts. John nodded and blinked and thanked. To his ears, they all sounded alike. And somehow, their words of comfort seemed to ignite a deep, throbbing resentment. He didn't want to get *through* this. Their sad smiles reminded him over and over again that his life was irrevocably changed.

His skin crawled. He wanted to run. Scream. Punch something.

What would happen if he did?

Finally, his mother ushered him back out to the car to head home.

"That was tough, wasn't it?"

Understatement. "Yeah." He cast a blank stare out the window, at the foreign world he'd thought he knew. They passed a store sign boasting Halloween Costumes on Sale Now. But he already had one. The "I'm-a-

Christian-of-course-I'm-doing-okay" disguise. Problem was, it felt too tight. But he couldn't take it off. Couldn't reveal how dark, how ugly and twisted his grief truly was.

What if he showed up at the wake in a Grim Reaper costume? His lip twitched with a half-smile. Now that would cause a stir.

Maybe he was going crazy.

"John?"

"Hmm?" He turned toward his mother.

"How are you holding up?"

He shrugged. "I'm tired. But I'll be all right."

"Hannah!" John bolted upright. Sweat rolled down his face and back. The sheets were soaked with it. His heart thumped against his ribs as he sucked in lungfuls of chilled air.

Even awake, the nightmare clung to him—the images digging into his brain like talons. Night after night, it chased him through a private, tarry world. Desperation clawed at his mind, and his ears bled with the cries of his wife and daughter.

He flung back the covers and stalked to the window, gazing down at his mother's front yard. His car sat parked in front of the mailbox. He could see the basketball hoop on the side of the driveway. How many games had he played with his dad? With Hannah when they were teens?

He rested his forehead against the glass. "I miss you, Hannah."

John closed his eyes as a tornado gathered inside him. He pushed off from the pane and let his gaze trail up toward the sky. "Do you even remember me?" he whispered, and looked out at the silent stars. "God?" The once-sweet name soured his tongue. He shook his head. "I did everything You wanted." He bit the inside of his cheek. "You could have stopped it. You could have saved them. But you...didn't."

A shudder worked its way up from the pit of his stomach, shaking him to the very core of his foundation. He released a slow breath through his nostrils, then closed the blinds.

Donning a T-shirt, John descended the stairs. At the foot of the staircase he scanned the living room—the homemade quilt folded along the back of the sofa, the family photos displayed on the oak mantle, the corner hutch housing Mom's collection of blown glass. He took it all in. Familiar, yet hollow.

Life had stopped being normal long before the fire.

He crossed the room toward the white-and-yellow kitchen, picturing Dad at the table with the paper. He'd delivered much wisdom from behind the business section—or his well-worn Bible. John's shoulders sagged under the memory. Did his father still read every day? Did he remember how? Or had disease robbed him even of that?

Shaking off the vision, John entered the kitchen. Three in the morning, but there'd be no more sleep for him that night. He started the coffee pot and went for a mug. The cupboard door creaked in protest, then refused to shut fully. John pushed it closed then watched it spring back open an inch. He could fix it if his mother had the tools. Was dad's tool-box still in the garage?

Three hours later, his mother shuffled into the kitchen in her bathrobe, a look of astonished confusion on her face. "John, it's barely six in the morning. What are you doing?"

John wiped the back of his hand across his forehead. "Did I wake you?" He set down the electric screwdriver and poured her a cup of coffee. "Here. Sorry about the noise."

She took the mug, eyes still wide as she scanned the room. He followed her gaze as it went from one dismantled cabinet to another.

"A door was popping open."

She nodded as her eyes slowly came to rest on him.

"And I fixed that sticky drawer. You really could use all new cabinets. Actually, there are a lot of things around the house that could use some attention. I can take care of it for you." He picked up the screwdriver and lined it up with the next hinge.

"You don't need to do that."

The drill revved. "I need to do something. I've got to keep busy, and this is all I can think of." He paused the tool but kept his back to her. "Please, let me do this."

A heartbeat went by in silence. "If it will help."

"Thank you." He gripped the cupboard door with both hands and wrestled it off its gummy hinges, then set it aside and faced her. Concern laced every line of her forehead, her brows drawn into a severe V. John pulled a paper towel off the roll and wiped his hands. "Don't look at me that way, Mom. Everyone is looking at me that way now. Like they feel sorry for me."

"Of course they do."

"But I don't need to see it in every face. It just makes it worse." He tossed the towel in the trash and poured the last of the coffee into his mug. The warmth of his mother's hand on his shoulder blade made him go still.

"I felt the same way when our friends found out about Dad."

He'd only been a teen when they got the news of Dad's early-onset Alzheimer's. At the time, John couldn't have imagined anything worse.

For a long moment, neither of them spoke. Then, setting down his mug, he finally turned to face her. God love her, she was trying not to give him pity-eyes, but her own grief made them red-rimmed and glossy. "Don't cry, mom. Please." He pulled her into an embrace.

"Oh, John..." She held him tight, and John closed his eyes and tried to draw a full breath. "God brought us through that shock, and He will bring us through this one as well."

John's jaw tightened. He squeezed her shoulders, then turned to retrieve his coffee and lower himself into one of the dining chairs. "What do you think of a nice beige oak? Lighten the room up a bit."

She sniffed. "Sounds nice."

He nodded and took a long drink, letting the caffeine do its work to keep him awake and functioning. "I'll run out for supplies after a quick shower. Get started on what I can."

"You have that appointment at two, remember."

Right, the insurance papers. He pinched the bridge of his nose, cringing at the thought of chronicling and itemizing his "loss."

"I'm coming with you."

"You don't have to do that."

"John..."

How was it that the tone of her voice alone could reach out to him? He closed his eyes and deflated. "Yeah, all right."

She was right, he couldn't do this alone. But her attentions hung on him like a heavy coat in the middle of summer. He wanted to breathe normally again, to not need the tender assistance that only underscored the reason for it. He felt claustrophobic. He couldn't go anywhere in this city without meeting with either memories or pity.

20

He straightened. *Or could he?*

That evening, after stuffing insurance forms in a drawer and throwing a tarp over the workbench in the garage, John pulled into the parking lot of the Life Care Center. Inside the cool walls, everything was just as he remembered. The same sunset paintings lined the halls, the same musty scent of old people mixed with Pine Sol hung in the air, the same face sat behind the welcome counter.

"John! Your dad will be so happy to see you."

He glanced at her name badge. "Hi, Shawna." She still remembered him, so it couldn't have been too long since he'd last been here. That's what he told himself anyway. "How's he doing today?"

"Today's been a good day. We had live music earlier, and he really enjoyed that. Come on, I'll walk you back." She led him to his father's room, gave the door a knock before opening it, then left them alone together.

Dad sat in a chair by his window, looking out at something only he could see. His bed was neatly made, his room tidy, but his hair was untamed and his sweater sagged around his chest.

John cleared his throat and swallowed his nerves. "Hi, Dad." His feet were nailed in place as he waited for a response. Would his father recognize him?

"Hey, Son." Dad's smile spread until it reached his eyes, and John exhaled his pent-up breath. He'd missed his father's warm smile more than he realized. Dad waved his hand inviting John to the chair beside his. "Have a seat. Let's talk."

"You look real good. How're you doing?" John rested his forearms on his knees and studied the new lines in his father's face. But despite the changes, he was still Dad.

"Fine, just fine," he said through his grin. "But how have you been?"

So like Dad to be more interested in what was going on in John's life than his own. Did he still pray for him every night? Not that he needed it. Little good it seemed to do.

"Well, it's been tough. Not gonna lie." John massaged the back of his neck and studied his shoe. Was he aware of the fire? John didn't see any trace of it in his eyes. Thank goodness.

They talked about sports and the economy. The conversation revealed his dad was a little displaced in time. No need to correct him.

"Any plans for a family of your own, Son?"

His windpipe closed as John reminded him about Hannah and Katy. "I, uh…I brought a picture. Don't think you've seen this one." He shifted his weight and pulled his wallet from his back pocket. "See? We had this taken when Katy turned a month old. Look, you can see her dimple. Just like her mama."

Dad beamed as he stared at the photo of Hannah holding Katy nose-to-nose. "Isn't that a sight? Beautiful." The pride swelling in his voice made the corner of John's mouth tip.

Yes, they were very beautiful.

He continued admiring the image as John looked around the room. Were they taking good care of his dad here? Did he have clean sheets? Fresh towels? Someone had made the effort to spruce things up— flowers, cards, a decade-old family portrait. His Bible sat on the nightstand. The same one John had grown up watching him read from each morning. He reached out, but stopped short of touching it, curling his fingers into a fist and turning on his heel to face the opposite wall.

A picture of the ocean met his gaze—complete with foamy waves, swirls of blue, a sun high above, and hazy white clouds stretched across the sky—and an ache rose up in John's chest. "I didn't fulfill my promise." He sank back into his chair, and Dad tilted his head and pulled his brows together.

"What promise is that, Son?"

"I promised Hannah we'd see the ocean this summer. If I got my raise."

His father reached out and patted John's hand. "Don't ever break a promise to your lady. Be a man of your word, Son. That's one of the first secrets of a good marriage." He handed the photo back to John. "And this one's a keeper, I can tell you that. Beautiful family, just beautiful. You should bring them with you next time."

"Yeah." John's voice pinched, but Dad didn't seem to notice. The reprieve from sympathy was refreshing, but it was time to get out of here. John couldn't play along anymore.

John awoke drenched in sweat, but at least he hadn't cried out. He stared at the ceiling, hiding from the questions boiling his soul. His faith was supposed to be strengthening him.

He showered, scrubbing away the images along with the sweat, then made his way downstairs as quietly as he could. But he needn't have worried about waking his mother at two am. She was up, sitting in the quiet living room with a pile of photographs on her lap.

She looked up at him with a pained expression when he entered the room. "I couldn't sleep. I was just looking at some old pictures. I wanted to put together an album for you."

John nodded and picked up a photo. His own albums, SD cards, computer...everything had been destroyed in the fire.

She sniffed and stretched her hand toward him. "Here's one of my favorites." The photo showed John with a guitar in his hands, and Hannah beside him, eyes closed, singing. "I loved listening to you two."

"She loved to sing." There had always been music in the house, like it was part of her DNA.

"I'll miss her voice."

"Me too. And so will her students." John took the photo from her hand and examined the image, softly running his fingers along Hannah's cheek, almost reverently. It seemed so long ago, though it was just last year—the first Sunday after Thanksgiving. He could tell by the single Advent candle glowing on the table.

"It must be the furthest thing from your mind, but I hope you'll still play this year."

John's shoulders tensed. He shook his head. "Don't ask me to think about that." Besides, his guitar had gone to ash in the fire, with the rest of his life.

"Of course." She nodded and lowered her gaze. "Forgive me."

John knelt beside her and took her hands in his. "There's nothing to forgive. We're going to process things each in our own way. I love you for doing this, making this album. Wanting some things to stay the same. But all I can see is that, they aren't." He stood. "They never will be."

John grabbed his keys from the side table then met her eyes. "I'm going for a drive."

His mother twisted the tissue in her hands, the protest shadowing her face melting away. "Okay. I'll leave the porch light on."

"Thanks." John kissed her cheek and she gripped his arm.

"I'll always leave the porch light on, Son."

A beat passed and he nodded solemnly. "I know."

In the driveway, he started the engine, looked at his mother's silhouette through the window, then backed out and headed toward the expressway. He clenched his jaw, wishing so badly for just one more embrace. One more chance to hear her laugh. One more conversation with his wife. "Hannah..." His voice bounced off the car windows. "Our favorite contestant on Survivor was sent home this week." Silence echoed back to him. "And that package from your granddad arrived a few days ago. All your old dolls. Katy bug will love—" His windpipe squeezed tight. "*Would have* loved..."

John's knuckles turned white on the steering wheel, and he exited the freeway just as the landscape began to blur. The abandoned drive-in theater beckoned him. A shot at privacy. His car lumbered over the bumpy lot, past the tall grass patches smattered throughout the run-down place. He rolled to a stop in front of the lone, torn forty-foot screen.

They were gone. It was all gone.

"God, why? *Why* would you do this to me? I was faithful to You, served You...and this is what I get?" He flung out his hands as his narrowed gaze swept across the floorboard and dash. Something poked out from beneath the passenger seat and he reached down for it, retrieving a pink pacifier. All he had left. There was no more car seat behind him.

John ground his teeth as a tornado gathered inside him. A chill shot through him as poisonous words formed in his mind. Words he'd tried to deny, to bury, but now could no longer restrain. He sent them up to heaven in a violent whisper. "I hate you." He raised his voice. "Do you hear me? I hate you!"

The rock in his throat devoured his rant. His body shook, racking him with a pain he never imagined possible. The world tilted with his admission, and the universe no longer made sense. Was anything real? Had his faith, his God, all been a mirage?

Chapter Three

John clicked open his pen and started writing. Lukewarm coffee sat nearby and a stream of light fell across the application on the table in front of him.

"Let me top you off." The waitress poured hot coffee over the cooling stuff in his mug, and John nodded silent acknowledgment.

Somehow, pages on the calendar had continued to turn. All the proper claims had been filed and processed. His life had been neatly quantified, his family's value appraised. His gut bubbled at the thought. Was nausea preferable to the numbness that pervaded his soul?

He'd deposited the insurance distributions in a separate account and ignored them as if they didn't exist. No amount of money, or anything else, could fix his world. And he wished everyone around him would quit trying. At least his mom had been okay with his skipping Christmas. He simply couldn't do it.

Hannah's birthday in March had been the worst. He'd stayed home from work and spent the day sleeping. Waiting for it to pass.

Nothing ever changed. Every day, the emptiness simply grew. He felt dead inside. If he wasn't caught in a wave of agony, he was numb. Jokes weren't funny. Food tasted bland. Colors were dull. Life had simply lost all meaning.

The only emotion he truly felt was in the nightmares that still stalked him every night. Every sleeping pill he could find had taken a turn at attempting to fight off the visions of Hannah and Katy writhing in pain. Nearly a year later, they very seldom worked.

It was time for a change. He flipped the paper over and continued writing.

Moving in with his mom had been the right thing. He knew that. She was dealing with her own loss of a spouse, and his presence made it easier on her. But he couldn't do it anymore. He had to get out on his own. To be alone.

So he'd decided to tap the bank account after all. Now, he sat at the local IHOP, filling out a rental application.

A bachelor pad.

That didn't feel right at all. In another life, he'd sat in this very restaurant as a married man. He'd brought Hannah in for the Rooty Tooty Fresh 'n Fruity breakfast. She sat across from him, blue eyes twinkling, blonde hair spilling around her face, devouring her food. She was in her second trimester then. The morning sickness was finally gone and she was ravenous. *Shut up!* she'd said when he couldn't stifle a laugh. *You'd be starving too if your body was creating a new life.* But she wasn't mad at him, she was giggling too. Always laughing, his Hannah. So joyful, so full of life.

He expelled a worn-out sigh and squeezed his eyes shut. When was the last time he'd laughed? He doubted he still knew how.

John signaled to the waitress. "Check please." The petite redhead nodded an acknowledgment. She probably drew second glances from most men, but John barely noticed. Beauty didn't move him the way it once had.

She returned with the bill and may have wished him a good evening, but he wasn't paying enough attention to be sure. The door opened with a whoosh and clanged shut behind him.

John wove his way through the neighborhood and cut the engine in his mom's driveway. The house of Smothering Mothering. He groaned. He didn't mean that. Mom was awesome. But he'd be glad for the privacy of the furnished apartment he'd found.

He plodded upstairs to pack his single suitcase. He wanted to finish before Mom got home from visiting Dad. How had she dealt so well with the slow loss of her husband, especially these last few years since he'd moved to the memory care facility? He shook his head. He couldn't go there right now. He rummaged through his room. Some clothes, comb, toothbrush—he didn't have much. Most important was the photo album Mom had put together for him. He wouldn't go anywhere without it.

He went downstairs and got to work on the dishes. Mom should have an empty sink. He dried a chipped dinner plate and stacked it in the cupboard, thinking how he'd need to get some dishes for himself now. Visions of registering for his wedding surfaced. Hannah had chosen their set from Kohl's. He shook off the memory.

Dishes done, he sank onto the sofa and turned on the TV, waiting for his mom to get home, and trying to stay out of his own head. He was pretending to watch a biography of Matt Damon when the front door opened.

"Hi, John. How was your day?"

"Good," he lied. "How's Dad?"

"Same. The Nielsens came by to pray with him. They said Pastor Barry is planning to visit next week. I think your father enjoys the visitors." Her eyes crinkled. How could she smile when Dad—*her husband*—was practically a vegetable? He didn't even know who she was half of the time. *You have to keep your sense of humor about things,* she often said. *Otherwise you'll just go crazy.*

He knew about that.

John cleared his throat. "Mom, I need to talk to you."

"Sure, honey." She swiftly joined him on the couch and leaned forward. "What is it?"

He cringed at the way her world stopped for anything he needed. He fiddled with the remote. "I found an apartment. Furnished. Talked to the manager today and…" He took a breath. "I think I'm gonna take it."

"Oh." She blinked several times. "Are you sure? I mean, there's no hurry, sweetie."

"Yes, there is." He pinched the bridge of his nose. "I can't *do* this, I can't be *here* and…I need some solitude. I love you, and I know you're grieving too, but…it's time. It really is." Her features softened as her resistance crumbled. "He said the application was a formality and I could pick up the keys tomorrow."

Her gaze hopped from his right eye to his left, then her chest expanded with a deep breath. "All right, then." She patted his hand and stood to remove her scarf and coat. After hanging them on the rack by the door, she faced him with a smile. "What should we do for dinner? Anything you want."

John glanced at his packed bag in the back seat, then pulled his car out onto the road. The keys to his new apartment were waiting for him. All he had to do now was show up and sign for them. Start trying to carve out a life for himself, somehow, in the midst of a town that didn't ever let him forget.

His body stiffened. How long could he survive like this?

He fiddled with the stereo, looking for something—anything—to fill the vacuum.

Something sparked in the corner of his eye. A flash of blonde. A familiar form. His heart seized and he ground the car to a halt, tires screeching and sending up smoke.

Hannah! There she was, pushing a stroller down the sidewalk.

His eyes went wide, his mouth gaping.

The woman turned her face toward him—an unfamiliar face—and gave John an odd look before hurrying on her way. John gave himself a shake and rubbed his forehead. *Get it together, man.* His grip on reality seemed to weaken every day.

Memories lived everywhere—the market, the coffee shop, the playground he and Hannah had imagined Katy playing at. More than a year later and the ghosts seemed more present than ever.

He blew out a breath. These streets were nothing more than a coffin nailed shut all around him.

His heart thudded. Sweat beaded on his upper lip. Spinning sensations seemed to yank him from his body, driving him toward madness. He couldn't breathe, he had to escape.

Don't ever break a promise to your lady, Son.

With a jolt, John twisted the steering wheel to the left and gunned it, pulled toward the western shore. He jetted up the ramp onto the interstate and flew into the fast lane.

His speedometer needle passed seventy—eighty—ninety. The highway extended as far as he could see, and the town that had destroyed him fell farther and farther away. Exhilaration rose mile after mile and his

mind dug into the desperate hope that somewhere else, in some other town, he wouldn't see her face everywhere he went.

When twilight gave way to darkness, John pulled in to the first halfway decent motel he saw. The room was small, with a tacky bedspread and matching curtains, but it was clean enough and he wasn't there for the decor.

So what *was* he here for?

Permanent escape? Temporary reprieve? He sat on the bed and pointed a blank stare out the window. Was he really thinking of driving all the way to the Pacific Coast? All he knew was, he couldn't go back. In the morning he'd call to quit his job, maybe let his mother know he'd be gone awhile.

Hannah and Katy invaded his thoughts. And for the first time since the fire, there was no one around to pretend for, so he invited the memories in, savored the sound of Hannah's laugh, the sparkle in her eyes. Listened to Katy's mewling cries, watched the two of them in his mind's eye as Hannah nursed their firstborn.

Their only born.

Would it ever stop hurting?

"Why did you take them from me?" The betrayal was raw even now.

The mini bar snagged his attention then. John had never been one for the hard stuff. Even in high school, he hadn't been a partyer. He'd always been Mr. Clean. It hadn't done him any good in the end.

He snatched a tiny bottle of vodka, unscrewed the cap, and took a swig. It burned his throat and cleared his sinuses. He coughed, then swallowed more. It slid down smoother.

Soon, his head swam. The sharp corners of reality rounded out; the hard lines blurred in his mind. The pain grew hazy. He released a long, slow breath, savoring the fading tension.

After months of tortured sleep, he'd found relief in the thing he'd sworn he'd never turn to. What did those rules do for him now? Anything that kept him from witnessing his family being burned alive every time he closed his eyes was a godsend in his estimation. Pun intended.

His eyes had trouble tracking as he glanced around the room. Determined not to dream, he downed some more before passing out on the shabby bedspread.

The thick hotel curtains blocked out the sunlight. He peered at the clock. Noon. The longest he'd slept since that fateful day. He smacked his tongue on the roof of his mouth and rubbed his eyes, eliciting a groan. His eyeballs throbbed in his skull.

Had he really gotten plastered in this crummy hotel room? Yeah, he had. But so what. He was used to the nausea anyway, and the headache was a small price to pay for the hours of dreamless sleep.

Throwing his legs over the side of the bed, he sat up. Too quickly. The room spun and he ground his teeth, closing his eyes until it settled. He scratched his day-old scruff, stretched his neck, then eased himself up onto his feet. He left the curtains drawn and lights off as he packed up, then double-checked the room for any stray belongings before heading out.

Downstairs, he choked down a toaster pastry from a vending machine, then stood in line at the counter to check out. He twisted off the cap on a bottle of water and popped a couple Excedrin while he waited. Mom was probably worried sick. He'd have to call her.

He settled his bill, then, suitcase in hand, donned his sunglasses and crossed the lot to his car. After sliding into the leather seat, he pulled out his cell and made the call he was dreading.

"I wondered when I'd hear from you. How's the apartment?"

He swept a nervous tongue over his lips as he searched for a gentle opening but found none. "I didn't take the apartment, Mom. I'm giving my notice at work and heading for the West Coast." A soft gasp came over the line.

"I made a promise to Hannah we'd see the ocean. And now…well, I've just got to do this." He rubbed his forehead. "A road trip will give me time to get my mind straight. I can stop and see all the tourist attractions along the way. Maybe I'll send you a picture of that big twine ball they have in Kansas." He forced a shallow chuckle, then released his breath. Time to bring it on home with the sincere soul-baring spiel.

"Mom," he cleared his throat—this part was a little too close to the truth, "Everywhere I go I see her. In the restaurants we visited, the roads we drove down. I see her in the faces of everyone around town. That's not good for me, you know? I need to be able to…" He shuddered at the lie on his lips, "to let go."

Her armor was pierced. John could almost hear the walls falling, the resistance expelled with her sigh. He closed his eyes and waited.

"How…how long will you be gone?"

"I'm not sure. But don't worry, Mom. This will be good for me, healthy." He poured on the honey as thickly as possible, making it easier for her to swallow. He made his promises and they said their goodbyes.

As John merged onto the freeway for another day of driving, he made it his goal to keep his thoughts on the road and get as far as he could. Line after yellow line zipped past, and the long stretches of nothingness liberated him. The silence didn't judge. The only pressure was his own need to keep moving.

Day after day he spent behind the wheel, savoring the relief, the sense of purpose as he catapulted himself toward the horizon. Toward the Pacific Ocean. Like he promised Hannah.

A new normal formed over the next few days. Countless hours on the highway were followed by nights at whatever bar he could find. It had quickly become a routine. A different town, a different drink maybe, but the same escape. He could even laugh once in awhile with the booze. It was a lifeline really, medicine for survival.

The sky went on forever, the flat landscape stretched over the earth like brown upholstery. John stuck his arm out the window, letting the wind pass through his fingers as he sailed through this tawny ocean. He leaned forward and turned down the stereo, then squinted into the distance looking for the next highway marker. Kansas. Eight hundred miles down. At some point the horizon would reveal a shoreline. He'd fulfill his promise, accomplish the goal.

His pulse spiked. *And then what?*

With a hard swallow, he shook his head, cranked up the volume, and pressed the gas a little harder.

Colorado and Utah ticked by and the flat, itchy countryside gave way to reddish plateaus and hills until steep mountains towered above him. The highway snaked through these rocks, winding around the fork-streaked masses like a river. John flew through until the stacked-pancake rocks turned to pock-marked ones and eventually back into the flat barren ground he'd seen too much of. But the progression of his scenery, and the nearing of his goal, made something shift inside him. Reluctance niggled at him.

A green Now Entering Nevada sign appeared and he eased up on the gas pedal, suddenly in no hurry. His gaze skimmed the tumble-weed-dotted landscape, seeking resolve. Reaching the Pacific signaled the end of his trip. Meant heading back home afterward, which was something he couldn't bear the thought of just yet. Swallowing what little moisture was in his mouth, he wondered how much farther before he'd see a bar.

Telephone poles appeared. The shrubbery multiplied. Billboards dotted the sides of the highway. And finally, civilization. Fast food joints and gas stations replaced the blanket of brown on the sides of the road, and John was joined by more and more traffic. The sun began to set, its light giving way to a million smaller ones.

Vegas.

He could always stop for a day or two. The ocean wasn't going anywhere.

Chapter Four

Las Vegas, Nevada

Pete jerked his head while drying another glass. "Hey John, I think that one over there likes you."

John followed his gaze across the hotel bar to a petite brunette sitting with two other girls. When she caught them glancing back, she locked eyes with John and lifted one side of her mouth in a suggestive smile.

John turned back toward Pete. "No way, man. Not interested, I told you that."

"Aw, come *on* dude. She's hot!" He set the glass on the shelf behind the bar. "I'm telling ya, the best way to get over one chick is with the help of another—know what I mean?" He held up a halting palm. "I know you don't like to talk about your past, and it's none of my business. But you've been hanging around here for over a month. Dude, you gotta move on. Look at her, she's practically begging!"

"Pete, you're sick." John chuckled at him. "Look, I'm telling you. I'm not at all interested. In her, or any of the girls around here that you try to push on me. Seriously. Okay?"

He raised both hands in surrender. "Okay, okay. I'm just trying to help out a buddy who is obviously in serious need of some fun."

"I'll be having plenty of fun when you bring me another kamikaze."

Pete dropped the subject and got to work pouring the drink, all the while shaking his head.

John stared out across the hotel lounge past the featureless faces around him. The distant plunking sound from the casino was merely white noise. No, he wasn't having fun—and when he did it was a counterfeit fun born of drink. Most nights the booze only dampened the throbbing pain.

But Vegas was the perfect place to park for awhile and nurse the pain. You gambled a little and they brought you free drinks. Or better yet, you carved out a spot at the bar and kept the refills coming in a steady stream.

"Here ya go, bro." Pete placed the drink in front of John who threw it back.

Half hour later, John was done with the crowd and ready for his quiet room. He had a good buzz going and wanted to enjoy it alone.

One more vodka tonic and he'd head up.

John scooted off his chair and dropped a chip for Pete, who was busy stirring a drink for a curvy blonde a couple feet away. No doubt, he'd leave his shift with her on his arm. He never left alone. Unlike John.

Pete nodded acknowledgment and John saluted goodbye.

The elevator dumped him out into the hall, and he pulled his card key from his shirt pocket. The door swung open against his weight, and he fell forward into his room, staggering to keep his footing. The swirling in his head was welcome as he struggled with his shirt buttons. He dropped onto the bed and closed his eyes, focusing on the fuzzy sensation he'd grown to love.

If only it wouldn't fade by morning.

He lay back on the bed enjoying the lack of awareness of his surroundings. His heavy-lidded eyes closed. The air conditioning unit kicked on and a door down the hall opened and closed.

John, my son, return to Me.

John's eyes popped open and he stared up through the blackness. He didn't think he was *that* drunk. After a few heartbeats, he closed his eyes again.

John, return to Me and I will give you rest.

His heart pounded as the words floated across his mind. He recognized that soundless voice. It belonged to *Him*—and John was still angry with Him. Would always be.

He had nearly forgotten that voice. Forgotten the many times in his old life when it had spoken comfort and strength into him. Or filled him with joy as he thanked Him for his blessings. Those things had become a fuzzy memory.

"Stop it. Leave me be. I don't want you anymore."

The inaudible whisper fell silent, but the memory of it pricked John's soul. Emptiness swallowed him, making him feel small. Alone.

I never felt alone when I followed Him.

The awareness stung. Even when Dad was diagnosed with early-onset Alzheimer's, and John had been scared out of his mind at the thought of losing him, God had strengthened him. And now, he missed God's comfort in spite of himself.

But John would not forgive Him. Ever. He'd curse God with his dying breath before he'd forgive Him for taking everything from him.

John clenched his jaw. With a pillow over his face and a curse toward God on his lips, he lay motionless until eventually, his pulse slowed and the rhythmic breathing of sleep replaced the jagged breath of desperation. And Hannah found him in his dreams.

John awoke basking in Hannah's memory. Her fair hair and clear blue eyes, her velvet touch. Until suddenly his head cleared and his thoughts focused sharply on the reality that she was dead.

His stomach clenched and a sour taste splashed the back of his throat.

He flung back the sheets and tripped to the bathroom, spewing the contents of his stomach. Afterward, he crumpled on the white-tiled floor.

"Hannah, Hannah…" Her name poured out of him over and over. What would she think if she saw him like this?

John ran his hands along his head and grabbed fistfuls of hair.

He threw his head back against the wall. The fact was she *wasn't* here and he would never be the same man he'd once been.

She was gone…and little Katy bug would forever be just six weeks old. He'd never hear her say *da-da* or help her take her first steps. There would be no tricycles, no piggyback rides. It would just be John, wretchedly alone, forever.

"Why?" A stream of expletives cut through the dark room. He raided the minibar, his consistent friend, and spent the next miserable half hour trying to deaden his senses.

But still the dream of Hannah's startled voice haunted him. *"John, what are you doing?"*

John sat in his room, head in his hands. Hannah hadn't haunted his dreams for three nights. The Voice, however, gave him no such respite. It had returned again last night, this sense of pleading, but John would have none of it. Time had not eased the pain…the wound in his heart had festered and spread.

His hands tightened into fists and he pounded them against the pain in his chest. Was there no relief? A harsh groan boiled over within him and his knees hit the floor.

No more of this! He was done. He wanted to be with his family again and he was ready, happy even, to face death. Tonight. To take his only way out.

The spinning thoughts quieted with his resolve and an odd sense of calm settled over him.

He rose, pulled his shoulders back, then grabbed his wallet and room key. He slipped out his door and headed to the bar to sort out the details.

"Hey Pete, Vodka, neat." John leaned his elbows on the slick cherry wood.

"Hey, bro, how's it goin'? It's been a few days."

"Not bad," John lied. "You? Anything exciting going on?"

Pete leaned in and dropped his voice. "Got my eye on this pretty little nymph." He gave a slight jerk of his head in the direction of a young woman with short dark hair and a tiny waist. She did look a bit like a nymph—or a pixie.

John raised his glass to Pete before downing the contents. "Hit me again."

Pete raised an eyebrow but poured more. John slouched on the stool and tried to think.

He'd been clinging to the end of his rope for a year and a half and his fingers were slipping. All that was left was to figure out how to let go. Something fast and certain.

He drained two more shots, oblivious to the world around him.

Pete tapped his palm on the counter in front of John. "Hey. You sure you're okay tonight, buddy?"

"Pete. I never have told you about Hannah." John raised his eyes to meet his friend's gaze.

"I know she messed you up pretty bad." He rimmed a margarita glass with salt.

John snorted. "You're half right. She was amazing." John shared bits and pieces of their romance in between other customers' drink orders and the girls flirting with Pete. None of them had anything on his wife.

Pete returned to pour, and John knocked back another shot. "Hannah was...unbelievably gorgeous. Blonde hair, eyes the color of the summer sky, perfect curves...I guarantee you I had the best honeymoon any man ever had."

Pete gave an amused laugh and John raised his eyebrows. "Dude, seriously. We waited. And the payoff was...let's just say, worth it." Just the memory of Hannah's skin against his sent a jolt of heat through his body.

"Well, good for you, man." Pete shook an apple martini for a tall redhead, flirted with the Pixie-Chick, then returned and filled John's glass. John swirled it around while Pete leaned forward to listen.

"A few months later, I come home and Hannah is all bubbly and excited. She hands me a gift bag with a purple bow. You figure out what was inside?"

Pete raised questioning eyebrows.

John nodded. "Pregnancy test. Positive. Figured about six weeks along. I was gonna be a *dad*. Can you imagine?"

John chuckled and shook his head. So many emotions had whirled through him at the news. His heart had pounded so hard. He was excited. Incredulous. Freaked out. But Hannah... She was glowing with joy. And God's voice had spoken peace into John's mind. He'd sensed God's assurance through his fears, that this was a blessing to celebrate. So they'd begun making plans.

"So...how'd this fairytale go bad?" Pete watched him, waiting.

John tapped his glass yet again. "Fill it up first."

Pete poured another but gave John a wary look. "Might want to slow down, bud. This is a record for you, and that's saying something."

John swished a hand at Pete, waving off his concern. "We had a little girl." He forced his voice through his pinched throat. With a smile, he stared out into the universe, picturing her little cherub face. "We named her Katy." The room tilted as John swung his head back to Pete and looked him in the eye. "Nothing I'd ever done, or could ever do in my entire life, could compare with that perfect little girl Hannah and I created together. Nothing." Despair clenched his jaw.

"Wow. I didn't know you had a *daughter*, dude." Pete whistled and turned his attention to the throng of girls on John's right in need of fresh cocktails. His Pixie-Chick was among them. He broke from the serious tone of John's story, exchanging flirtatious grins and cracking a few jokes. John didn't care about any of it. He stared into his glass for a long moment then chugged the clear liquid.

He was lost in some alternate world where Hannah and Katy still existed. He focused on his baby—every chubby roll on her arms and legs, every wisp of gold hair. He tried to picture her dimpled grin but couldn't form a clear mental image. The details of her smile were fading.

No. Guilt sucker-punched him. He tapped his knuckles on the sides of his head but couldn't see her. Eyes squeezed shut, he rubbed his temples.

John.

That voice intruded again into his thoughts. It had never echoed in his head out in public.

John.

It came like an anguished plea. But John's pain was *His* fault.

Behold, I have loved you with an everlasting love.

The intrusive Bible verse chafed, made him falter in his resolve. But he was coming to the part of his story that would give him the ammunition for what he had to do.

He lifted two fingers for another drink.

A woman slid into the seat next to John. He ignored her presence. Arm heavy, he lifted his glass to his lips.

His new neighbor swiveled toward him. "Hi. You alone tonight? You're way too attractive to be sitting here by yourself."

"Yep." John stared at his drink. "I'm alone."

"Me too. I'm not very good at it." Her soft laughter sounded wonderful, even in John's state of mind. "How about if we're alone together? I'm April."

"John." He mumbled his reply with barely a sideways glance.

"I like that name. It's nice to meet you, John." The melody of her voice caught him off guard. "Buy me a drink?"

John traced the rim of his glass and shrugged. "Sure, why not."

"Bartender—I'll have a Midori Sour."

"Coming right up. But uh, don't bother with that one. He's not interested."

"Don't be rude, Pete." John took his eyes off his glass and the room swayed.

"Sorry, just trying to help—and failing again, apparently." Pete handed the lady her green cocktail.

"Thanks. And thank *you*." She turned towards John.

"Yeah. So, uh…April, right? You on vacation?"

"Nope. I'm a native. Well, a transplanted native. Haven't been here very long—a few months or so. What about you? Business trip, weekend getaway, poker tournament?" Her eyes danced. Flirting, trying to draw him in.

"None of the above. I'm also a new transplant." *Soon to be uprooted,* he reminded himself. He took a sip of his Vodka and looked away. Her eyes felt too familiar.

She tilted her blonde head to one side, catching his gaze, and pressed her straw to her lush lips. "So what do you do?"

"You're lookin' at it." He tried to keep the acid out of his tone. "What about you? Work at one of the shows?"

She threw her head back and let out a laugh like a beautiful melody. John was unable to repress a slight smile.

"I don't think so. I've worked as a bar waitress and that sort of thing. But I'm keeping my eye out right now for…other opportunities."

John studied her then. Blonde, blue eyes, full lips parted in an alluring smile. Her hair was a little shorter, but she reminded him so much of Hannah.

Her forehead creased. "Who's Hannah?"

He'd said that out loud? He blinked slowly. "She was my wife." His tongue was heavy, warping his speech. Pete would cut him off soon if he didn't hide the effects. Maybe he should switch down to a Rum and Coke.

"Oh. Divorced?"

"No. She's dead." It came out on its own, like the cork popping off a bottle.

Pete and April both froze, eyes wide, and exchanged a look. April turned to her drink and Pete's gaze bounced around John like he wasn't sure what to do next.

"I'm so sorry." April's voice was low.

Pete cleared his throat. "Dude, that sucks. I...I didn't know."

John shrugged. "How could you?"

Pete leaned forward and dropped his voice to a near-whisper. "So where's your daughter?"

John fixed his stare straight ahead. His lips flattened into a straight line. "Katy too." The filthy words choked him. He tipped his glass and washed them down, then dragged the back of his hand across his mouth.

April shifted in her seat, as if she wasn't sure the conversation was meant for her ears. Her resemblance to Hannah slammed John with cruel force. Even the way she carried herself—with tact, not wanting to butt into his business, but clearly moved. A strange flicker of emotion sparked, but he shook it off.

He expelled a breath, needing to let it all out, the story. Like saying goodbye.

He closed his eyes. "They died in a fire." He'd said it. For the first time, he'd said it aloud. Somehow, voicing the horrid facts lent them existence. "They burned and I wasn't there to stop it." The muscles of his face contorted and he dropped his head, pretending to clear his throat.

"More." He tapped his glass. Pete gave him a sideways look before adding one finger more. John gulped it, feeling it sail smoothly down. He set his elbows on the counter, head in his hands. Two detestable beads of moisture rolled down his cheeks and then a gentle hand rested on his arm. His first human touch in what felt like ages.

He looked up into sad, compassionate eyes. April exuded Hannah's spirit like the embodiment of her reincarnated soul. Her concern wrapped itself around the deepest part of him.

She *saw* him. John felt exposed, but didn't mind. He couldn't look away from her eyes. An odd sort of fascination grabbed hold, and it confused him.

"I'm honored that I remind you of her." April gave him a soft smile. "She must have been a wonderful woman. Why don't we drink to Hannah and Katy?" Pete poured out two more drinks and April lifted hers in the air. "To Hannah and Katy."

"To Hannah and Katy," John echoed, still staring at this surprising woman.

When he turned away, the room again skewed. He shook his head to clear it but the dizziness worsened. He focused on the small TV screen hanging in a corner of the lounge where the Chicago Bulls were on fire. He watched them score a three-pointer and grimaced. "Ah, come on, Pacers."

"I don't think this is their year." The feminine voice tickled his senses.

He slid an assessing glance at April. The urgency he'd had just minutes ago, to let go of this life, had disappeared. Like one of those drowning rats, right when he wanted to give up, the universe threw him a thin lifeline. The undeniable impulse to keep treading water gripped him. Of course it was pointless. He'd eventually drown. But suddenly he wasn't in as much of a hurry.

Inwardly he cursed himself for being a coward. But outwardly he tried to listen to April's chatter about stupid television shows.

"And people actually vote—it's like a really big deal. Who wants to own the world's ugliest dog?" She dipped her head and stifled a giggle. Her laughter was a drug John was quickly becoming addicted to.

How was it possible that she would look and sound like his wife? Maybe he was just that desperate to see Hannah again. He listened closer and laughed in earnest a moment later. The sound was strange in his own ears.

"I like you, John. You're easy to talk to." She grinned. "I wouldn't mind another drink though." April lifted her empty glass in a discreet but

41

unmistakable gesture. Was that some kind of code, to buy a lady a second drink?

John told Pete to get her another, then returned his attention to April. She crossed one silky leg over the other and fixed her gaze squarely on him. A rush of warmth shot through his body and his stomach muscles tightened. She lowered her eyes for a moment. Was she blushing? Of course not.

Pete delivered her cocktail and she brought the straw to her lips. John found himself studying her mouth and another wave of heat radiated out from his chest. He cleared his throat and turned away. What was he doing?

She trailed her fingers along his arm, sending little bolts of lightning through him. "What's wrong?"

"Nothing." He turned to her and his eyes drifted again to her mouth. He couldn't seem to help it. Her lips curved into a seductive, knowing smile.

Automatically, John's gaze swept over her body, admiring her curves. Ashamed, he brought his focus back to her face, and was met with half-lidded eyes that held an unspoken invitation.

It had been a long time since he'd seen that look in a woman's eyes—in his Hannah's eyes. But he recognized it well. His breath caught in his throat and he swallowed hard. She reached out to run her fingers across the back of his hand, which clutched his glass in a choke-hold.

She inched toward him in her seat. The smell of cigarette smoke was replaced with her sweet perfume, and John couldn't find his breath. With a coy tip of her mouth, she leaned closer, the scent of her hair swirling around him. Her lips tickled his ear. "Why don't we go somewhere else to talk?" Soft fingertips traveled along his arm and his heartbeat quickened. He nodded.

What am I doing?

April took his hand and slid out of her chair, leading him along behind like a puppy. They rode the elevator up to the fourth floor while John concentrated on keeping his balance. He shoved his hands in his pockets and the woman who looked like his dead wife looped one arm through his, running the fingers of her other hand up and down his neck.

Uncertainty ate at him, and it seemed a hundred pairs of eyes were on them, but he couldn't pull himself away. The doors opened and they drifted down a hallway.

"This is me." She pulled the keycard from her purse.

Flee, my son!

The warning only fueled rebellion in him. Locking his jaw, he squelched his misgivings and marched inside. The door clicked shut.

April set her purse on the coffee table. He watched her glide across the room and noted the curve of her hips swaying beneath her skirt. A surge of fire licked through his veins, awakening a profound craving, a physical hunger that had been lying dormant, until now.

She returned and faced him and he shifted his weight. What were they doing? She caught her lip between her teeth and looked up at him with unmistakable desire.

It was Hannah's eyes that locked onto his, Hannah's hands that ran tentatively over his chest, setting his blood on fire.

He eased his hands from his pockets and brushed his fingertips along her back. Gazing down at her, his own longing reflected in her glowing eyes—like a deep, unquenchable thirst. How long had it been since he'd held a woman? She pressed herself against him and he sucked in a ragged breath. His pulse thrashed in his ears.

"John." Her voice was low and sultry. She lifted gentle fingers to his brow and ran them through his hair. "I want to comfort you... Let me."

Her hands explored the muscles of his chest, his neck, his arms. And his flesh responded. With a hand on the back of her neck, he tilted her face up toward his. His breath was unsteady as his mouth hovered above hers. The first touch of feminine lips ignited his body, destroying all restraint.

He saw only Hannah, and he kissed her deliberately. Deeply. Voraciously.

Her mouth trailed to his jaw, tracing a line down his neck and back up to his ear.

"Hannah..." The name spilled out as he turned his feverish attention to her neck.

"Wait..."

Struggling for control, John stared down at her, still wrapped in his arms. She flicked her gaze away then kissed his neck once, twice. He closed his eyes.

"I—I need rent money..." Just a whisper as her fingers played along his back. "Do you understand?"

A moment passed before he realized what she was saying. He nodded. Holding her face in both his hands, he drew her up until her breath mingled with his. "Hannah..."

Somewhere in the distance, he heard her faint reply.

"April."

Then she melted into his arms.

Chapter Five

John rolled over, and a jackhammer let loose in his skull. He froze, hoping to coax it away, then blew out an even breath as the pain eased by the tiniest of fractions. Sunlight lanced through the window and stabbed his eyes, but he gritted his teeth and forced them open. Rubbing his temples, he turned his head away from the window to escape the bright blade.

Hannah?

He gasped. Golden hair draped the pillow beside him, and the sheet over her slender form rose and fell with each breath. He blinked, but she didn't disappear. This didn't feel like a dream… Had the entire past year and a half been a horrible nightmare?

Memories found shape through the familiar fog of a gigantic hangover. The suicide plans. The bar. Talking about Hannah and Katy. And…and…

No. Please, God, no!

John hadn't prayed in months, and that brief, desperate plea was the best he could muster when the horror of his actions pierced the haze in his brain. Sitting up sent a crack of lightning through his skull, but he didn't care. He scrambled out of the bed and stumbled back as images played out in rapid-fire sequence, forcing their way into his unwilling consciousness. Each detail became sharper, etching into his brain until he thought it would bleed.

A prostitute? I paid money to…

His eyes cut to the dresser and the wad of cash sitting on it. The bills he'd counted out for…

No!

His throat closed, and he barked out a revolting cough, which brought with it another memory he didn't want to acknowledge. He'd called her…*Hannah!* Defiled his sweet wife's name. Oh God, was this real? Was this happening?

Clamping his mouth, he stumbled toward the bathroom.

Violent spasms wracked his body, ejecting the meager contents of his stomach. Even when nothing was left to vomit, the retching continued. He clung to the slippery toilet rim as wave after wave of guilt and disgust washed over him.

Shaky legs gave out and he crumpled onto the cold linoleum. Dismal shame shook him in the deepest part of his soul. Even as that stranger—April, a prostitute, a woman of the night—lay asleep in the bed, John lay covered in his own vomit, wriggling like a worm on the dirty bathroom floor.

He wept. For Hannah, for Katy, and for himself—for the loss of the man he once was, the man Hannah had fallen in love with.

Then he released the one cry he'd been avoiding all along.

"Oh, God. Oh Lord, I'm sorry. I'm so sorry. Oh, God!" Remorse gripped him. "Oh, Lord Jesus, forgive me, I've been so wrong."

Tears fell, collecting on his chin until they dripped into the puddles of vomit. He could do nothing except keep crying. He didn't try to stop. The pain had its way with him until he felt a still, small voice whisper across his soul.

Welcome home, my son.

Hurtling away from Vegas, he headed south on I-15.

Running again.

He was so tired of running. But he couldn't go back to Indiana. Not back to his past.

Miles of cacti and scrub brush surrounded him—more than enough nothingness for a man to lose himself in. He could start a new life. All new, along with this second chance God had given him.

For the first time since losing Hannah and Katy, a glimmer of hope flickered to life. John rolled down the window and enjoyed the sense of freedom—and the presence of God—in the wind that whipped his hair.

Suddenly, an image of blond hair draped across creamy skin flashed in his memory. His stomach dipped and shame tugged him toward a dark pit. His hands tightened on the wheel.

"God, I need your help here. I just want to start over. Be a better man. I can't do it on my own."

He relaxed his grip. Peace settled over him and he drew in a deep, satisfying breath. God was his rock now. Anything was possible.

Stomach rumbling, he pulled off the freeway for a bite to eat. He cruised through a residential district in a clean, friendly-looking town. School was out for the day and the sidewalks were full of kids walking home in clusters. Emerging out onto the main road, John stopped at a red light and looked to his left. An immense church building stood watch on the corner, a large cross displayed out front. The marquee read "All Are Welcome."

John snorted. *Yeah, right. Even guys like me who screamed profanities at God and drowned myself in liquor? No way.*

People like you are why I sent my Son.

John's cheeks puffed out. *Yeah, but that doesn't mean Penny Parishioner would be comfortable sitting beside the dregs of society.*

He took in the crisp church grounds, a strange sense of longing washing over him—to belong, to feel at home. He hadn't had that since...

He swallowed and looked back out at the church building. The sign below the marquee listed their Sunday service times and below that, in larger block letters: "Midweek Bible Study Tonight at 6:30 p.m." John shifted his gaze away. He was hungry for God, but he didn't belong with that crowd anymore.

He parked in front of a Mexican restaurant tucked into a shopping center. Seated at an outdoor patio table, he people-watched while devouring a plate of tacos. Afterward, he refilled his Coke—no rum— and hit the road, headed back toward the freeway.

But that Bible study sign wouldn't leave him alone. It kept nagging at him, this tug to turn around and go back.

It seemed ridiculous. There were hundreds of churches across the state, or the country for that matter. He should get things together, find an apartment, a job, *then* he could find a church to attend.

The hairs on the back of his neck pricked. Why couldn't he shake the feeling he'd be missing out on something if he didn't go to that service, in that church, in that town...*tonight?*

He groaned and flipped on his blinker. *All right, all right.* He'd have a few hours to kill, but for some reason he couldn't explain, he needed to be in that church when the evening service started.

John spent those hours exploring the town—walking through neighborhoods and enjoying a large park with rolling hills and a pond in the middle—and still he was early to the service.

A man in a brown sweater vest and khakis, carrying a satchel and a Starbucks cup, crossed the parking lot in the direction of the sanctuary. John followed him through the entrance, where a round of friendly faces greeted him. Half a dozen people with name tags and stacks of bulletins stood in the foyer.

A middle-aged woman smiled at him. "Welcome to Christ Community Fellowship." Her eyes crinkled around the edges and made John feel welcome.

"Thank you." He shook her hand.

"Do you need a bulletin?"

"Sure, yeah." He took the tri-folded paper she held out to him.

"Enjoy the service." She grinned again before turning to the next person entering the building.

John passed through the double doors into the main sanctuary. The place was three times bigger than his home church with walls covered in modern decor. Did this many people always turn out for a midweek study? He scoped out the room and headed for a spot in the back.

A muscular-framed man approached from the aisle and took the seat beside John. He raised his chin in greeting. "Hey man, what's up?"

John returned the man's smile. "Not much. You?"

"Well...I'm here, ya know? One of those weeks ya really need a refill to make it to the end. But it's all good. God's good, man." His smile widened to reveal off-white teeth set against his dark skin.

John jetted a silent breath. "Yeah. He really is."

"Name's Derek." A large hand extended toward John and he grasped it, noting the edge of a tattoo peeking out from the man's sleeve.

"John."

"Good to meet you, man. Don't think I've seen you around here before, but it's a big church."

"It's my first visit. Saw the sign out front and got curious." Though unfamiliar with his surroundings, John felt at ease. As much as was possible given the secret he was carrying.

Derek's head bobbed. "That's cool, that's cool. It's a great place to be, man." He held John's gaze for a beat then squinted. "I think you'll like it."

John smiled. He already did. "Thanks."

Derek turned toward the front and lifted an ankle onto his knee.

The lights dimmed and a team of musicians took the small stage. John bowed his head as the lead guitar player prayed, then stood with the congregation as the music began. It pounded and pulsed like the heartbeat of God. These weren't the hymns from back home. John closed his eyes and listened. Electric guitar, drums, even a violin—not what he was used to in church, but holy in its own way. He smiled as the music seemed to transport him into God's presence.

But in the quiet moment between one song and the next, the accusations whispered at him again. He had no right to be here. No right at all.

The pastor—a short, stocky man in his sixties—took the podium and opened his Bible. His rich, baritone voice reminded John of his grandpop and he shifted in his seat. The pastor looked out over the congregation as he spoke, catching John's eye.

With a sharp inhale, John stepped past Derek and headed toward the exit. He kept his head down until a voice startled him.

"Don't like the sermon?"

John turned to find Derek's steady gaze pointed at him. He shook his head. "Don't deserve the sermon."

Derek nodded then looked toward the crowd. "There's a lot of people here. And a great many of us are relentlessly haunted by our sin."

John's pulse throbbed in his throat. He could almost taste the liquor on his tongue. He shook his head, unable to form a reply.

"We all wear masks, man. Everyone's got junk hidden inside—anger, pride, lust, selfishness, you name it."

The words painted a picture that looked too much like him—and the mask he'd worn for friends and family back home.

Derek smiled at him. "God wants to change you from the inside out, not the outside in. Just focus on Christ, man."

John stared at him. Who was this guy?

"Grace, dude." Derek clapped him on the shoulder.

Grace. The word came alive, stinging John's eyes.

"You gonna stay for the message?"

John blinked and ran his tongue behind his teeth. Without a word, he gave a quick nod to the man who had dared to speak truth to a stranger.

The rest of the hour flew by and John absorbed every word.

When the communion tray came to him, he took his portion as if for the first time. He bowed his head and thanked God for the nudge to turn back around and come here tonight.

After the closing prayer, Derek turned to him, eyes glowing. "So whatcha think?" His eyebrows twitched upward.

John didn't know how to answer. He swallowed and nodded. "It was good."

Derek rubbed his lips together and grinned. "Mmhmm. Think you'll be back?"

"I'd like to."

"Like I said, it's a great place to be." His expression turned sober. "Especially for guys like us." He gave a quick nod, then revealed his off-white grin again. "Maybe I'll see you next Tuesday."

"Tuesday?"

"Check the bulletin." He stepped into the aisle. "Nice meeting you, John. Take care."

"Yeah, you too."

Derek disappeared into a pocket of people exiting the building. John opened the trifold and scanned a series of announcements until he found the weekly schedule. Each day listed several meetings or events. When he read Tuesday's lineup, he did a double take. Leaping from the page were the words *Recovery Group*.

John wandered out of the sanctuary with the hairs on his forearms standing on end. Stars winked in the night sky as he crossed the parking lot.

God had planned this whole thing for him? He lifted his gaze into the glittering night and shook his head. This…this was incredible.

He dropped into the driver's seat and studied the bulletin again. Almost every day offered an event of some sort. Bible studies, home groups, various ministries. The men's group was meeting for breakfast the following morning. They probably had pot lucks, too.

His throat ached as he started the engine and headed toward a motel.

Maybe…maybe he'd go to that breakfast in the morning. And afterward, maybe he'd fill out an apartment rental application.

Chapter Six

"Wow. Pastor Dan…" John flipped through a few of the silver-lined pages of the new Bible. "You didn't have to do this."

The pastor's eyes sparkled. "You're welcome, Son. Now you don't have to use the loaners all the time. Don't be afraid to mark this up with notes or highlights or whatever. It's meant to be studied, not left on display."

John tore his eyes from his name engraved on the cover and looked at his new teacher. "Thank you."

The older man patted his shoulder and nodded.

John took his seat in the back of the sanctuary, rested his foot on his knee, and waited for Sunday service to start. Between the men's breakfasts, Recovery Group, and Sunday and Wednesday services, in less than two weeks this place had already become like a second home. Complete with a growing sense of family. John scanned the crowd and thanked God for those who had so quickly accepted him.

Feet shuffled and half a dozen low conversations buzzed as Derek lowered his large frame into the seat beside him. "Hey man, what's up?" Derek jerked his head in greeting.

"Not much. Settling in to the new place. Snagged a couch at Jerome's and could use some help getting it up the stairs."

"Yeah, just say when. You gonna be at Recovery this week?"

"Course."

"Cool. So how'd your interview go?" Derek reached down to stick his Bible under his chair.

John spread his hands. "You're looking at the new Home Depot Special Services Associate."

"Awesome! Pound it." He held up his fist and bumped John's knuckles. "Praise God."

"Totally. Thanks for the prayers."

"Any time, man."

The lights dimmed and the worship team filed onto the stage. A beam of light shone on one end of the platform and a young woman stepped into the center of it. No microphone. No instruments. She simply stood there, erect, in long flowing skirt and bare feet.

She was stunning.

John closed his eyes and shot up an apology. He was there to worship, not be distracted by a pretty face.

A hush settled over the room after the opening prayer. John attuned his ears to the front, waiting, eyes still closed. An occasional cough cut through the air against the backdrop of rustling fabric as people shifted in their seats. Then the drums pounded out a beat and John opened his eyes. His gaze was again drawn to the dark-haired beauty on stage. The music continued and her hands rose and gestured in graceful rhythm.

Sign language—in an elegant performance unlike anything John had ever seen.

The woman put her entire being into the motions, her fluid movements like a dance. He leaned over to Derek. "Who is that?"

Derek gave him a sideways glance. "I don't know her name. She goes to the College and Career Group." He smirked before taking up his singing again.

John studied her. Waves of deep brown hair flowed around her as she moved. Slender arms curved and floated, and a heart-shaped face pointed up toward Heaven. Her bare feet added something genuine to her worship.

As the congregation sang of offering, her open palms rose high before her arms flung open wide, presenting herself to God. The striking imagery brought the words to vibrant life within John. The lyrics sang of bowing down before God, and she nearly touched the floor in an expression of absolute surrender.

Something almost magical was taking place. Her face glowed with such joy that John almost felt he was intruding on a private moment between the signer and her God. *He* wanted that joy, that spiritual intimacy. His voice rose a little louder, a bit rusty from disuse, but carried by waves of emotion, as he was drawn deeper into worship by her mesmerizing, heartfelt expressions toward the Lord.

Even after the music ended and she left the stage, John was dazed. He rested his forearms on his knees and struggled to focus on Pastor Dan as he launched into the sermon. And when the woman returned to the spotlight for a closing song, John was again hypnotized.

"Quit staring, big guy." Derek's eyes flickered with mischief.

John rubbed his forehead, hiding an embarrassed smile. His conscience stung. He should be solely focused on God right now. No distractions.

God was overhauling John's inner world, but he was still a work in progress. Though his rage had evaporated, he still felt like he was walking around with a hole in his chest. A hole that just weeks ago he would have filled with alcohol, and lots of it. He still struggled. And he knew he had no chance at making that pain go away on his own. If anything broke his focus on God…he didn't want to imagine what would happen to him.

He tucked his new Bible under his arm and filed out into the foyer behind Derek. John gave him a light punch on the arm. "Hey, I'll give you a call about that couch. Have a good one."

"Yeah you too, man. See ya." Derek smiled and they parted ways.

Fifteen minutes later, John tossed his keys on his kitchen counter and grabbed a pop from the fridge. The cool fizz tingled his nose as it chilled his throat. He plopped into a kitchen chair and scanned his one-bedroom apartment. It was a nice little place, but it wasn't like the home he'd once had.

As he took a swig from the can, a shaft of afternoon sunlight beamed through the window and bounced off his wedding band. He set the drink down on the table and twisted the gold around his finger. It had felt right to put it back on when he left Vegas—a visual cue to be a man Hannah could be proud of. But maybe it wasn't a good idea to hold onto what was gone. Maybe he needed to find a way to let go. If he didn't, how would he ever heal?

As he nudged the ring over the first knuckle, the image of feminine fingers lacing through his stabbed his eyes.

He shoved the ring back down and ran his hand over his face.

How could he live in the forgiveness of God when the Enemy had a way of bringing April's face to mind—often more than *just* her face?

His shoulders rounded under the weight of shame. He grabbed the can of Coke and brought it to his lips, wishing for a moment that he had some rum to go with it. *God, I'm so weak.* Half an hour removed from a worship service and these were his thoughts?

Fill your mind with Me, my son.

John swung his feet off the chair in front of him and marched across the living room to the stereo. Praise music soon filled the air, and John closed his eyes, concentrating on the words. Absorbing them like a sponge. He could almost hear Hannah's voice singing the lyrics.

She was right. Music truly was medicine for the soul.

But even as he felt his spirits rising, he knew he'd face these demons again.

John's first week on the job was more challenging than he'd expected. Office politics, new personalities, a bitter sales associate who'd been passed up for John's position, suppliers he had no relationship with. All things that would work themselves out in time. But Friday night found John parched, and driving through an area of town a few miles out from his normal route.

He knew why he'd chosen this road, but he could handle it. Even taking a second pass by *Bill's Tavern* wasn't something he needed to share with the recovery group. Not if he didn't go in. Which he wouldn't.

But the thought of a nice gin and tonic set his mouth to watering.

He gripped the steering wheel and tried not to look again at the neon sign glowing in the window. The muscles of his arms twitched as he wrestled with the impulse to turn into the parking lot. One smooth drink to relax. Just one. It wasn't a sin—even Jesus drank wine.

A street lamp flickered. John shot one more glance at the bar, everything in his spirit telling him to go home and everything in his flesh telling him to go on inside. Sweat beaded his forehead. Summoning all his willpower, he gunned the engine and sped away. A split-second later he found a stop sign bearing down on him. Too fast.

A blue Civic seemed to materialize out of thin air, and John's lungs seized. Time slowed to a crawl as his imagination flooded him with the grotesque image of Hannah's lifeless body, her empty eyes casting blame on him.

He slammed his brakes, braced for the impending sound of crunching metal. Hannah's form, pinned beneath smoldering two by fours, dissolved into the vision of someone trapped amidst twisted steel and broken glass. A jolt and high-pitched screech carried the two cars through the empty intersection and onto the side of the road.

All went silent.

John sucked in three quick breaths. "Oh, God." Eyes wide, mouth agape, he stared through the windshield at the car in front of him. "Oh, God." His fingers were numb as he unbelted himself and flew out of his car toward the other vehicle. A woman's head was leaned forward on the steering wheel.

No! Not another death.

John's heart beat against his ribs. His unsteady legs carried him closer. The lady sat back and rubbed her neck, and relief trickled down John's spine. He puffed out his cheeks, taking stock of the actual situation confronting him, rather than the terrorizing visage supplied by his warped fears.

Still, his muscles quivered with adrenaline. "Are—are you all right?"

The woman turned to him, eyebrows drawn tight. He inhaled sharply as recognition sparked. That face…the woman from the worship team. With a growl, John buried his hands in his hair. What had he been thinking?

She rolled her window down and opened her mouth to say something, but John spoke first. "Are you hurt? Do you need a doctor?" He assessed her features, searching for evidence of pain, injury, anything he needed to fix.

Her eyelids fluttered and she shook her head. "Yeah, no. I'm fine."

She opened her door and John retreated to give her room.

"Oh, I'm…I'm so sorry." What was he even *doing* over here? Rubbing his forehead, he turned and paced. What if she'd been seriously injured? What if… He spun and paced again. His head was pounding, and his mouth watered, screaming for that gin. He swore under his breath. *John, you idiot!*

Turning, he splayed his hands out toward her. "I'm so sorry. I didn't even see...I'm sorry."

She shifted her weight and cocked her head, watching him. "I'm fine. Really." Her eyebrows lowered. "Are *you?*"

He didn't have a scratch, but his hands wouldn't stop trembling. "Don't worry about me." He exhaled through flared nostrils.

"All right. We're both okay. That's good." Her gaze went to his shaking hands, and he balled them into fists at his sides. "And the damage doesn't seem too bad. So...let's relax."

John shook his head, then looked away. Relax? He couldn't relax knowing he'd come a hair's breadth from vehicular manslaughter. It was seriously stupid of him to have been on this street, let alone to have floored the gas.

She touched his arm, regaining his gaze. "Let's check it out."

His heart still thumped as they walked the circumference of the cars to assess the damage. Just a few dents, easily fixed. Nothing like the terrifying outcome his mind had feared. He closed his eyes, unsure whether what he felt was relief or disgrace. Probably both.

With a huff of foggy breath, John sat on the curb and rubbed his face. How could he still be thinking about that drink? First he's circling around his temptation zone, and then he crashes into someone from church. And not just anyone, but the pretty signer whose open worship took him straight into the presence of God.

She sat beside him and touched his arm. Her nearness and touch affected his breathing, adding betrayal to his list of failures.

"Would it be all right if I took a minute to pray?"

He nodded. "Yes. Please."

With a gentle hand on his shoulder, she spoke. "Lord, thank you for watching out for us. For protecting us. Now I pray that You would calm us down and bring us peace, that we might feel Your presence."

John's pulse slowed as he listened. The craving for alcohol—any alcohol—subsided. By the time she said "amen," his breathing had steadied. The tilt-a-whirl sensation of the event slowed to a stop as his thoughts centered on God.

He puffed out his cheeks and expelled a ribbon of air. "Thank you. I needed that."

"I could tell." She gave him a soft smile and his neck warmed.

He stood and wiped his hands on his pants, then blew into them, noticing the unusual chill in the air for the first time. "By the way, my name is John. I go to your church."

"I thought you looked familiar. I'm Jenni." She extended her hand. It was warm and steady. And baby-soft.

He cleared his throat. "Again, I'm so sorry I hit you."

She waved her hand in front of her face. "That's what insurance is for."

"Right. Insurance." He pulled his wallet from his back pocket. After they exchanged information, John walked her back to her car door. "I just want to make sure it starts up okay before I leave."

She tipped her face toward him, a curious smile on her full lips, and their gazes locked. "Thank you."

What was that look in her pretty brown eyes? "No problem."

The engine started up fine and John got back in his own vehicle. They each pulled onto the road and he watched her turn left and slowly disappear.

Even then, John felt her calming touch and her prayer, like a handprint on his mind.

Lifting the paper she'd given him, he read her name: Jenni Dupont.

He managed a shaky chuckle. "Good to meet you, Jenni."

Chapter Seven

Six Months Earlier

April Johanson's chipped nails strummed on the table. She made the mistake of glancing at the kitchen clock. Nearly ten p.m. He should've been home hours ago. The tiny diamond on her left hand seemed to sneer at her.

Shoving away from the table, she popped up and stomped to the kitchen. No answer on the cell phone, not replying to texts. She foil-wrapped the rest of the meal-gone-cold on the counter, stuck it in the fridge, rinsed her plate, and wiped down the counters. Fire coursed through her veins as she straightened the kitchen chairs, then fluffed the couch cushions. Arms akimbo, she stood at the edge of the hall, blinking furiously. A visual sweep of the room showed everything in order. Time to face the obvious.

She'd be going to bed alone…again.

Teeth, hair, flannels—still the house sat silent. This place had seemed so tiny when they'd first moved in together. Now, it felt big and lonely.

After more than a few cleansing breaths and a dozen different positions, April faded into sleep.

The front door rattled and her eyes flew open. Her heart pulsed in her temples. She strained to listen. The digital clock glowed 2:08 a.m. She propped herself up on her elbows.

"Stupid keys." Robert's grumbling carried through the walls, and the doorknob clanked again. Dropping her head back onto her pillow, April let out her breath. Okay, it wasn't a crazed thief. Just her irresponsible fiancé who would be in big trouble in the morning. She rubbed her eyes and dragged herself out of bed and into the living room.

Robert stumbled in, leaving the door open. When he noticed her, he stopped and rolled his glassy eyes before dropping onto the sofa. He reeked of booze.

Seriously? Again?

Her jaw clenched. She fingered the two-month-old engagement ring. It seemed to mark the beginning of the change. Of Robert's becoming more and more like one of her mom's loser boyfriends.

She crossed her arms over her chest. "Hey."

"Where's dinner?" He looked vaguely past her.

Her eyes burned. "There's lasagna in the fridge…I'm going back to bed."

"Something the matter?" He glared at her, no doubt expecting her to lay into him about the late nights and the liquor.

She released a sigh. "I'm not doing this tonight, Robert."

"Oh, of course you aren't *doing this tonight, Robert.*" His face twisted in mockery. "Okay, Miss High and Mighty. What—can't be bothered to waste your breath on me? Go ahead and say it, Your Highness." He stood and stumbled towards her, leaning a heavy hand on the arm of the sofa.

April's cheeks grew hot and her pulse roared. She narrowed her eyes and took a deep breath. One-one thousand, two-one thousand, three-one thousand. He was too drunk to carry on a rational conversation. Best wait till morning. "There's nothing to say. Goodnight."

Robert drew himself to his full height and glowered at her. "You're not gonna tell me what a loser I am? How immature it is for me to stay out so late?" He made finger quotes on the word immature. "Don't act like you're not ticked. Either spit it out or go heat me up some dinner." He jerked his head in the direction of the kitchen.

Her nostrils flared. "Do it yourself!"

"Oh, so you *are* mad?"

"Yes! I'm mad. Okay? I'm furious. I shouldn't have to go to bed not knowing where you are. Or when you'll be home, if at all." She held up her ring to show him proof. "You smell like a brewery all the time. I despise the way you look at me, if you can even see me. Hello—I'm the one in the middle!" Her lip curled of its own accord. "You wanna fight, but you can't even stand up straight." Pathetic. "I hate nights like this and sometimes I think I even hate you!"

His eyes flashed. She sucked in her breath, wishing she could suck back those words.

"Is that right? Well, what are you gonna do about it? You gonna threaten to leave? Gonna tell me to get help? Spare me."

Her throat constricted. Why hadn't she kept her mouth shut? She didn't hate this man. He meant everything to her. She just hated her life looking so much like her mother's.

She shook her head. "No. I'm...just tired."

She pinched the bridge of her nose. Things would settle down and they'd be fine. He was just living out the last of his bachelorhood. She crossed the room to lock the front door. When she turned back, he grabbed her wrist, pulled her close, and pressed his soft but beer-tasting lips to hers.

See? They loved each other. He just needed to sleep it off. Things would be fine tomorrow.

She returned his kiss then gave him a sweet smile and pulled away.

"Where you goin'?"

"I told you, I'm going to bed. I have to work tomorrow." And tomorrow couldn't come soon enough. All this drama...she wanted it over.

Robert studied the length of her through squinted eyes, stirring a curious dread like a bubbling cauldron in the pit of her stomach.

"Well, I'm starving. The least you could do is heat me up some dinner."

Her jaw clenched. This was stupid.

"Hey, I don't ask for much from you. I work hard and I take care of you and you can't even make me something to eat? What good are you? I swear sometimes I don't know why I'm even with you. I deserve a lot better, April. A lot better."

He was drunk, so she swallowed a stinging retort.

While Robert took a seat at the dining table, she headed into the kitchen. She may only earn half his salary, but she had a job. She grabbed the lasagna from the fridge and got down a plate. It's not like she couldn't take care of herself, she'd been doing it her whole life. It was just nice not to have to. She cut a large piece and started the microwave.

"Do you have to make so much noise in there?"

Trepidation rose. Her eyelids fluttered and she chewed her lip as the microwave dinged. Why couldn't things be the way they used to be?

She pulled a fork from the drawer without clanking the other silverware, then placed the meal on the table in front of Robert. "Want something to drink?" Or had he had enough already?

He cocked his head and looked at her. "What do you think? Ya know April, you're lucky I stick around. No one else would put up with you." He spoke through mouthfuls of lasagna. "And your stupid questions."

She fought to hold her temper and her tears. It was only the beer talking. Robert would never hurt her on purpose. She brought him a glass of milk.

"I mean, seriously, look at you." He shook his head.

April sat down at the table, not wanting to make things worse by leaving while he was speaking.

"You gotta admit you're pretty pathetic. You're not even that good lookin'. I could do a whole lot better, I'm sure you know that. You know that, right?" He pointed his fork at her and waited for an answer, a strand of mozzarella clinging to his goatee.

"Yeah," she bit out, "sure." Was she that plain? Could he be out of her league? She gave herself a mental shake. No—Robert had told her hundreds of times that she was beautiful.

This was the last time she was going to listen this. Tomorrow they'd have a sit-down. He had to understand how much this was affecting her.

He'd apologize in the morning, she knew. He would feel terrible and take it all back. He'd grovel and she would soak it in and pretend she didn't hurt. But never again would they do this dance. He'd get counseling or enter a program or something. She wasn't going to budge this time.

She looked at that disgusting string of cheese hanging off the corner of his mouth and wanted to let loose on him. To tell him that he was the lucky one, not her. But she bit her tongue and kept quiet. He was making it difficult to do; he seemed to be itching for a fight. He eyed her as he ate, as if on the prowl for something to pounce on.

His icy glare sliced her heart. "What are you thinking? You think I don't mean it?"

Angry tears sprung to her eyes. But was she angrier at Robert, or herself?

"Oh come on, are you crying? You're going to stoop to that now? Trying to make me feel guilty?"

Somewhere inside her, a fuse lit. It traveled from her gut to her lips and exploded from her mouth before she could stop it. "No! I just want you to shut up for once! If you're going to do this to yourself, at least leave me out of it. When you're plastered like this it's you who is pathetic!"

His palm came down hard on the table. "Watch it, sweetheart! Or God help me, I'll…"

God? Yeah right.

She held up her palms and shook her head. "I try to be patient and understanding, Robert, but you can be such an idiot sometimes."

The slap across her face nearly knocked her out of her seat. She covered her cheek with her hand, eyes wide.

"Shut up!" He held a thick finger in front of her nose.

Her mouth opened, but no words came. Her cheek prickled. Her mother's voice rang in her ears—*welcome to my world.*

She blinked at him, speechless. Robert mouthed-off when he was drunk, but he'd never raised a hand to her.

She knew she should let it go. She'd learned that much growing up. But no. She pulled her hand back to return the favor.

He seized her wrist and snorted. "Don't even try."

Lava coursed through her frame. With a sharp inhale she tried to wrench her hand free but his grip was firm. He stood, tipping his chair over in the process, and yanked her up with him. Her eyes widened. With both her wrists now in his possession, he plowed forward and pushed her ahead of him.

Her back thudded against the living room wall. She gasped, heartbeat faltering, and blinked at the scowling face in front of her. What was this? "I'm…I'm sorry," she managed.

Robert pinned her arms above her head and squeezed. She winced as he brought his face down to hers. He couldn't really be doing this. Not her Robert.

"Don't you know that you can't do anything to me?" His stubble grazed her ear as he hissed. "You're powerless, April. You're nothing. I'm in control here. And I only keep you around for one reason." He brought his lips to the nape of her neck.

Reflexively, her knee flew up. Hard. He stumbled back, doubling over.

April stood panting, rubbing her wrists. Relieved the crazy spell was broken. She shook her head. "You're a sorry drunk, you know that?"

Robert lifted his head and locked on her eyes. His face darkened. "And you know what you are?" The air exploded with vile, hideous words that made April want to cover her ears.

"You need help."

He grabbed his plate and chucked it, marinara sauce splattering the furniture. She ducked as it crashed into the wall behind her head. Before she could recover from her shock, he came at her—rage flashing in his eyes.

Terror struck her core.

He rammed her, thumping her to the ground. A kick to her stomach drove the air from her lungs. She curled around herself, gasping. Coughing.

She crawled toward the recliner, hoping to pull herself up. But Robert yanked her by the feet, dragging her across the rug, burning the skin on her back. Before she could cry out, he straddled her, holding her down with his full weight.

"Robert…" With the little air she had, she screamed and pushed against his legs. "Get off! You're hurting me!"

He raised a fist high above her and her eyes widened.

"No!" She lifted her hands and turned away as his knuckles crashed into her temple. Stars flashed through her vision. His fists hammered away and all she could do was use her hands as a feeble cover. She thrashed and pounded on his thighs and tried to wriggle out from beneath him. It was no use. Blow after blow crashed into her forearms, her face. Searing pain shot through her jaw. Another crack to her cheekbone. Panic rose like bile in the back of her throat. Was this how she would die?

"Robert, please! Stop! Don't do this!"

An iron-clad fist connected with the side of her head as she tried in vain to find shelter behind her arms. He released a frustrated grunt and grabbed her flailing arms in a vice grip. His nails dug into her skin and he slammed her wrists to the floor above her head. Her hands tingled, but the hitting had stopped.

A warm trickle trailed from her mouth. "Oh, God!" *I don't want to die.* She tried to catch her breath between sobs. Her pulse roared in her head. Moisture ran down into her ears.

Robert stared down at her with evil eyes, his sweat dripping onto her face. A vein in his forehead pulsed.

Who was this monster? Where was the man who loved her?

His expression shifted, his eyes hooded and dark, and his breath deepened. He released her and stood.

"Get up."

At his barking command, April scrambled to her feet, stumbling on shaky limbs. Her body trembled, the metallic taste of blood covered her tongue, and by the pain in her side she was sure he'd cracked a rib.

His fingers twitched. "Come on." He grabbed her arm and pulled her toward their room. "Sit." He thrust her onto the bed and she winced as she landed.

Her heart galloped. She wanted to bolt, but she sat, frozen. She stared down at her hands and silently begged mercy from the God she didn't believe in. Robert sat beside her and jerked her chin up, studying her face. His gaze traveled from her forehead, past her eyes to her mouth.

What did he think of his handiwork? Would the apologies come now? Would she forgive him if they did?

He leaned close, his hot breath reeking of stale liquor, churning her stomach. His lips pressed into hers, rough and possessive. April pushed against his chest but arms of steel pulled her close and he kissed her harder.

She tasted rancid malt-and-hops, and her busted lip throbbed against his mouth. She wriggled in his unyielding grasp as panic exploded through her body. Oh God, please no! Fresh tears rolled down her cheeks and she moved her head away.

Robert wove his fingers into her hair and yanked her head back, sending a shock of fire through her scalp. She cried out in pain.

"Knock it off, April! Don't fight me."

So she didn't.

An hour later, with Robert finally passed out on the bed, April threw clothes into a suitcase, swiping furiously at the hot dampness on her cheeks. She ached in more places than she could've imagined, but no way would she be a statistic. After emptying his wallet, she limped out of the apartment.

Dawn was still an hour away and the parking lot was awash in the glow of street lamps. Breathing fast, she tried not to think of what would happen if he caught her. An alley cat hissed as she approached a row of shrubs. She jumped, exhaled, then continued on.

The car-port lay in sight of the bedroom window. She held her breath and squeezed her eyes shut as she twisted the key. The engine turned and she peeked up at the beige curtains. Not a flutter. She crept out the complex gates, then punched it full speed toward the highway.

She wouldn't be coming back. You couldn't count on anybody else to come to your rescue. April had learned that much growing up. She didn't have a lot of money, but it was enough.

It would have to be.

April's chest thumped. Logic told her she was safe now, that the forsaken desert road would lead her miles away from Robert. But her nerves and her imagination had her jumping at every set of headlights that gleamed in her rear-view mirror. For hours she focused on the New Mexico highway stretching ahead, pressed onward by the simple need to get as far away as possible.

When the gas light came on, she had no choice but to roll into a shabby-looking service station. Dawn brought a hazy lowlight to the skyline, illuminating her far-from-home surroundings. Her fingers rattled the keys when she moved to cut the engine. She held her hands out and watched them shake uncontrollably. The shiver spread through her till her teeth chattered, and not from cold. She wiped damp palms on her jeans and grabbed a deep breath, wincing as her ribs expanded, then got out of the car and headed inside to pay.

The smug station sat in the middle of nowhere, and had the prices to prove it. Might as well be asking for her firstborn. She opened her wallet and thumbed through the bills. Another stop like this and she'd be out of money in a day.

She shook her head and pulled out two twenties. "Forty on number three, please."

The stringy-haired attendant grabbed the cash without a word and punched some numbers on the machine. "Receipt?" He eyed her like she had two heads before dropping his gaze to the ticker tape emerging from the register.

"No thanks."

"You're all set then." He turned his back to attend to who-knows-what on the other side of the workspace.

April dipped her head and left to pump her gas. What was with the way that guy looked at her? Weirdo.

Her stomach growled. She'd need some fueling up too. She scanned the block as she filled her tank and noted the golden arches a half mile down the road. When she got there, she pulled down her visor to check her reflection. Her hand flew to her mouth as she caught sight of her blotchy face. Purpling was starting to appear below her left eye and her fat lip was uglier than she had imagined.

No wonder the gas attendant had looked at her like that. Gingerly, she lifted her fingers to the cut on her mouth, testing it. She hissed at the sting. Her eyes were puffy and red-rimmed. She pulled the compact from her purse and tried to camouflage her complexion as best she could. She dabbed on some lipstick to hide the cut on her bottom lip then reassessed her reflection. She should be able to get through the doors at least. The drive-through would be better but Mother Nature was calling and if she waited another hour the breakfast rush would bring more eyes to dodge.

She lowered her head as she stepped inside. The smell of french fries twisted her stomach but she headed to the ladies' room first, thankful to find it empty. A minute later, she turned on the tap to wash her hands, then leaned down to splash her face. Strands of blood-stained hair fell into view. She shuddered and positioned the crusty lock under the running water, rubbing out the offense and gulping back a sob at the red swirling down the drain. Tears would spill if she didn't pull it together. Then how would she look?

Grabbing a brush from her handbag, she smoothed her frenzied hair. Then she brought out her small makeup kit and got to work. Smearing Cover Girl across her cheekbones, she rubbed circles into her blotchy pink and purple skin. Her lower left eyelid was turning an ugly shade of gray, and was swollen enough to feel the extra skin when she moved her eyes. She stood back and studied the covered bruises. Concealer could only do so much, but from far away she might escape stares.

A flashback of her mother in a similar state invaded her thoughts.

April watched her for a moment with new eyes, then blinked the picture away. She was not her mother. She'd be nobody's punching bag.

She dusted bronzer in the hollows of her cheeks for an almost-healthy glow. Blue eyeliner reduced the redness. The fat lip called for neutral lipstick, inside the lip line to minimize its new size. Though it stung to apply, the effect was worth it.

She pulled in a satisfied breath, cut short by the sharp pain in her ribcage. From a couple feet away she should pass for okay. Somehow, that made all the difference. She exited the restroom and approached the counter to order.

More money whittling away, but a person had to eat at some point.

Back in her car, she scarfed down half her burger then cranked the engine and headed toward the freeway. She ate while she drove, ignoring the pain clicking in her jaw with every bite.

But the reality of the situation began to weigh on her. What if Robert came looking? Where was she going to go? Robert knew all her old Las Cruces friends and she hadn't heard from Mom in years. She'd be no help anyway. If only Uncle Jim were still alive. She pushed away the memory. She had no one. She needed a plan. She didn't have enough money to travel far. Gas alone would eat her cash. And her debit card would put Robert on her trail.

A green road sign grew on the horizon. April squinted to read it, then felt the corner of her mouth twitch as an idea formed. The Nevada state line was about an hour away. Las Vegas crowds.

Perfect.

The January sun hadn't yet set and the city welcomed her like a soothing oasis. Palms lined the streets and sunlight reflected glamour off the sides of the buildings. The whole town seemed to be shouting promises she knew it couldn't keep.

Though cash was precious, she desperately needed a shower, and the Vegas Club Hotel and Casino was boasting a low-rate room.

April ventured in, covering her face with her hair as she approached the counter.

"Hi! Welcome to the Vegas Club Hotel and Casino. How can I help you?" The bronzed Barbie behind the counter must've had one too many cappuccinos.

Exposed under the lobby lights, April glanced around for gawkers. "I'd like one of those twenty-three dollar rooms if you have one."

She ran her tongue along her cut lip as she held out the cash. April didn't lift her eyes to see the woman's expression, and she didn't hear what was said about amenities. But after some tapping on a keyboard, the receptionist held out a receipt and plastic card.

"Here's your key. Would you like help with your luggage?" Her plastic smile was back, all of her teeth filed into a perfect line.

April shook her head. "No, I got it. Thanks."

"All right, elevators are right over there." She pointed with a zebra-striped acrylic nail and April followed her line of sight.

"Thanks."

She toted her suitcase and duffel bag to the elevators, grimacing with every step. When she arrived at her room at last, she closed the door behind her and released a grateful sigh. She leaned back and closed her eyes, waiting for a sense of calm. Instead, an earthquake rumbled in the pit of her stomach and spread through the rest of her body. Her knees wobbled and threatened to give way. Robert's grimy stench enveloped her, choking her.

She tugged at her shirt, yanking it over her head. Water. She needed water. She tore off her clothes and scrambled into the bathroom, then froze in front of the mirror.

Her breath caught in her throat. Tears came without warning as she stared at her reflection. Her weary makeup revealed black-and-blue marks along her cheekbones and one eye. A large purple boot impression branded her torso. Her neck boasted the tell-tale sign of his stolen gratification. Finger marks remained where he had clutched and pried and handled.

He still had her, she wasn't free.

Resisting the urge to scream, she covered her mouth with both hands and stared into her own pitiful eyes. Muddy lines ran down her reddened cheeks.

Stop it, stop it!

Her palm met the counter-top and the tears obeyed.

The room filled with steam as she turned on the shower, as hot as she could stand. She stepped in and let the heat raise goosebumps over her. Her muscles loosened under the steady stream. The shampoo smelled like coconut, but failed to transport her to a Hawaiian paradise. She scrubbed her scalp until it burned, watching the suds swirl down the drain, knowing it wouldn't be enough. After scouring every inch of her skin till it was raw, she still felt just a shade cleaner than filthy.

She dried off then scooped up all the complimentary soaps to pack into her purse. Nestling into the soft red sofa, she sucked in a cool breath as her heart rate slowed. Robert was probably livid by now. The thought brought a strange satisfaction. A modicum of peace finally seeped in. She climbed under the covers of the queen sized bed and pulled the blankets up to her chin.

She was safe. No rattling keys tonight.

Exhaustion poured over her like a bucket of wet cement and within seconds her eyelids were too heavy to open.

The sun went down, again, along with April's hope. She climbed into her Toyota and threw her head back against the seat. This wasn't where she figured she'd be a week after arriving in town. Her determination and careful spending were supposed to pay off.

What was Robert doing? Did he realize she was gone for good? Had he called anyone looking for her? Maybe he'd reported her missing. Or... maybe he was glad she was gone.

A tear slid to the corner of her mouth, the saltiness filling her with self-pity.

She missed the man she'd been duped into loving—and hated herself for it.

With a sniff, April wiped her nose with the back of her hand then cleared her throat. No more crying for him.

She recalled the first morning she spent in Vegas. Waking up in a big warm bed, finding her muscles stiff and sore, pulling her sleeves down over the bruises as she stood in front of the billboard-like menu of the hotel's café. She knew then and there that her wallet would grow cobwebs within days if she plunked down for three square meals and another night or two in a hotel. Even a cheap one. A good deal was only good if you could afford it. And she couldn't.

An unattended server's cart had stood off to the side. Plates of half-eaten omelets, toast, pancakes, and fruit made her stomach rumble just looking at it. After a quick glance around she'd pushed embarrassment aside then swiped a piece of toast and an untouched slice of cantaloupe before she could change her mind. Cold limp toast had never tasted so heavenly.

She wrapped her arms around her middle and reminded herself she had to be self-disciplined. If she couldn't do that she'd end up running home to Robert. Wasn't that always one of her mother's excuses? That she couldn't afford to support herself? That a few slaps now and then were a small trade-off for being taken care of? Not April.

She looked at the newspaper on the seat beside her, the few want ads already crossed off. When she'd first headed out with chin held high to pound the pavement, she'd given no thought to the possibility that a week later she'd have zero leads on any sort of employment.

The receptionist position required proficiency in Excel, the job at the drugstore had been filled. She'd even answered an ad for a nanny but the mom bristled at the way her husband looked at April.

She looked down at her bare finger, cursing her stupidity. Why had she left her engagement ring on the kitchen counter for Robert to find instead of hawking it for a few hundred bucks?

She was running out of time.

With a growl, she started the engine then meandered through the city looking for somewhere to pass some time. She needed a drink. Just one. She'd nurse it awhile, put off hunkering down in the backseat of her car for as long as she could. She'd pretend, for just a few hours, that life was different.

About a mile outside The Strip, she spotted a bar that caught her eye. Jake's. Small and secluded, it looked like the kind of place she could hide out in for a while.

She threw a few toiletries from her duffel bag into her purse and headed toward the entrance. Opening the door, she blinked till her eyes adjusted to the dim lights. Sweaty men of all shapes and ages sat at tables with their heads bowed over their glasses.

She took a few steps toward the bar, rolling her eyes at a couple women who giggled and tossed their hair. After hoisting herself onto one of the barstools, she peered through the smokiness toward a man in a cheap suit who sat at a piano at the far end of the room tapping out a bluesy tune she didn't recognize.

"What can I get you, beautiful?"

April snapped her head around and locked gazes with a strikingly handsome bartender. His hooded eyes traveled over her face.

Heat crept into her cheeks. "Uh…Can I get a white russian?"

"I think I can do that." He flashed his perfectly white teeth and expertly got to work spinning bottles and bounce-pouring her drink. "Here ya go, on the house." He winked.

"Thanks." He had no freakin' clue how much that free drink meant to her. She took a small sip, resisting the desire to gulp it down and ask for three more. He watched her, hazel eyes glancing at her from the side in between filling customers' orders.

He returned and leaned forward on the counter, his shirt sleeves outlining his muscular biceps. "So, I don't think I've seen you here before."

"Nope—first time." This guy couldn't possibly be flirting with her.

He grinned. "Thought so. I'd remember that face." Or maybe he was. She rewarded him with a smile. The dim lighting must have helped hide the bruises under her concealer. She hoped. "So… how long are you in town for?"

"Oh, uh…I just moved here."

"Really?" His brows inched up and a playful smile spread across his face. "Well now, that's interesting."

A dry laugh sputtered from her lips. "Oh yeah, it's interesting all right." She sipped her drink.

He cocked his head of sun-bleached hair. "So, what do you do?"

"I'm still looking for work. No luck so far. If I could get paid for filling out applications I'd be all set."

He quirked an eyebrow and grinned. "Since you bring it up, we have an opening for a waitress right here. Want an application?"

April's eyes went round. "Um. Yeah. Sure." Working in a bar was never one of her life's ambitions, but neither was being homeless and alone.

He pulled an application from beneath the counter and handed it to her. "Ya know, I can interview you right now even without you filling that out."

"Oh really?" She raised an eyebrow back at him.

"Sure. I'm a good judge of people, doing what I do. You seem like a decent person, I think I can trust you."

"Oh yeah?" She laughed. "You can tell all that by the two or three sentences I've spoken?"

"Yep."

"In that case, let the interview begin."

"It's already finished. When can you start?" He grinned again.

"No teasing now."

"I'm not. I'm totally serious."

"What?" She blinked. "Aren't you going to ask me questions?"

"Okay. Can you carry a tray of drinks from the bar to the tables?"

"Well sure, I guess. But I've never waitressed before. Isn't there more to it?"

"You'll pick it up. Most important is that you're friendly and can flash that beautiful smile at the customers. Ask one of the other girls if you like. Lisa over there's been here for two years." He inclined his head toward an auburn-haired waitress. "So like I said, when can you start? Assuming you want the job."

April's forehead wrinkled. This was…was this really happening? "You don't have to talk to the owner or manager or something?"

"Nah. Jake leaves this kind of thing up to me. He trusts my judgment and so far I've given him no reason not to."

She looked toward the redhead, Lisa, scooping up tip money from an empty table. The woman smiled and sauntered over to the next group of middle-aged men waiting to place orders, tucking the cash into her apron pocket.

"Tomorrow, if you want." She turned back to the bartender.

"Great." His eyes danced under the bar lights.

April bit her lip, thoughts swirling. Had she really just landed a job? This had to be a good sign.

"Be here at two p.m. You can bring that application back then."

Moonbeams shot out from her body. "Sounds good." She extended her hand and he grasped it.

"By the way, what's your name?" He was still holding her hand. And whether wrong or right, she liked it.

"April. April Johanson."

"Nice to meet you, April. I'm Ryan. Moore." He held her hand a moment longer before letting go. "Enjoy your evening." He nodded to her, then got back to work pouring drinks and entertaining customers.

April turned around to face the open room and smiled at the piano man. Maybe things *were* going to turn out fine. She took another sip of her drink and grabbed a handful of free pretzels. Then she slipped into the bathroom where she rubbed hotel toothpaste around her teeth with her finger and splashed her face. Ryan jutted his chin in farewell as she left.

As she walked to her car, April bit her lip on a grin and swung her purse back and forth. Starting tomorrow, things were going to be different.

The sounds of traffic woke April from her curled spot in the back of her car. She scrambled up to the front seat then eased her car down the main road to an alley where she set the brake and opened her suitcase. Moving quickly, she peeled off her T-shirt and wriggled out of her jeans in the cramped space behind the steering wheel, replacing them with her nicest outfit. There was nothing to be done about the wrinkles in her skirt and blouse.

Her one full meal today would be scrambled eggs and toast with a glass of orange juice. She'd get these from one of the many cafes along the Strip. But first she used their facilities to do her makeup. The bruises were fading, that helped. With her rumpled clothes and flat, dull hair she looked only half-way decent but it was the best she could do.

A couple hours from now she'd start her first shift at Jake's. Anticipation bubbled up in her belly. This was her fresh start.

She lifted her chin, feeling just like Mary Tyler Moore singing "I'm gonna make it after all!"

April shook her head and laughed. What a dork. But at least she was smiling.

Chapter Eight

April tucked a five dollar bill into her apron and carried a tray of empty glasses to the front of the bar. Waitressing had turned out to be a pretty good gig. There were good days and bad days as far as tips went, but overall she couldn't have asked for a better job. Her boss was gorgeous, the other girls were nice, and the customers—well, most of them were all right too.

"Hey April—how about you bring over another round for me and my buddies, sweetheart?" Mark. A middle-aged, brown-haired divorcee who considered himself a ladies' man. He'd made April the target of his affections and had been obnoxiously flirtatious all week.

"Ugh." April rolled her eyes, but Ryan just laughed. She smacked his arm. "Stop, it's not funny. I'm sick of that guy. He gives me the willies. Maybe I can pawn him off on Laura or Stacy."

"He always leaves a good tip, doesn't he?"

True. She quirked her mouth to one side. The more attention Mark got, the bigger his tip. And April needed all the money she could get. First and last months' rent plus a security deposit—not to mention dishes, utilities, a mattress at the very least—it was taking longer to save up for than she'd realized.

She looked up at the ceiling and puffed out her cheeks. "Fine."

On went her doll's mask. She ran her fingers through her hair, adjusted her top, and loaded a tray with the four beers.

Maybe she'd even try turning it up a notch. Moving toward Mark's table, she used her best cat-walk. His eyes swept over her approvingly as she swayed her hips. She wanted to gag, but she slid him a coy smile and turned to his friends.

"Here you go, boys." Had that cooing voice really come from between her own lips?

She leaned over and passed the first drink to the dark one, a beautiful exotic-looking Jamaican, who gaped at her chest. He raised his eyes to find her watching his gaze. She lifted a brow and tipped her mouth, encouraging the cad. At least he had the decency to clear his throat and look away. The scrawny blond kid, barely legal, laughed and lifted his beer for a long, foamy drink. There seemed to be only one non-perv at the table—the muscular guy, brown hair and eyes, who thanked her politely before lifting his glass.

She then moved to Mark and bent low to set his mug in front of him. Bringing her face next to his, she purred, "Let me know if you need anything else." She watched his gulping reaction. Men could be reduced to mush so easily.

He slapped her rear as she turned to leave. "Will do, sweet-cheeks."

She hid a cleansing breath before looking back over her shoulder. "I certainly hope so." She raised an eyebrow and held his gaze for a beat before sashaying back toward Ryan.

Behind her, the table erupted with hoots and howls.

"Oh man! Did you see that?"

"Yeah, that's what I'm talkin' about."

"Dude, order some wings or something and get her back over here."

Ryan shook his head and chuckled. "Going for the jugular, aren't you?"

April splayed her hand on her chest. "Whatever do you mean?" She grinned, then shrugged. "I need a good tip." And that was the kind of thing they came for, she'd learned.

"Well, you certainly deserve it after that performance. I almost want to tip you myself."

"Thanks." They exchanged a look then erupted into hushed laughter.

Stacy hurried over. "Ryan, I need two cosmos and a dry martini." She lifted her black hair with one hand, and fanned her neck. "Hey April, how's your evening going?" Her green eyes sparkled with mischief and she poked April in the ribs. "I saw you over there. You keep stealing all the big tippers and I'll have to start one-upping you!"

"Oh, I dunno…there's plenty to go around. You can have the little one." She nodded toward the barely legal kid.

"Hmm." Stacy pouted, peering through the crowd. "Doesn't look like he could afford me." She took the order Ryan set on the counter and sauntered back toward her waiting customers, winking at the scrawny blond as she passed Mark's table.

Back and forth April went between the bar and the tables, filling drink orders and flirting with the customers. Tips rolled in. At the end of the night she counted out over three hundred bucks and bit her bottom lip to keep from squealing.

They wiped down the cherry-wood counter tops and refilled the salt shakers, then she clocked out and said goodnight to Ryan and Stacy before heading "home."

April stopped in at her usual spot—the restroom of the liquor store two blocks down from Jake's. The bathroom was a single-stall and she could lock the door while she brushed her teeth and removed her makeup.

She pulled several paper towels from the dispenser, pumped the soap, then ran them under the faucet. After pulling off her shirt, she ran the wet paper towels behind her neck, down her chest, under her arms. A lemony fragrance wafted up, helping her feel cleaner than she probably was. The last drops of her travel-size shampoo weren't enough, so she pumped more lemon soap into her hands, bent over the sink, and scrubbed her scalp.

Half of the day's tips would probably go to restocking a few essentials.

Stripping out of her work clothes, she stepped into sweats and pulled her wet hair into a ponytail. Then she slung her purse over her shoulder and headed out.

The lights of the city twinkled in the night sky. Vegas never got quite as dark as it should because of them. Casino after casino, hotel after hotel, like a string of Christmas lights they stretched down the street toward the horizon. She'd gotten used to the eccentric people, the tourists, the papers littering the sidewalk. Her tired feet settled into a steady rhythm.

After another couple blocks she got to her car and turned the key in the lock.

"April?"

She froze, heart tripping at the familiar voice, then turned in a slow circle. Ryan's brows pulled together and he glanced over her shoulder into her car windows.

April pulled her upper lip between her teeth. "Hey, Ryan." She smiled. "What are you doing?" Would he notice the tremble in her voice? Or the makeshift pillow in the backseat?

"Well to be honest, I followed you." He'd *followed* her? "I was going to see if you wanted to grab something to eat, but you left so fast. I was trying to catch up with you when I saw you go into that liquor store, so I waited for you outside. I'd about given up and left when you came back out."

Her pulse throbbed in her throat.

"You had changed your clothes and taken off your makeup and...I didn't know what to think. So I followed you. What's the deal?" He cocked his head and stepped closer.

Her mind raced as she searched for a plausible reason why someone would use a liquor store's facilities to get ready for bed. "Well, I dunno. I wanted to get out of my work clothes I guess. Why on earth would you *follow* me like some stalker? That's...that's creepy, Ryan." Her voice cracked and she passed a panicky tongue over her suddenly parched lips.

He dipped his chin and looked right through her inner shield. "April...are you living in your car? What happened to your apartment?"

And just like that, the jig was up. Shoulders drooping, she closed her eyes and exhaled. "I never had an apartment." She examined her scuffed shoes. "I've been working so hard to save money—and I almost have enough, I really do. Please don't say anything, Ryan. Please." If they found out she'd used a fake address on her application... She clutched her hands and chanced a look at Ryan.

Pity radiated from his eyes. He scanned her face and glanced from her to the car and back again. Her upper lip slipped between her teeth again as she waited for him to say something. Anything.

Finally, he grabbed her hand. "Come on."

"Come on where?" She blinked and wrinkled her forehead.

"Back to Jake's. You aren't sleeping here tonight. I'm taking you to my place—Don't worry, I'll sleep on the couch. Nobody will know. And don't argue with me about it, I'm not leaving you here to sleep in your car."

For one heartbeat she resisted, but her will dissolved. She swallowed past the tightness in her throat, overcome with new admiration and gratitude. Who knew the smokin' hot bartender was also such a decent guy?

"Let me get my things." She grabbed her duffel bag and locked her car, then stopped. There'd be gossip for sure if she were seen climbing into Ryan's car with a duffel bag.

He must have read her thoughts. "Hey, why don't you sit tight and I'll go back to get my truck. I'll pick you up here in a few minutes."

"Okay. Thanks, Ryan."

Ten minutes later he pulled up in an old black Dodge Ram. Spot free and shining under the Vegas lights, it was obvious he babied it. Soft rock music sounded in the background as he rolled down the window and told her to hop in. She opened the door to the faint scent of his cologne.

She climbed in, palms sweating. "Thanks."

"No problem."

Her bag perched on her lap as he drove. They didn't speak. An empty can of Dr. Pepper rolled on the floorboard by her feet—guess he only babied the outside. The visor in front of her sported a CD holder filled with music she couldn't see well enough to make out. A bottle of cologne nested in the center console. She wiped her hands on the sides of her sweatpants.

This was too weird. Being there. In Ryan's truck. But being in his personal space also felt like a strange privilege. And for the first time in weeks, she wasn't going to be sleeping in her car. Gratitude wound itself through her discomfort.

They arrived at his place in under ten minutes, but by the time April got out of the truck, her nerves were stretched to the limit.

He threw her bag over his shoulder. "Come on."

She followed up the concrete stairs and along the outdoor hallway. He stopped in front of number 208 and unlocked the brown-painted door, pushing it open for her. She hesitated, then stepped past him into his apartment. The scent of his cologne mingled with a hint of old food and stale beer.

"Make yourself at home. You want something to eat? I have leftover pizza in the fridge."

"Sounds good." She lowered herself onto his black leather couch, hands on her knees, and looked around. The one concession to décor hung above the big screen TV—a beautiful picture of the ocean. The only other thing on the walls was a light up Budweiser sign. Several empty cans—soda as well as beer—sat around the stacks of *Sports Illustrated* and *GamePro* scattered across the glass-topped coffee table. April reached for a *Car and Driver* magazine but dropped it when the microwave dinged.

Ryan appeared and handed her a plate with two pepperoni slices. "Want something to drink?"

"Maybe some soda or something. Anything you have is fine. Thanks."

"No prob." He disappeared for a moment and returned with a can of Coke, then dropped down beside her.

They talked about that night's shift and laughed at some of the customers. He didn't ask why she was living out of her car, just kept the mood light, the conversation shallow. Her shoulders relaxed and she leaned back into the cushions while polishing off her pizza. Only one more thing would make this night perfect.

"Mind if I use your shower?"

"Go for it." He nodded toward the hall.

The hot water—and soap—felt so good on her skin that she had a hard time getting out.

She pulled her sweats back on and combed her hair. Plush brown carpet pampered her feet as she came back out to the living room. Ryan had set up his bed for the night on the couch. He wore only a pair of sweatpants—one muscular arm resting behind his head, the other pointed at the TV flipping through channels. When he looked up and smiled, butterflies fluttered in her belly.

"Hey, the wet look suits you." He lifted his eyebrows.

Heat rushed into her cheeks and she forced a casual laugh.

"Bedroom's down the hall. I figure you probably want to get to sleep."

She nodded. "Yeah, I'm wiped out. Guess I'll see you in the morning." She paused. "Ryan?"

"Yeah?"

"Thank you."

"No sweat." He gave a crooked grin and she headed down the hall.

Something about sleeping in your car for weeks makes a warm bed more comfortable than you ever imagined. She sprawled out, enjoying the large space, then curled up with a nice, big comfy pillow. It smelled like Ryan. A smile spread across her face and she closed her eyes, breathing it in.

Instead of morning traffic, the delicious scent of eggs and bacon woke her. Sunlight streamed across the pillow still wrapped in her arms.

She dressed and brushed the morning tangles from her hair, then hurried to the kitchen. Ryan stood in front of the stove, one hand holding the handle of a pan and the other working a spatula. His shirt hadn't yet reappeared and April couldn't help admiring the view. She cleared her throat to get his attention.

"Oh, hey—good morning." He shot a bright smile over his shoulder. "Eggs are almost done. Hope you like scrambled cause that's the only way I make 'em." He dished up the eggs, added a couple pieces of bacon, and passed her the plate.

"Thank you, sir." April grinned and seated herself at the tiny kitchen table. Something between them had shifted. They were no longer just co-workers, but friends. It was a welcome change.

"These are great." She spoke between forkfuls of eggs. "You should be a chef." Much better than the fake-tasting eggs at the cafe.

"You flatter me, *ma chérie*."

April smiled then bit into her salty bacon, trying not to groan in pleasure as it melted on her tongue. A proper woman should be repulsed by the grease, but she loved the bubbling fatty ends. Her deprived taste buds screamed for more, as did her shrunken belly.

Ryan watched her with an amused smile as she polished off the last bite. "I love a woman who knows how to eat."

Her cheeks warmed. "It's not like I licked the plate."

"Don't be embarrassed. Have as much as you want." He gestured toward the three pieces of bacon left on the table. "Please."

"Not gonna argue." She reached for one more slice. "Thank you."

A smile passed between them and April found herself imagining what it would be like having breakfast with Ryan every day. She'd always been able to take care of herself, but…she was lonely.

She gave herself a mental shake. *Chill.* Neediness did not wear well on her.

They finished eating, took turns using the bathroom, and then locked up and headed out. Ryan dropped her off at her car. "See ya at work."

"Yeah. Okay." She stood there a moment, chewing her lip. Should she give him a hug? A handshake? But before she could decide, he turned and got back into his truck.

He looked at her and she waved as he drove away.

April was headed toward the suit signaling for his check when the front door swung open.

"Evening, Jake." She grinned at the boss as he stepped in.

"Hey there, sweetheart." He dipped his head before disappearing into the small office behind the bar.

Her customer was pulling out his wallet as she approached. He didn't look up at her. He'd been aloof since the moment she greeted him and now seemed in a hurry to leave. She didn't get the feeling he was a good tipper, but maybe she'd be surprised.

She placed his bill on the table and tried to make eye contact. "Anything else I can do for you, just let me know."

"Here." He handed her his credit card without glancing up.

Stifling a sigh, she offered a pleasant thank-you and turned toward the front. Oh well. A table of over-privileged college guys had racked up over a hundred bucks in expensive shots. Their type were her bread and butter.

She glanced toward their table. Empty. Her lips puckered. *What in the world…?* She scanned the establishment from one dark corner to another. Guys didn't go to the bathroom in groups, right? A knot formed in the pit of her stomach.

Stacy approached, grumbling, from behind. "Crummy tippers tonight." She deposited empty glasses behind the bar then looked at

April, worry lines appearing on her smooth forehead. "Hey. Are you all right?"

April stared at her. "Did you see those three frat boys at table five?"

Stacy grinned and folded her arms across her chest. "Yeah, they're cute. Why?"

"I…I think they skipped out."

"They dashed on you?" Stacy's face went flat. "Are you sure?"

"I don't see them anywhere." Both women looked out across the room.

"Oh, honey. I'm so sorry."

April blinked and shook her head. "They'd ordered over a hundred dollars. I can't afford that! Stacy, I can't afford that."

Stacy gave a sad smile and twitched her eyebrows. "Maybe Jake will make an exception? Or discount the tab?" She rubbed April's arm. "I don't know what to say. It happens to the best of us."

"Yeah." But not everyone was living on the street, skipping meals to save up for four walls and a roof. April draped an arm across her middle and gripped her elbow. "I guess I should focus on the rest of my customers if I don't want to lose tips."

"Just do what I do. Adjust your top and get your flirt on."

April gave a humorless laugh that came out more like a huff. She forced her lips to curve up and headed back out.

A few steps later her shoulders sagged, along with her smile. The weariness of her plight seemed thicker than ever and her eyelids felt hot. She sniffed and rubbed her nose.

Suddenly, the little hairs on the back of her neck stood on end. She lifted her head and found Ryan watching her. It wasn't the first time that evening. He smiled sympathetically and goosebumps broke out on her arms. He saw too deep when he looked in her eyes.

He saw everything.

April blinked and hurried to one of her tables. What she wouldn't give for a pound of chocolate right now.

For the next two hours she did her job, robotically, dreading the math to come at the end of her shift. If she gave up her morning coffee for a week, that would cover about a quarter of what she was going to be docked. Maybe she could pick up an extra shift. A Friday night would be awesome but those were highly coveted.

She was lost in thought when a hand touched her elbow, making her jump.

"It's almost quittin' time." Ryan was near enough that she could smell the cologne radiating from the skin at the hollow of his neck. "You know you're coming home with me. Right?"

"Shh." April slid a glance around the room. "Talk a little louder why don't you?"

"I won't let you sleep in your car, April." His voice was low but it felt like a microphone was shoved into their conversation. He touched her hip and leaned close to her ear. "I'll pick you up at your car ten minutes after clocking out, okay?"

His nearness made her pulse hiccup. April chewed her lip and gave a slight nod. Her secret was out—Ryan's eyes wouldn't let her forget it. Why pass on the hot shower and warm bed? Besides, she liked being looked after. When she wasn't the object of whispers and stares, anyway. Out of this public environment, she could enjoy Ryan's company. Maybe let him in a little.

After all, secrets were lonely things.

Half-empty boxes of Chinese takeout sat on the coffee table, the remnants of dinner. Ryan's treat. After they'd cracked open their fortune cookies, and after she'd groused about the nefarious frat boys who'd stiffed her at work that day, he'd fired up his video game console and challenged her to some virtual bowling.

"What's better than a little bit of fun to get your mind off things?"

Booze. And ice cream.

Half hour later, she'd changed her mind. April didn't usually turn to video games after a bad day, but it was working.

Ryan raised his game controller and took aim on the screen. When he pulled back his arm, April poked him in the ribs.

"Hey, no fair!" His bowling ball careened into the gutter. April threw her head back and hooted, feeling the ache in her heart release with the laughter. Best therapy she'd ever had.

That and the hot soapy shower she took after ten frames of bowling.

She plopped down on the couch and flipped on the TV while Ryan took his turn in the bathroom. She'd grown up on the late-night oldies— Taxi, Dick Van Dyke, Barney Miller. Watching them now brought a familiar comfort. Ryan joined her for an old re-run of M*A*S*H. It was like she'd known him all her life, the way she relaxed around him. Laughed. Put her bare feet up on his coffee table.

The show ended and Ryan turned off the screen. "So…" He locked his eyes on hers. "Do you think you'll ever tell me how this happened to you? Living in your car?"

April looked down and picked at her fingernails. "I'd rather not."

The simple question brought the unspeakable memories raining down on her and she closed her eyes against them. Ryan reached for her hand and rubbed his thumb along her fingers. Her shoulders shook.

"Shh, it's okay."

He pulled her into a hug and she buried her face in his T-shirt. When she regained control of her emotions, she turned her head, laying her cheek against his chest. Soaking in the warmth of human contact.

His fingertips ran up and down her back, soothing, while she listened to his heartbeat. Steady, calming. Its rhythm changed as he stroked her still-damp hair. The air sizzled. Her breath caught and she sat up. Looked at him. That gentle look on his handsome face.

He lifted his fingers and brushed the hair from her cheek. His eyes darted to her lips and he lightly traced their outline with his thumb.

This was it. Oh my word, he was going to do it. Her heart raced. She held her breath as he leaned forward and touched his warm lips to hers, a rush of heat racing through her body. Her eyes closed and she dared to gently press into his feather-soft kiss.

The gentleness gave way to a burst of intensity as his hungry mouth moved over hers before traveling along her jaw to her neck. April could barely keep up with what was happening. His lips greedily made their way down to her collarbone. He leaned in, pushing her back onto the sofa. Pinned.

She blinked. Moved her hands from around his neck and placed them against his shoulders. "Ryan, I can't." She breathed the words into his hair. "I'm sorry, this…is too fast for me."

"April…" His raspy whisper sent tantalizing sensations shivering through her. "Don't say that." He kissed her neck and she exhaled and closed her eyes. *Maybe…* His mouth found hers again and her lips moved with his of their own accord.

No. She couldn't. "We can't."

"Yes, we can. We should." His skillful hands took liberties she hadn't offered, and he pressed his rough cheek to hers. "Don't fight it."

Feeling trapped, panic stole her breath. She clutched the back of his T-shirt in both her fists. Tried to pull him away. But he only groaned and ran his hand along her thigh.

No! Oh God, please!

"Robert, get *off*!" With one quick explosion of strength, she shoved him, rolled off the couch, and scrambled to her feet, panting.

Ryan grabbed her wrist and looked up at her, brow wrinkled. "Who's Robert?"

Had she said Robert? Whatever. "Just let me go."

He released her wrist and blinked a few times. "April…"

"I'm out of here—"

"Stay. Let me help you, I'm your friend." He stood and reached toward her but she stepped back. "If you stay with me, no one else will find out you're homeless."

She bristled. "Are you *threatening* me?"

"What? No—"

"I'm leaving. I *thought* you were my friend. But I don't do well with threats. Or men forcing themselves on me." She squared her shoulders and jutted out her chin. "So how's this—you leave me alone and no one *has* to find out you tried to rape me."

His eyes grew wide at the accusation and he buried both hands in his hair. "What! Are you nuts? It's not like that. I wasn't going to—"

"Oh yes you were, Ryan." She'd seen that look before. That unstoppable, unreasoning, take-what-I-want look.

"That's…you're crazy!"

Crazy? Yeah right. She shook her head and shot one last sneer his way. Ryan didn't get up when she heaved her duffel bag over her shoulder. She flung open the door and slammed it behind her, then hurried down the stairs and out onto the street, jogging in the direction of her car.

How had this happened to her? *Again?* And Ryan of all people! Her body quaked, and her head throbbed. The best friend she had in this city. Her *only* friend. That's what she got for believing someone cared.

Her eyes itched as she walked the several blocks to her car. Life was *not* going to get the better of her. She was her own hero, like always.

Hadn't she taught herself to scramble eggs at five years old? She could certainly figure out a place to live. No more waiting.

She plunked a couple quarters into a newspaper vending machine along the way. The apartment hunt started now.

Chapter Nine

"Well, if you can be here by seven, I'll wait for you." The apartment manager on the other end of the line didn't sound too thrilled with April's schedule.

"I'll be there. Thank you." She ended the call and slid her pay-as-you-go phone into the pocket of her black-washed jeans. A small luxury from the Goodwill store. If tips were half decent today, she should have enough to work something out. With any luck, she'd sign a lease for a place right around the corner from work—tonight.

She separated strands of hair in the rearview mirror before stepping out and closing the door. Adjusting her purse over her shoulder, she blew out a breath and started walking. The bar came into view and a shiver ran through her.

Ryan.

She didn't want to face him. Interact with him. She placed a hand on her belly to calm the frantic buzzing. What if he confronted her here? What if she was fool enough to listen? Her stomach lurched, but she pulled herself together. No, she was nobody's fool.

Holding her head high, she swung open the door and marched inside. Ryan stood behind the bar, talking and laughing with Jake. His eyes flicked to April, smile gone, before he turned and got to work wiping down the counter.

"Hi, Jake." April smiled in the boss's direction, ignoring Ryan. "Don't usually see you here this early."

"I had some business to take care of today." Jake headed toward the back office. "April, can you come here a minute?"

"Sure." She followed him into his office and he closed the door behind her.

Then he fired her.

April looked through the window of her Toyota, her heart mirroring the rain outside. Beside her on the console lay her cell phone plugged into the car charger, and under that, the newspaper she'd so confidently purchased a few nights before. Useless now. Nobody would rent to her without verifiable employment. Not to mention the lack of character witnesses.

Her stomach growled and she tried to ignore it. To not care. But who was she kidding? This stank. She'd worked so hard saving up money but it wasn't enough, and it was all falling apart. Her scalp itched in want of a good shampooing. She rested her head on the steering wheel, unable to bear the thought of sleeping in the car one more night. But what was she going to do? The only people she knew were Ryan and…

Stacy.

Her head snapped up. Stacy would most certainly let her crash at her place for a couple days. But even better… April bit her lip as the idea clicked into place. Hadn't Stacy complained about bills and rent lately? *What if…*

Sure, April didn't have a job, but she had some cash and she and Stacy had always gotten along well. She flipped open her pre-paid and dialed the number.

"Hey, Stace, it's April. I want to run something by you."

Okay, here goes.

The last thing April had wanted was to need anybody but, well, here she was. Stacy was nice, hopefully this would work.

She pulled the parking brake and toted her suitcase and duffel bag down the path toward building C. The rain had let up but she had to pick her way around puddles left in the pavement. When she rounded the corner, Stacy bounded toward her and pulled her into a hug.

"Roomie!"

April laughed and gave Stacy's hands a squeeze. "This is gonna be fun."

Stacy led the way and opened the door to a cozy apartment. April took off her coat and glanced around at the landscape photography covering the walls.

"I took those myself." Stacy offered a coy smile and shrugged. Who knew she had an artistic streak?

April arched her brows and nodded. "Wow. Impressive."

She followed Stacy around as she gave the ten-cent tour. Modest living room, just big enough for the brown faux leather couch and TV. A simple kitchen with white tile and cupboards. They crossed over an area rug sprucing up the plain beige carpet as Stacy showed April to her new room. A desk and chair stood against one wall but she'd have to get a bed and nightstand.

"Settle in and I'll order a pizza." Stacy pulled her phone from her pocket.

April grinned over her shoulder and dropped her bag on the floor. "Sounds fantastic."

She bit her lip and turned in a slow circle. This was her space. Her *home*. A smile started in her belly and reached up to her ears.

While Stacy finished ordering a medium thin-crust with everything from Pizza Shack, April scanned the DVDs piled in the entertainment center. A chick flick was definitely the way to go tonight. How long since she'd indulged in a cheesy romance?

It didn't take long for them to dive into an impromptu girl's night in. They propped up their feet, pizza in hand, and fired up *City of Angels*. Nicolas Cage filled the screen and stirred April's soul.

"*I would rather have had one breath of her hair, one kiss from her mouth, one touch of her hand, than eternity without it. One.*"

Her throat thickened just as she heard the sniffle beside her. She turned to Stacy and they both laughed through their tears.

April blew her nose on a napkin. "Now why can't I find a man like that?"

"You mean an angel? I don't think they exist." Stacy turned toward me. "Or maybe you just mean Nicolas Cage."

"No, I mean a man so devoted he would give up everything to be with you, even for one brief moment." She sighed deeply. All the men she'd ever met were interested in one thing. Themselves. *Treat you nice in the beginning, then use you.*

"Girl, no man is ever going to turn your life into a fairytale. But no matter what, there's always rocky road." With that, she popped up and disappeared into the kitchen, returning a moment later with two bowls of ice cream and snapping April out of her funk.

"Mmm. You're right." Silky chocolate soothed the ache and the crunch provided a strange release for the tension. Throw in some soft marshmallows and the result was absolute bliss.

Heavenly. She spooned another bite onto her tongue and smiled. She had a street address, a set of keys, a blanket to sleep under. What could be better?

When the dishes were done and the lights turned out, April snuggled up in a fluffy blanket and listened to the buzz of the refrigerator—a refrigerator full of food that wasn't from a drive-through—and promised herself that she'd *never* sleep in her car again.

Music thumped below a din of voices. The air buzzed with the collective energy of a hundred people and problems melted away. At least for tonight.

April tipped her head to Stacy, duly impressed, as Stacy handed her a green drink. "You are *so* the queen of bar hopping."

"I know." She giggled, then sashayed away.

Stacy was a girl who knew how to get what she wanted. They rarely paid for anything when they went out. Tonight they'd ended up at a club off Fremont Street, having a marvelous time.

April sat at the bar sipping her Midori Sour—on the house—and watching Stacy shake it on the dance floor with a guy she'd been flirting with all night. April sighed and turned away.

"Having a good time?" The tenor voice came from an attractive blond with deep-set brown eyes and a strong jaw. He slid over next to April.

"Trying." She bit her straw and looked up at him through her lashes.

"Let's dance a few…" He cocked his head toward the center of the room and took her hand. Depositing her drink on the counter, April trailed along and let him slip his arm around her waist as she moved to the beat.

One melody faded into the next before he spoke. "What's your name?"

"April. What's yours?"

"Ethan." He stuck close, hand on her back, attention more on her moves than on keeping time with the music. But he wasn't a total klutz, and what girl doesn't like commanding attention? Especially from the cute ones. Maybe she'd even give this guy her number. Let him take her out on a real date. Who knew. She could make room in her life for dating now that she had an address.

They danced several songs before stopping to catch their breath back at the bar again, where he bought her another drink.

He downed a shot of tequila then looked at her in a way that made her warm all over. "You're a great dancer."

"Thanks." She swallowed and broke eye contact.

Stacy stood a few feet away in deep conversation with her acquired date—her hand on his arm, in to hear him over the thumping music. She caught April's eye and winked, looking from her to Ethan then back again. When she wiggled her eyebrows, April stifled a laugh and shook her head.

She sipped her cocktail, and Ethan leaned down to whisper in her ear. "Can I take you back to my place?" He pulled back and looked into her eyes, a hungry half-smile on his lips.

Fast mover. "Uh, I don't think so." April laughed, making light of the offer, hoping to spare his feelings. Couldn't he just ask for her number and suggest they go out sometime? She'd say yes if he did.

He lifted a lock of her hair and rubbed it between his fingers, then leaned in close again, his lips grazing her earlobe. Desire shook through his voice. "I could make it worth your while."

April quirked an eyebrow at him and twisted her mouth to one side. He glanced over his shoulder, then rubbed his thumb against his fingers. "I've got cash."

Her eyes popped. She stiffened as she pulled in a quick breath through her nostrils. Had he really just said that?

Too disgusted to speak, she sneered at him, but he only stared back with hopeful expectation lighting his eyes. He was actually waiting for a response! Well, she'd give it to him. She splashed her drink in his face and, with a flourish, spun on her heel to retrieve Stacy.

"We've gotta leave." Hooking her arm in her friend's, she dragged her to the door.

"What's wrong?"

"I'll tell you on the way. Come on."

Stacy looked back at her nameless date. "Sorry, guess I gotta go!"

They rushed out the doors and through the parking lot, April's cheeks still hot with rage. *Of all the insulting…low-life…*

As they drove, April unloaded her complaint to her captive listener. Though Stacy offered sympathy and called Ethan a choice name, she didn't seem too fazed. How could she not be as indignant about this as April was?

At the apartment, April threw herself face first onto the couch. "Ugh. Where do I *find* these guys? How do they keep finding *me*? Men are so stupid!" She wailed into the pillows, then sat up and looked at Stacy. "Do they think of anything else? I mean, seriously. Did he think that would work?"

"You could take it as a compliment."

She shot Stacy a deadpan stare.

"Well, what happens in Vegas…you know the saying. Don't be so surprised." She sank into a chair. "Lots of guys come from out of town with a wallet full of cash, expecting to buy whatever they want in Sin City. They're usually only here for the weekend, so they say and do whatever they want. Especially at the clubs. One of the biggest draws of this city is the legal prostitution. That guy was probably just trying to circumvent the gatekeepers."

April sneered and shook her head. "I'm sick of men and their one-track minds."

"Well, there's always women."

"Not what I meant."

Stacy kicked off her shoes and shrugged. "Eh, whaddya gonna do? Look, don't worry about it. Let's go to sleep and tomorrow we'll find you that new job."

April blinked then nodded. Stacy had a way of keeping things in perspective. Why should this guy get under April's skin? She knew who she was. And she was on the brink of her brand new start. It was taking a little longer than she thought, but it was happening.

Straightening her spine, she went to her room to climb under the covers of the new bed she'd purchased. It had taken almost all her remaining cash, but it was hers.

And tomorrow was a new day.

And so was the next, and the next, and the next. Unfortunately, each "new day" yielded the same results: Zilch. Rent day came and went, not caring how it affected her pride. With no money to cover half the bills, she'd become a free-loader and she hated that.

"Any luck?" Stacy was lounging on the couch when April got back from what she'd thought was going to be a real interview.

"No. They wanted someone with a business degree to work in their corporate office." She hung her purse on the hook by the door. "I picked up an application for a fast food place on the way home."

"Don't bother, it's not worth the time." Stacy stuck her pencil between her teeth and continued working on her crossword puzzle.

April paced the room. "I know, but I'm running out of options."

"There's always Ethan's offer." Stacy lifted the corner of her mouth.

April frowned. "That's not even funny."

"Sorry, just trying to lighten the mood." Her gaze dropped to her crossword puzzle book. "You do need to figure something out though. I can't afford to cover you again."

The muscles in April's neck tightened and she collapsed into a kitchen chair. "I know." She laid her head on her arms.

"Tanya down at the restaurant mentioned she was looking for a place."

April's head popped up but Stacy raised her hands in defense. "Don't worry, I told her I already had a roommate. But…she has money. *Steady* money…" She bit her lip.

She didn't have to say any more. April *had* to come up with the rent this month. With a groan, she buried her face in her arms again.

Stacy came and patted the top of her head. "Well, sorry your day was cruddy. Wish I didn't have to work tonight. But I better scoot if I'm gonna be ready in time."

April didn't look up but heard Stacy's door shut behind her. *What am I going to do?*

She made coffee and took her mug to the small kitchen table where she could see outside through the window. The weather was beginning to warm, the trees filling out in full, leafy green as the month drew to a close.

She sighed again. Though Stacy tried to be cool about it, she was in an awkward position and April felt the strain on their relationship.

If she didn't get a job lead this week…

She tried to summon Mary Tyler Moore but she was apparently in hiding.

April would never make it on her own.

Maybe leaving Robert hadn't been the best thing after all. He might have gotten help—therapy or rehab or something. It could have worked. At least she would've had a roof over her head that didn't constantly threaten to disappear.

Oh shut up, April. Don't be an idiot like your mother. She shook her head and gulped her lukewarm coffee. Of *course* Robert would have kept drinking, and no doubt would have hit her again. She might have ended up in the hospital. Or worse. She had to remember that.

Far better to be struggling and alone than to be with a monster.

April pounded her fist on the table. No matter what she had to do, she would make this work. She *would* find a job and she would not for one second regret leaving Robert.

She still had a week. There had to be a job for her a little deeper into the barrel.

April flung open the door and peeled her jacket from her arms, tossing it on the couch. No job, no money, no rent…no roof. This was the way of the world, right? She'd been given a deadline and it had come down to this.

Heartsick, she crossed her arms over her chest and paced the living room. When Stacy got home from work she'd have to tell her.

She didn't get the job. She couldn't pay.

Heaving a sigh, April stomped toward her room. Might as well start packing now and get used to the idea of sleeping in her car again. Sure, Stacy probably wouldn't kick her out on the spot, but the tension would be more stifling than her cramped back seat. Why put off the inevitable? She was out of options. Stacy needed Tanya and her reliable rent money.

She slammed her door, then slapped it with her palm. Stupid world. Like wax, her anger melted into fear. What if she never made it back off the streets this time? *What if I end up dying there?*

A despairing sob caught in her throat but rather than stop it, she let it come. She plopped onto her bed and bawled for five long minutes, fully immersed in her own suffering.

Okay, stop! You aren't a child.

She balled her fists by her sides. "You aren't helpless. You are *not* a victim! You'll do whatever it takes, remember? Whatever you have to for this to work." *Whatever you have to.*

She inhaled sharply. The answer was so obvious. So simple.

It had been foolish to dismiss the idea before. Of course, she hadn't been this desperate then. Things had changed. But…could she do it?

A new kind of determination carried her toward the bathroom. In the shower, she ran the razor from her ankles to her upper thighs, not stopping until her legs were smooth and stubble-free. Her heart pounded as she dried off and rubbed lotion into her arms and legs.

She applied extra makeup, accentuating her best features, and paid extra attention to her hair. The outfit she chose drew attention to all the right places.

Her knees shook as she slid into a pair of sexy heels. "Calm down. Just see what happens." She could always change her mind…it wasn't a done deal.

Not yet.

She scribbled out a note for Stacy and left it on the kitchen table, then cast one last, assessing look in the mirror. Satisfied, she grabbed her keys and headed out.

She'd find the perfect, intimate atmosphere to engage in quiet, flirtatious conversation. Maybe it would happen like before and it wouldn't even have to be her idea.

She picked a medium-end hotel and booked a room for the night. Sauntering through the casino lobby, she followed the echoes of happy hour. Tonight, she was aware of each man she passed. Felt his hungry, appreciative gaze on her.

In a perfect world, she'd be smitten with an impossibly gorgeous god-like creature who would fall head over heels for her. He would be loaded, and generous, and the whole evening would be more like a whirlwind romance than...anything else.

The lobby opened up to a swanky bar. April took in the rich tapestries adorning the floor. Across the room, floor-to-ceiling west windows overlooked the city lights. Stunning crystal chandeliers illuminated the area.

No hard wooden chairs here. Instead, plush overstuffed couches and armchairs invited guests to make themselves comfortable and stay awhile. A far cry from Jake's.

An older, portly man with a bald spot sat alone at a small round table near the center of the room. Nearby a cluster of younger girls held fruity drinks and giggled while being fawned over by a group of alpha males. One of them would probably make a perfect target.

Target?

A tiny shudder rocked through her and her feet refused to move. She swallowed and brushed the hair out of her eyes then scanned more of the room. A bartender with black hair, dark eyes, and full lips tended to a small crowd of customers. One thin girl, with dark curly hair and olive skin, seemed to be trying to catch his eye, but he was busy mixing drinks and winking at a voluptuous brunette with a spunky pixie-style haircut.

To their left, a man about her age sat alone, blond head down, seemingly in a world of his own.

Well don't just stand here like an idiot. She forced herself to move to an empty barstool a few seats away from the pack, her eyes skipping again across each person in sight. The blond guy was quite attractive. As he talked with the bartender, she stole a good look at him.

His hair could use a trim but was pleasantly disheveled. He swept the room with a blank gaze, showing off light eyes, and his scruffy jaw line was finely cut. A dark blue button-down shirt stretched tight over broad shoulders. He hunched over his drink and stared straight ahead, a look of sadness shadowing his handsome face.

"Hel-lo. How are you this evening?"

Startled by the bartender's greeting, she looked up to see his angled smile. This guy must get a lot of tips.

"Fine, thanks." Her smile wobbled.

"What can I get ya?" His eyes skimmed her.

"I'm not sure what I want yet." *Not sure at all.*

"No problem. Let me know if you want me to make a *suggestion.*" His words held a layered meaning but April wasn't interested in this guy, even with his charm and undeniable Adonis-like qualities.

"I'll let you know." She dismissed him gently, trying not to damage the image she needed to construct.

He moved on to the next customer and her gaze drifted toward the pack of giggling girls and amorous guys. One of the men ran his fingers down a girl's arm and she swatted him away. He'd probably appreciate more willing company. She should move closer and catch his eye. But she *couldn't* move.

She gulped, eyes drawn back to the blond-haired man. For whatever reason, she found herself much more interested in this mysterious guy who had barely glanced up since she'd arrived.

Chapter Ten

April blinked her eyes open, head throbbing when she turned it. The other side of her bed was empty. She gathered the rumpled sheets around her and stood. Her garments were strewn across the room, one heel on a chair and its match on the floor nearby. She ran a hand through her bangs to clear her hair from her face as her gaze fell on the green stack of bills on the dresser. A smile twitched on her lips as she fanned out the cash. *Should be enough for Stacy.*

She blinked. Suddenly the money turned to acid in her hands and she dropped it back onto the dresser, recoiling.

No. This was wrong. She had to give it back. To John.

John Douglas. His name brought a new, dreamy smile to her face. Her conscience pricked at the way she'd taken advantage of him and she frowned. She hadn't expected to feel bad for the guy. Men always took advantage of her, it was her turn. Yet he was different. His memories of his wife, his love for her…he was romantic. And so gentle.

She closed her eyes, remembering his unhurried touch, his tender kiss. He had to be the first man she'd ever known who seemed capable of true love. Last night may have just been a fantasy, but she felt a connection with him. They'd both been dealt a pretty bad hand in life. Surely he felt it too.

Where was he, anyway?

She wriggled back into her dress and wandered to the bathroom. The faint smell of vomit crinkled her nose. Poor guy—must have been the booze. But better to get sick than violent. Robert rarely puked, he just got mean.

She picked up her brush and pulled it through her morning tangles.

How long until he got back?

Her hand froze mid-stroke. What if…he wasn't coming back? Sure, she'd asked for money, but being with him hadn't felt like a one-night-stand. Not to her. *But that's what it was supposed to be, you idiot.* She blinked. Maybe he hadn't felt the same magic she had. Maybe he up and left. Like she was nothing.

No.

She tried to shake off the idea but failed. Maybe she was in denial. Maybe she had been too business-like. This *had* been a business transaction, right? It's what she'd intended, wasn't it? She wasn't anything to him.

What had she become—a hooker?

She snatched several quick breaths. Such an ugly…dirty…*honest* word.

The room spun and she dropped the brush to grip the countertop. Who was she kidding? Last night was not a romantic encounter.

The truth sobered her. She felt as defiled as the night she'd left Robert. Only this time, she'd done it to herself. Her reflection glared back at her. She wasn't the strong, self-reliant woman she'd told herself she was when coming up with this plan. Not even a little bit.

Crumpled, low-cut dress. Day-old eyeliner. She was nothing but a dirty whore.

She dropped her head. Tears burned her cheeks and hiccupping sobs shook her shoulders. Why had she ever done it?

The worst part was that she really liked John. She'd taken advantage of a truly decent man and convinced herself she was helping him. Convinced herself it *meant* something.

April turned the knob on the sink for hot water and soaked one of the stark white hotel washcloths. She lathered it with soap and scrubbed her painted face, leaving the cloth blackened with her bawdy mascara. But her clean, pinkened skin couldn't disguise the harlot she was.

What was the difference between her and Ryan? Hadn't Ryan tried to "help" her? Persuaded her he was a friend and that it meant something. Even though she didn't want it—not the way he did. How was she any different? She hadn't used physical force or threats, but she'd used weapons of her own—seduction, emotional manipulation, physical enticement. She put John in a position to be taken advantage of and got what she wanted—rent money.

So what if she got caught up in his fantasy, wishing she was Hannah and that he was really hers. So what that she felt sincere pity for him. She'd used him. Degraded herself. And it could never be undone. Never be erased.

She gathered her things and the door clicked shut behind her. Her head hurt, her stomach hurt, and her heart hurt as she headed home. When she walked in the door, Stacy glanced at her and cleared her throat.

"Hey, um…I've got to get the rent over to the manager today and I—"

"Here." April handed Stacy the cash and watched relief pour over her. "I'm sorry I'm still ten bucks short, but…"

"Wow, April, this is great! Where did you get this? Did you find a job?"

"No job yet. But don't worry about it." She waved her hand in front of her face. "This should cover me for a little longer, right?"

"Yeah, but…" Stacy's brows pulled together. "Where did it come from? Did you have to sell something?"

Yes. April swallowed the stone clogging her throat. "I don't want to talk about it, Stace. Just take it."

"Oh…all right, I guess. So, still no job?"

She closed her eyes and took a breath. "No Stacy, no job. Give me a little longer on that. Okay?"

Stacy started to speak but closed her mouth as April sulked off into her room. She set her purse in the corner of the room and stripped out of her dress, pulling on some worn jeans and an oversize sweatshirt instead. She had to get the previous night out of her head. To let it go. It was over and she couldn't take it back.

She leaned against the headboard of her bed and ran her fingers along the blue and gold floral bedspread. "What's done is done. The rent is paid. So get a grip." She'd bought herself some time. She should celebrate.

After sulking and staring at her ceiling for a couple hours, April convinced herself to get up out of bed and move on. Keep living. Like she always did.

Stacy's pedicured feet were propped up in front of the TV as April emerged from her room. She dropped down beside her and took a deep breath. "Sorry for my mood earlier, Stace. Wanna have a girls' night? We could watch a movie...*Never Been Kissed?* You like Drew Barrymore."

"Sure." She shrugged. "Sounds fun. I'll get the popcorn."

"And I'll get the rocky road." She sure needed it.

Stacy laughed. "You and your rocky road."

The laundry sat neatly folded on the coffee table, the counters gleamed, and the floors boasted perfect vacuum lines. If April had trouble paying her share of the bills, the least she could do was handle the chores. Besides, cleaning was a nice break from job-hunting. She must have applied for work at every business within a ten-mile radius. Thankfully, her poor little Corolla was holding together like a champ, despite being overdue for an oil change and having a balding tire.

Her cell phone rang as she finished emptying the dishwasher and she pressed it to her ear. "Hello?"

"Yes, hello. Is this April Johanson?"

"Yes, it is." She stacked the last cereal bowl and closed the cupboard door.

"Hello, Ms. Johanson, this is Dr. Bergstein's office calling. We received your application and I'm calling to set up an interview."

"Uh..." Her mouth went dry. The optometry office was about ten miles outside of the city and she'd held little hope for hearing from them. "Yeah—I mean, yes. When did you have in mind?"

They set up the appointment, then ended the call. A surge of adrenaline coursed through April's body despite her efforts not to get too excited. She'd been on countless interviews and had come close to a job offer more times than she cared to recall, but still...

"Hey April, how was your day?" Stacy came through the door and tossed her keys on the counter before heading to the fridge.

April hid her smile and shrugged. "Eh."

"Anything promising?" She popped opened a wine cooler and took a drink.

"Well…" April's sing-song voice caught Stacy's attention. She arched her eyebrows. Waiting.

"I have an *interview* Thursday." April squealed. Stacy joined in, grabbing her hands, and jumping up and down with her.

"And the best part is, it's at a doctor's office—no more flirting with sweaty drunks to get my paycheck! No offense."

"None taken." Stacy rested her hands on April's shoulders and stared into her eyes. "This is going to work out. I feel it."

April nodded. "Thanks. I hope so." Then things would finally be on track.

April sat in her car for a minute before heading up to the apartment. Stacy had worked a late shift last night but she would be up by now. And she'd pounce the second April opened the door. What should she say? She pulled out her keys and unlocked the door.

Stacy snapped her head up when April stepped inside. She stared, waiting. April tossed her purse on the coffee table, feeling Stacy's eyes drilling into the back of her head. She braced herself and turned.

Stacy shook her hands in front of her, looking about ready to burst. "*Well?*" She practically shouted, throwing her hands in the air.

"Stacy…" April released a long sigh. "I got the job."

Stacy's pink lips stretched into a smile that took up her entire face. "Fantastic! Oh, I knew you could do it." She threw her arms around April, squeezing and rocking her side to side.

April closed her eyes and clung to her friend. Did Stacy understand how much this meant to her? Did she have any clue how desperate she'd been? Stacy's joy reinforced April's own giddiness. She laughed and then cried—like she'd won the lottery instead of getting a receptionist job. To her, it was even better. All the stress of the past months came out in one big release. She was employed. In a respectable field with room for advancement. This time she was sure it was going to work out.

And she was ready.

Chapter Eleven

Riverside, California

Jenni pulled on a silk robe and headed for the kitchen thinking about the kids she'd be meeting that morning.

"You nervous?" Her mom came up beside her and pulled her hair back from her shoulders.

"No, I'm not nervous. I love this part." She smiled and bit into a bagel.

"Good. Will you be home for dinner?"

"Yes, but it's Thursday, so I'll be leaving again right after."

"Right. The church."

"Mm hmm."

Her mom lowered her own bagel into the toaster and dragged a mug from the cupboard. As she shuffled toward the coffeepot, morning light slanted into red eyes that squinted tiredly over dark circles.

"Didn't you sleep okay?"

She added a little milk and shook her head. "I was up half the night with your Aunt Mary is all."

Jenni winced. "Just a hard night, or…?"

"No." Mom sipped coffee. "She ran into Uncle Dave. And *Ariana*."

Poor Aunt Mary. *Please give her strength, Lord.*

"Men only think with one organ, Jenni, and it isn't their brain."

"Mom, you can't believe that's true. Men fall in love too."

"Of course they do, sweetie. But they're weak. And when life gets tough, you can count on them reverting to their basest instincts."

"Sometimes maybe, but I think there're still some good men out there."

She smiled. "There are. And they're much easier to find when you're young and beautiful than when you're old and spent. So quit your dillydallying and reel one in already."

"You're not old. And neither is Aunt Mary."

"Yes, we are. And you will be too, before you know it. So do us all proud and bring something home from that church of yours besides Bibles and tracts. You've been going there for years now and have yet to meet someone."

Jenni quirked an eyebrow. "That's not why I go there. And I *have* met Someone."

"You have?" Her mom's eyes brightened.

"Yes. His name is Jesus."

Her mom groaned. "Oh Jenni, that's not funny."

"I wasn't trying to be." She grinned and wiped a sponge along the counter, clearing the bagel crumbs. She had a few friends who were single, attractive, and character-driven, and if friendship should ever develop into something more, well, then so be it. But she had learned to be discerning. Cautious with her heart. She didn't match her mother's hurry.

"At this rate I'll never be a grandmother."

"Not unless there's another virgin birth."

Her mother shook her head. "Have we scared you off so completely?"

Her parents' divorce, her aunt and uncle's split, there was enough pain in her family on the relationship front, but Jenni hadn't given in to cynicism.

She returned the sponge to the sink and rested her hands on her mother's shoulders, looking her in the eye. "No. I'm just not on the prowl. I've got plenty of other things occupying my heart. And right now, I gotta get ready for one of them." She kissed her mother's cheek. "I'll see you tonight."

Half an hour later, Jenni entered the special education building at James Monroe Elementary.

"It's good to meet you in person, Jenni," Miss Lisa, the teacher, greeted her at the classroom door.

"You too." Jenni stepped inside. Eight third graders sat at little tables and peered up at her like wide-eyed fawns—hesitant, hopeful, and adorable. Two through extra-thick glasses, one from his perch in a wheelchair. Three wore hearing aids.

Miss Lisa leaned close. "Don't worry if some of them seem chilly toward you. I have a couple of kids who are a bit withdrawn."

"No problem," Jenni assured her. She could relate. Sometimes she felt like an instrument missing a mouthpiece, in need of a fine-tuning in order to play. These children were the same, and love was the key to making them sing. She smiled warmly at them as their teacher introduced her.

"Good morning," Jenni spoke and signed in American Sign Language at the same time. "I'm so happy to be here with you today."

Two of the three deaf children smiled extra wide as they realized she spoke their language. The third, a little blonde girl, sat stoic.

Unfazed, Jenni continued. "Who here likes music?"

Five hands shot into the air. Jenni looked directly at each of the kids in hearing aids. "Do you like music?" She signed and pointed at them. They stared at her in bewilderment. "Music you can *feel*, in your body." She made the signs for *drums* and loud vibrations, widening her eyes. "I love music, and I think everyone should have the chance to experience it." She opened the shoulder bag she had set beside the desk and withdrew two percussion instruments—a small drum, and a set of claves, laying them on the desk. "This is all I could bring today, but it's a fun introduction. Who wants to try first?"

She started around the room to give each child a turn at hitting the drum or striking the claves. The first two deaf children banged them tentatively at first, then grew more bold, smiling at the pulsations they created in the air. The little blonde exerted just as much force, her eyes riveted to the instruments, but remained expressionless.

As Miss Lisa looked on, each child tested out the percussions, becoming more animated as the minutes slipped by. Finally, Jenni stowed the small instruments back in her bag then pulled out a book. "Now I thought I'd read you one of my favorite stories from when I was your age."

With Miss Lisa turning the pages for her, Jenni signed and read aloud the story *Giraffes Can't Dance*, complete with over-the-top facial expressions and lots of giggles from her audience. She made extra eye contact with the sullen little blonde girl and was eventually rewarded with a gentle lift of the corners of her mouth. When the story ended, the kids clapped and smiled, and Jenni glimpsed the sun breaking through the cloudy wall between her and the more guarded ones. She then spent several minutes answering questions about herself, and chatting with the kids, making special effort to engage the blonde. Her time was up much too soon and Jenni packed her things back into her shoulder bag.

"Class, what do we say to Miss Jenni?" The teacher prompted, verbally and through sign language.

The children responded with a mixture of vocal and ASL thank you's. Jenni's heart warmed at the sight of their glowing faces. No, more than warmed. It burned with a passion to love them. To give them everything they needed to find joy and connection in a world that largely didn't understand them. The same way she had felt isolated, hidden with her pain, before God had grabbed hold of her and refused to let go.

"You're welcome," she signed. "I hope you'll invite me back again. Next time I'll bring bigger instruments." She raised her eyebrows and nodded toward the group, connecting her gaze specifically with each of the hard-of-hearing children. "Maybe a guitar or my friend's bongo drum. I think you will like that a *lot*."

A couple of children hugged her around the waist before she left. The little blonde girl tapped her arm, then her hands launched into rapid conversation about dancing giraffes that evolved into giggles. Joy wound through Jenni's heart. She knew, even if the girl didn't, that they weren't just talking about silly stories, they were building trust, connection, self-expression. Their fingers stilled, and words gave way to small, warm hands wrapping around Jenni's middle. She squeezed back, her heart brimming.

"Thank you so much," Jenni signed.

The girl pointed to one of the desks. "Will you sit by me?"

At the front of the room, Jenni noted Miss Lisa watching them, eyes wide with wonder. "I would love to, but I have to go to work now and can't stay. Next time, okay?"

The girl frowned. "Soon?"

"I'll do my best."

"Okay back to your seats, everyone. Time for our math lesson." With a touch to Jenni's elbow, Miss Lisa pulled her aside out into the hallway. "That was Emma you were talking to just now." Her eyes filled and she blinked. "She's usually the least communicative child in my classroom. To see her connect with someone like that" —she shook her head—"is very special."

Jenni searched for words. "Moments of connection are my favorite part of working with these kids. They're like…violins without strings. They don't know the music locked inside of them, but if you can show them…"

"It makes all the difference," Miss Lisa finished for her.

Jenni nodded. Giving a voice to those who felt they had none was the reason she'd been drawn to ASL in the first place. She knew the pain and loneliness of being unable to express what was inside, knew that the pain would find a way out in one form or another, and how unhealthy some of those forms could be. She was grateful, so grateful, for the grace that had saved her from herself and then planted the seed of compassion in her heart. She smiled. "I had a wonderful time, thank you."

"No. Thank *you*."

As Jenni crossed the school parking lot, she spotted the dented fender of her car and pulled out her keys. The rest of her day was mapped out before her—a four-hour work shift, then dinner, then worship practice at the church—but as the fender reminded her, you never could tell what surprises you might encounter in a day.

John's face came to mind then, surprising her. He seemed like a decent guy, one starting fresh. She'd seen him at church often, talking to a friend, praying with the pastor. He bore the unmistakable countenance of a new believer. Whatever his story, he was looking to the body of Christ for support. She heeded the prompting she felt to pray for him, then turned onto the road and prayed to be ready for whatever might come her way.

Music sounded through the auditorium as John pushed open the sanctuary door. Looked like the worship team was practicing for next Sunday. John was earlier for the men's study than he'd thought. Musicians dotted the stage and played to the empty room. Musicians…and their sign language interpreter. The music reverberated in his bones before fading away to silence.

The lead guitarist removed his Gibson from across his shoulder. "All right, guys, that'll do it. See you Sunday morning."

The team chatted as they packed up their stuff. Jenni laughed with one of the vocalists, and John smiled at the sound of it. She reached for her water bottle and jogged down the steps of the stage. Toward him.

"Hi, John."

"Hey." He jerked his chin in greeting and returned her smile.

She pinned him with her gaze. "How have you been lately?"

Something in the way she said it made him squirm. "Fine, thank you. I called about the accident, but my insurance said they haven't heard anything from yours yet. They couldn't find a report. Did you lose the info, or is there something I can help you with?"

"Eh. The damage is so minor, I'm not even going to bother."

"Well, if you decide to take it in, please go ahead and file a claim. My insurance guy will take care of you. Or just give me the quote and I'll cover it outright. It was completely my fault." His ears burned with residual guilt.

"It's called an *accident* for a reason, John."

"No. I had no business taking that street in the first place. You have no idea."

Gentle fingers came to rest on his forearm. "Hey, nobody's perfect. That's why we need God, right?"

That about summed it up, yes. "Yeah…like every second of every day." John had so much to overcome, so much to leave behind. And zero chance of success on his own.

"Can't argue with you there." Her expression went soft, contemplative, and she fiddled with the silver bracelet on her wrist. "He carries us."

She held his eyes for a moment, making him feel exposed. Vulnerable. Did she sense his struggle? Have one of her own?

He looked away as he passed a hand over his scruff of his cheek and forced lightness into his tone. "Well, He usually has to *drag* me."

Laughter bubbled from her lips. "The scrapes should heal, though."

"And the scars are a reminder." He grinned.

The laughter drained from her eyes and she nodded soberly. "They are." She stared at him, as if searching for something behind his eyes, then seemed to give herself a little shake. "Well...I, uh...I should get going." She snatched her bag and draped a cardigan over her arm. "See ya later."

"Bye..." He took a quick breath. "Jenni?"

"Yeah?" She looked back over her shoulder and their gazes latched and held.

The air around him buzzed, his lungs felt like they had a slow leak, and he couldn't think of anything to say.

Without seeming to notice, she was still toying with that bracelet, turning it around and around on her wrist. Did it mean something? What had jolted her a moment ago? He wanted to find out, to fix whatever it was, but it wasn't his place. He had no right to ask. All he had was a strange ache to keep her talking.

And the even stranger sense that one day, she'd let him in on whatever burden she was carrying.

With that odd sensation whipping through him, he finally found his tongue. "Don't speed."

Her mouth quirked. "I won't."

John studied the angles of her face, then the sway of her hair as she walked away. A deep longing rose up from somewhere within him, but for what, he didn't know.

How could he even look at another woman? Despite the fact he'd finally removed his wedding band, it felt like cheating every time he saw Jenni and felt the heat wash over him.

He clenched and unclenched his fists, then rubbed his palms on his jeans. He needed to focus on God right now, on sobriety. On strengthening the faith that had crumbled so easily under pressure.

He needed to keep his distance from Miss Dupont. But he had a feeling it wouldn't be easy.

"I still get angry sometimes." John dribbled the basketball between his knees, out of Derek's reach.

"That's all right. It's a process." Derek lunged across the asphalt but missed the steal.

"Not sure I'll ever get over it."

"Getting over it isn't the thing. It's getting *on* with it. With your life."

John swiveled around Derek and took the jump shot. The ball swished through the net. Derek snatched it on the rebound. "You don't need to stay stuck in this place forever."

"I get that. I do. It's just…" He stopped and wiped his face across his sleeve. "I'm not sure what I'm supposed to be doing, and honestly it scares the tar out of me." He paused to suck in air. "I've always had a plan, ya know? Marry Hannah, buy a house, a dog, have a couple kids, then grandkids, and later retire to Tallahassee or something. Boom, boom, bam."

Derek dropped a muscled hand on John's shoulder. "Life has thrown you a curveball to be sure. Just stick close to God. He's got the map."

"Believe me, I'm trying." Man, was he trying. If he could keep Jenni out of his head, it'd be a whole lot easier. But how was he supposed to do that when he had to watch her on stage every Sunday? And she always made a point to check in with him, ask how he was doing. As if she knew he was going through a rough patch.

He smacked the ball away from Derek and jogged down the court.

It wasn't just her beauty that had snagged him. It was the way she loved Jesus. But that wouldn't be his excuse to focus on her instead of God. He stopped at half court and took aim. Air ball. "Just wish he'd give me a peek at that map, know what I'm saying?"

"I hear ya. He don't always work like that."

John shot Derek a sardonic smile. "Yeah well…not sure I approve of that."

"Give me the ball, bonehead."

"Come and take it."

The sun beat down on the back of his neck as John worked to outmaneuver his friend. Sweating, feet pounding across the court, his stress siphoned away through the use of his muscles, which no longer shook with demands for alcohol.

This new life was going good. He just had to stick to the game plan and focus on today. On God. And not get preoccupied with anything—or anyone—else. No matter how hard that was.

"I don't know, Tori." Jenni lifted a hanger from the rack and held the dress up against herself. "It's the way he looks at me sometimes." She tipped her head as she gazed at her reflection in the full-length mirror, then looked at her friend. "He hasn't tried to come on to me, or expressed interest, but…when our eyes meet…something happens. It feels like I've known him for years, even though I barely know him at all."

Tori pulled off a shoe then pointedly arched a brow. "Are you saying *you're* interested?"

"No. I'm not saying that." Definitely not. She clapped the dress back onto the rack and fingered through the row of maxi dresses. "I'm only saying there's something different about him, about the way we connect. It's strange."

"He's handsome and mysterious and you're intrigued. What's so strange about that?"

For Jenni, everything. "You know I don't lose my head over cute guys. But you're right, I'm intrigued." Safer than interested, anyway.

"As well you should be. It's even fine to be more than intrigued. So get to know him. When was the last time you went on a date? Wasn't it like January that Blake took you out?"

"Yeah, but it wasn't really a date." She'd even paid her own way to be sure.

"Only because you didn't let it be. We both know that he wanted it to be a date, though."

Jenni shrugged. Blake was a good guy, but there was nothing there but friendship.

"And it's been years since Aiden. Girl, do you plan on becoming a nun?"

"I'm too young to be called an old maid, thank you very much. Aiden was a huge, blistering mistake that I don't care to repeat." She pulled out a blue dress, examined it, and hung it up again. "And I won't, because I'm not a dumb twenty-year-old anymore." No more blind love leading her into heartbreak.

"That's right, you aren't. So trust yourself. Trust God. Keep your heart open and see what happens. Maybe this mystery man will surprise you."

"I don't know about that." Jenni held up another dress, this one with large Hawaiian flowers covering the skirt. "What do you think? Too much orange?"

Tori twisted her mouth to one side. "A little. Though if anyone can pull it off, you can."

"Hmm, I don't think so."

Tori put the shoes back on the shelf. "Well, these pinch. Nothing here for me today. I'm heading home to my cat and my DVR."

Jenni laughed. "Okay. See you this weekend."

"Sounds good, and hey, let me know if anything interesting happens with you-know-who."

"If anything interesting happened with anyone, I'd let you know."

When John entered the sanctuary the following week, he wasn't expecting to find it empty. Worship practice must have been postponed or canceled this week. Disappointment filled him and his eyes lighted on the acoustic guitar standing in the corner.

His fingers suddenly itched to pluck the strings. He ascended the steps and wrapped his palm around the neck of the guitar. He lifted it slowly, the familiar weight and feel carrying him back in time. At the end of the stage, he lowered himself to the floor, legs hanging over the edge, and propped the instrument on his thigh, positioned his fingers, and dragged his thumb across the strings. A haunting E minor rang out, stirring his emotions. He switched to a G and closed his eyes, moving through a series of chords until a song formed. He could almost hear Hannah's voice accompanying him. Could see the joy on her face as she sang.

He wasn't much of a singer himself, but he parted his lips and let the words come, softly. Hannah had always said it didn't matter how well a person could sing, music was born in the heart, something that gave to the soul the more it was released. She was right.

"I didn't know you played." The feminine voice cut in.

His fingers stilled and he opened his eyes to find Jenni watching him. "It's been a while."

She lowered herself beside him, dangled her crossed ankles, and planted her palms on the edge of the stage. "Please, don't stop on my account. Keep playing."

Darting his tongue over dry lips, he began another song.

A moment later she joined in. She had a lovely voice. John had never heard it before. Her role was always sign language interpretation on stage, never singing in front of a mic. As he watched her face, something stirred inside him. She caught his gaze and her eyes smiled as she continued the melody. Their music efforts blended into one, her vocals pacing his chord changes seamlessly, like a dance of sound. He'd only felt that with one other person.

Hannah....

He tensed and his fingers slipped on the strings. He flattened his palm over them, silencing the instrument.

Jenni gave him an inquisitive look, and he shrugged. "Sorry. Guess I'm out of practice." Needles pricked his eyes as he stood and replaced the guitar in its stand. He shouldn't have picked it up in the first place.

"That's okay. I thought you played beautifully. Until the end there." Her grin jolted him even further.

"Thanks." He swallowed against the dryness in this throat, unable to return the smile.

Jenni came to him, brows drawn in concern, and touched his arm. "Hey." Her topaz gaze searched his. "Are you all right?"

Face taut, John simply nodded. There was no way to explain to her what was happening. Why his heart was boxing his ribs or his hands were slick with sweat.

"Psalm thirty-two. Read it when you have a chance. Let God surround you with songs of deliverance." She squeezed his arm and smiled.

Their gazes tangled, and for a long moment he couldn't look away. Which did nothing for his accelerated heart rate. Finally, he broke contact and stepped back. "Thanks. I, uh, gotta get going. I'm supposed to be somewhere. But I'll see you Sunday, 'kay?"

"Okay." She assessed him again. "Take care, John."

"You, too."

John hurried out to his car, head spinning, chest aching. Confusion warped his mind—sadness, nostalgia, longing, and hope blurred together in a formidable mass. But was he being pulled down into a pit…or out of one?

Chapter Twelve

"So. You're here early." Derek gave a wicked grin as families trickled in for the Sunday service.

"I value punctuality."

"Sure. Whatever you say. And uh…you sittin' up front today?"

So, Derek had noticed he'd chosen a seat closer to the stage the last couple Sundays. But he didn't know the reason—there *wasn't* a reason. And no, Jenni wasn't it.

He ignored the bait, and pointed toward the third row. "Yeah, my stuff's right there if you want to join me."

John and Derek took their seats as an electric violin sent out a restrained, velvety tone. A piano's reflective sounds joined in, and the vocalists began singing about the greatness of God. Jenni acted out what their collective voices declared.

John closed his eyes. Worship music always affected him in a deep, mysterious way. God seemed bigger and his worries smaller. Hannah had known the power of music. Had often called it one of God's greatest gifts to mankind.

After a handful of songs, he was ready to take in the Scriptures. To really hear it. The pastor's message sharpened his focus on who God was and what kind of man John wanted to be. What having faith meant. It looked a lot different than he'd always thought.

When the service concluded, John stood and stretched his legs.

Derek clapped him on the back. "Have a good one, man."

"See ya later, Dare."

John headed for the exit, his spirit satiated. The worshipers milled about in clusters outside the sanctuary. A few kids stood at the donut table, picking at crumbs and bits of frosting. John watched them a moment, then began threading his way toward Jenni. Just a quick hello.

She stood with her back to him, chatting with a friend. Sunlight bounced off the bare skin of her shoulders as she gathered her hair in her hands and twisted it up on her head, wrapping the ends around and around before tucking them in. His pulse spiked and he looked away from her soft neck, out toward the hedges on the other side of the courtyard.

"Hey, John!" Jenni had turned and was walking toward him with a grin that made his chest ache. "I was just thinking about you."

Warmth spread through his muscles. "Oh yeah?" Her scent spiraled through the air around him. Perfume, or maybe shampoo—something sweet and feminine and very appealing.

"Did you check out that—"

"Psalm?" He finished for her.

"Mind reader, are you?"

"Shh. Don't blow my cover."

"Oh, right. If anyone found out there was a man who could read a woman's mind, the very fabric of the universe could unravel."

"Yeah, you don't want that on your conscience."

Her laughter unwound something tightly knotted within him, eased a tension he hadn't been aware he carried. "I did read it, yes. Psalm thirty two...songs of deliverance. It was perfect."

"It's one of my favorites. I've spent a lot of time in the Psalms."

"I pretty much live by them. You know that part about the mule? That was me. But I'm learning to trust God's leading. Less painful than being pulled around by the bit."

"Yeah, ouch." One corner of her mouth inched up. "Is that the part that spoke to you? For me it's the verse about God being my hiding place. Protecting me. But I love how the Scriptures can speak to each of us in just the way we need."

Her face lit up when she smiled, drawing his attention to her exotic features. High cheekbones, angular jawline, perfect teeth behind perfect lips. Lips that were moving again with words he'd best not miss. He refocused on what she was saying...

"So, now I'm looking for a ride home." She combed her hand through long, dark hair.

He nodded. A beat passed. "Sorry, what do you need?"

A grin slid up one side of her face. "A ride home. I rode with Tori today. We had lunch plans with a few friends but I got a text that my aunt needs me to babysit. I'd rather not hold Tori up by making her take me home first. So I just thought…I'd ask you." She crossed an arm across her chest and gripped her elbow as if nervous to be asking.

His instant eagerness was met with a mental reprimand. He should stay away from her. From the way she made him feel. But somehow he found himself smiling down at her. "Of course." After all, he'd hit her with his car and still she was the one encouraging *him* at every turn. He couldn't say no. He didn't want to.

"Great, thanks so much." She signaled to her friend that she'd found a ride.

Alone in the car with Jenni? The thought held great appeal. And he chided himself for it.

Jenni turned back toward John, noting the redness of his neck. "Okay, ready when you are."

She followed him out across the parking lot, her stomach suddenly dipping. But she shook it off as she approached his car. When he pulled open the passenger door, Jenni faltered for a moment before climbing in.

"Watch your fingers." John waited then closed the door, and Jenni, slightly stunned, paused to relish the simple act as he came around to the driver's side. Nobody had ever opened her car door for her before.

John tapped his thumbs on the steering wheel, seeming as nervous and awkward as she felt. "So, hey, you were fantastic this morning."

His guileless remark warmed her cheeks. "Thanks." She tucked a lock of hair behind her ear.

His eyes slid to her as he started the engine. "The way you sign like that…it's amazing. It must've taken a long time to learn."

Amazing.

She flexed her toes and grounded her thoughts. "About three years now. I love it. It feels like singing, but without using my voice. If that makes any sense."

"Makes total sense to me; it *looks* like singing. Like whole-body singing. It brings the worship to life, shifts it into a whole new gear." He shook his head. "I've never experienced worship like that."

"Really?" She studied his profile. "I feel like music comes in so many forms, and all of them are powerful. Healing."

"I feel the same way. Music calms storms in the soul."

Hot dang, that was poetic. Goosebumps broke out on her legs, and she rubbed her knees. "You should play your guitar more often."

His gaze cut to her, a mysterious shadow behind his eyes But before she could translate the look, he answered. "I don't have a guitar anymore, so…"

"Oh, that's a shame. I enjoyed listening to your music."

A thread of silence stretched until John coughed. "So, do you use sign language in your job too, or…?"

"No, not yet. Hopefully someday soon. When I finish school and start my career. But it certainly isn't a required skill working at Just Juice."

"Oh, I know that place. Down on Cherry Avenue, right?"

"Yeah, that's the one. Not very glamorous, is it? But it's pretty flexible with my classes."

"No, that's awesome. I love juice. I mean, who doesn't, right? It's sweet, it's cold, it's refreshing. I'm thirsty just thinking about it."

Her cheek twitched. "Wow. Okay, then. If you're that big a fan, I'll make sure you get the friends and family discount."

"Yeah?"

"Of course. Just come by during my shift sometime."

"How can I say no?"

"I guess you can't." She blushed, aware she was luring a handsome man to her workplace via discounted smoothies. But he was simply a new friend and she was being friendly. She shifted in her seat to face him. "So, what about you? Where do you work?"

"Home Depot."

"Home Depot, huh? Do you get to drive that big beeping truck thing up and down the aisles? I've always wanted to try that." She pointed out the window. "Turn left here."

He chuckled. "No, I'm back in the office. Special services associate. I handle special orders for customers— vendors, installers, that kind of thing." He looked at her. "Not very glamorous."

"It pays the bills, right?"

"Right."

"So how did you get into that line of work?"

He shrugged. "I always enjoyed working on home projects. Guess that started with my dad. Nothing like getting that perfect finish on your deck flooring, or transforming a plain porch into something special with intricate spindles."

She watched his profile as he talked, the way he went on about character being reflected in the design details.

"You can tell a lot about a person when you help them design their home." He shot her a glance, which snagged for a moment on hers before returning to the road.

He cleared his throat again. "Anyway, I spent a lot of time at home improvement stores with my dad as a kid, worked at one through high school, then college, eventually putting my business degree to good use negotiating with wholesalers, suppliers, overseas imports. Turns out I had a knack for it." He paused. "And it's a way to feel close to my dad."

Hearing him talk about the father-son bond warmed a cool place in her heart. Did families like that still exist? Where kids had fathers they could admire? "I guess it does more than just pay the bills then."

He dipped his chin, an unreadable emotion darkening his blue eyes. "Yeah..." There was pain there. But she was smart enough not to pry.

"So what are you going to school for?"

"I'm working on my master's in education. Thinking of working in elementary. Special needs. So until God steers me somewhere else, that's the path I'm on." She smiled. "But you never know, I could end up moving to Zimbabwe or selling Tupperware. We'll see where life takes me."

"You sound open to anything. Kind of adventurous."

"You won't catch me skydiving or anything. I just *try* to remind myself every day that I gave God control of my life. He's better at it than I am."

He looked at her, eyes probing. "Yeah. I guess we all should do that."

That strange feeling overtook her again. The connection. And her heart fluttered. Outside her window, her neighbors' homes slid by. "Oh." She pointed to a white stucco house with brick facing around the garage door. "That's me."

He rolled to a stop, though she wished they had a few more miles to go. Miles to spend talking, getting to know him.

"Nice place. Love the brickwork."

"My mom's. I'm still living with her while I finish school." Reluctantly, she gripped the door handle. "Thanks for the ride, John."

"My pleasure."

She stepped out and closed the door, then leaned onto the open window. "Don't forget to stop by for a smoothie."

"I'll be there." His lips curved into a smile that made her heart skip a beat.

"See you soon then." The thought pleased her. But time would reveal whether he really meant to stop and see her or not. Whether he was interested in …being friends.

John stared after her as she glided up the walkway and disappeared into her house. The sweet, feminine, very appealing scent of Jenni's perfume faded with her absence.

What a remarkable woman. She had a smile that nearly undid him and eyes that seemed to look straight through him all the way to his backbone. And for some odd reason, she seemed to enjoy talking to him.

He put his car in gear and made a U-turn, humming to himself—until Hannah's face flashed across his mind's eye. His smile faltered.

Hannah would always be in his heart. He knew that. But this…survivor's guilt or whatever it was, was slowly killing him. How could he move ahead without feeling he was leaving her behind, erasing her? The question looped through his mind like a song on repeat. Maybe what he needed was a way to honor her memory.

John signed the check and popped it into the envelope. Donating to the local music non-profit felt right. Amazing, actually. And he'd taken the first steps needed to start a memorial fund in Hannah's name specifically for the purpose. Already he felt peace, like somewhere up in heaven, she was smiling.

He dropped the donation in the mail on his way to the office, then, in between work calls, spent the morning reviewing information for Hannah's memorial fund. She'd have been so pleased with the idea, but he lacked a targeted focus. Hannah always thought that music should be accessible to everyone, sometimes even giving free vocal lessons to kids who couldn't afford it, but there were several organizations already supporting free or low-cost music activities in the community. He'd love to find a need that wasn't being met yet, and use Hannah's memory to fulfill it.

It would come. He just had to keep looking.

John's gaze drifted from the purchase order on the monitor to the clock displayed at the bottom corner of the screen—11:58 a.m. He tried to finish entering an order for travertine tiles, but his thoughts were a jumbled mess, returning again to his afternoon plans. To the smoothie awaiting him.

Jitters overcame him. He took a swig of his soda to keep his fidgety hands busy. He had to chill out. Jenni was a friend, nothing more.

Okay, so...*why* had he worn cologne today? Dumb move for a guy trying to convince himself he wasn't interested in a woman. But he couldn't worry about that right now. He had somewhere to be. He slapped his laptop shut and grabbed his keys.

Fifteen minutes later, he pulled into a parking space and exhaled. The sun was high overhead, filling the landscape with hope and promise, yet John felt nervous as a cricket in a frog pond. Why was he really here? What did he *want* from Jenni?

He passed beneath the Just Juice sign and into the shop. Jenni stood behind the counter in a yellow cap, orange polo, and black apron. Youth and vitality radiated from her and John easily pictured her surrounded by giggling five-year-olds. She'd make a great teacher.

She glanced John's way as she finished helping a customer. When the elderly woman left, John stepped up and leaned onto the countertop. "You didn't tell me you were an assistant manager. I'd say your job just became much more glamorous."

Jenni laughed. "If you say so. Know what you want yet?" She pointed to the menu board above her head.

From her? No. He grabbed a straw from the dispenser and began tapping it against the counter. "I'm always impressed with the variety you guys offer. Hard to choose."

"My favorite is the Peachy Peach."

"That sounds good. Can you leave little chunks of peach in it?"

"For you? Absolutely. But you might have trouble with that straw."

He tossed it on the counter with a grin. "Straws are for sissies, anyway."

She chuckled, then set to work blending two of the drinks. One for each of them he presumed.

"Here you go. One Peachy Peach with chunks. No charge." She handed him his cup then removed her apron. "Come on, I'll take my fifteen-minute break. I want to show you something."

"Okay."

They went outside and strolled past the other shops in the strip mall.

"So you finally came." She bumped him with her shoulder. "I was starting to worry."

"Worry? Why?"

She shrugged. "I thought maybe you were only humoring me. That maybe you don't enjoy our conversations as much as I do." Her gaze skittered away from his as she took a long sip of her drink.

John stopped her with a hand on her elbow and turned to face her full on. "Jenni." He nearly laughed. "Why do you think I get to Bible Study so early every week?"

A smile spread across her face and nearly knocked the wind out of him. "To talk to me?"

"Well, there is that whole 'studying the Bible' thing too. But yeah, I come early to talk to you."

A lingering quiet settled over them as they looked at each other. Then she brought her straw back up to her lips, a look of concentration crossing her face as she turned to start walking again. John kept pace with her, wishing he could read her thoughts. Wondering what to say next.

"Does that weird you out? What's that face mean?"

"Oh, no. I just got a peach chunk stuck in my straw."

He laughed in a release of tension. She pulled the straw out and tossed it in a bin. "See, I can be a manly man, too."

John wagged his head. "Jenni, you're a lot of wonderful things, but you're definitely *not* manly."

Her lashes fluttered as she lowered her eyes from his. "So tell me, John, how long have you lived here?"

"About a month and a half I guess." Actually, he knew exactly how long—it'd been six weeks and two days since he drove in on a Wednesday, walked into church, and never left.

"And where did you live before?"

His ears pulsed with the sound of slot machines and clanking shot glasses. Definitely a topic for another day. "I'm originally from Indiana."

"I hear it's beautiful there. I imagine you grew up much different than I did here. Any brothers or sisters?"

"Nope." Why did he feel like he was being interviewed? "Only child."

"Me too, though I always wanted a sister."

She tucked her hair behind her ear and looked up at him. "Look, here we are. This is what I wanted to show you."

John followed her line of sight. A three-tiered fountain covered with intricate vines in an Italian-inspired motif sprayed water into the blue sky. "It's beautiful."

"I've always loved this fountain. Ever since I was a little girl. I still like to make wishes." She pulled two pennies out of her pocket and gave one to John. "Come on." She led him to the outer edge of the waist-high pool where she closed her eyes and squeezed her hand into a fist. John took the opportunity to study the soft texture of her cheek, the arch of her brow. Then she opened her eyes and pitched the coin up to the top level of the fountain. She gave a satisfied nod then turned to him. "Your turn."

"Not sure I can match that throw, but…" He blew into his hand then chucked the coin into the air as she had. It bounced off the top tier and landed in the second. "Uh…that's not an accurate reflection of my athletic ability."

Her soprano laugh sounded beside him. "It still counts, don't worry. My wish was for a little blonde girl I met recently to find the music inside of her. What about you?"

"I thought it was supposed to be a secret."

"You don't have to tell me if you're scared."

"Scared? No. Smart? Yes. I'm just protecting my investment."

She dropped her chin and laughed, and John joined her. Then his eyes skimmed her smiling lips and he sobered. "Actually, I wished for my dad to never forget he has a family who cares about him."

"You really love your dad, don't you?"

"I do. He, uh…he has some health issues. But his faith is strong. Always has been." He looked out toward the clouds clinging to the edge of the horizon. "He's a really good man."

"I bet he is." Jenni regarded him with an unblinking gaze. "Because from what I've seen, he passed that trait on to his son."

John's gut tightened. "Thanks." His voice came out hoarse and he coughed.

Jenni's smile dissolved as her eyes rounded. "Shoot…" She checked her phone, then gave him a defeated look. "Sorry, but I have to get back inside."

Already? He needed more time with her. "Of course." They turned back toward the store and stopped outside the glass door. "Thanks for the smoothie."

"You're welcome." She caught her bottom lip between her teeth for a moment, lingering.

His pulse jumped. "Maybe we can do it again? When you have more than fifteen minutes to spare."

She nodded. "I'd like that."

"Maybe I should get your phone number."

"Not a terrible idea." Her eyes sparkled.

He pulled out his phone. "Here, you wanna just…"

"Yeah." She punched in her number and her fingers brushed his when she handed it back. "Now call me so I have yours."

He did, and she pulled her cell from her pocket when it vibrated. "Okay, got it."

Her smile heated his blood. Strands of hair floated about her face and grazed her neck, stirring in John a dreamlike desire to reach out and trace their path. He smiled and backed up a few steps, waving as she disappeared into the shop.

Shrugging his hands into his pockets, John moved toward his car instead of standing there like a goofball, staring in after her. What was that? Had he just…was that flirting? Was Jenni sending him signals or was he off his nut?

He shot one last look toward the shop and his eyes connected with Jenni's. She quickly dropped her gaze back to her workstation.

Heat flooded his body. He was definitely not off his nut.

Chapter Thirteen

Well, *that* was definitely different.

Jenni scrubbed orange pulp off the store counter, fighting to ignore the buzzing in her belly. But holy moley, was her heart pumping. He'd been coming to worship practice just to see *her*. She'd suspected but hadn't quite believed.

They had exchanged phone numbers. And was that talk of setting up a...date?

Okay, slow down there, pardner. She blew out a slow breath. The lighthearted banter was fun, and an adrenaline rush was fine, but she wasn't a teenager anymore and she wouldn't lose her head like one. No. She would finish her shift, go home and walk her dog, practice for this week's song set, and not think about John.

The next few hours allowed her pulse to settle as she distracted herself with customers and coworkers then clocked out. But when she walked in the front door, and her mother met her with a smirk.

"What?" Jenni asked as she hung up her purse.

"Claudia told me. So who is he?"

Jenni inwardly groaned. Her mother's friend Claudia worked at a boutique in the same shopping center as Jenni and must have seen them walking. She should've known she might set off the rumor mill.

"Just a friend from church, Mom. That's all."

"Sweetie, don't play dumb. Snag him and snag him quick."

"People don't want to get *snagged*, Mom." She shook her head in bewilderment as her mother followed her to the living room.

"Nonsense, of course he does. Why else would he be buzzing around a juice bar?"

Jenni planted a hand on her hip and tipped a smile. "Maybe for the juice?"

"Uh, yeah. Right. I know my daughter is not that naive." She brushed a lock of hair off of Jenni's forehead, her smile going soft. "Oh, honey. I always hoped you'd find a nice, uncomplicated man at that church."

"Church is chock-full of complicated people." Jenni shook her head at her mother's faulty ideas about Christians.

Her eyebrows hiked up. "Well, Claudia's daughter met her fiancé at a night club and you can imagine how *that* is going. But not you. It'll be smooth sailing for you in comparison."

"Mom," Jenni spoke through a chuckle. "John and I are friends. That's all." *So far.* She bit her lip and bent to scratch Sadie's head as the dog jumped up on Jenni's knees.

"John? You've mentioned that name before." Her eyes narrowed in thought. "Wait. Is this the same John who rear-ended you a while back?"

"One and the same, yes." She filled Sadie's water dish.

"Maybe it was fate. Kismet. What a romantic story that would be, huh?"

Jenni rolled her eyes and leaned her hip against the counter.

"Okay, or maybe you are just friends and your mother is driving you crazy." She kissed the side of Jenni's head.

"Just a little. But I love you anyway."

Las Vegas, Nevada

Feet aching, April rolled her ankle under her desk as a woman strode toward her, a boy of about seven beside her.

"This is *not* what I was told last month." The unkempt mother shoved two sheets of paper across the counter then adjusted the toddler on her hip.

April took up the forms and glanced over their contents. An Explanation of Benefits from the woman's insurance provider, and a bill from their office. "What seems to be the problem, Ms. Fletcher?"

"I was specifically told the composite fillings were covered by my plan. But *this* is saying I have to pay twenty bucks per tooth. That's sixty dollars I don't have." Her face flamed, wide eyes quivering with a sheen of tears. The woman looked like she hadn't seen a good night's sleep in days and April's sympathies stirred. She put on a gentle tone.

"Ma'am, the composites are covered, but not at a hundred percent. See? Without insurance, they would have cost one hundred and seventy. Each."

"Someone should have told me about this. I was misled." The child in her arms lurched forward and grabbed one of the flower-topped pens from the counter. "Stop it." She snatched the pen and shoved it back in the jar. "I can't pay this. I need you to do something."

"I'm sorry, Ms. Fletcher. You'd have to talk to the financial coordinator and she isn't here right now. Would you like me to have her call you tomorrow?"

Ms. Fletcher shifted her weight and blinked several times. "Yes. Thank you. I'm sorry, I don't mean to be rude. I just…it's difficult right now." Her mouth pinched shut. "If there's anything your office can do to help me with this, I'd appreciate it."

April nodded. "I understand. I'll pass along your message." She smiled and watched as the small family shuffled out the exit. Though it wasn't her place to deal with this sort of thing, she crossed her fingers they'd be able to accommodate them in some way. April understood financial difficulty all too well.

The waiting room sat empty, at last. Despite a few challenges, her first time running the front desk alone had gone better than she'd feared. She stifled a yawn and rubbed her eyes. Was it time to go? She glanced at the clock on her screen. Five minutes. She got up and entered the waiting area to straighten the magazines.

Dr. Bergstein came in from the back and replaced a file folder in its spot on the wall. "Thanks for doing that, April. We really appreciate that you keep things so neat and tidy out front here."

"My pleasure." A smile touched her lips. Renewed her confidence.

"You can go if you want. I'll lock up."

"Thanks, Doctor. I'll see you in the morning." She gathered her purse then covered another yawn with her hand as she reached the door. This job was going great. She loved the people, the atmosphere. She could certainly imagine working here a good long while.

By the time she lugged herself up the stairs to her apartment, she was ready to drop. Her eyes wanted to close and her stomach felt a bit unhappy. A cold drink, a hot shower, and a soft bed were on the agenda tonight. She screwed off the top of a water bottle and brought it to her lips.

"You're just coming in and I'm just heading out." Stacy entered the kitchen smiling, then reached around her and grabbed a Pop Tart from the counter. "Hey, you don't look so hot. A bit green really. You feeling all right?"

"I'm just not used to the nine-to-five thing yet." April chugged the ice cold water, then capped the bottle.

Stacy's forehead puckered. "I don't think so. You look flushed. I think you're sick. I felt a little something coming on last week too, but I dodged it."

She shook her head. "Uh uh. I can't be sick. I just started this job."

"I'm sorry to tell you this but you're sick."

April moved to the living room and kicked off her shoes. "My probation period lasts three months. I can be sick then." She sank into the recliner, eyes closed. A fishy scent wafted through the window from the apartment next door and, as if in reply, her stomach did a horrible tuck-and-roll and acid shot up her throat. *Uh oh.* Her eyes popped open and she propelled herself toward the bathroom.

"Watch the rug!"

Nice, Stacy.

A moment later, she sank back on her haunches. Okay, she *was* sick. Great. She dragged the back of her hand across her mouth and blew out a long, shaky breath. Probation or no, she had the flu. Was the universe conspiring against her?

Groaning, April gripped the cool edge of the counter and pulled herself off the floor. Brushed her teeth. She dried her hands on the red terry towel on the wall and shook her head. This was lame. So much bad luck should not be heaped upon one person. How would it look if she called in sick so soon? She couldn't. She climbed into bed and curled onto her side, clutching her belly.

In the morning, she forced herself to go in to work. Maybe it was a twenty-four hour thing. After all, she hadn't woken through the night feeling ill. But three trips to the bathroom later, she was sent home. She slept on and off until Stacy came in to check on her.

"Girl, you look awful. Have you checked your temp?" She placed her hand on April's forehead. "You don't feel too warm. But maybe you should call a doctor tomorrow. Get some Tamiflu or something."

"I can't afford a cash visit, are you crazy? Besides, I don't run to the doctor for every little thing. People get sick, it happens."

"Right. Well, do you want some Sprite or crackers or anything before I go?"

"Yeah, that sounds good. Thanks." April tugged the blanket up under her chin as Stacy went to get the snack. What would she do without her tried-and-true friend?

Stacy stood over the bed, worry lines creasing her brow. "You don't seem any better. You need to see a doctor."

April released a weary sigh. "I know, but I can't. I won't get insurance benefits for a couple more months—if I even make it through probation. I've missed so much work because of this."

"Yeah, you've been hugging that toilet bowl every day for over a week. I'm worried."

"I'm…" An ominous cloud settled over April. Her heart drummed inside her chest. *No. Impossible. There is absolutely, positively, no way.* Her tongue went dry. "…I'm sure I'm fine. I'll let you know if I need anything."

Stacy pressed her lips together in a defeated smile. "Okay…I'll be in the living room."

"'Kay."

She closed her eyes but her mind was wide awake now. This was stupid. Talk about paranoid. But no matter how ridiculous, she'd never be able to sleep until she put her mind at ease.

She slid her feet into some flip-flops and shrugged into a hoodie. "I'm gonna pick up some soup and stuff."

"Oh, I can make a run to the store if you want. You should stay in bed."

April shook her head. "Thanks, but I've been so cooped up I think getting out of the apartment for a few minutes will be good. I won't be long."

"If you're sure…"

"I'm sure. I'm getting a bit of cabin fever. Back in a bit." She slipped out the door before Stacy could protest further. The trip took just fifteen minutes. And five minutes after that, she sat in the bathroom staring down at the two little blue lines shaking in her hands.

Okay, not the flu.

The walls seemed to press in around her. A ringing sound filled her ears. Her chest heaved.

That shameful night haunted her enough without *this*. She focused again at the plastic stick in her hand, as if it might have changed. But it hadn't. Her mind retreated behind a shield of numbness, a thousand questions bouncing off without making it into her head. Her pulse tripled as she squeezed her eyes shut. "Stacy?"

Stacy appeared and leaned on the bathroom door jamb. "Yeah?"

April swallowed hard then stared up from her perch on the toilet lid. She had no words. Just…held up the proof.

Stacy's mouth dropped open and in a flash she was beside her, stroking her hair. "Don't worry, it's okay…" Comforting fingers crossed April's brow. "It's all right. *Who…?* Never mind, it doesn't matter. We'll get you through this."

April pressed her lips together. She knew who the father was. He might even still be staying at that hotel. He'd seemed like a long-term resident. Not that it mattered because she wasn't going to tell him.

Better if he never knew.

Stacy continued to rub her back and stroke her hair while April sat in shocked silence. The drip of the bathtub marked the passing time, and the blankness of her mind began to fill with scattered pictures. Dreams sucking down the drain. The image of Ms. Fletcher in all her rumpled glory, battling over her child's twenty-dollar fillings, sent a wave of panic through her. She stared at the test, a single thought spinning through her head.

She *needed* her job. And she could *not* have a baby.

As soon as her paycheck came she'd take care of...*this*...and forget it. Forever.

Jenni hugged her friend Natalie then picked up her Bible. "Bye, Nat. I'll see you later." She turned to find John approaching. "Hey there."

"Hi." His blond hair was perfectly styled, his blue eyes glinting in the sun. "Listen, I don't know if you have any plans, but...you wanna grab some lunch, or coffee, or something?"

She smiled. "Sure." She'd been hoping he'd seek her out today. Because, yes, she *was* intrigued. Perhaps even, she dared to give birth to the thought, interested.

"Mexican food?"

"Love it. And I'm starved. But you'll have to drive since I carpooled again."

"Great. I'm parked right there whenever you're ready."

She picked up her purse and Bible from the planter beside her. "I'm ready now. I'll text Tori that I don't need a ride home." She was sure Tori would consider this an *interesting* invitation. Flashing him a smile, she followed him to his car where he opened the passenger side door for her.

Again, their eyes met, and butterflies danced in her belly. "Thank you."

"Of course."

She slid into the passenger seat, and John reached down and lifted the fabric of her long blue sun-dress, tucking it into the vehicle where she arranged it around her ankles. Once she was situated, he closed the door. And Jenni took a deep breath.

Ten minutes later they entered Miguel's Mexican Restaurant. The scent of beans and sizzling carne asada wafted through the air as they were seated at a corner table by the window.

After placing their orders, Jenni pinched a tortilla chip and crunched into it. "So, how are things?"

"Good actually." John bobbed a chip in salsa. "I'd say real good." He popped the chip into his mouth and reached for another. "Work's…good. Everything is—"

"Good, I know." She smirked and she reached for another chip. He seemed a little nervous, uncomfortable, and she couldn't tell whether it was because of *her*, or something else on his mind. "I hope things continue that way for you, then. I get the feeling sometimes that you've had your share of struggles."

"Insightful." He brushed the salt from his hands, then pushed his shoulders back. "You know, Jenni, I'm glad you accepted my invitation to lunch, because…I've been wanting to thank you."

"Thank me? For what?"

"I came to this town to start over, get a fresh start. You were one of the first people I met, and you've always made me feel…" He took a breath. "…welcome. Encouraged me when I really needed it."

"You're a good man, John. Whatever fresh start you're seeking, it's available."

His gaze broke away. "They say people don't really change."

"In a certain sense, maybe. But if that were true, where would the hope of Christ be? And I know that hope is very real." Her thoughts drifted back to her own days without Christ, without hope. "I think you know that, too."

A beat passed and John picked up his glass and took a drink of soda. "You have a talent for saying just what I need to hear. I want you to know, whether you realize it not, you've played a big part in getting me where I am today."

She cocked her head. "What do you mean? Doesn't seem like I've done all that much." He was the one proving chivalry wasn't dead, making her feel like a lady. Intriguing her.

John cleared his throat. "Jenni, there's things about me you don't know. Not specifically. I have the feeling you might have wondered or guessed but I'll just come out and say it." He pushed his glass aside and leaned toward her. "I was a drunk. Before I moved here."

She'd expected something like that, had pieced together the signs, but she'd also been able to tell that his faith was genuine. That God was at work in him. Though she sensed he carried shame.

He looked her in the eye and continued. "This Wednesday will mark seven weeks sober for me. Seven weeks back walking with Christ. And so many times since I arrived, when I was struggling—really struggling—it was you who'd show up and share a scripture or say something that gave me strength to get through it."

Warmth spread through her chest and Jenni leaned forward and looked him in the eye. "Thank you for sharing that, John. For entrusting me with it." It was a big confession, one she didn't take lightly, and one that showed her his commitment to change was absolute. "I have so much respect for you putting it out there like that. And I'm…humbled…that I have been able to be of encouragement to you."

He nodded. Their waiter appeared at that moment, delivering their steaming plates and providing a reprieve from the heavy mood. When the waiter left, Jenni reached across the table.

John took her hand and smiled. "Let's pray."

After *amen*, they dug in. Scooping bell peppers and grilled chicken into a warm tortilla, John looked across at her. "So tell me, how long have you taken ballet?"

"How did you know I took ballet?"

He tapped his forehead. "Mental powers."

She snickered. "Oh, right. I forgot about that."

"No, it's obvious from the way you move when signing. I meant to ask you before." He bit into his fajita.

"Well, I *did* take ballet lessons. For years. Since I was a little girl. I stopped after my junior year of high school but I guess it still comes out at times."

"It does. I'm sure you were great."

"Thanks. These days it's nothing but school, work, and church. Dance requires a lot of time and dedication and as much as I loved it, I wasn't willing to sacrifice any more for it. Maybe someday I'll have a little girl who I can introduce ballet to. I'd like that."

Something, some indiscernible look, clouded his eyes. He coughed and turned his attention to his drink.

She shook her head. "If that's what God has for me. And that's a big *if.*"

With a brief smile, John sat back and cast a thoughtful gaze on her. "I think you'll get that family someday."

"Mental powers again?"

He smiled a little more. "I'm no fortune teller, Jenni, but I believe God will give you the desires of your heart in His time."

Jenni's pulse tripped. Her mother's ridiculous word rang in her ears—*kismet*.

She shivered. "I…try not to hold on too tightly to any of my dreams. Because you never know." She had a lot of experience with broken dreams.

"That's very true."

She took another bite of her enchilada and deflected the conversation to John. "Okay, your turn. What's Indiana like and what made you want to move to Southern California?"

"Indiana is great. People are friendly, it's beautiful. Not so packed and condensed as it is here. It's a whole different feel, living there."

"Yeah, so…why did you move?"

John took his time chewing, leaning on his elbow with his fork in the air. "Well, long story short, I ran away. I went through some difficult things in Indiana and I needed to get some distance to clear my head." He took a sip of his soda, reading the question in her eyes, but offering no further explanation.

She didn't want to pry, so she simply nodded. "I'm sorry for whatever you went through." Whatever it was likely connected to his drinking and he'd offered enough just sharing that. She scooped a bite of refried beans onto her fork. "So what about now? What does your future look like?"

He released a slow breath, head shaking. "I don't know exactly. I'm taking life one day at a time, trying to stay in the center of God's will. For now, He has me here, and I'm enjoying it very much." He paused. "Especially when I have the pleasure of your company."

Her cheeks warmed, and he grinned. "What's Jenni's story? How did you come to faith?"

Ah, the meaty stuff. "Well, I've been a Christian since junior high and I don't have any gripping tales of horror that got me there."

"No old gang ties then?" He teased.

"What gave me away?"

He wagged a finger at her then tapped his forehead.

She snorted. "Right. I keep forgetting."

"But seriously, I'm interested to hear…if you don't mind sharing."

"Okay." She enjoyed talking about what God had done in her life. "Well, I didn't grow up in a Christian home, but my best friend growing up was a Christian, and often invited me to church. I'd attend if I had stayed the night at her house. Then, the summer between seventh and eighth grades, my parents filed for divorce." She escaped his eyes and began constructing a mound out of her refried beans. "Things were bad at home, and I wasn't coping well. At all." Maybe someday she'd reveal her coping methods, but now was not the time.

She shook off the shadow and pushed on. "That's when my friend got me to a junior high retreat." She chuckled, patted the summit of bean hill with her fork. "I was having a pretty good time, but I think it had to do with the cute boys there. But that whole weekend I felt like I was missing out on something, you know?" She clutched the fork handle as though clinging to the memory—that moment she'd first sensed her deepest need. "These kids had something I didn't have. I didn't get it. I felt like…like I was outside with my nose pressed up against the glass watching the rest of them sharing something…extraordinary.

"With what was going on in my life, that was the first time I'd been open to hearing about what my friend believed. So I listened. The teachers talked about God, about needing a Savior, about Jesus." She brought her fingers to her chest. "I knew I needed Him. Desperately. They did an altar call; I wasn't going to go forward." Her eyes misted over and she paused a moment, reliving the moment. "But I was watching the other kids who had gone forward. Some were crying, some were simply standing with their eyes closed up there at the front, but all of them had this look on their faces—like they were seeing God or something."

She looked down at the mess she'd made of her lunch. "And I wanted that; I *needed* that. So I stood and took a step, shaking like the San Andreas Fault. My friend grabbed my hand and I started bawling like a baby—out of nowhere. So she walked with me up to the front and I accepted Jesus."

Releasing her fork to the table, she met his eyes and smiled. "And I've been in love with Him ever since." She smiled. "So that's my story." Most of it, anyway. She adjusted the bracelet on her wrist, turning it till the words faced up.

John nodded solemnly.

"More than you bargained for when you asked, huh?" She laughed softly.

"Not at all. Sounds like a powerful experience."

"Yes. It was."

The next hour passed quickly, with easy conversation and stomach-dipping glances. When the bill came, John insisted on paying, though Jenni had fully intended to cover her share. But she relented at his persistence. Did that mean this *was* a date?

They arrived at Jenni's house and John walked her to the door. A hanging basket of jasmine scented the porch with a heady aroma that punctuated the emotion of their entire afternoon. Jenni jiggled a brass key in the lock.

"Does the key tend to stick?"

"Only when I need to use it."

The door opened and she looked back over her shoulder. John's forehead bunched as he ran his thumb over the door's strike plate. "I think I can fix this for you, if you want. Do you have a screwdriver?"

She took in his stubbled jawline, his masculine hand leaning on her doorframe, and her heart cracked open. "I'm sure I do."

She hurried inside, rummaged in the kitchen drawer, then ran back to him on the porch. "Will this one work?"

"Perfect." He set to work loosening the screws on the strike plate and resetting its position, then placed the tool back in her palm. "All set."

"That was fast."

He shrugged. "It was a simple fix. Let me know if there's anything else you want me to look at."

Just me.

What the what? Startled at her line of thinking, Jenni stared at her feet and gave herself a shake. "I'll keep that in mind." She looked up at him, her blood surging to her head. "Thanks for lunch."

He explored her eyes. "You're welcome. And...if you didn't hate it," a crooked smile appeared, "maybe we can do it again?"

She schooled her stammering heart. "I didn't hate it, and yes...I'd love to do it again."

"Great."

Neither made a move to leave, they just stood there, smiling at each other.

John's gaze seemed to follow the strands of hair floating about her face and neck, tightening Jenni's stomach muscles. He cleared his throat. "Well, goodbye then." He wrapped her in a friendly hug, which, along with the scent of his cologne, she enjoyed a bit too much to make sense of.

"Bye, John." She lowered her gaze to the newly mended door knob before she opened it, then glanced over her shoulder at him one more time as she slipped inside.

Wowza.

Chapter Fourteen

Jenni pressed the door closed, listening as it clicked into place. A flutter danced through her stomach. Her pulse had soared with John's hug goodbye. And the way he had looked at her just now...she needed a paper fan to cool her neck.

She gave herself a mental shake then set her keys on the entry table, catching her reflection in its mirror. Her cheeks were stained red. She swiftly covered them with her hands. This wasn't like her. She didn't go giddy around handsome men. So why did she feel flushed and dizzy around John? *Because he's not just another handsome man.* She flattened her palms against her abdomen and blew out a puff of air.

The sound of claws clicking on the linoleum made her turn. "Hey, Sadie girl. Whatcha up to, huh?" She knelt to scratch behind the cocker spaniel's ears, then planted a kiss on her fluffy head.

"Hi, Jenni." Her mom strolled toward her from the hall.

"Hey, Mom." She heard the melody in her own voice as she glided toward the living room.

Her mother wore a knowing smile. "That was John out there, wasn't it?"

"Yeah, he fixed the door."

"The sticky lock? That was nice of him."

"And he took me to lunch."

Her mother raised an eyebrow. "So...was it a date?" A grin stretched across her face and made the flutters tiptoe back through Jenni's belly.

"I don't know. Not really. We're just friends…I think." She scrunched her forehead and looked toward the front door. For a moment there, it certainly had felt like a spark of something more passed between them. But it was subtle, nothing overt, and maybe all in her head.

"Oh, Jenni, you must see that he likes you. And I haven't seen you smile like that in years." She shot Jenni a smug look and tapped her knee. "When do I get to meet him? Maybe you'll give me that grandbaby yet."

Jenni tossed her head back. "*Mom.*"

"I'm just saying…" She raised her hands in mock defeat.

Jenni shook her head. "You're too eager to marry me off. Or more precisely, have me start popping out babies."

"I am not. You're exaggerating."

Was she? Mom was always pushing Jenni toward a friend's son, or a young co-worker—or the UPS driver. *He's cute, Jenni. Let him take you out.* Or *Lydia says he just got promoted to project manager.* Or *Did you see those biceps?* Jenni didn't care about any of that stuff.

…Okay, yeah, she *cared.* But it wasn't the only thing that mattered. She'd seen enough decimated lives to know that she'd rather have no one than have the wrong someone. She'd live with the flak. Some of her friends called her picky. Some, scared. Maybe they weren't altogether wrong, but Jenni preferred to think of herself as…cautious. Content to wait. Those were good traits, right?

Her mother wasn't as patient. She never could understand Jenni waiting on God in this area of her life. Then again, why would she?

But Jenni's heart didn't behave normally around John. She had some sorting out to do, that was for sure. She rose from the couch. "I'll be in my room if you need me."

"Oh, actually, Mary's just putting Tessa down for a nap in your room. I hope you don't mind."

"Not at all. But I didn't know Aunt Mary was coming over today. I didn't even notice her car outside."

"You were distracted," she teased, then tipped her head toward the hall. "Mary just wanted some family time." Something in her mother's tone told Jenni that her aunt was struggling, and no wonder. Jenni still had a hard time processing the fact that Uncle Dave, a man she'd loved and trusted, had been having an affair for eight years. And chose last Thanksgiving to drop the bomb that he was leaving Aunt Mary to be with his mistress. Jenni pressed a hand to her stomach, then busied herself refolding the blanket hanging on the back of the couch. Being a single parent couldn't be easy. Especially with both a toddler and a teenager.

Mom straightened a candle holder on the mantle and eyed her in the mirror. "Jenni...you'll do better than we did. Don't worry. Just remember to check the closet for skeletons first and you'll be fine."

"Hey." She eyed her mother with a dip of her chin. "No background checks."

"I only did that once. And I was dating a cop at the time, what do you expect?"

"Just promise me you'll stop trying to direct my love life—"

"Or lack thereof..."

"Or lack thereof...and leave it to me to decide who and when and if I decide to date."

Her mother faced her with hands on her hips and angled her head. "I'll try."

Jenni pinched the bridge of her nose. *Oh, Mom.* That was the best she was going to get. She glanced toward the kitchen. "So, is Christy here?"

"In the backyard on her cell phone."

Jenni slid the glass door open and stepped outside. Shafts of sunlight striped the patio through the lattice covering and a light breeze sent the wind chimes into song. She spotted Christy on the bench swing, staring out across the yard with a grim look on her face. Wisps of dark hair fluttered in her eyes, but she didn't seem to notice or care. She didn't even seem to realize Jenni had approached.

"How's my favorite cousin?"

Christy blinked as if stirred awake. "Hey, Jenni." She scooted over so Jenni could sit beside her then looked down and picked at the frayed thread on her ripped jeans. "I was hoping you'd be here." The strain edging her voice didn't go unnoticed.

Jenni looked into her reddened eyes. Something wasn't right. "What's going on?"

"I just...wanted to talk to you."

The catch in her voice set off alarms in Jenni's head. But Christy was only thirteen. *Going on eighteen.* She shook off the thought. Surely whatever was wrong couldn't be too serious, right? She spoke gently. "Okay…talk."

"I did something stupid and now my whole life is ruined." Christy's breathing increased and she blinked rapidly.

Lord, please be here right now. "What do you mean?"

Christy glanced toward the house as if checking for eavesdroppers, but they were alone. She moistened her lips and looked back at Jenni. "Sometimes we go hang out at my friend Misa's house. Her mom is never home. We turn the music up loud and watch movies we're not supposed to and just goof around. No big deal. But last night…" She hesitated, looking down at her hands. "Scarlet invited some boys from school to come. They convinced Misa to get into her mom's liquor cabinet. I swear, we'd never done that before. But we just wanted to have a little fun." She pressed her lips together and looked away. There had to be more to the story. Christy wasn't just suffering a guilty conscience. She'd said her life was ruined.

"Okay." Jenni forced her muscles to relax. "What happened next?"

A throttled sob came from Christy's throat. "I don't know! Not exactly. I can't remember."

Jenni's heart sank to her stomach, then bounced red-hot back into her chest. If one of those boys had put his hands on her little cousin… She bit her lip to keep silent so Christy could finish.

"When I woke up all my friends were giggling at me. Scarlet was snapping pictures. I looked down and saw they'd propped a bottle of Jack Daniel's in my hand. Scarlet says she's gonna post them online!" A tear dropped onto her flushed cheek. "I look completely wasted in the pictures. Everyone will see it. What if my mom finds out? She'll kill me! My life is over."

Jenni's heart thumped. Christy was too young for this. It seemed like just last summer she was playing with Littlest Pet Shop toys. Jenni exhaled a prayer and spoke with more composure than she felt. "Christy, do you think anything might have…happened…while you were passed out? Were the boys still there?"

"No. Tiff swore to me nothing like that happened."

"And you trust her?"

"Yeah. For sure. She wouldn't lie about something like that. I'm a thousand percent sure."

Jenni nodded and found her breath. Barely. "Well then, it could have been a lot worse. But those girls are obviously not your friends. You need to drop them. And I think you should tell your mom."

Christy snatched her hands out of Jenni's, eyes wide. "No, I can't tell my mom. She'd ground me for life and besides…" Her face fell. "I don't want her looking at me different. You wouldn't understand." She shook her head and looked away.

Jenni sighed. "I have a pretty good idea. I was thirteen once, not so long ago. My parents were going through their divorce and I did a lot of things I shouldn't have. I felt alone. Like I didn't have anyone to talk to. So I always want you to come to me, okay? You can trust me."

"I know. I do. But I can't tell my mom."

"Secrets like this can be dangerous." Jenni toyed with her bracelet. "The truth sets us free. You know, what finally helped me was realizing that God truly does love me. I wasn't alone. *You* aren't alone."

"Jenni?" Christy searched Jenni's face. "Do you think I'm bad?" A quiver teetered on the edge of her voice.

Jenni reached up and stroked Christy's hair. "I skipped Algebra class for a week, and I stole cigarettes from my mom's purse and lit up in the backyard. I don't think you're bad."

Christy's brows rose with her skepticism. "You smoked?"

"I tried a few times. Luckily it didn't take."

"I never would have guessed."

Nobody would have. She'd hidden her pain well. Even now there were some things she didn't like to recall. "There's a lot you probably would be surprised to learn about your favorite cousin."

Christy's eyes widened with interest. "Like what?"

"Well…like how when my parents used to argue, and I could hear them screaming through the walls of my bedroom, and I felt alone and scared, and didn't know how to express that… I turned to the edge of a razor blade."

"No way. Not you, Jenni."

She lifted her brows and nodded. "Yes, me." Jenni rubbed her lips together and tried to gather her thoughts. Christy needed to hear. "One particularly bad night…I…grabbed the razor in the shower…pressed it into my skin…" she looked Christy in the eye, "and swiped it across."

Round eyed, Christy squeezed her hand.

"As it bled, it felt like…a release. All the emotions that I held inside could now come out in a physical form." She covered Christy's hand with hers. "I couldn't talk about it, get it out in words, so I got it out that way, and it was awful. I had to wear long sleeves all summer to hide it. And who knows what would've happened if the habit had gone on for long. But it was later this same summer that my friend Tori took me to the church camp, where I became a Christian." She shook her head. "I don't like to think about where I would've ended up if I hadn't let God help me at that point in my life."

"Wow."

Jenni rubbed Christy's back. "Yeah. I know you're going through a lot right now too. I've been there, kiddo."

Christy balled her fists and pounded them in her lap. "Okay. But I just have to figure out how to stop those pictures getting online, and I *promise* I won't ever do something like that again. Please don't say anything."

"Look, I'm not sure what to do about the pictures. And I still think you should talk to your mom, but…I'll keep your confidence for now."

"Oh, thank you." Christy's relief was visible.

Jenni patted her knee. "Hey, maybe you'd like to come to church with me next week though?"

"Maybe. We should go inside before my mom comes looking for me." She wiped her face. "Jenni…I love you."

"I love you too, little cuz." Jenni wrapped her arms around Christy's neck and squeezed her tight. "Always."

Christy sniffled. "Thanks."

Oh, Lord, she needs You so badly.

The rest of the afternoon and evening was spent listening to Aunt Mary recount her latest online dating disasters in between her complaints about the inadequate child support she was receiving, and her disparaging comments about Uncle Dave's girlfriend. Jenni watched Christy's jaw tighten at the mention of her father, and saw the way she pushed her food around on her plate at dinnertime. She was quick to leave the table, offering to entertain two-year-old Tessa in the den. Aunt Mary had reason to feel wounded and angry, but she didn't seem to notice the part she played in hurting her own daughter. Jenni wondered if she should find a way to broach the subject. But would her aunt be too hurt and offended to listen?

When Jenni closed her eyes that night, her heart ached for her family. A family torn apart and void of true hope. Maybe God would use the situation with Christy to bring them all closer to Him. Or maybe they had a long way yet to fall. She shifted onto her side and stared out her bedroom window at the dim outline of backyard shrubs. She had several friends at church who faithfully stood with her, praying for her family on a regular basis. Maybe she should share these new concerns about her cousin with someone.

But as she lay there pondering in the dark, she was surprised to find that the person she most wanted to share her heart with wasn't Tori or Nat…it was John. Her breath hitched at the realization. To lean on John? Seek encouragement from him? Yes. She did, she wanted that. A smile stole across her lips as she rolled onto her back and stared at the ceiling. John, with his knowledge of the Psalms, his own personal connection with them. With his ardent love for and dependence on God. John, who opened her car door, picked up the tab, and wielded a mean screwdriver. Who had a way, in a short amount of time, of making her feel taken care of whenever she was with him.

He's become a good friend, God. Possibly more? She swallowed against the sudden tightness in her throat. Well…God only knew.

After years of waiting, she was afraid to hope.

Jenni stood in front of the bathroom mirror and buffed mineral powder over her face, then dropped her stippling brush back into her makeup caddy. That was all she needed for a simple day of blending fruit. She twisted a section of her hair and pinned it back with her favorite Hawaiian blossom clip, then reached for her bracelet. It had been a gift from Tori years ago, shortly after she'd become a Christian. The words inscribed in pewter were much-needed today. *I Carried You.* A fact she treasured and never wanted to forget. Especially when life became uncertain.

She slid it past her knuckles and onto her wrist, then ran her fingers over the barely visible scars just above. The imprints of her life without

God. Of how much pain she'd shoved inside and then released behind locked doors. The same adolescent pain she now saw in Christy.

She whispered a prayer. "Thank you for carrying me."

As she grabbed her purse and opened the front door, she held on to two truths. One, that she would never be done saying thank-you to God for all He'd rescued her from. And two, that He would carry her through anything life brought her way—including navigating a possible relationship with John Douglas. Would he call her after yesterday's "was-it-a-date"? Stop in for a smoothie?

Jenni shouldered her phone to her ear as she fished out her house keys. "No, he didn't stop by today."

"You sound disappointed."

"Yes—I mean, *no*. Why would I be? It's fine." She turned the lock with ease and opened the door. "Did I mention he fixed my front door lock?"

"Yes." Tori laughed. "Do you have any idea how fun this is for me?"

Sadie greeted her at the door, jumping, dancing in circles, and wagging her little stump tail. Jenni patted her head. "Ready for your walk, girl?"

"Excuse me?"

"I meant the dog. But you can join us by phone, if you stop teasing."

"I can't help it. I've never seen you like this. You think you're playing it cool but I've known you too long for that to work on me. I can read you like a Jumbo Tron and you *like* him."

"I barely know him."

"But you want to."

She groaned. Yeah, she did. She clipped on Sadie's pink leash and headed out.

"Okay, fine. You got me..." Sadie pulled her down the block—past the rose bushes decorating the neighbor's walkway, and the Jacaranda trees adding purple splashes to the yards. The vivid colors that surrounded her seemed to reflect the emotions swirling inside as her thoughts hovered around John. "Tori…" She lowered her voice. "I can't stop thinking about him."

"Ha! I knew it! Continue…"

She let Sadie lead the way as John filled her thoughts. "That man is something else. Hard working, upright, thoughtful, sold-out for God, never inappropriate toward me. And his eyes…"

"Ooh…what about them?"

Jenni gave herself a shake. "But I don't want to be stupid." *God, please don't let me do anything stupid.* Like fall for someone only to get hurt.

"You won't."

"I know I have issues. I'm aware of my walls. But just look at my mom, and Aunt Mary…their lives have been destroyed by the men they loved."

Jenni hadn't been privy to all the details of her parents' divorce, being so young at the time, but Aunt Mary's had been on full display. For months after Uncle Dave left, Aunt Mary tried to win him back, to convince him to choose her over his lover. That kind of humiliation and pain…Jenni refused to go through.

"Jenni…you can't do that to yourself. Come on, girl, take a risk."

"The very fact that I want to is what scares me. But…"

"But what?"

"But something about John…makes me want to tear down some of my walls."

"Ooo…this is good, Jen. This is real good."

A smile slid into place. "So you approve then?"

"Psh. You have to ask that?"

She breathed a laugh. "Guess not."

"I gotta go, but listen. I want up to the minute reports on anything and everything that happens between you two, okay? Up. To. The. Minute. And if you start to chicken out before you've even tried, I'll be here to smack some sense back into you. Be brave. You can do this."

"Thanks, Tori. See ya."

She shoved her phone into her pocket. Maybe it *was* time to tiptoe into the unknown and see if a blessing awaited her.

Maybe.

Maybe, maybe, maybe.

Jenni silenced a groan. She hadn't been so preoccupied with a man in…well, ever.

She hadn't dated anyone seriously in over three years, and that had ended badly. Her relationship with Aiden was doomed from the start, and the whole time, she'd known deep down that the Lord wasn't in it. But she had ignored all the warnings in her spirit and let herself fall for him anyway.

When it ended she sank into a depression for two months. She'd been just as depressed that she'd ignored God's gentle warning as she was about the break-up itself. It had been the first time in seven years she'd been tempted to reach for a razor blade. Through God's grace she came through those two months and her walk with Him was stronger than it had ever been. But she wasn't going to make the same mistake again. Were there men out there who were decent and honorable and faithful? Absolutely. But as her mother said, they were hard to find. And appearances could be deceiving.

A revving lawn mower pulled her from her introspection and she looked out over a recently-hosed lawn glittering in the afternoon sun.

Sadie trotted beside her, tongue lolling out of her smiling mouth. Carefree. The way Christ wanted His followers to be, in Him. Jesus' words filled her heart and mind. *"Come to Me, all you who are weary and burdened, and I will give you rest."* She smiled. Matthew 11:28. Those famous, simple words that filled her with profound longing and gratitude.

Maybe they'd be a comfort to Christy as well. Jenni would send this verse to her in a card, the old-fashioned way, as soon as she got home.

They reached the front door and Sadie looked up and licked her muzzle, happy for the adventure. Bending, Jenni kissed her furry little head as she unclipped her leash. Sadie's nails tapped across the kitchen tile toward her water bowl while Jenni pulled out a blank note card from the writing desk.

Mom wouldn't be home for a couple hours, so Jenni sealed the card then curled up with her latest Francine Rivers novel, losing herself in its pages until dinnertime.

But even Francine couldn't keep the question from forming in her head…would he call? When? And if he asked her out…would she be ready to say yes?

Well that was a dumb question. Because she certainly had no intention of turning him down.

Chapter Fifteen

"Was it wrong? Inappropriate?" John held the phone tight to his ear with one hand and pinched the bridge of his nose with the other.

"What? Hey, as long as you're putting God first and keeping your priorities straight, you can trust Him to take care of the rest. You aren't doing anything sinful taking Jenni to lunch."

"I just don't want her to get the wrong idea."

"What idea would that be? That you like to eat?"

"Derek, it's not just lunch. I'm attracted to her. Really attracted to her." He ran his hand through his hair. "Really, *really* attracted to her."

"You don't say?" Derek chuckled. "Look, it's not wrong to develop feelings for someone new. Hannah's been gone, what, two years almost? You've told me yourself she wouldn't expect you to stay single forever."

"And that's true. It's just...I don't know."

"You're just scared, man. I get it. Sometimes God does things we don't expect—He works in mysterious ways, as they say. Just because you didn't expect this doesn't mean it's bad. My advice is to be diligent in prayer, and beyond that don't let yourself get wrapped up in guilt and fear. That's the enemy's bag of tricks, not God's."

John released a long stream of air through his nostrils, weighing what Derek said. "Thanks. I guess I needed to hear it." He leaned back in his chair and clicked off the phone, the weight lifting off his shoulders. He was a single man. He was allowed to take a woman out. But if a relationship with Jenni would hinder his walk with Christ, or if it wasn't God's will for any reason whatsoever, he didn't want it. He bowed his head right there at the kitchen table and prayed for wisdom and inner peace.

Scraping his chair back from the table, he entered the kitchen and selected a flavored coffee pod from the rack. While it brewed, he fished out his cell phone and scrolled down to Jenni's number. He'd added a photo beside her name, and even from a thumbnail image her eyes did something peculiar to him. He hesitated half a moment, thumb hovering above the call button. She might think he was coming on too strong or too fast. But he just wanted to talk to her, to hear her voice. He added a splash of cream to his mug and dialed.

"John, hi." The gladness in her voice put his concerns to rest.

"Hi yourself." He sank onto his sofa and propped his feet up on the coffee table. "How was your day?"

"Well, I juiced some stuff," she teased. "Walked the dog, read a book...wondered if you'd call."

"Oh?" His chest swelled. "Then I'm sorry to have kept you waiting, my lady."

She laughed, and the light, feminine sound reverberated through his body.

He cleared his throat. "So what kind of dog do you have? Wait, let me guess."

"Okay."

"Uh, not a toy breed. I think you'd go for something weightier, so to speak. Less wimpy. Although I don't picture you as the Mastiff type either. I'd say something in the middle range—friendly, loyal, lots of personality. Uh...I'm going to guess, maybe a beagle."

"Wow. Interesting analysis. You know they say dogs are a reflection of their masters. I guess I'm flattered you don't find me wimpy. And I have to say, you aren't too far off. It's kind of scary actually. But I don't have a beagle. I have a cocker spaniel."

"Ah, even better. Yeah, I can see that. Cockers are supposed to be people dogs from what I've heard. Not to mention cute."

"So you think I'm cute?"

"Uh, I meant the dog. Is probably cute."

"So you *don't* think I'm cute?"

"I didn't say that. Of course I do. I mean—"

A snicker sounded from her side of the line. "I'm teasing, John. Relax."

The little imp. "That wasn't nice. Have some mercy on a guy, would ya? Gaw*lee*."

"Did you just say 'golly'?"

"And now the Midwest boy gets dissed by the Cali girl. Anyone have some lemon to squeeze on this paper cut while we're at it?"

She was laughing hard now, forcing words out between breaths. "I'm sorry…I'll stop. Really."

He joined in, mingling his laugh with hers and noticing how good it sounded together.

Their conversation weaved through topics like favorite TV shows and breakfast cereals, the price of gas, and the new cross they'd hung on the sanctuary wall. Talking to Jenni was effortless. Words just flowed.

At some point, he got up, poured half a mug of cold coffee down the kitchen sink, and took the phone to his room. Their conversation grew serious as she spoke about herself—her childhood, her parents' divorce, her worry over her young cousin and the crowd she was spending time with. John gave what encouragement he could, though he had little experience with adolescent girls. It sounded like what the girl needed was a father, and he choked up for a moment as he realized he no longer was one. Still, he had to admit it felt good having Jenni look to *him* for support for a change, instead of vice versa. And it felt good to give it.

He also felt a hitch in his gut. She seemed to open up to him without reserve, while he kept so many secrets buried. But when was the right time to mention you lost a family? So he let her keep talking and let himself keep getting lost in the sound of her voice and the details of her life. He had a deep desire to know everything.

He registered soreness in his neck and took a glance at the clock. "Whoa." He blinked. "It's one in the morning…I guess we should say goodnight."

"Seriously? Oh, wow. Yeah…I guess we should."

Her deflated tone told him she was just as reluctant to hang up as he was, and sent a knot to his gut. "Well, goodnight."

"Sleep tight."

"Don't let the bedbugs bite."

He set his phone on the nightstand, rolled onto his side, and smiled as he closed his eyes.

John pulled on his robe and bounded into the kitchen. Waving away the fruit flies buzzing around the banana tree, he opened the fridge and grabbed the hazelnut creamer. Then he snatched a mug and set it under his single-cup brewer. Did Jenni like coffee?

With drink in one hand and Bible in the other, he settled onto the sofa. Reading scripture and praying every morning had become a habit—one he looked forward to more and more each day. One that kept him focused. And if he was going to keep spending time with Jenni, he needed to keep that focus.

Self-doubt still rose up on occasion to needle him, but right now, today, deep peace flooded him. A warm comfort settled in his chest as he looked ahead to seeing Jenni again.

"What do you have for me today?" John grinned as Jenni handed him a smoothie.

"Lemon Limelight." She hung up her apron, then stepped through the glass door he held open for her. The summer wind rustled through the leaves in the trees and the blue sky seemed to smile down on them as they strolled toward the fountain.

"Okay, here goes." John sucked on his straw then scrunched his face in an involuntary pucker.

Jenni giggled. "Not your favorite?"

His eyes squinted shut. "No, I can't say that it is. Hoo-boy, that's sour." He tried to laugh with her but was too busy trying to rid his tongue of the offending flavor.

"Here, drink some of my Bananarama to get the taste out." She pointed her straw toward him and he didn't hesitate to lean down and take a sip.

"Ah, much better. Thank you."

"You're welcome." She chuckled again. "Sorry for the bad pick. Next time we'll stick with peach or berry, I promise." She brought the straw back to her own lips and John's neck warmed. What was he, twelve? Sharing a straw should not so easily register on his sensuality meter. But thoughts of connecting his mouth to hers in any form left him charged and in need of distraction.

They reached a stone bench near the fountain. "How about we sit a spell?"

She raised the back of her hand to her mouth, covering a snicker.

"I mean, let's take a load off. Is that better?"

"No. I actually like 'sit a spell.'"

"Just because you like to laugh at me," he teased.

"Only sometimes." Her laughing eyes simmered. "I like the way you talk."

Did she now? "I'll try to believe you."

"Are you going to sit there all day?" She reached into the fountain and launched a splash of water toward him.

"Hey!"

She matched his laughter, then stepped up onto the lower ledge of the fountain.

"What are you doing?"

"We're not *that* old yet. Come on up. Feel the mist."

John shook his head. "You're going to fall in."

"Are you scared?" She slanted her eyes at him.

John smiled at her pretty profile as she tipped her face toward the pinnacle of the water cascade. "All right, I'm coming." He left his drink on the bench and joined Jenni on the fountain. His torso lurched to the left as he found his center of gravity. "Okay, so maybe *I'm* going to fall in. Then won't you feel bad?"

"No. I like laughing at you, remember?" She snickered and jerked away as if he might come after her.

"Yeah, you *better* keep your distance."

She slid a step back his way. "Never."

His laughter caught in his throat. Had she meant that the way it sounded? The way he wanted it to?

Swallowing hard, he dug around in his pocket and produced a coin. Rubbing his thumb over Jefferson's face, he made himself a deal. If it landed in the top tier, he'd ask her out on a date. A real one. If not, he'd go home and take a cold shower.

Jenni wobbled toward him, jutting her arms out for balance. "Hey. Got another coin for me, or are you going to hog all the wishes?"

He squinted at her. "I don't know, it's a pretty good wish."

"So's mine."

They stood in a playful face-off, one of her brows arched high and nothing but the sound of falling water filling the air between them.

He produced another coin from his pocket and laid it in her open palm. "Maybe our wishes…are one and the same."

"Maybe they are." The slight curve of her lips sent his thoughts back to imagining how they'd feel pressed to his own.

He coughed and pointed his eyes upward. "Okay, you wanna go first?"

"How about we go together?"

He looked down at her, standing beside him, and nodded. "Good plan."

They each took their coins in hand, and Jenni gripped his shoulder for balance as she took aim. John cocked his arm back too, fighting the distraction of her touch. "One, two, three!"

As their coins went soaring, Jenni folded at the waist, arms flailing in circles as she fought to regain her balance. Both coins glanced off the top tier and landed in the second. "Oh no!"

Jenni gripped his shirt sleeve, eyes wide, and John twisted toward her, locking onto her upper arms in a steadying hold. "I've got you."

She laughed and grabbed hold of his forearms in return. "That was too close."

Her proximity sent a now-familiar rush of heat through his body. "Maybe we better get down?" His voice came out low, husky.

"Probably wise," she whispered. But she didn't make a move.

They were still holding on to each other, and John's breathing hitched. The coins hadn't reached the top, but he didn't care anymore. Jenni was in his arms, sort of, and it felt so right, so good, he needed more. What might she do if he kissed her? Right here, right now? He could so easily lean in and connect, find out what she felt for him, what he felt for her.

But didn't he already know what this feeling was? "Jenni?" His nerves rattled his bones.

"Yes?" Her gold-dusted eyes riveted to his and her fingers gently pressed in tighter on his arms.

"Would you like to go out to dinner sometime?"

A smile stretched her lips. "I would."

"Tomorrow? Five thirty?"

She nodded. "Perfect."

"Good." His heart struck against his ribs as he studied the depths of her eyes. She was so beautiful, even in her bright orange polo and yellow cap. He grinned. "For now, I think you're due back inside to juice stuff."

She sighed. "You're right."

They released each other and hopped down from the fountain. After escorting her back to her shop, he crossed the parking lot to his car. His gut clenched. He'd just asked her out on an honest-to-goodness *date*. Was he ready to be more than friends?

Arms tingling, Jenni opened the front door to John standing on her porch. His eyes widened as his gaze traced her from head to toe.

Self-conscious, she offered a smile. "Are you okay?"

"Yeah." He blinked then scanned the length of her again. "You look…beautiful."

Heat poured into her cheeks and she smoothed her copper dress, dropping her eyes. "Thank you." She swept her gaze over him—his neat hair slightly mussed, brick red tie around his neck, black shirt and slacks. "You don't look so bad yourself."

"Thanks." He continued to stare for a moment before his throat bobbed, and he offered his arm and escorted her down the steps.

She slid into her seat and carefully arranged the folds of her dress. Then John closed her door, trotted to the driver's side, and navigated them toward the restaurant. He couldn't seem to keep his eyes off her, and Jenni felt her neck heating. He had never looked more masculine, more ruggedly handsome, as he did when he looked at her that way. Like he wanted to pull her close and claim her with a kiss, but wouldn't take anything he hadn't earned.

What *would* his kiss be like?

They were seated near a bank of windows and placed their orders. The air was warm and clear, the sun still golden in the summer sky. They couldn't have ordered a more perfect evening. But in truth Jenni could've been looking through muddy rain and eating hot dogs and mac instead of steak and swordfish, and she would've enjoyed herself just as much.

Throughout the meal, the way John listened to her, smiled, made her laugh… She hadn't felt such strong attraction since Aiden, and in that case she'd known deep down he was wrong for her from the get-go. But this. This felt natural.

"I'm glad you asked me here tonight, John."

"I'm glad you said yes."

She smiled. "I don't date a lot. I guess I'm a bit cautious that way. But you…" she looked straight at him, "you put me at ease somehow."

"Good," he answered softly. His eyes traced her brow then reconnected with hers. "I like you, Jenni. A lot." His Adam's apple rose with a nervous swallow and Jenni smiled.

The pulse in her throat hammered. "Same here."

The waiter stopped and refilled their water glasses, and Jenni finished her last bite of swordfish.

John pushed his empty plate aside. "You guys have so many great seafood restaurants here."

"We are sort of a coastal city. More so than Indiana anyway. Makes for more seafood offerings, I suppose."

"Yeah I'll have to get to the beach eventually. I've never seen the ocean."

"What?" Her mouth hung open. "Never? As in, *ever?*"

He shook his head.

"You're serious?"

"Yep. I came all the way from Indiana to see the Pacific but somehow still haven't gotten myself down there. There's this juice place that seems to take up most of my free time." He grinned.

"Okay, this just won't do. Not that I'm complaining about the visits but we *have* to get you to the beach." She twisted her lips. "You know, some of the college group from church are going to the beach tonight for a bonfire…maybe we could go?" And wouldn't Tori just love to see them?

"That sounds perfect."

She smiled. Indeed it did.

John inwardly cheered at the thought of prolonging their evening with a beach bonfire. From the moment Jenni had stepped out onto her porch looking like beauty personified, he'd wanted the night to last forever. Her silky dress matched her bright brown eyes and flowed over her slender frame, over every feminine curve, like liquid gold. And her pink lips were so tempting.

They arrived as the sun was just beginning to set, casting beautiful oranges and yellows onto the wrinkled sea. John's feet sank into the sand with each step as they plodded toward the crackling fire. The smell of burnt wood rose in smoky billows. A loud pop was followed by sparks drifting up from the center of the pit.

"Hey, guys. We decided to stop by." Jenni greeted the group and introduced John, then found a spot on a shared blanket for them to sit.

"This is incredible." He shot her a smile as she cupped a handful of sand and let it pour through her fingers. The salty breeze, and Jenni's nearness, intoxicated him. The breaking of waves on the sand mixed with the crackle of the fire, creating a powerful ballad.

"I enjoy the beach, but I probably take it for granted. It's nice to just sit and soak it in once in a while."

With Jenni close beside him, John rested his arms on his knees and took in the scene he'd imagined for months, years. The vastness of the ocean mirrored that of its Creator, who stretches out His fingers to hold the universe in the palm of His hand, yet died for him.

How could he have had such a small view of God all those years? Thanking Him for earthly blessings yet failing to see beyond the here and now. Sure he'd claimed otherwise, but ultimately John's faith had been more about how to structure his eighty-some-odd years in this life rather than about what lay beyond.

But God had pursued him, straightened him out. And cast his mistakes into the sea.

"It's big, isn't it?" Jenni ran her finger over a small shell in her palm. "The ocean, and God's love for us."

He stared into the depths of her eyes. "I was just thinking the same thing."

Her cheeks, pinkened by the cool breeze, lifted in a soft smile. Somehow they'd drifted toward each other. Her face, her lips, were nearer to his than a moment ago, hovering so close he could feel her breath, and John's gaze skated to the pulse hammering in her throat.

Behind them, a guitar suddenly twanged. Jenni inhaled and straightened, and John cleared his throat—and his head.

One of the guys strummed a worship song and John found himself caught up in the music, anticipating the chord changes, imagining the feel of the strings beneath his fingers. A few people sang along. From the corner of his eye, John caught Jenni studying his face, watching him take it all in.

"Do you want to walk with me down by the water? Your first visit to the beach wouldn't be complete without getting your feet wet, and maybe finding the perfect seashell."

She'd slipped out of her heels as soon as they'd arrived. Now, John removed his shoes and socks, rolled up the bottoms of his pants, and followed Jenni down toward the ocean's edge.

Soft, warm powder engulfed his feet, gradually becoming firmer and cooler as they approached the water. "This feels nothing like the course, grainy sand at the lake back in Indiana."

"I imagine not."

He took a few steps away from her toward the water and the first wave stretched across the shore to touched his toes with icy fingers. He sucked a breath through his teeth. "Yikes."

Behind him, Jenni laughed. John shot her a playful scowl. "I'll be ready for the next one."

"Mm hmm." She crossed her arms and leveled him with a smirk.

"I don't see you offering your feet to the arctic water. Why don't you come closer?"

"I'm good. This experience is for you; I've been to the beach plenty of times."

He raised his brows. "You aren't scared, are you?" He took a deliberate stride toward her, and she scurried backward. "Come on, just a little closer."

"No… No, that's okay."

She squealed as he scooped her up with an arm under her knees and marched toward the water.

"You wouldn't dare!"

"Wouldn't I?" He swung her back and forth, pretending to take aim toward the oncoming waves.

Jenni clung to his neck, plastering herself to his chest. "Oh my gosh, don't let go!"

His sudden awareness of her tightened his muscles. He stilled his arms and looked into her eyes. "I won't."

As she stared up at him, her fingers moved the tiniest fraction across the back of his neck. Pulling in a deep a breath, John gently lowered her to her feet. She said nothing, just remained at his side and faced the horizon as another cold wave approached, then another.

His heartbeat steadied under the hypnotic cadence of the water rolling up over their feet and then shrinking back into the sea. As Jenni lifted her face to the wind, John bent his toes into the wet sand and watched the ocean rinse them clean. He stooped to pick up a shell, brushing the sand from its grooves. "This one's nice. No chips." He held it up for her to see.

"That *is* a good one." She reached for it. "Not bad at all."

John knelt to search for more while Jenni made lines in the damp sand with her toe as if hoping to uncover one. Her flexed calf passed his field of vision and suddenly seashells weren't so fascinating. He tore his eyes away from her shapely legs and moved them back to the sand.

Tearing his thoughts away wasn't as easy.

She knelt beside him. "Ooh, look at this one." The wind whipped her hair and surrounded him with her scent. She laid a hand on his arm, branding his skin with her gentle touch, and held up a shell in her other palm.

Her smile faded as the air thickened with crackling tension. The only thing keeping him from reaching out to touch her cheek was the wet sand coating his fingers.

They both stood and brushed off their hands. Jenni looked down at her toes. "When I was a little girl I used to dig up sand crabs and see how many I could gather before it was time to go home."

John smiled and tossed the shell and snatched it out of the air. "You'll have to show me next time."

"I'll bring the shovel if you bring the bucket."

"Deal."

They drifted along the shore, stepping over seaweed and past occasional sandcastle remnants, saying little as they looked out over the red horizon. John peeked at her, hair blown back by the salty breeze. The wind had freed several strands which danced around her face, and he envied them the chance to skim across her silken cheek.

Without a word, John moved his hand to graze hers. She coyly hooked her pinky around his, and with that velvet touch, inspired him to press his palm to hers, to lace his fingers between each of her delicate ones, the feel of her skin against his warming his blood and somehow making sense of his world again.

They stopped to watch the edges of the sun dip below the horizon, a gauze of purple, pink, and orange stretching toward them in a stunning display. John's gaze drifted to Jenni's face, watching her admire the sky, and every muscle tightened. He took a steadying breath, tried to clear his thoughts. But when she looked back at him, the desire in her eyes sent his pulse skyrocketing.

Everything else seemed to vanish. It was just the two of them. And now there were no sandy fingers to stop him from touching her. And no uncertainty to hold him back. He grazed his knuckles along her cheek and tucked a lock of hair behind her ear, skimming his thumb over her earlobe to her jaw. Sweet heavens, she was soft. Her lashes lowered as she gently leaned into his touch, then looked up at him again with questioning eyes.

Whatever the question, his answer was yes.

His lungs filled with electrically-charged air, and he watched Jenni's shoulders rise and fall with her quickened breath. When her gaze landed on his mouth, he did the only thing a man could do. He held her face in his hands, tasted her breath, and bent toward her waiting lips.

First contact stopped the world. He drew her close, palms gliding to the small of her back, keenly aware of her closeness, of his hunger. Her fingers caressed his temples before sliding into his hair, heightening his response. She was sweeter than he'd imagined, nearly too much to bear, and he took his time cataloging every nuance of her tender kiss.

She trembled, a soft hum coming from her lips into his, teasing his senses, hinting at how much of her there was to discover. Unhurried, he gently pressed in for more, savoring her, searching…and challenging his self-control. But God help him, he would not cross any lines. Even if it killed him.

With a strength not his own, he stepped back and pointed his face toward the ocean, trying to regain his senses before turning to her again. He scanned the horizon and steadied his breathing. They had officially entered new territory, and some things needed to be said now, rather than later.

"Jenni." He still didn't look at her. "I have to tell you something. About me. It's not easy for me to talk about, but it's important that you know." He peeked at her. Her smile from a moment ago had been replaced by a creased brow. She looked at him with a tilt of her head, but waited in silence, as if bracing for bad news.

John took a deep breath and forged ahead. "I was married...before I came here. Her name was Hannah." The name still brought a wistful grin to his face. "And I had a daughter...Katy." He stole another glance as she pulled her head back, appearing stunned. Confused. Her mouth opened but she didn't speak.

A horrifying realization occurred to him—she might think he'd *left* his family back in Indiana. "Oh, no. I didn't divorce Hannah."

She blinked, shaking her head like this wasn't making sense.

John took her hand. "You remember I told you I'd gone through something difficult back home..."

She nodded, a look of fear swallowing her features. He gulped back the boulder in his throat.

"Well, they..." Could he say this to her out loud? "I...lost them...before I came here." His chest tightened, but he steadied his voice and forced the rest of the words past his lips. "There was a fire."

He felt the familiar sting in his eyes. Jenni's hand flew to her mouth and she shook her head. John had lost his voice. He looked at her and tried to confirm the awful truth without words. Her eyes widened with shock, maybe fear, and then softened with pity as full understanding dawned. Watching the transformation on her face was painful. The fresh understanding brought a sharpness to his loss, cutting open the scars on his heart. He stared at his feet and pulled in a steadying breath.

How awful was it for her to hear this right now, tonight, in a moment like the one they'd just shared? But he had to tell her. He'd be stealing that moment, deceiving her somehow, without her knowing this vital piece of him.

He studied her face. Had he made her uncomfortable? Ruined everything?

Jenni curled her fingers around his arm and when he looked, her eyes glistened.

She brushed dampness from her cheeks with trembling fingertips. "John, I'm so sorry. I...don't know what to say." She slowly shook her head, then pulled her brows together. "Thank you for trusting me with this." Her voice was a hoarse whisper. She pressed her palm to his cheek. "I wish there was something I could do."

Treasuring her compassionate touch, John placed his hand over hers and closed his eyes. "Thank you... You already have." He pulled her fingers to his lips before lowering them, still clutched in his, down to their sides again, then steered them back toward the bonfire.

"I'm sorry I had to ruin the moment out there." He wished he hadn't had to. "I just...thought you should know."

"Don't you dare be sorry. Besides, you didn't ruin anything. Not for me." She gave a coy smile and bumped him as they walked. "It was...perfect." She lowered her head and caught her bottom lip between her teeth.

The corner of John's mouth turned up in a satisfied grin.

Perfect.

They walked back to the bonfire, silent about the kiss they'd shared, and what it meant, in the shadow of Hannah and Katy. But she didn't let go of his hand when they approached the others and that told him all he needed to know.

"Hey you two, you're back just in time to roast marshmallows." Tori, with a suspiciously wide grin on her face, held out the plastic bag, and Dana handed Jenni two long skewers.

Tori leaned in toward Jenni. "Although it looked like you already had your dessert." She'd lowered her voice, but not enough to keep John from hearing. He fought to contain his smile as Jenni elbowed Tori in the ribs, then pinned him with apologetic eyes.

"May I?" He took the skewer from Jenni's hand and lanced a marshmallow, then eased it out over the flames. "FYI," he whispered in her ear, "I always have room for dessert."

Jenni's eyes flitted to him, then back to the fire, and she turned her skewer. "I uh…I think I'm okay with that." Her lips twitched.

After several of the crispy, gooey desserts, they said goodbye to the remaining bunch and trudged through the sand back up to the parking lot. The briny wind had grown cold, raising goose bumps on Jenni's bare arms. John wrapped his arm around her shoulders and tried not to think of all the ways he'd like to keep her warm.

When they arrived back at her house, he stood with her on the porch as she fished her keys from her purse.

After finding them, she looked into him with those honey-brown eyes. "I had a great time tonight, John."

"Thanks for taking me to the beach." He smiled. "I look forward to next time. Digging up those sand crabs you told me about." He tapped the tip of her nose.

She grinned back at him, eyes sparkling. Lingering.

Waiting for him.

Chest aching with anticipation, he lowered his face to hers, then hooked his index finger under her chin and paused briefly for permission.

Her eyes closed, and her breath suspended.

Mouth bending with pleasure at her invitation, he angled her face up and grazed his lips across hers.

The softness of her mouth, the inquisitive exploration of her lips on his, spiked his pulse. She circled her arms around his neck, and together they moved in flawless rhythm, a melody and harmony, as if their souls had merged to one.

Her hair was silk beneath his fingers, stirring a forgotten craving, a demanding need. He deepened the kiss and she responded with a shuddering breath that sent a familiar, heady rush coursing through him. One that had to be controlled. But his body balked at the command to stop, at the boundaries that had long since become foreign to him, begging to hold her just a little closer.

His body strained against his resolve until, with agonizing effort, he pulled away. She mirrored the backward motion without opening her eyes. When she slowly raised her lashes, the flushed look on her face almost sent him back for more, but he had too little self-restraint left to allow it. He dragged in air, stunned by the electricity between them. How could he have questioned whether there was more than friendship between them?

He cleared his throat, the fog beginning to clear from his brain. "Wow."

"Yeah." Her eyebrows shot up. "Wow."

Together they let out a whispered laugh as he touched his forehead to hers.

John straightened. "Well, on that note...I'll say goodnight." He lifted her fingers to his lips. "And I'll call you tomorrow, if you'll be around."

"I'll be around. Goodnight, John." She smiled then slipped inside and closed her door.

John sat in his car for a moment, replaying the way her lips felt on his, the way her eyes pierced through his armor into his soul. Something huge had changed tonight.

His heart.

He was falling in love. And he was terrified.

Chapter Sixteen

Jenni sank back onto her pillow and sighed. If she closed her eyes she could still feel John's arms around her. The night had been wonderful. The sand, the water, the sunset, John's hand in hers... The memories sent a shiver the length of her body. She ran her fingers along her lips. She'd never been kissed like that before. Though, granted, her experience was limited.

She'd imagined John's kiss more than once, but nothing could have prepared her for it. For the gentleness of his fingers trailing her cheek, or the bolt of lightning shooting through her core at the touch of his lips. Always the gentleman, he'd moved slowly, shown restraint. Delicious restraint that only magnified the desire trembling just under the surface. And assured her with the unspoken promise that it would wait.

Oh thank you, God, for that fender-bender.

Grabbing a deep breath, she attempted to settle her soaring heart rate as Sadie jumped onto the bed and snuggled beside her. Jenni wove her fingers through the creamy fur and pulled her head from the clouds, to John's past. The shock of it slammed her all over again. Such unimaginable loss. Her heart ached for him beyond words. No wonder he'd turned to alcohol to numb that kind of pain. It was incomprehensible.

In the arena of life experience, she was still just a child compared to him. Five years difference in age didn't sound like much. But he'd been a husband, and a father. Now a widower. While she still lived in her childhood home with her mother. What did she have to offer?

Love?

Pulling her sheet up to her chin, her gaze fell on her fuzzy cheetah print slippers. Had she been shopping for them when John lost his baby girl? John had lived so much life already while she was so insulated, so…unable to relate. How could she possibly be the right woman for him? Maybe it was all a mistake.

Oh God, I don't want it to have been a mistake.

Her phone rang, as expected. "Hi, Tori."

"So I guess it went well, huh?"

"It did…"

"That's not quite the enthusiastic response I was expecting. Anything wrong?"

She swallowed the doubt lodged in her throat. "No. It's just… more complicated than I expected."

"It always is."

But…he'd been married. What if he wasn't over her? What if when he was with Jenni, he was thinking of his wife? "I don't know, Tori…what if this is a mistake?"

"Did it feel like a mistake while he was kissing you on the beach?"

"No. It felt…right."

"Now there's the sigh I was expecting."

Jenni couldn't help smiling. "Guess I'm just a little over-cautious."

"Pray about it. And relax. It'll be okay. No one's signing any contracts or anything."

They ended the call and Jenni puffed out her cheeks. *Okay, Lord. Show me the path You have for me.*

Be still and know that I am God.

The verse filled her mind as clearly as if God had audibly spoken. Her muscles relaxed. God had her in His hand. He'd take care of everything if she just kept her focus on Him. Peace washed through her.

Sadie licked her fingers, then curled into a ball at the foot of the bed. Jenni rolled onto her side and stared out the window. She breathed a laugh. Ridiculous to get so worked up after one kiss. *Two, actually. Both way above average.*

Her heart did another somersault. Yeah, she had it bad.

John stood beside her on the beach. The wind whisked her hair around her face as she stared deep into his blue eyes. He gathered her into his arms, and she held his face in her hands as she poured all of herself into his kiss. The whole world in that moment consisted of the beating of her heart, the crashing of the waves, and…her cell phone? *Let it go to voicemail.* It grew louder and louder, and the sound of the waves faded further away, until finally she realized she was at home in her bed.

Just a dream. Disappointed, Jenni threw off the covers and dug through her purse for her phone. John's name shone on the screen, and her stomach did a cartwheel as she answered.

"Hello?"

"Hey. I was about to hang up."

"John." She couldn't keep the smile out of her voice. "I'm glad you didn't hang up."

"Did I wake you? I'm sorry."

"No, no. I'm awake." The dream image resurfaced, spreading heat to her cheeks. "I just had to find my phone."

"Good. Listen, I don't know if you had plans this morning, but do you want to get breakfast?"

A smile scrunched her cheeks. "What time?"

"I can pick you up in an hour if that works for you."

"Perfect."

The call ended and Jenni burst out into the hallway, colliding with her mom. "Oops, good morning."

"Morning, honey. Should I make breakfast?"

"Uh, no. I sort of have plans."

Her mother crossed her arms and turned her head, eying her with a discerning grin. "With John?"

"Maybe."

She lifted one eyebrow.

"Okay, yes. And I only have an hour to get ready."

"That's two dates within twenty-four hours." The other eyebrow rose. "He must really be something. When do I get to meet him?"

"Soon. I'll introduce you when he gets here. But right now I have to hurry."

Her mother gave an amused look before letting Jenni pass.

Jenni took a quick shower, dried her hair, and applied just a touch of makeup. Would John look at her the way he had last night? A grin tugged at the corners of her lips when she recalled how he'd been nearly speechless when she first opened the door. That was a look she'd like to see again. She pulled on her favorite pair of jeans and a flattering pink top, then slid on her bracelet. As she waited for him to arrive, her nerves kicked in. Last night had been wonderful, but she needed to slow down. Proceed with caution. She closed her eyes and shot up a prayer.

The knock at the door made her jump. John stood there, dressed in black jeans and a blue-grey polo, looking even more handsome than she remembered. His gaze swept over her and the tilt of his mouth set her stomach fluttering and somersaulting. "Hey, Jenni. You look nice."

"Thanks." His eyes told her his thoughts had returned to the previous night, and her lips twitched.

Her mom appeared, and Jenni gestured toward her. "John, this is my mom, Laura."

Her mother reached out her hand, enthusiasm in her eyes. "Nice to meet you, John."

"Nice to meet you, Ms. DuPont." John shook her hand.

"Call me Laura."

"Laura, then."

"You're the one who fixed the door. Thank you."

"Oh, it wasn't a big deal. Happy to help." He smiled, then turned to Jenni. "You ready?"

"Yep." Jenni grabbed her purse and stepped outside.

"Bye, honey." Her mom leaned on the door with a goofy grin on her face, as if Jenni were heading off to the senior prom. "It was nice meeting you, John." At least she didn't take a picture.

"You too. Goodbye, Ms. DuPon—er, *Laura*."

"Bye, Mom." Had Jenni really made herself that much of a hermit that a breakfast date warranted this much eager excitement from her mother? Apparently yes.

The door closed and Jenni followed John off the porch, her ballet flats tapping their way to the curb. John opened her door and Jenni settled in, greeted by his masculine scent. Once on the road, he slid a glance her way. "You look good today."

A smile rippled through her. "Thank you." He'd said that once already, but she'd take it again. They pulled into the parking lot of the Waffle House and John turned off the engine. "Just a second."

He jogged around to her side to open her door, as if he were a limo driver, and she, a movie star. Jenni loosed an internal sigh. Indiana boys sure were raised right. She'd have to thank his mother.

When he offered his hand, Jenni gladly slipped hers into it, the touch of his skin awakening a hunger for something other than waffles. *Too much too fast. Too much too fast.* But her heart, for once, didn't seem to be listening. Surely he could hear the pounding in her chest. Hopefully her palms wouldn't start sweating.

The smell of bacon and fresh waffles welcomed them at the door. With only a few tables in use, they were seated right away. As the hostess cleared the extra sets of silverware from their table, Jenni scooted into their booth, shaking off her nerves. *It's John, you dope. Since when are you this nervous around him?* But she knew the answer to that already: Since he'd kissed her senseless.

Did he plan to do it again?

When the server came for their drink orders, Jenni decided to skip the coffee—and the coffee breath—just in case. She looked over the menu. "I think I'm in the mood for orange juice this morning."

The server left and John slanted his gaze at Jenni. "Really? *Plain* juice for the queen of nectars? You know it will never live up to that amazing peachy peach."

She laughed. "You're right, that was delicious. Juice—it's my sole talent, I'm afraid."

"Definitely not. After last night, I can say there's at least one other thing you're *really* good at." His brows shot up for an instant and flames sprang to life in her cheeks.

"Yeah I guess I do roast a mean marshmallow."

He shot her a half-cocked smile, then opened his mouth to retort just as the server interrupted to deliver her juice.

"Cheers." Jenni quenched her suddenly parched throat then redirected the conversation. "So do you have any hobbies? Besides handyman stuff?"

He nodded. "Basketball. Pacers all the way, baby."

She wagged a finger. "Oh, no. You're in California now. Time to switch to the purple and gold."

"Not gonna happen. A Pacers fan wouldn't be caught dead rooting for the Lakers. So you'd better get used to it now."

Had she? She smiled at the thought, then held her hands up in mock surrender. "Okay, okay. I can see you need more time. Do you play too?"

"Derek and I do a little one-on-one now and then and he's trying to get a few guys together to play once a week. We'll see how that goes. Should be a good time—for me anyway. I always smoke him." He raised one muscled arm up over his head and mimicked a jump shot. Suddenly all Jenni could think about were those strong, masculine arms encircling her, holding her close. She felt the flush in her cheeks and met his eyes to see if he'd noticed. His sly smile told her he had.

Busted. She'd been cursed with tell-tale cheeks—they always gave her away.

She rubbed a hand over her throat and tried to recover. "So, what are your plans for the summer? There's tons you probably want to see— Disneyland, Knott's Berry Farm. Do you like roller coasters?"

"Love 'em. I used to drag Hannah to Holiday World any chance I got." His gaze went soft, distant. "She couldn't stand coasters, but I made her ride them anyway." He breathed a laugh and Jenni's stomach knotted.

She pasted on a smile and busied herself running her fingers up and down through the condensation on her glass. "Maybe the San Diego Zoo instead. It's always been one of my favorites."

"Yeah, sounds great. And maybe I can get you to a basketball game."

"I'd be rooting for the Lakers."

"A little rivalry could be fun. I won't judge."

She laughed, her uneasiness evaporating. "Gee, thanks."

After their breakfast, he paid the check and guided her out the door with a palm on the small of her back.

Once outside, he took her hand. "If you have an hour to spare, there's something I want to do."

She stopped while he got out his keys. "Like what?"

"You'll see." He released Jenni's hand for her to climb into the car, then waited till she was safely settled to close her door.

When they pulled up to their destination a few minutes later, Home Depot was the last place she expected to see. She shut her door and looked over at John, who wore the expression of a child on his way to Chuck E Cheese. "So…what are we doing here?"

He shrugged. "I used to love Saturday mornings building stuff with my dad. Come on." He held his hand out and she took it, letting him lead her into the home improvement store. Strangest date ever.

When they'd stepped through the doors, John paused, lifted his face, and inhaled deeply. "Ah…smell that?"

"Saw dust and paint fumes?"

"No. Creativity."

He led her toward the back center of the store where long tables had been set up. Small squares of wood lay on them, and tools, and Jenni's eyebrows came together. "What's this?"

"Our Saturday morning project." He grinned then grabbed a work apron from the table, slipped it over her head, and reached around her waist. His nearness made her head pound, and he smiled down at her as he secured the apron ties, giving them a little yank. She stumbled into him and her hands flew to his chest as she steadied herself.

They both froze. "Sorry," she whispered up at him.

"Don't be." His hint of a smile made her heart skip a beat, then she followed his gaze down to where her hands were still plastered against his…very firm chest.

Red faced, she withdrew them and inched backward with a shaky smile. Her legs would not hold her up much longer if she didn't get some distance. She pivoted toward the table and busied herself examining its contents. "So…how do I help? What do you need?"

"Well, first, you won't be *helping*…you'll be building. And second, you'll need this." From somewhere under the table, he produced a hammer and held it out to her with both hands.

She stared down at it. "It's pink."

He smiled. "Yep. And it's yours."

"You…bought me a hammer?"

"You're welcome."

She poked out her lips and nodded, then wrapped her fingers around the handle. "Thanks."

Definitely the strangest date ever.

A few other people—mostly fathers and grade school children—trickled in and took up places around the table. A bittersweet sense of yearning flowed beneath the crackling hum between her and John.

As the instructor greeted people, John pushed a box of nails toward her then set one piece of wood against another. "Here you go."

Cupping a hand toward John, Jenni spoke out of the side of her mouth. "Is now a good time to admit that I've literally never used a hammer before?"

"After today, you won't be able to say that anymore."

Touché.

He grabbed his own box of nails and wood pieces and set to work.

Jenni watched his profile, the look of concentration lowering his brows, the nail held between his lips. She scooped out her own nail and positioned it, raised her hammer...

"Whoa, wait." John set down his tools and took her wrist in his hand. "You really haven't used a hammer before, have you?"

"I warned you."

He circled around behind her so he was looking over her shoulder, his right hand holding her wrist, his left covering hers as she gripped the nail. "Gentle at first." His breath tickled her ear and she struggled to concentrate as he guided her to tap the hammer on the head of the nail until it sank into the wood. "There you go. Once it's secure, you can swing a little harder. But not too much. It's a birdhouse, not a railroad track."

"Thanks." She turned her head and found herself staring into his eyes. Blue eyes that skipped to her mouth, then crinkled with his smile. Her pulse hammered in her throat.

"Any time."

A heartbeat passed with his arms still around her. "I...think I got it now."

"Oh. Right." He withdrew and returned to his place beside her, then picked up with his bird house where he'd left off.

Jenni rolled her shoulders and grabbed another nail. For the next several minutes, they worked on hammering, sanding, and gluing the various parts of the birdhouses together. The children prattled; the parents did most of the work themselves. John talked about his family, his dad, building derby cars and tree forts, and Jenni reveled in every minute of it.

She lifted her bird house and examined it with a frown. "I think I messed up. It's lopsided. And this nail is poking out here."

A little boy across the table giggled before being hushed by his father. John laughed too, but not in a mean way. "Not bad for a first try."

"No?" She laughed along with him then reached for another nail. Maybe she could fix it.

"No, not at all. You should've seen the first project Hannah made." He shook his head. "Oh man, was it a dreadful mug tree."

Jenni's smile plunged down into her stomach. "Oh." Her fingers shook as she tried to hold the nail steady.

"But she got better. And so will you." With a nod, John returned his focus to attaching the little perch of his own birdhouse.

Steady... She cleared her throat. "So...you used to do this kind of thing with Hannah?" She kept her eyes down, on her pile of nails, but stole a sideways glance at John.

"Occasionally." He squeezed a bead of wood glue onto the spindle that would serve as a perch.

Were they reenacting a date he'd had with his wife?

Jenni looked at him then, waited for him to meet her eyes, for what he'd just said to register with him...but he appeared oblivious.

Was this kind of thing just part of what it meant to date a widower? She wasn't actually jealous of a dead woman, was she? No, it was fine. It didn't mean anything. It wasn't a comparison. Not really.

She pinched the nail and tapped it with the hammer, then hit it harder once, twice... On the third strike, her hand slipped, and pain ripped through her finger. She gasped, pulling her hand against her chest. "Oh, ow ow ow ow..." She hissed.

John spun toward her with concern in his eyes. "Are you all right?"

"No," she squeaked. She shook her hand trying to dislodge the pain but it wasn't working. She grimaced and shook her hand again.

"Let me see."

Her finger throbbed with its own pulse and tears sprang to her eyes, but Jenni allowed him to take her hand. John's brows lowered as he gingerly turned her hand side to side and examined the injured digit. His touch was soft, careful, almost sensual, and Jenni's breath hitched. He brushed his finger over the top of her hand, momentarily distracting her from the heat pounding in her fingertip. "Well, it's not broken, so that's good."

"It still hurts."

"I think I can fix that… May I?"

She nodded, and he locked his gaze on hers as he lifted her sore finger to his lips. The gentle kiss cut off her air supply and diverted her attention from the pain, but the throbbing heat increased, traveling throughout her body. Her legs weakened when cool air washed over her skin as he gently blew over her fingertip.

"Better?"

She nodded.

"Good. How about we call it a day here and finish these up later?"

"Yeah." She forced air back into her lungs. "That's a good idea."

He set about cleaning up her work station, while Jenni evaded the glances of a couple of the other men who were hunched over their own projects. Her heart was knocking around her ribs like a set of drumsticks and she tingled all over.

Holy moley. Best…date…ever.

Her pulse had returned to normal by the time they were back in John's car. She pressed her hand to her cheek, cooling the sore finger.

"Should I take you home to ice that, or do you want to suffer with me a little longer?"

"Hmm, tough choice. I guess I'll suffer."

He smiled, reached across the console, and carefully laced his fingers through hers. "Aren't I lucky?"

They picked up a loaf of day-old bread and drove to a nearby park. The sun had warmed the late-morning air as they started up over a grassy hill. John settled onto a bench in front of a small, man-made pond and patted the spot beside him to welcome Jenni. He opened the plastic bag and they each took a slice of bread, tearing off chunks to toss to the mallards that were already converging on them.

"I haven't done this since I was a kid." Jenni laughed at the quacking hoard swarming them.

"It's been awhile for me too." John reached for a piece of bread and flung a chunk several feet away. A goose began honking to scare off his competition and Jenni pulled in a contented breath. John had a much better idea of what a date should be than most. This was perfect. Or would be, if he'd kiss her again.

Hey, you wanted slow, remember?

She growled inwardly at the self-reminder.

The ducks were demanding little things and the loaf went quickly. When they finally realized the food was gone and wandered away, Jenni leaned back against the wooden bench and listened to the rippling water and rustling leaves.

John tossed the last of his crumbs and wiped his hands on his pants, then inched closer to her, his leg brushing hers. He took her hand then, and gave her a look that made her head spin. If he didn't kiss her soon, she was going to die.

She grinned, trying not to be overtaken by tremors when he tucked her hair behind her ear, then teased her earlobe. Then he leaned in, and, finally, melted her like caramel with a touch of his lips. She traced the contours of his face, thinking she would be perfectly happy doing this forever, but it was over much too soon.

He leaned back with a slow exhale and looked out across the water. His eyes dimmed as his thoughts seemed to take him somewhere else. Perhaps to…her?

Jenni fought the cage that wanted to go back up around her heart. She touched his hand, trying to focus on his need instead of her own. "What's wrong?"

"Nothing. It's just…" He shook his head as if searching for words. "I don't understand…I didn't expect…" He turned back to the water, and Jenni pressed her fingernails into her palms.

What? What was he unsure about?

"I've been praying about us for awhile now. Even asked advice from a friend. Because I have these feelings for you, but…"

But. A tiny word that could change so much.

Jenni straightened her spine and steadied her voice. "But, what?"

"But my love for Hannah was deep…real. So I don't understand how…" His palms came up then dropped back to his lap.

There it was. The confirmation she'd feared. She swallowed against the rock in her throat. He still loved his wife, and didn't know how to move on. "John…I think maybe…maybe this is a mistake." She scooted away but he clasped her hand.

"Wait…what are you saying?" His gaze locked onto hers, the space between his brows wrinkling.

She chewed her lip. It was better to lay it all out now, before either of them got hurt. She wasn't about to try and *convince* him to move on from the past, with her, no matter how much she wanted him to.

"There obviously is something here, between us, but *you need more time*, I get it." She pulled her hand from his. "Look, don't worry over last night. We had a great date, and it was probably a big step for you, but maybe it's best if we're…just friends. For now."

Panic flashed behind his eyes and twisted her heart. "I don't want to be just friends with you, Jenni."

She stood and pointed her face toward the breeze, wrapping her arms around herself. "I don't think you know what you want quite yet. And that's okay, John. It's really okay."

He stood and turned her around by her shoulders. "But I do know. You, Jenni. I want *you*." He shook his head, brows knit tightly together. "I thought I was being clear, but…" He held her face in his hands and stooped to look her in the eye. "I'm just trying to say I feel so lucky to be blessed this way a second time. I mean, after Hannah—"

Her eyes closed. *Second.* She sighed. "But John…" She pressed her fingers to her temples. "I can't just step into her role. Pick up where you two left off…"

"What are you talking about?" Confusion pinched his brows. "Why would you think that?"

She hesitated, not wanting to make it harder. "Back at the store, you… Forget it, that's not important. The love you had for your wife, that loyalty, it's…*beautiful*. You have every right to hold onto that." She forced herself to meet his troubled gaze. "But whether you realize it or not, you've been talking about Hannah like you wish she were here…" her voice fell to a pained hush, "…instead of me. And I just…I can't do that." Could he understand? "I can't compete with an idealized memory. I can't be second place to a ghost. I don't think you're ready. Or maybe I'm not, I don't know."

His eyes rounded with understanding. "Oh, Jenni. I'm such an idiot. I did sort of compare you to Hannah, didn't I? With the woodwork." He pinched the bridge of his nose. "I never meant… You aren't in second place, love. Not by a mile." He brushed the hair back from her face, and her heart thrilled at the word *love*. "I was careless with my words, but I didn't mean to hurt you. Trust me, I *know* how I feel about you." His eyes pleaded, and she felt her heart twisting within her.

She pressed her fingertips into her palms; she had to stay strong. "And I know how I feel about you. But I'd need you here, in the present. I don't want to share your heart, even with someone who's gone. I'm just not built that way. I'm not strong enough and I don't think I ever will be. I can't compete with her."

"You're not competing with Hannah." He framed her face and pressed his lips to her jaw, eroding her walls. "Oh, Jenni, you're not. I promise. I'm just so humbled and, and amazed, that God's allowed me to…" He burrowed his fingers into her hair and rested his forehead against hers—his breath smelling like mint, not coffee and onions. "Don't do this, Jenni. Please, believe me," he whispered. "I'm so ready."

A shiver ran through her middle as Jenni studied the depths in his eyes. He was terrified. Of losing her. And she wasn't ready to lose him either. Not before they'd even given it a chance. She might come to regret it, but she wanted—*needed*—to believe him.

She nodded. "Okay… let's see where this goes."

John pulled her close, tucking her head beneath his chin with a deep sigh. She wrapped her arms around him and listened to the beating of his heart. This spot felt made for her, and she never wanted to give it up. Would he one day tire of her insecurities? "John…I'm sorry for being overly sensitive."

"No. *I'm* sorry for being so stupid," he breathed into her hair. "I should've considered your feelings before I spoke. It can't be an easy thing for you, to be with someone with the kind of past I have. But I'll work hard to make you believe…" He stepped back and whispered his gaze over her face. He brushed his fingertips along her cheek, leaving a trail of electricity in their path. "You're all I see, Jenni. Nothing else."

Her stomach flipped as she looked into his blue eyes. He leaned down till his lips were achingly close, hovering just shy of touch. The air crackled as Jenni gripped his collar and rocked up on her toes to close the distance. Moving her lips over his, she relished every sparkling sensation coursing through her.

If this was going to work, she had to learn to not flinch so easily. She pushed back the haunting apprehension, buried it in a corner of her heart. The part of her that feared she'd always be shadowed by Hannah's memory. Right now, in John's arms, only one question circled her thoughts.

Just how long does it take to fall in love?

Chapter Seventeen

Las Vegas, Nevada

"Want me to come with you?" Stacy tucked a leg under her and faced April on the couch.

"No thanks, I think I'd rather be alone." April forced a bleak smile. "Everything I've heard says it's a simple procedure. I'll be okay."

Stacy squeezed her hand. "Of course you will. I'll cook stir fry tonight. And we'll have ice cream too. Whatever you need, I'll be here for you when you get back."

April took a deep breath. "Thanks."

An hour later, her cab pulled up in front of a plain white building. It was smaller than she expected, with only a smattering of cars parked in the lot. A few young trees were tied to stakes along the sidewalk. It looked clean enough she supposed. After paying the fare, she stood there alone and took in the shrubs and the friendly sign above the entrance. Then focused on the glass doors. Her heart beat in double time and her palms began sweating.

You'll be fine, it's no big deal.

But dread suddenly wound its hot tentacles around her gut. Nothing would be the same after this. There'd be no going back. But what else could she do? She looked down at her shoes padding over the concrete walkway, feeling like she wasn't the one controlling the path her feet carried her down. But she lifted her chin and repeated her mantra. *You'll be fine, it's no big deal.*

Movement registered in the corner of her eye. Great, a protester.

The woman held a picture—an ultrasound image of a fetus with the words Did You Know? emblazoned across the top. April dropped her head and kept walking, but curiosity got the best of her and she looked back to the sign.

At five weeks your baby's heart is beating. The brain and lungs have begun to develop.

At six weeks, your baby's eyes have lenses and her nostrils are formed.

Wait, what? That had to be a lie. Scare tactics. Sensationalism. Guilt trips. She scrunched her brow and averted her eyes, but she couldn't help herself. She stole another peek.

At nine weeks your baby has fingerprints.

A sharp inhale. Did it…have *fingerprints*? Her hand fluttered to her abdomen and she counted backwards…nine weeks. It had been nine weeks!

Her head swam, the world tilted, then her legs gave out, dropping her to the ground. She flattened a palm on the concrete, gasping. Her lungs burned for air. What was happening?

The woman with the sign rushed over to where April was slumped on the sidewalk. "Are you all right?" Alarm rang in her voice. But there wasn't enough oxygen in the world for April to give her an answer.

The woman rubbed her back. "Shh. Breathe. I think you're hyperventilating. Here, put your head between your knees, and breathe slowly…long, even breaths. Purse your lips."

April did as she was told and soon her lungs found the thin promise of relief. When her breathing steadied, she looked up at the stranger's face. "My baby has fingerprints."

April called Stacy to come pick her up but offered no explanation. Silence dominated the car ride home. Inside her womb, a new person with fingerprints all its own, was growing. The same way everyone started out. She watched the traffic, mesmerized by the vast sea of people surrounding them.

Finally, Stacy spoke. "So…what happened?"

"I couldn't go through with it."

"I...I could go back with you. Maybe you just needed support. I know it's not easy. But it's not as bad as you think, really. We could set up a new appointment, and—"

"No. I'm not going to go back, I'm not doing it."

Getting fired was no surprise to April. That's what happened when employees spent more time in the bathroom than the front desk, doing their job. But her heart sank as she picked up a newspaper and scanned the Employment section. Like her trips to the porcelain throne, this was too familiar. Only difference now was that she wasn't the only one counting on her.

She took a minimum wage job for a couple of weeks but the pock-faced shift manager overreacted when, in a moment of weakness, she scarfed down a burger in the back room without paying for it. And her hard luck was receiving no commiseration from Stacy. April tried to come up with a plan, to talk it out with her best friend, but Stacy wouldn't listen.

Leaning on the entryway to the kitchen, arms crossed over her chest, Stacy's eyes glinted steel. "April, be reasonable. You can't take care of a baby if you can't even take care of yourself."

April pressed her lips together and looked out the kitchen window, Stacy's words like a thousand needles pricking her heart. Did she think April didn't know that?

Stacy cocked her head and huffed. "I certainly can't have a baby *here*. Quit being so selfish. Do what you know is right. It wouldn't be fair to bring a baby into the world like this. Think of the horrible life you'd be giving it."

April picked at her fingernail. "Did you know it already has a tongue—and a brain?"

Stacy pressed on, unfazed. "You're making it harder than it has to be. It's still not too late. You need to end this *now*."

April whipped her head toward her. "I'm not killing my baby."

"April, it's not a baby!"

"Don't feed me that line, Stacy. This isn't some abstract concept, it's *my child*. It's got a beating heart. Fingerprints. And it's growing inside of *me.*" She flattened her hand to her chest. "I'm supposed to have a *choice*, right? That's what you're big on. I choose to keep it! So mind your own business and shut your mouth."

A wave of nausea forced her to stop and sprint to the bathroom, effectively knocking her off her swagger.

She turned on the tap and looked at her reflection. What was she going to do?

April opened the bathroom door, and Stacy looked up from her spot on the couch. She twisted her mouth to the side. "Sorry."

"It's okay," came the automatic response. But it wasn't.

Chapter Eighteen

Riverside, California

Reaching over to her nightstand, Jenni grabbed her phone and checked for messages.

Good morning, darlin'. Call me when you wake up.

She hit the Call button and bit back a smile as she waited for John to answer.

"Hey, sleepy head." His voice sent instant sparks through abdomen.

"I think I liked darlin' better than sleepy head."

"Well, *darlin'*, I like imagining how attractive you must look first thing in the morning with your hair all a wild mess. Mm hmm, your bed head is quite appealing in my imagination."

"Your imagination is going to get you into trouble."

"Probably. It's a battle I'm willing to fight, for you. Listen, can you do something for me?"

"Like?"

"Can you block off next Saturday for me?"

"The whole day you mean?"

"Yes, the whole day. I have something special planned."

"Ooh, what is it?"

"Can't say. It's a surprise. But you might want to dress up a little."

"Sounds intriguing." She raked her fingers through her tangled locks. "I'm in."

"Good." She heard the smile in his voice. "Okay, I've got to get going. You have a good day, babe. I'll call you later."

Her mouth quirked. "Okay. You too."

She ended the call and pulled back her covers. Something special planned? Anticipation tingled her spine but she bit back her excitement. She still had to keep her head, though every day was harder. John was all kinds of perfect. Faithful. Attentive, Spiritually minded. Honorable. Handsome beyond all reason. And true to his word, he'd made her believe *she* was all he was thinking about when they were together. He lavished attention on her, went out of his way to show her, time and again, that she held a distinctive place in his life.

She stood on weakened knees and assessed her 'bed head' in the mirror. Frizzies stuck up in back like a halo and a weird curlicue popped out on one side. Definitely not as attractive as John must imagine. But she smiled knowing that he *did* imagine.

At what point did a woman know a man was *the one*? And why did that sound so corny?

Jenni shook her head to clear it of these too-deep thoughts, and shuffled into the kitchen in her PJs and slippers.

"Hey, princess." She filled Sadie's dog dish then reached for a mug from the tree. Coffee spun and swirled up to the top, inviting her to inhale deeply.

Having the living room to herself, she plopped onto the sofa to enjoy the stillness of the morning. Lovable little Sadie jumped up beside her and rested her chin on Jenni's lap. She scratched Sadie's ear. "How's my sweet girl?" Then she ran her fingers through the soft fur while reading her daily devotion. Maybe the wisdom she needed would come to her in its pages.

When her mother woke and joined her on the couch, Jenni closed her Bible and took a deep breath. "Mom? Can I talk to you?"

"Of course. What is it?" Her mother set down her coffee mug and faced her with a knowing gleam in her eye.

"I want to talk to you about…John."

A smile lifted her cheeks high. "You two have quickly become two peas in a pod, haven't you? I'm all ears."

Moments later, Jenni twisted her hands in her lap and watched her mother's face go slack.

"Are you serious? A fire?"

Jenni nodded. She and John had agreed that it was better to have his past out in the open than to risk an awkward revelation later. Speaking of it was harder than she thought it'd be, but she wanted it out of the way so she could talk to her mom about what she *really* wanted to—her growing feelings for him.

Her mother shook her head. "That's terrible, Jenni. Awful." She dropped her gaze and pulled in a breath. "I should've known it was too perfect." Her eyes pinged back to Jenni's. "Honey, listen to me." She took Jenni's hand in her own and stroked it. "He's handsome, and kind, and the first man in a long time to catch your attention." She gripped Jenni's hand tight. "But you need to think long and hard about what you're getting into."

"I know. Believe me. And I have."

"Have you? Because Jenni, a person doesn't go through a thing like that and come out unscathed. He's going to be working through those issues for a long, long time. If it were me, I'd walk away now, while you can."

Jenni's eyes widened. "You can't seriously be saying that."

"It might sound harsh, but you have no idea what the ripple effects of a tragedy like that could be. Haven't you lived through enough drama? I'm worried that what he needs is a licensed therapist, not a girlfriend. Not my daughter."

Jenni pulled her hand away. "Mom—"

"Don't look at me like I'm a monster. I like him too, dear. I do. And he deserves to find happiness again someday. But I don't want to see you shouldering a burden like that. I love you too much."

"Stop. Please."

"Honey…do you think he's stopped loving his wife? Stopped missing her?"

"I think he's ready to move on."

"What if he's not?" She shook her head. "I know a thing or two about men, about baggage, and I see heartbreak ahead for you if you're wrong."

"I'm not."

"*Jenni.*"

"I'm *not*." She stood and pulled her shoulders back. "I can't do this with you this right now. I've got to go."

The sun had long since chased away the morning dew from the grass on the sprawling hills. Jenni kicked off her sandals and crossed her legs beneath her as John lowered himself beside her. She squinted up at his face, a smile blooming on her cheeks. "This is a fun idea. I love the outdoors."

"Me too." He opened the insulated bag beside them and handed her a sub sandwich and a bottle of lemonade.

"Thanks." Far in the distance, she could see a few children playing tag, running in and out of the trees. And over at the baseball diamond, a couple of guys having batting practice. A jogger went by with his golden retriever trotting beside him.

A contented sigh parted her lips.

"Beautiful day, isn't it?" John chewed and looked out over the park as well.

"It really is. Then again, every day has looked beautiful since…"

"Since we kissed on the beach," he finished for her.

She licked a crumb from the corner of her mouth. "I was going to say since the semester ended, but…"

"Ooh, ouch."

She laughed and leaned over to plant a smooch on his lips. "Kidding, kidding."

John polished off his sandwich and pulled out a container of ripe red strawberries from the tote. She watched the wind rustle his sandy blond hair, watched the sun glint off of his cheekbones and brighten his eyes until they rivaled the brilliance of the summer sky. She brushed her hands on her napkin and cleared her throat. "Can I ask you something? That day I found you in the sanctuary with the guitar…you said you hadn't played in a long time. I can't help wondering, why not? You were good."

A crease formed between his brows as he plucked the stem from another berry. "I used to play for my wife, and our daughter. I'd play, and Hannah would sing, and together…it was like magic. Music was sort of

189

woven into our lives. But after the fire..." His jaw clenched as he swallowed. "My guitar went down with everything else, and I simply lost the desire to play."

Layers of heartache pulsed through Jenni's chest. Hurt for John and his losses mostly, but behind it the selfish sting of another woman's memory, another life he'd cherished.

Her mother's warning came to mind, but she dismissed it, longing somehow to comfort him. Jenni placed her hand over his. "But you *did* play. Maybe you're starting to find it again. That desire."

"Maybe." He met her eyes and squeezed her hand. "When you joined in, a breath of life entered the song. Everything came together when you added your voice, it felt like the most natural thing in the world. It brought back memories and I didn't know how to process that."

A lump formed in her throat. "Memories aren't all bad. In time, they'll hurt less. And you'll be ready for new ones."

His eyes were clear and untortured as they pierced hers. "I know. They already do hurt less. And I'm already collecting new ones." He lay on his back with his arms under his head and stared up at the sky. "Like the first time I saw you. My friend had to help me pick my jaw up off the floor."

A laugh worked its way up her throat, easing the tension there. "You're exaggerating."

"Barely. Derek elbowed me in the ribs and told me to quit staring. But I couldn't."

Heat pricked her cheeks and she knew they were pink. "Oh yeah?"

"Yeah. You were wearing a long, turquoise skirt, we were singing about surrender and I was completely decimated by your beauty. How you expressed worship from a whole new perspective, mixing everything good about this world and the next, I just didn't stand a chance."

Oh, there went another piece of her heart. She gulped down some lemonade then brought her knees to her chest, arranging her skirt around her ankles and trying to slow her heart from falling for this man at such breakneck speeds. But it was no use.

She rested her cheek on her knees and smiled at him as he sat back up beside her. "No, I guess you didn't."

She snickered and he cocked his head, tossed a strawberry stem at her, then joined her laughter.

"I still love watching you sign."

The sun warmed her face as Jenni watched John pluck a blade of grass and twirl it around in his fingers.

"How do you sign grass?" He asked, as he positioned the blade between his thumbs and blew into it, making a whistle.

She brought her palm up to her chin to demonstrate. "Like you're lying in the grass."

A bird chirped from somewhere overhead, echoing the song in Jenni's heart.

"What about...flower?" He plucked a dandelion from beside the edge of their blanket and held it out to her.

With a tilt of her head, she took it, her lips twitching into a smile. With her right hand, she made the flat O shape and rotated it in front of her nose. "Flower."

His smile tingled her belly and she looked out at the horizon. A gentle breeze swayed the green treetops and raised goosebumps on her skin.

On the blanket beside her, John stretched out on his side and propped his head in his hand. "It must've taken a long time to learn all of those signs."

"It wasn't too bad. I caught on pretty quickly, especially through music." She brushed off her hands and mirrored his position, straightening her skirt over her calves. "Music...is so powerful. Everybody should have a way to enjoy it, even if they can't hear it."

"Yes, they should." A sober expression filled his features. "I believe that."

She breathed deep and squinted out at the horizon. "If I could have any job in the world, it would be music therapy for the deaf."

His eyebrows rose. "Really? I've never heard of that."

"If I had the means, that's what I would be working toward, rather than classroom teaching."

"So why don't you?"

She shrugged. "I wouldn't know where to start. Teaching special needs presented a clearer career path. Starting a whole music therapy program from scratch would take a lot of resources that I just don't have."

"I might be able to help." His brows lowered and he cleared his throat. "Hannah loved music, too. Thought everyone should have access to it, so she often gave free voice lessons to kids at church. Had us donate instruments to the Sunday School classrooms. So, a little while back, I started a memorial fund in her name to support musical causes, honor her. But I hadn't yet found a specific outreach to support. I'm thinking...maybe I just did. I have funds earmarked for a music charity, and I've already met a few people who might know where to start."

She stared at him, completely dumbstruck. "What are you saying exactly?"

"I'm saying I want to fund a music program for the deaf, with you leading it."

"You do?"

He nodded.

The full weight of the idea settled in her chest and brought on a wave of butterflies. She blinked at him. "You *really* think we could do this?"

Excitement radiated from him. "Yes, I do. I say we start researching it this week." The sparkle in his eyes spun her head.

"Wow... This could help so many kids! I might be able to really make a difference."

His gaze whispered over her face. "You have such a beautiful soul, Jenni." With a smile lifting one of his sun-kissed cheeks, John picked up a strawberry and held it to her lips. She bit into it, then he pulled it to his own mouth and did the same.

"How do you sign strawberry?" His voice rumbled low, and sent a shiver down her spine.

She held out her index finger and pretended to twist a berry from it. He scooted closer, till she could feel the heat radiating off his chest. Good night, was he beautiful to look at. He captured a strand of hair blowing beside her face and tucked it behind her ear. Her breath caught as he caressed her cheek with his knuckles.

"How do you sign...kiss?" He traced her lower lip with his thumb, then moved achingly slow toward her mouth. The first touch of his lips was always sweetest. Her pulse raced as he explored and savored her in ways that left her reeling.

He tasted like strawberries and sunshine and everything right in the world. And his lips, his caresses, made her feel beautiful, cherished, adored. Was this real? Was this man really hers? His fingertips skimming her throat answered *yes*.

Wrapping his arm around her waist, he held her tight, then laid her on her back and continued his expert attentions, trailing his lips along her jaw and the hollow spot behind her ear.

She banished the sudden awareness that he sure knew what he was doing, that he'd had plenty of practice. Experience that she did not. Now wasn't the time for insecurity. She stroked his cheek and drank him in. If the time ever came, and she was already fantasizing about wedding announcements and taking his last name, she had no doubt that she'd figure it out. And that he would be a patient teacher.

Jenni slid off her sandals and left them at the foot of the stage. She flexed her toes over the carpeted floor. "Did I tell you he built the deck on his parents' house? He and his dad did it themselves. They were apparently very close."

"Were?"

"Are. But his dad has Alzheimer's, early onset, so in some ways he's lost his father. But family is very important to him. His parents are still married. Almost thirty-five years!"

"Wow, that's impressive."

"I know, right? He was a camp counselor as a teen, he's played the guitar since he was twelve, he loves his mother…" A dreamy sigh made its way out of her mouth.

With a bemused grin, Tori plugged in her bass guitar and shook the cord out around her feet. "So you've been solving the mystery of the mysterious new guy, huh?"

"You could say that." Jenni clamped her teeth over her bottom lip to hide her smile.

"And to think, I was there to witness the birth of your romance on the beach that night. So tell me how it's going between you two."

"It's going perfect. He's so romantic. He's got some big surprise for me on Saturday. Oh, and guess what else? He wants to help me start my own music therapy program for the deaf."

"Wow. Sounds like he's all that and a bag of chips."

"Oh, Tori." Jenni closed her eyes and moved her head side to side. "He's...amazing." Warmth unfurled in her belly as Jenni let her mind fill with John's image, the memory of his touch, the way he made her feel.

"Uh oh," Tori snickered. "I'm not sure what we're talking about here. But by the flushed look on your face I'm thinking we need volunteers for round-the-clock chaperons." She wiggled her eyebrows.

Jenni brought her hand up to her throat, heat prickling her cheeks. "Might not be a bad idea." She glanced around at the others on the stage, all busy setting up their instruments, and drew close to her friend to whisper, "His lips have completely ruined me for any others. Holy moley that man can *kiss* like you wouldn't believe."

From the corner of her eye she saw Isaiah, the lead guitarist, turn toward them and smile wide, his hand up by the side of his head as he adjusted his in-ears monitor.

Jenni felt the blood drain from her face. Her eyes bounced from Tori to the microphone beside her. "Is that *on?*" she whispered violently.

Tori checked the mic then smothered a laugh, turning it toward Jenni. Green light. "Yep." She laughed freely, as did Isaiah, while Jenni wished she could melt into the floor and disappear.

John chose that moment to waltz into the sanctuary and smile at her.

"Hey, bro!" Isaiah greeted him with a lift of his chin and a crooked smile. "Good job, man."

"Hey, uh...thanks?" John twitched his eyebrows at Jenni as if to ask what that was all about.

Jenni shook her head and covered her cheeks with her hands as John approached, took the stage steps two at a time, and stood beside her. "Hi." Her voice came out shaky and breathless and someone behind her chuckled.

"Give her a smooch, John." Tori egged him on. "We don't mind."

"Your friends are weird," he said as he drew her into an embrace. "But they have good ideas." And before she could brace herself, he covered her mouth with his and weakened her knees. But it lasted only a moment before John was touching her cheek and backing away. "Better let you get back to rehearsing."

"Nice!" Isaiah called out.

Tori, Isaiah, and the others began clapping and Jenni shot them a wild-eyed silent plea.

"What is *with* your friends?" John's smile shook her insides until a laugh bubbled up from her throat.

"Nothing. Ignore them."

She knew her cheeks were stained red, but in that moment, she decided she didn't care. Not one wit. She rushed to catch John before he made it back to the bottom of the stairs, grabbed his shoulder to turn him around, and dove in with another kiss full on the mouth. She pulled back and grinned down at him from her place two steps above, chest plummeting with her deep sigh. "Yep. *Totally* ruined," she declared for all to hear.

His eyes took her in, glanced around at the others, then returned to hers. "Okay. I don't care what's going on. I think I like it."

Jenni threw her head back and laughed.

Tension hung in the air around her and even Sadie was keeping a safe distance from the dining room. Jenni shouldn't have told her mom about her and John's plans to get the music program started. But somehow Jenni had thought her mom would share her excitement.

"And now you're going to get tangled up in business as well? These are big changes, Jenni. Too many so quickly. What's gotten into you?"

Jenni closed her eyes and willed her pulse to remain steady as her mother's words hit their mark and bruised her heart. They *were* big changes—but good ones.

"Take a minute to think, would you? Because *I* think this is a bad idea. You don't know yet if this...*relationship* is going anywhere. He even admitted he has a drinking problem? Come on."

"*Had*, Mom. Had." Oh, the price of transparency. "Can't you be happy for me?"

Her mother shook her head, forehead wrinkling. "No... I wish I could, I've tried, but... He's got way too many issues." Her voice sounded pained. "And it's not your job to fix them. You *can't* fix them. You do see that, don't you?"

Her night had gone from wonderful to strained in about ten seconds flat. Jenni rested her forehead in her hand and tried to form a response while pushing cold peas around her plate. Would this battle with her mom go on forever?

She looked up at her mother and spoke with a calm, measured tone. "Mom, please. I understand what you're saying, but—"

"Do you really? Because I don't think you do. You're on a dangerous path here. One that will only lead to trouble sooner or later. I'd like to see you get out before you lose more of your heart to him."

Too late for that.

Jenni stuffed a bite of pot roast in her mouth and chewed, camouflaging her twisting features. Why couldn't her mom just trust Jenni's judgement?

Her mother sighed. "Jenni?"

Jenni locked onto her eyes. "Mom, I love you. But I'm a grown woman. I know you're only looking out for me. But sooner or later you're going to have to accept that John's not going anywhere anytime soon. This…this is different. This feels real." As if her whole life had been a dress rehearsal leading up to this.

Jenni held eye contact until her mother cleared her throat and placed a forkful of mashed potatoes on her tongue, closing her lips around them.

Silent moments passed, then she stood. "Would you like some coffee?" She carried her plate to the kitchen and Jenni followed, knowing this was her mom's way of bridging the divide between them.

"Sounds good." The scrape of her fork against the plate as she sent the scraps into the disposal joined with the gurgle of the coffee maker as it began brewing. Soon the kitchen was permeated with the strong aroma of their favorite Italian blend. They'd end the evening mutually enjoying the hot drink, speaking little, and allowing their hearts to find that place of familiar connection. But Jenni knew her mom still felt apprehensive.

Truth be told, Jenni still faced insecurities of her own sometimes. Who wouldn't? The difference was, she had the Lord to bring them to. If only the rest of her family had that source of strength as well.

Chapter Nineteen

Jenni stole another glance at John as they cruised down the freeway. He looked incredible in his dark brown suit and copper tie, coordinating perfectly with her dress. She couldn't keep her eyes off him.

And where was he taking her? An hour of driving and she still didn't know. Dressed up all fancy-like and it was barely noon. She ran her thumb along the back of his hand.

"So guess what... I spoke to the director of Orange County Music Therapy Services and told him what we're trying to do. He offered to help and wants to meet with you."

"Seriously?" Her eyes rounded. OCMT had an extensive reach of services, but nothing in their county.

"Yeah, we chatted for awhile about your vision and your focus on the deaf community. He thought that was fantastic. He even said if you need an internship, let him know."

"John, I..." Her eyes tingled and she blinked in effort to keep them from spilling over. "Thank you. Nobody has ever done something like this for me before. I have to admit I didn't expect you to be so involved when you offered to help me build this dream. But you..." She blinked again. "You always surprise me."

"I wouldn't just write a check and forget about it. Jenni, if this is your passion, I want to be a part of it in whatever way you need... It's important to you." He checked his mirrors than gave a resolute nod. "And that makes it important to me."

She drew in a breath of astonishment as, eyes still fixed on the road ahead, he reached for her hand.

He glanced at her. "So, how's Christy doing?"

Jenni let out a breath, shifting her thoughts to her cousin as John turned off the highway onto a main road. "Well, I haven't heard anything new. She's still seeing that sixteen-year-old. Not that she is technically allowed to date, but they text constantly and she is completely obsessed with him."

Her cousin hadn't come to church with her yet, though Jenni continued to invite her. Christy was on a dangerous path and Jenni feared what it might take to wake her up.

John squeezed her hand. "I've been praying for her, and I'll *keep* praying."

"Thank you. That means a lot." She smiled, then turned toward him in her seat. "So, when do I find out where we're going?"

He chuckled. "When we get there."

She narrowed her eyes in a mock glare.

"Be patient." He kissed her knuckles.

"No fair. How can I stay mad at you when you do that?" She dropped his hand to run a finger along his scruffy cheek.

"No fair," he echoed. "How am I supposed to concentrate on the road when you do that?"

Smiling, she took his hand again and leaned her head back against the seat. "Is it much farther?"

"Nope." He released her hand to pull his wallet from his back pocket just as he slowed to turn in to a parking lot. One nestled in the shadow of the Pantages Theater.

Jenni's eyes rounded as she noted the theater sign. She turned to John, mouth agape. "What?"

A satisfied grin smothered his face. "I wanted to celebrate. We've been together for one month and I wanted to take you somewhere nice."

All this for one month of togetherness? "Wow. I've been dying to see *Wicked*."

"I know." He gave a cunning smile. "We have good seats too. Come on."

They approached the entrance and he opened the door, guiding Jenni inside with a hand on the small of her back. She sensed his watchful gaze on her face as she took in the red carpeted floor, the intricate archways, the exquisite chandeliers. *Beautiful.*

They made their way up the grand staircase to find their seats. Had it not been for John's steadying hand she would have tripped for lack of watching her footing—her eyes were drawn to the intricate details of the auditorium.

The house lights dimmed, replaced with color, and Jenni perched on the edge of her seat to soak it all in.

The show took her breath away. It was all she'd hoped it would be. She wasn't sure what amazed her most—the theater, the show, or the man beside her. Definitely the man.

Intermission came and they walked out to the lobby to stretch their legs. In a quiet corner, John ran his hand up and down her arm. "How do you like it so far?"

"It's awesome. The sets, the lights, the special effects, it's just...*wow*." She threw her hands in the air. She'd always been a sucker for stage shows, but she'd had very little experience with professional productions. No question this was magic compared to community theater.

"So you're happy with your surprise?" He smiled like a little boy, obviously pleased with himself.

"Are you kidding? I'm *thrilled*. My mom will probably flip out when I tell her. She's been dying to see this too." She bit her bottom lip and scanned the ornate lobby walls one more time.

John's face grew sober and he tilted his head. "How *is* your mom?"

Jenni shifted her weight. "Uh, she's good. We've had some really good conversations lately. She even said she'd think about coming to church with me sometime." She didn't bring up the lingering tension over Jenni and John's relationship.

"I hope she does."

The lights flickered, signaling the end of intermission. John hooked a finger under Jenni's chin and planted a quick kiss on her lips before they headed back to their seats. She loved it when he did that.

His kiss still turned her insides to mush and she had to work on steadying her steps as they wove through the crowds and past the knees of those in their row.

Hours later, the cast came out for their bow and the audience gave a standing ovation.

As they exited the theater, Jenni shook her head in awe. "I mean, the costumes. The music. That was incredible. Thank you so much."

John plastered a smug grin on his face. "The date's not over yet."

"Where are we going to eat?"

"That's another surprise."

She laughed. "Maybe I can guess." Jenni eyed him as they got into the car. "Red Robin? Cheesecake Factory?"

"Nope." He was enjoying this too much, and she couldn't stand not knowing. Okay, maybe it was kind of fun. But she was getting impatient.

Soon, the ocean came into view and Jenni bit her bottom lip. *The beach.* She should have guessed.

They found a spot to spread out a blanket, then took off their shoes and walked along the water.

John turned to her with a devilish sparkle in his eye. "I think we should start a new tradition." One corner of his mouth inched up. "I'd like to believe it's our responsibility to find the best beach locations for romantic kisses."

Her belly tingled. She studied the lines of his jaw, the shape of his lips, and ran her hands up over his chest and around his neck. He circled his arms around her waist and looked into her eyes with an intensity that told her she better brace herself.

She released a tiny squeal when John lifted her off the ground then pressed his mouth to hers. His hold was strong. She wasn't going anywhere. Muscles relaxed, she hung suspended in the air, kissing John for all she was worth, her fingers in his hair and their hearts beating together wildly. When he lowered her back to her feet she wasn't sure she'd be able to stand. But somehow she managed, as he cradled her face in his hands and tortured her with his self-control. The lapping of the waves serenaded them, salt flavoring the air.

His kisses slowed, and he pulled away to look at her. His blue gaze was deep, intense, and made Jenni almost forget where she was. He ran his fingers along her swollen lips and Jenni closed her eyes and released a shaky breath. Then he lowered his lips to her ear.

"I love you, Jenni."

Her breath caught. His confession was a match setting her on fire all over again. "I love you too," she murmured.

The words had been ready and waiting on her lips, and releasing them into the universe felt like magic. She trailed her fingers into his hair and held him close, their heartbeats combining into a near audible thudding.

John nuzzled her neck, and placed a tremulous kiss on her shoulder. She was highly aware that his restraint meant that bringing his lips to hers again would've been too dangerous. But part of her longed for that danger. Desperately. Thank God for John's integrity. She wasn't sure she could trust herself to stick to her own convictions at the moment. But she had complete trust in John. He'd never let things go too far.

John smiled as he unlocked Jenni from their embrace, and led her by the hand back to the blanket, where a basket of food awaited them.

It couldn't get much better than this. Jenni's insecurities about John's late wife had faded completely away. She knew in her heart he loved her the way she loved him—completely and without reserve. And she couldn't wait to see what the future would bring.

Jenni breezed into the house, tingling all over. Her mother reclined on the couch watching the news, Sadie curled up beside her.

"Hey, Mom." She sat down on the other side of the dog.

"So did you have a nice time?" An obvious lack of enthusiasm made her question almost painful.

"I had a *wonderful* time. It was perfect. Please stop worrying and give him a chance. Accept that he's a part of my life. John is a great guy, I promise. Guess where we went. You'll be so jealous!"

Her mother's chest fell with her sigh. "Honey, I don't dislike John. He seems like a really nice man, and if you'll remember, it was me who pushed you to go out with him in the first place. But…I keep thinking about his past. He's coming to you with a lot of baggage. And I don't want to see my baby girl get hurt."

Jenni groaned, running her fingers through Sadie's fur. "Mom, please not this again. John's past isn't 'baggage'. He's not damaged goods. His faith has carried him." She worked her throat. "He went through something extremely painful. But have you considered that he may have come out better for it on the other end?"

"Sweetie, how can you be so sure? You haven't really known him that long. What you *do* know should frighten you more than it does. You don't want to be living in the shadow of his past. Who knows how it might come back to haunt you." Her mom's voice was low, soothing almost. "He may never fully get over something like that. You have no idea what you're taking on."

Jenni frowned and shook her head. Those shadows *had* scared her at times. But what her mom didn't understand, *couldn't* understand, was the transforming power of the Holy Spirit. She couldn't grasp the concept that John's "baggage" had been laid down, handed over, given to Christ.

A lengthy silence hung in the air until Jenni tilted her head and found a playful tone. "Mom…do you want to know where we went or not?"

Her mom gave a resigned smile. "Okay, tell me where you went."

"The Pantages."

Mom's jaw dropped. *"Wicked?"*

Jenni nodded. "Uh huh."

She spent the next half hour gushing over the play, and the romantic picnic. She left out the words they'd spoken to each other, the territory they'd crossed into. But she didn't hold back all the other romantic bits. Sharing moments like this with her, Jenni's heart pulsed with the hope that one day her mother would come to know the Lord. And find a measure of the healing and joy Jenni had found.

At the sound of the doorbell, Jenni closed the music therapy pamphlet and stuck it in her desk drawer.

Aunt Mary, Christy, and baby Tessa arrived to celebrate Mom's birthday. They clamored inside and unburdened themselves of purses, diaper bags, and wiggly toddler, then settled into the living room. Christy took her sunglasses off the top of her head, her dark hair getting stuck in the frames for a moment. She smoothed her flyway's then gave Jenni a hug, their bond whispering in her eyes. Jenni pecked her on the head. "How's my favorite cousin?"

She grinned. "Who, me or Tessa?"

"Har har. Very funny." The doorbell rang again and Jenni greeted John on the porch.

"Hey, you." With a coy smile, she tipped back her head and lifted on her tiptoes to meet his lips. After the briefest of moments in his arms, she ushered him inside and made introductions, while Sadie jumped up and licked his hand. Brave man to take on a house full of women.

"Happy Birthday, Laura." John offered Jenni's mom a smile impossible to resist. For most.

"Thank you, John. It's nice you're here. Make yourself comfortable."

"Yes, have a seat." Jenni pointed him toward the living room with an encouraging smile. "I'll be right back."

After plating some chips and guacamole, and pouring John a cup of ice-cream punch, she returned and joined him. Sitting on the armrest of the couch beside her man, Jenni rubbed his back while Aunt Mary regaled him with stories of her as a little girl.

"Ahem." Jenni tried to give her *the stare*, but Aunt Mary avoided her gaze. "You guys are going to run him off."

John patted her knee and winked. "No way."

Sadie scratched at the sliding glass door and Jenni rose to let her out. Tension poured over her in waves. She loved that John was here, but her mother still had her reservations and Jenni wasn't sure what to expect.

"You look nervous." Christy had sidled up behind her without Jenni even noticing.

"Maybe a little." She crossed her arms over her chest and leaned against the wall.

Christy looked over her shoulder toward the couch, where John was talking to Aunt Mary. Tessa sat on her mother's lap and John leaned forward and shook her foot.

"He's smokin'."

"Christy!" Jenni hushed her giggle.

Christy shrugged. "Well, he is."

Jenni put a hand on Christy's shoulder and turned her around. "Okay, enough of that. Let's get back to the party." She steered her cousin back to the living room where she took a seat in the recliner beside the couch. After Jenni settled back on the arm of the sofa, Christy caught her eye and shook her splayed fingers in front of her chest, mouthing the word *hot*.

Jenni coughed to divert John's gaze from her impetuous cousin.

"You okay?" He handed her his cup and she took a sip.

"Thanks."

"So, John." Aunt Mary handed a pretzel stick to Tessa to gnaw on. "You're helping Jenni with some sort of music thing?"

"Yes, a music therapy program for the deaf. But she can tell you more about it than I can; I'm just her sidekick."

"You're definitely *not* just a sidekick. You're more like the engine. This wouldn't be happening at all without you." She squeezed his shoulder and looked around at her family, chest swelling.

Mom came into the room and turned the stereo on low. "So how are you involved then, John?" A Johnny Cash song hummed through the speakers as she settled in a seat across from them.

"Oh, through a memorial fund I started for charitable music programs."

"Memorial fund?" She cocked her head, then straightened. "Oh, yes, your *wife*."

Jenni tensed at the way her mother emphasized the word. She gave a subtle shake of her head but Mom just settled an unflinching gaze back on John. "What was her name again?"

"Hannah." His smile looked pasted on, and he directed it at Jenni.

Mom's eyebrows formed a deep V. "Hannah. Such a pretty name. I bet she was a beauty."

Jenni's stomach twisted while her mother crossed her legs and kept her eyes pinned on John.

"Yes, she was." John shifted in his seat and reached for his punch. He drained the cup and set it on the coffee table in front of him.

Did she have to do this now? Test him like this?

Mom's brow twitched as she caught Jenni's eye. "It must be pretty painful still." She emitted a commiserate grunt from the back of her throat that kicked up Jenni's pulse. "I can't imagine getting over a thing like that. I suppose you never do, really. Such a terrible loss."

Christy, eyes round and mouth clamped, looked from Jenni, to her mother, then back to John. Mary busied herself with Tessa's shoelace.

John glanced at Jenni, then back at her mom. "I don't know about getting over it, but I'm getting *through* it. With God's strength and with your daughter."

Her mother paused for a moment. Was she conflicted? Satisfied? "Well, good for you. I don't think I would've been ready so soon to get back into the dating game…" She held her hands open toward the two of them.

"Mom…" Jenni sprang to her feet, face burning. "That is *enough*."

"Honey, it's okay." John laced his fingers through hers and pulled her back down to sit. He rubbed circles on the back of her hand with his thumb, then looked up at her mother. "Ms. Dupont, I know my background is uncomfortable, hard to process. I'll just say that I was swallowed by grief for a long time before I was ready for God to put me back together."

Her mom nodded slowly, a discomforted look on her face as though caught with her hand in the proverbial cookie jar.

John sat straighter and looked her in the eye. "But I think I'm a better man now than I ever was before. Because that's how God works. Believe me when I say I would never hurt your daughter."

"I never said…" Mom dragged her tongue along her lips before clamping her mouth shut and Jenni silently cheered.

"You didn't have to. Ms. Dupont, Hannah and Katy will always be in my heart, *helping* me love Jenni the way she deserves." He locked his gaze on Jenni's and smiled, making her heart skip. "You see, she's brought love back into my life. And that's something I've learned not to *ever* take for granted."

"I'm…glad to hear it." Mom ran a hand over her necklace, clearly embarrassed.

John looked at Jenni, then mouthed the words, "I love you."

She leaned down and planted a kiss on his cheek.

Only the soft sound of Elvis Presley's "The Wonder Of You" punctuated the stillness in the room. Couldn't have timed it more perfectly. Finally, Aunt Mary cleared her throat. "Well, who wants more Chex Party Mix?"

The tension ebbed, the conversation finding its way to more normal topics. Jenni prayed the worst of it was past. Whether it was guilt or shock, Mom didn't attempt any more jabs, and even engaged John in a conversation about hardwood floors. And Jenni counted that as progress.

"Okay, everyone, it's present time." Jenni led her mom to the chair with a balloon tied to it while Christy opened the camera on her phone.

"Don't post any of those until I approve them," Mom wagged her finger at her niece as Mary placed the gifts in front of her on the table.

They watched her open each one—a new pair of earrings from Jenni, a Kohl's gift card from Aunt Mary, and a "Best Aunt in the World" picture frame from Christy and Tessa.

Then John grinned and handed her an envelope, Mom's earlier passive-aggressive display seemingly forgotten. The room quieted and Jenni shot him a quizzical look. She'd told him he didn't need to bring a gift and he'd said nothing about getting one.

Jenni's mother took hold of it with a tilt of her head. "You didn't have to get me anything."

"I know. But I wanted to." John smiled then gave Jenni a sly wink.

As Mom held the envelope, Jenni could see the surprise in her eyes, the crumbling of her defenses. Looking to John, Jenni mouthed, "What is it?" But he just raised his eyebrows and inclined his head toward her mother.

Jenni watched her mother open the flap and peer inside. Mom's eyes rounded as she slowly pulled out a set of theater tickets. She turned her wide eyes to John, covered her mouth, then splayed the tickets across her chest. "He got me tickets to see *Wicked*."

"Wow, what a gift." Aunt Mary bounced Tessa on her hip. "Sure beats mine. You trying to make me look bad?"

John chuckled. "Sorry. Should I take them back?"

"No!" Aunt Mary snatched them from Mom's hand. "There's two here, right? Did I tell you how pretty you look today, sis?"

Maybe Mom's armor had finally cracked. She turned a stunned smile on John. "I don't know what to say." She pressed her fingers to her lips as she looked down at the tickets, then turned her palm up and met his eyes. "I can't believe you did this. But thank you."

Jenni's cheeks lifted as she rose from her chair to hug John. Turned out he was navigating her family quite well. Better than she could've hoped. He grinned, obviously pleased that the gift had gone over so well.

With the gifts opened, Aunt Mary hoisted Tessa onto her hip and headed down the hall to change her diaper. Wadded paper littered the floor around Mom's chair so Jenni scooped it up to toss in the trash. She passed John on her way to the kitchen and stopped him with her gaze. "You are the most thoughtful man in the whole wide world."

He gave a sheepish look then ran the back of his forefinger along her cheek.

Aunt Mary came by and herded them both over to the dining table. "Come on, everybody. Time to light up the cake. Who has the fire extinguisher?"

Mom smacked Aunt Mary's arm then wagged a finger toward Christy. "Watch out for Tessa. Little sisters are the worst."

"It's our job." Mary laughed and hugged Laura before lighting the birthday candles.

As they were singing, Jenni caught John watching her in a way that wakened her insides, made her muscles tighten deep in her belly. Did he have any idea how much he affected her with just a look?

After the cake was eaten, John insisted on doing the dishes. Once he'd slipped into the kitchen, her mother slid her gaze to Jenni, raising her eyebrows and smiling. "He's really something else, isn't he?"

"You finally noticed." Jenni grinned at her mother.

"Well he certainly knows how to make my daughter happy, I'll give him that much."

She might not have admitted it out loud, but Jenni had hope that her mother was beginning to embrace John—baggage and all.

The party ended, and Jenni's heart swelled as she walked John to his car.

"What's on your mind?" He poked her in the ribs. "You're quiet."

She grinned up at him. "Thank you."

"For what?"

"For being you. Sweet, thoughtful, caring, wonderful, gorgeous you."

He leaned back against his car and pulled her into his arms. "I didn't do anything to deserve such high praise from you."

She laced her fingers around his neck, stretched up on her toes, and kissed him.

"But I'll take it." He locked his arms around her waist. "You know your family is probably watching through the window."

"I'm sure they are. I guess that will keep us in line then." She pulled his head down and kissed him again, breathing in the scent of his cologne.

He tapped the end of her nose, a corner of his mouth tipping. "Thanks for inviting me. I'll give you a call tomorrow."

"Okay. I love you." Oh, how good those words felt.

He held her face in his hands. "I love *you*."

Chapter Twenty

John patted his stomach, almost regretting the extra cheddar-bay biscuit he'd consumed, but not quite. He smiled down at Jenni, leaning against his side. "Are you getting sleepy?"

"Not at all," she said dreamily. "Dinner was wonderful." Her eyes went soft as she looked at him. "And the ring is gorgeous, thank you." She splayed her fingers, examining the topaz ring on her right hand.

"You're welcome. It's not every day you get to celebrate a four month anniversary."

The last few months had been incredible, better than he believed he'd experience again.

Jenni laid her head against his chest and John caressed her arm, skimming his fingers up and down her shoulder.

Nuzzling into him, she fingered the bracelet on her wrist, spinning it around and around.

John squeezed her closer to his side. "I've never seen you without that bracelet. Is there a story behind it?" He smiled and pressed his cheek to the top of her head.

She inhaled as though to speak, but paused.

"Jenni?" He turned to look at her.

"There is a story behind it. I'm just not sure if now's the time to talk about it."

"Uh oh, it wasn't a gift from an old boyfriend or something, was it?"

"No."

The timbre of her voice made his spine straighten. He'd hit a nerve and somehow knew it was important. "You can tell me anything." He removed his arm from around her and shifted his body until they were facing each other.

And he waited.

Her lower lip was between her teeth as she slid the bracelet off and handed it to him.

He took it from her, examining it, and read aloud the words engraved on it, "I carried you." He looked up at her, but her eyes were fixed somewhere below his chin. "It's a beautiful message…what does it mean?" His heart slid into an awkward rhythm, sensing the weight of whatever it was God had carried her through.

Fear and shame colored her features as she placed his fingers on the delicate skin of her wrist, just beneath where the bracelet usually rested. At first he sensed nothing out of the ordinary. Just silky skin that under other conditions might light his blood on fire. But as she brushed his fingertips back and forth along her wrist and then higher on her forearm, he noted the subtle pattern; thin, slightly raised lines marred her otherwise flawless flesh. He blinked, then gently lifted her arm and squinted to examine the nearly imperceptible scars.

"Is this what He carried you through, love?"

Lifting her eyes to his, she nodded solemnly and whispered, "Yes." She blinked and rubbed her lips together, then started sharing her story. As she opened up about how deep and dark her pain had been, and the path God rescued her from traveling, John's heart was ripped in two. Even all these years of distance, tears still clung to her lashes in the retelling.

"I tend to feel things deep. Too deep. I've never been strong. But the Lord is strong on my behalf."

John nodded. *That*, he knew for himself.

Her eyes were pools of liquid gold as she exposed her heart. "I still struggle to express my emotions, especially strong negative ones. But I've learned it's important not to stuff them inside. And that I'm never alone in them, despite how it might feel. I wear that bracelet so I never forget."

They got lost in each other's eyes for a long moment and Jenni worked her throat, shame etched in the lines of her mouth. Maintaining eye contact, John lifted her hand from her lap, turned it face up, and pressed his lips to her wrist. To each line, each moment of desperation. Her chest expanded, then plummeted as she watched him slowly, methodically, accept her past, her pain, embracing all of her—scars included. Just as she had done with him.

John's heart thudded hard as his senses awakened to the feel of her. When he lifted his face to hers, her gaze skipped to his mouth and she released a shuddering breath that spiked his blood. The pulse at the base of her slender neck hammered and he pressed a kiss there, feeling each heartbeat travel from her body to his. She tipped her head, inviting him to continue. Wrapping her in his arms, he kissed along her neck, her jaw, then captured her mouth and let the movement of his lips express what words could not adequately describe.

He loved her. Pure and simple. Though there was nothing simple about it.

The low moan in the back of her throat caught him by surprise and halted him in his tracks. "Quick," he whispered, "say something about your mother."

She began laughing, quaking against him.

"Babe, that's not helping."

She kissed him again and spoke against his mouth. "Well, *you* started it."

"Yeah but I'm not going to finish it." Not tonight anyway. But maybe, if God allowed it, *someday*. Someday he might claim her fully.

"I know. And I trust you."

"Then trust me...it's time for a distraction."

"Okay, um...how's *your* mother?"

"Aaaand, that'll do it."

Her eyes sparkled then went soft. "Thank you." The teasing was gone from her voice, but neither was it sultry. It was raw, exposed, real.

John unwrapped her from within the circle of his embrace and took both her hands in his. "I love you, Jenni. In case you couldn't tell." He threaded his fingers through hers.

"Oh, is that why you shower me with gifts?" She grinned. "Looks like I know *someone's* love language." She grinned, a spark of mischief in her eyes.

"You look like you have a secret."

"Maybe I do." She scooted forward and stood. "Okay, you wait here. I'll be right back."

He narrowed his eyes and watched as she went out the front door. A minute later, she poked her head back in.

"Okay, close your eyes," she commanded from the doorway.

"What are you up to?" Brow creasing, John did as instructed. He heard the door close, heard her footsteps bringing her closer, something rustling nearby, felt the couch move under her weight.

"Okay, open them."

He did, and found her sitting straight up beside him, hands laced beneath a smile. Then he noticed something propped near the coffee table, and did a double-take.

"Jenni..." He raked his eyes over the bright red bow affixed to the shiny black acoustic guitar standing before him. His eyes pinged to her, biting back a nervous smile, then returned to the instrument.

"Do you like it? Is it okay?"

Speechless, John lifted the guitar to his lap and ran his hands over the sleek wood.

"I didn't know what you'd like, but...Isaiah said this was a good one."

He pulled his eyes from the instrument to her face. "Jenni, this is a *Martin*."

"Uh huh."

"I don't know what to say. This is quite a gift. I don't think I'm qualified to own one of these." Or if he was ready to own a guitar of any kind.

"But you are, John. It's time to move forward, to embrace life. All of it."

His heart thudded against his ribs as the weight of her words sank deep into his spirit. He had moved forward, mostly, but some things had yet to be reclaimed. And Jenni saw that, understood it even before he did. *Thank you for bringing her into my life.*

With a slight nod, he adjusted the tuning then positioned his fingers and began plucking out a series of notes within a chord. How had he been so blessed, after all he'd done? Only by the grace of a God who loved the unlovable.

Emotion built within him, and as his fingers coaxed out a melody, he glanced up at Jenni, who beamed then closed her eyes to listen.

John cleared his throat. "All to Jesus, I surrender...all to him, I freely give..." He eked out the words in a low, throaty whisper, letting the lyrics take root in his heart.

At the refrain, Jenni joined in, "I surrender all..." He locked his eyes on hers while their voices, joined as one, swelled in volume— "I surrender all..." the melody prepared to climb higher...higher, and he sang now in full voice, reverberating in his chest, "All to thee, my *precious* savior..." John's heart shattered in praise as he watched Jenni, radiant, worshiping with him, fingers moving as she sang, "I surrender all..." His voice had thickened with emotion and choked itself out, but he kept playing. Kept supplying the music for Jenni's voice and hands, overcome, until he reached the end of the song and let the final chord slowly fade away to a holy hush.

Finally, he cleared his throat and set the guitar in its stand. "Thank you, Jenni," he signed in ASL to her wide-eyed surprise. Then he took a breath and focused on the movements he'd been practicing. He pointed to her. "You are beautiful," he moved his hand before his face in the sign for *beautiful*, "compassionate," his fingers undulated out from his chest, "an inspiration," his fists moved up, as if drawing something good out from within him, as she truly did, daily. "I am blessed," he signed. He'd received back from the Lord much more than he deserved. A mended heart, a beautiful woman who loved him, the gift of song restored. Her eyes swam but her face was lit by her smile.

Having run out of signs to share, he dropped his hands.

"John..." Her throat bobbed. "Thank you. That was amazing and it means more to me than I can express."

He dipped his chin. "You're welcome. It doesn't compare though with what you've given me." He gestured toward the guitar. "I didn't know I needed that, but I did."

"You're welcome." She took his hand and laced her fingers through his. "You've earned it. Especially after putting up with my family." She slanted puckered lips to one side and rolled her eyes.

"No concerned mother could scare me off. I wouldn't give you up for anything. Not for the world." He leaned in and kissed her, his blood heating when she combed her fingers through the hair at the nape of his neck.

He deepened the kiss, pouring his heart into every movement of his lips over hers until she broke away and whispered, "I should go."

John looked deep into her eyes. "But baby it's cold outside…"

She snorted on a laugh and shoved his shoulder, then shimmied up and out of his arms.

"Good night."

Indeed it had been. The kind that gave a man a lot to think about.

Jenni was lost in thought as she robotically rolled the vacuum back into the closet and shut the door. Replaying her favorite parts of the previous night. How safe John made her feel when she shared her heart, her secrets, with him. Exposed her past. How warm all over when he kissed her scars.

She jumped when her phone rang, then fished it out of her back pocket to answer. "Hi, Tori."

"Hey, how was last night?"

A smile tugged at her mouth. "Amazing." She coughed to clear her head of the potent recollection of his velvet kisses. "We went to Red Lobster, so that started things off well."

"Did you get the crab alfredo or did you branch out and try something new?"

"I had lobster, but the food wasn't the best part." She held her hand out in front of her as she walked toward the kitchen. "He gave me a ring, Tori."

A gasp carried over the line. "A *ring*? Well, that's—"

"Not that kind of ring," Jenni hurried to say. "Oh, it's gorgeous though. I can't wait to show you. It has a topaz stone in the center and catches so much light. And he was so romantic, Tori. He chose the ring for the honey color of the stone. To match my eyes, he said." She nibbled her bottom lip, remembering the way she'd melted at his words, admired the gem—and the man—through a veil of tears.

"Okay, I'm officially jealous."

"I don't blame you." She grinned and leaned a hip against the counter. "You know what else he did?"

"Um…if it's about his blush-worthy kisses, then no. Three's a crowd, girl. I already know how *ruined* you are."

"Stop that!" She could hear Tori trying to hold back her snickering. "I can hear you laughing."

"I'm not. But should I take you off speaker before letting you proceed?"

"Tori…"

"Okay, sorry…I'm done. Tell me."

"He taught himself some ASL and signed to me." Her throat constricted at the memory.

"He did? Jenni, I think you have a keeper."

"So do I. But I'm having trouble getting anything done." She thought about him so often it was hard to concentrate on anything else. It had taken three attempts to get through the reading for her educational psychology class that day. His face materialized in her mind's eye and warmth blossomed in her belly. "He is so deliciously distracting."

"Well go take a cold shower and get back to work. I'll see you later."

"Take care." Grinning, Jenni put the phone back in her pocket and pulled the furniture polish and rag out from under the kitchen sink.

She misted the dining table and buffed circles into the wood with the rag. Light from the setting sun streamed in through the window and ricocheted off her ring, scattering sparkles onto the ceiling and eliciting a smile from her lips. She paused in her task and rocked her hand back and forth, playing up the effect. Unable to resist the temptation, she wiggled the ring past her knuckle and held it a moment before sliding it into place on her left hand. Would the day come when John slipped a ring on *that* finger? She held her hand out in front of her and angled her head, admiring the sight and savoring the tingling sensations coursing through her. A happy sigh escaped her lips before she realized it was coming.

"Jenni?"

She startled at the sound of her mother's voice behind her and quickly pulled her hands toward her middle. "Hmm?" Pasting on a casual expression, she turned to see her mother's soft eyes on her.

"I…I want you to know how much I love you. And that I'm happy you've found someone. John's been good to you. And *for* you." Her eyes went to Jenni's hands, fingers attempting to conceal the ring until she could move it back to the right hand. She lifted her gaze to Jenni's. "I can tell he's not going anywhere any time soon." She stepped closer and gave Jenni's arm a squeeze.

"Thanks, Mom. That means a lot to me. John *is* a good man." She raised an eyebrow and looked at her sideways. "I tried to tell you."

"Honey, I never disliked John. I just…worry about what he brings to the table."

Would she ever let this go?

"Truth be told, I still have my concerns, but…I can see for myself how much he loves you." Her lip twitched as she moved toward the kitchen sink, and Jenni twisted the ring off and returned it to its proper place.

Her mother continued. "Besides, I would be hard-pressed to pass that up if I were in your shoes…he's quite the hottie." She tossed a smirk over her shoulder and wiggled her eyebrows.

Jenni's cheeks flamed. "*Mom.*" Tori's teasing was one thing, but her mom? No.

"What? I'm not blind, Jenni. He's very appealing." She pulled up on the water lever then turned back to face Jenni. "I understand why you've fallen for him so hard. That's all I'm saying. I've seen the way you two look at each other. You could cut the sexual tension in the air with a knife."

Jenni gaped at her mother. "Mom, just stop. Please."

This was not a conversation she wanted to have with her mother. Especially since it was *so* true. She moved to the living room to straighten the throw pillows, willing her mom to drop the subject. But instead, she trailed in behind her.

"Don't look so mortified. Physical compatibility is a very important ingredient to a healthy relationship, honey, there's nothing to be embarrassed about."

"Mom." Jenni straightened and pressed her fingertips to her temples. "We're not…I mean, we don't…" Oh, dear God, she didn't know what to say.

"Sweetie, you're twenty-four years old." She gave Jenni a dead-pan stare. "I wasn't born yesterday. No need to pretend for me."

"I'm not. *We're* not."

Her mother cocked her head. "You've been dating John for months. I'm not naïve. I'm not trying to make you uncomfortable. I'm *happy* for you. Really, I promise not to say another word." She turned away with a mischievous smile.

"Good. Because I'm not sleeping with John. Purity is important to me, to both of us. It's more than a quaint notion, it's part of our faith. Let's leave it at that and never have another awkward conversation like this one ever again."

Her mom popped back into the living room, the hint of a smirk still teasing her eyes. "Whatever you say." She disappeared back to the kitchen and dishes soon rattled as she loaded the dishwasher.

Sadie whimpered and pawed at the back door, a welcome diversion. After letting the dog out, Jenni decided she'd cleaned enough and went to her room, heavyhearted more than embarrassed. She still had some reading to do for class, but first, she turned on the lamp on her nightstand and opened her Bible, turning to the Psalms for encouragement.

Her mother was certainly a product of her generation. Though she wasn't seeing anyone now, she'd dated plenty of guys over the years and brought home more than a few. Some after the first date. But that had mostly been in the first few years following the divorce and Jenni suspected it was her mother's way of proving to herself she was still desirable. But still, all these years later, though it had never brought her fulfillment, her mother saw nothing wrong with it. Even assumed it of Jenni.

Jenni shook her head in dismay. Being surrounded by people who didn't understand God's way of doing things, who didn't know and trust Him, sometimes Jenni felt so alone.

She poured out her heart in prayer for each member of her family— Christy, her mom, Aunt Mary, even little Tessa. Especially for her, still too young to not be tainted by the world around her. She could have a different kind of life, if only her family would come to know Christ.

And something was changing in the air, she could feel it. As if life was on the brink of something big.

Lord, what do you have planned for me and those I love?

Chapter Twenty-One

Las Vegas, Nevada

April closed the baby book and dropped it on her bed. Time to squeeze into her skirt and head out. Stacy had secured the arrangement. It was far from ideal, and the last couple weeks had been beyond awkward, but April had no choice. Off-the-books tips at Jake's was better than another fast food gig.

April sucked in her belly and tugged the zipper closed. She ran her hand over the bulge in front and tilted her head. Sixteen weeks along, second trimester. From the outside, few could tell she was pregnant. But inside…her little bean had eyebrows, could suck its thumb. According to the books, she might feel movement any time now. She rubbed her lips together, head shaking. That was gonna be bizarre.

"April?" Stacy called from the kitchen. "I'm making tilapia, want some?"

"No way. Can't handle the smell. I'm leaving for work in a minute, can you wait till I go? And open the kitchen window when you're done?"

"Yeah, I guess."

April slid into her shoes and checked herself in the mirror one last time as she prepared for another day working with Ryan. He'd apologized at her first unofficial shift, begging her to believe he wasn't that kind of guy. Part of her almost believed him, wondering if she'd misconstrued that fateful night. But the larger part of her repeated she was nobody's fool. She'd accepted his apology out of necessity alone.

Ten minutes later she rolled into a parking spot and set her brake. Pulling down her visor, she spread gloss on her lips and separated her bangs. In the mirror she spotted Ryan just heading inside. She ignored him, snapping her visor back in place and climbing out of the car. After their little heart-to-heart, Ryan pretty much stayed away from her altogether, other than filling her drink orders. It was as good a system as any.

On the days April felt good physically, it was easy to slip back into the old groove. Flirting, darting back and forth between the customers and the bar. Tips those nights weren't bad. She caught up on rent at least.

Tonight wasn't one of those nights. Her round-the-clock nausea might have eased up a bit, but her energy tank seemed to have a leak. And strong smells made her stomach lurch. She was exhausted, and she couldn't think.

As she delivered an order to one of her tables, a cute guy with rippling pectorals scowled. "Hey, I ordered a rum and Coke, not a beer."

She forced a smile. "So sorry, let me take care of that for you." She'd already messed up three orders in the first two hours. Worst ever.

It didn't take her long to swap out the order at the bar and head back, hoping the mistake wouldn't show up in her tip.

"Here ya go. Let me know if I can get you anything else." She winked, but he didn't engage.

Smoothing her hair off her forehead, she approached the next table where a heavy-set man was flagging her down over his empty bowl of peanuts. He waved his arm high in the air, his stench roiling her stomach. She covered her mouth and ran for the ladies' room, where she pulled in several clean breaths, clearing her sinuses of the offensive odor.

After composing herself, she stepped back out onto the floor. Thank heavens, someone else had brought that man his refill. She spotted a familiar face and her spirits lifted. "Hey, Mark. Long time no see." She lifted a corner of her mouth in a suggestive smile. Maybe tonight's bottom line wouldn't be so bad after all.

Mark turned to her with a wolf-like grin, his gaze sweeping over her body. He blinked and frowned. "Huh. April." He dipped his chin and turned back to his drink.

"Need me for anything?" She purred.

"Not that I can think of."

This was not the Mark she remembered. "Let me know if you change your mind."

Her forehead wrinkled as she approached Ryan at the bar. "Mark's acting weird tonight."

Ryan's gaze shifted as if he were uncomfortable. Was he avoiding eye contact with her?

She planted a hand on her hip. "And so are you. What's the deal?"

Ryan cleared his throat. "Thing is..."

April crossed her arms over her slightly rounded belly and stared at him through narrowed eyes. "Do you have something to tell me?"

"Well, yeah." He rubbed the back of his neck. "See...customers have been complaining. You've been messing up a lot of orders. Everyone saw you run from the big guy's table. You're not able to draw in the male customers like you used to either. No offense but they don't come here for the family values."

Customers didn't like that she was pregnant? Well, too bad.

"The thing is, you aren't an official employee. If complaints get back to Jake, that's bad for me. He finds out about this arrangement and I lose my job. So you can see I have no choice here. I have to let you go."

April dropped her chin and stared at him. "What?"

"Look, I'm sorry. You knew this was a temporary gig. You got caught up on bills, right?"

"So just like that?" She blinked rapidly.

"You can finish out the night, of course." He dried a glass and set it on the counter. "I said I'm sorry."

Sorry? Was he capable of the feeling? He wasn't sorry at all. He'd assuaged his own conscience and decided he'd done enough penance. Unbelievable.

"Whatever." She stalked away, shaking her head.

She left with her meager tips and the twenty Ryan had shoved into her hand on the way out. What a hero.

The apartment still smelled faintly of fish when she returned. And Stacy was waiting for her with a scowl. Ryan must've called.

"Stacy, please."

Her lip curled. "You're going to have to figure something out, April...again." Ice hung at the end of her sentence.

"I know."

April turned toward her room. Why was Stacy acting this way? April missed her friend so much. But Stacy always seemed *this close* to losing her patience.

Over the next several weeks, April tried to reach out, to fix things, but Stacy was never more than cordial at best. Indifferent, even bitter, at worst. The job hunt was going nowhere. *She* was going nowhere. Her only source of joy was the life inside of her. Every night she flipped through the pregnancy books she borrowed from the library, a quiet awe filling her as she studied the baby's development.

"Hey, Stace, look at this." April held the open book out in front of Stacy. "This is what it looks like. Right now. Isn't that so cool?"

Stacy shrugged. "Yeah. Neat."

"You barely glanced at it. Come on, it's really cool. It looks like a newborn, just a little skinnier, but can you believe that?"

"I saw it, April. It's cool. Hey, can you go in half for a pizza tonight?"

April slumped on the couch. "No, sorry. I was going to either scramble an egg or make a PB and J." She'd worked a few temp days last week but it wasn't enough for her rent, let alone food. And she was running out of clothes that fit, too. She hadn't gained much actually, a fact she blamed on her small frame, but at almost twenty-one weeks it was definitely time for some maternity pants. She'd have to stop into the Goodwill store soon.

She pushed herself up and went to the kitchen. Five minutes later she was salting a couple scrambled eggs on a paper plate. As good a dinner as any, she supposed. At least she was getting protein, and the smell didn't set her off.

She propped her feet back up on the coffee table and nibbled at the eggs.

Her belly fluttered. She froze. *Was that...?*

After holding her breath for several seconds, she forked another bite. Again the strange, rolling flutter.

She spread her hand over the left half of her lower belly. A little thump, like...popcorn. A smile stole across her face and misted her eyes. "Stacy, come here! Quick."

"What's wrong?"

"Nothing. Feel this." She grabbed Stacy's hand and held it to her stomach. "Shh. Just wait."

Stacy looked nervous, then bored. Then finally, that little thump. April beamed. Stacy's eyes rounded before she snapped her hand back and turned away.

"What's wrong?" April's forehead wrinkled.

Her voice was tight. "Nothing. It's just…it's weird."

April stared at her. How could Stacy not think that was amazing?

That night, she lay in bed unable to sleep. She always figured she could handle just about anything, but now…she felt so alone. She wasn't going to get through this, was she? She chewed her lip and blinked. The only one who seemed to care at all about this baby was her. And she had nobody. She swiped the heels of her hands across her eyes. There was no one left who would help.

She sniffed. Or was there?

Running her hand over her rounding belly, she admitted the truth to herself. There was one other person out there who *might* care.

April wove through the lobby to the lounge and found the dark-haired bartender, Pete, on duty. Lucky break. He and her one-and-only *john* had seemed to know each other rather well. She'd arrived early enough to beat the evening rush and only a few patrons were at the bar. They looked to be mostly the business crowd, quietly discussing work over a few drinks.

"Hi," she croaked, approaching the bar.

"Hey there, what can I get ya?"

"Just some Pepsi." She hoisted herself up onto the barstool and looked him in the eye. "Do you remember me?"

He set a glass of Pepsi down and squinted at her for a moment, then recognition dawned in his face. "Yeah. You're the girl from that night. April, right? It's been awhile." He smiled.

Yeah, twenty-three weeks. "It has." She put on a casual air. "So uh, have you seen John lately?"

"No, he left a long time ago." He clacked his tongue. "Don't think I've seen him since that night actually."

"Oh." Her voice fell, shoulders slumped. Pulse roaring, she pressed her fingertips to her temples. Her hopes had been higher than she'd admitted to herself. When Pete's eyebrows pulled together and his head cocked to one side, she turned her face away.

"You okay?"

Pete's forehead was creased with concern, his dark eyes soft. She shouldn't confide in him, but the emptiness inside her said she had nothing more to lose. She looked into his eyes and took a deep breath. "Well…"

She stood and pulled her shirt tight around her stomach, showing off her bump.

"Oh." Pete's brows hiked up and his eyes darted from her belly to her face a few times. "Oh. Wow. And you…think it might be his?"

"I know it's his." She ran her fingers under her lashes, attempting to keep twin mascara lines from running down her face. To save a shred of dignity, if it wasn't too late. But the last of her pride was slipping away, along with her hope. "Any idea where he went?"

"Uh, not really." He shifted his gaze and April knew he was weighing his words.

"Please," she whispered.

He looked at her again, and swallowed. "Look, he didn't tell me where he was going, he was just gone. But he used to talk about crossing over into So Cal and heading toward the coast. Not sure how that's going to help you much though." He scratched the hollow of his cheek. "He drove a navy blue Camry."

She rubbed her lips together. "Thanks."

"Sure."

She dropped a few bills to cover her soda then stood and shouldered her purse.

"Hey, I hope you find him."

She gave a slight nod, then left, mind reeling. Blue Camry somewhere in California? She knew this was a bad idea.

Chapter Twenty-Two

Riverside, California

John smacked the alarm, slid his legs over the side of the bed, and ran his hands over his face. No time to hit the snooze today. He stretched his neck, rolling his head in a full circle, before he stood and grabbed his robe, shrugging into the comfortable sleeves on the way to the kitchen.

The oniony smell of last night's dinner was soon overridden by the scent of coffee as he brewed up his morning cup of energy. He'd hardly slept a wink last night.

He tossed the stirring spoon into the sink with a clank, then took a seat at the kitchen table. His Bible still lay there, open to the passage he'd been reading last night. The one now highlighted and underlined several times.

Proverbs 3:5-6:

Trust in the LORD with all your heart and lean not on your own understanding;

In all your ways acknowledge Him, and He will make your paths straight.

He pulled in a breath through his nostrils. He'd been careful the last six months to keep God at the center of his life, to acknowledge Him in everything—in all his ways. God would fulfill His promise to direct his paths.

This certainty, this peace he felt... John had to trust it came from God. Because one fact grew clearer each day. He didn't know exactly what his future held, but he wanted Jenni in it.

Another verse sprang to mind and he flipped through the worn pages until he found it.

Psalm 37:4-5

Delight yourself in the LORD and He will give you the desires of your heart. Commit your way to the LORD; Trust in Him and He will do this.

John set down his mug, grabbed the highlighter, and ran it over these words as well. He had honestly sought to make God's desires, his desires. So he'd continue seeking God, commit his way to Him, and then there was nothing left to do but trust that God would both direct him and give him the desires of his heart.

And, well, he knew what his heart desired. But was it too soon?

He moved to the living room bookcase, pulled out the carefully preserved photo album, and slowly opened its cover. It seemed only right to take a moment with Hannah and as he did, a deep assuring peace wrapped around him like a down comforter. He closed his eyes and pulled in an unhurried breath.

Knowing there was safety in a multitude of counselors, John reached for the phone. Mom would be up, probably sitting with her Bible and coffee like he was. She answered on the third ring.

"Hello?" Her sweet voice filled the line, awakening aching memories of home.

"Hey, Mom, it's me."

"John? How are you, honey? It's so good to hear from you."

"I'm doing good—it's great to hear your voice too. How's Dad?"

"Overall he's doing well. They've had a hard time getting him bathed; he's started getting combative with the orderlies. So they call me down to help with that. He's usually happy. Most of the time he knows who I am, sometimes he doesn't. He asked about you the other day. I told him you would visit soon."

John pushed down the lump in his throat, fending off the sadness of mourning his father while he was still alive. "Maybe I'll come for Christmas."

"I would love that. But I also know you have a full life down there and I am so thankful to the Lord for that. How are things with Jenni?"

John passed a hand over his chin. "That's why I called actually. I wanted to get your advice. You know, your 'godly counsel.'" He drummed nervous fingers on the table. "You've always given me that. And I need it now."

"Okay…what is it?" Her voice held a smile.

John rapped a finger on the table like a drumstick. "Mom. I know this is might sound crazy. I've only known Jenni six months." He paused for a moment. "But I have this sense that this is *right*. That God put us together." The line was disturbingly quiet. "That He even has a real future for us…as in forever."

She didn't jump in. Was she clueless as to where he was going with this? In horrified shock? Or something else? He pulled his shoulders back, straightening in his chair. "I'm thinking of asking Jenni to marry me and I want to know what you think about it."

"John." Her voice held a grin. "If God has given you a peace about this, then why do you doubt Him? If you are asking whether *I* approve, the answer is yes. I do."

His breath cut short. Of all the people he might ask for guidance in this, he thought his mother might have advised him to slow down.

"I've never seen you as committed and strong in your faith as these last six months. I've watched the Lord do a *miracle* in your life, John. A miracle. Putting it back together after it had been pulled to pieces. He's been creating something beautiful in you, and a part of that has been Jenni. If you were expecting me to disapprove and try to talk you out of it, you're mistaken. All I will say is that I trust you to abide in Him, and I trust Him to guide you."

John cleared his throat of the emotion gathering there. "Thanks. I…I wasn't expecting you to be so enthusiastic." He smiled. "So let me get this straight, you're *not* going to tell me it's a mistake?"

She chuckled. "No. If the two of you don't feel it's a mistake, then neither do I. Truth be told I've been expecting this for awhile now. I give you my full blessing. I can't wait to meet her! And, honey…Hannah wouldn't want you to be alone."

"Thanks, Mom."

The call ended and John sat for a moment, shaking his head in amazement. He pounded his fist on the table then scraped his chair back and stood.

"Okay, Lord, let's do this."

Subzero air-conditioning blasted John's face as he stepped into the mall. He stood there in a daze. Was it just him, or were there an overabundance of jewelry stores here? Five feet inside and already three shops fought for his attention.

He approached a small storefront with one man sitting behind the glass counters, working on some sort of machine. He looked up and smiled. "Can I help you with something today?"

John coughed. "Yeah, I'm looking for a ring?" He hadn't meant for it to come out like a question. His palms were sweating and he wiped them on his jeans.

Understanding sparked in the man's eye. He dipped his chin conspiratorially. "An engagement ring?"

"Yes…an engagement ring." The words felt strange and exhilarating on his lips.

The man proceeded to show John an assortment of rings, trying to get an idea of what he was looking for. John hadn't a clue. The first was simple and elegant—a white gold band set with a square diamond. It was beautiful in its simplicity, but Jenni's needed more personality.

The second boasted a circular diamond surrounded by six small ones, forming a sort of flower. Another ring held a topaz in the center with two diamonds flanking it on either side. Neither were quite right.

John moved on to the next store and another dizzying array of choices. He learned more about jewelry and diamonds than he'd ever cared to know. Oval diamonds, marquise diamonds, pear shaped diamonds, emerald-cut diamonds, the list went on and on. This wasn't going to be easy.

He took a break for lunch and headed for the food court. Soy sauce, french fries, and Philly cheese hit his nostrils and rumbled his stomach. More choices to make and his head was spinning. He stood in line for a chicken bowl, staring across the horizon of the mall. Why did they make this so hard? It was never hard in the movies. It was always spontaneous and perfect. His brain was on such overload that he gave the cashier the wrong change.

He hadn't had to worry about ring shopping for Hannah—they'd been gifted a family heirloom as a wedding ring for her. It was a beautiful piece passed down to her from her grandmother. John smiled at the memory.

He chewed slowly, weighing his options. He refused to leave without finding a ring today. And there was only one place left to visit before making his purchase. He tossed his trash and headed there.

And there he found it. The perfect ring for Jenni. A large, one carat, princess-cut diamond in the center, framed by a square of smaller diamonds, set in platinum, with still more small diamonds encrusting the band. Dazzling…like her. It might take him years to pay for it but he didn't care.

He ran his tongue along his dry lips and nodded at the sales lady. "This is it."

Her eyebrows hiked up. "This one? Do you know her ring size?"

"Six, I think. Will I be able to take it with me now?"

She grinned. "Yes, sir. We do have this in a size six. And if she ends up needing it resized, just come on back in and we'll take care of that for you."

"Okay." He rubbed his forehead. This was happening.

Like a strange out-of-body experience, he swiped his credit card and signed the papers. The salesperson then handed him the small plastic bag, inside of which was a cardboard box, holding a black felt one, which displayed the ring John hoped would surround Jenni's slim finger and proclaim to the world she was his forever.

Elation surged through him as he thought about that night's dinner date. He checked the time. Five hours was too long to wait to see her. He rubbed the back of his neck then climbed into the car. The temperature on the dash read ninety-two degrees. A nice cold smoothie sure sounded good.

When he arrived at *Just Juice*, Jenni's face lit up brighter than the diamonds on her ring.

"I didn't expect to see you until tonight." She came around the counter and pecked his cheek, then glanced at the clock. "I'm due for a break. Want me to make us a couple drinks? Take a walk?"

Perfection.

He took her hand and kissed it. "That's exactly what I want."

They strolled in between shoppers, John's mind wandering to the ring he'd offer her tonight.

She bumped him with her shoulder. "Hey, are you all right?"

"Of course. Why?"

"I don't know, you seem preoccupied. Is something wrong?" She furrowed her brow, scrutinizing him.

"Not at all. Everything's fine."

She looked at him quizzically. He needed to distract her.

He took her face in his hands and kissed her, slow and tender. "Better?"

She smiled, her worry lines smoothed away. "Oh, yeah."

"I love you."

Her cheeks flushed pink. "I love you too."

"Pick you up at six?"

"Mm Hmm."

He dropped a light smack on her lips. "Get goin'. People need just juice."

"Don't they, though?" She grinned and sauntered back toward the shop.

April gripped her stomach as a wave of nausea rolled over her. This stress was no good for her, or the baby. The apartment was positively oppressive. She needed out and really, what was holding her in Las Vegas? Nothing. She could be broke and miserable anywhere. If she could somehow find John in California, maybe he'd help. Maybe he'd be even be happy about the baby.

She allowed dreamy images to fill her head. At least they were something to cling to.

Since talking to Pete, she'd been laid up in bed most days. Staring at the wall in a bleak haze. She had no appetite and couldn't keep down half of what she ate anyway. Worry began to gnaw at her when she pressed her fingers into her belly. The movements were getting stronger but by now she thought she'd be getting huge. Then again, what did she know?

Well, she seriously had nothing left to lose. She could lay around stressed and depressed, or she could at least try to find her baby's father. So she peeled herself off the couch and drove to the closest library.

The obvious first step was a simple phone search but it proved useless. He either kept his number unlisted, or had it under a different name, or he didn't have land-line at all. This was going to take a little more digging.

She sat in front of the library's computer screen and typed into the search bar. "All right, let's see what we can find," she muttered as her fingers tapped the keys. "John Douglas...fire...Indiana." Click.

A dozen links popped up. News articles recounting the tragedy that took Hannah and Katy. Heartbreaking photos. She bit the inside of her cheek. Hannah did look a little like her. April scribbled down whatever facts she could find. His hometown, the name of his high school, his parents' names, the church where the services were held. But how would this information help? She tapped the end of her pencil on the desk.

An idea sparked. Excitement swelled. If she had the guts, it could work. And April had the guts to do just about anything when necessary. Her fingers flew across the keyboard as she entered another name into the search box of the online phone book, a smile stretching her lips as the results filled the screen.

His mother was listed.

She dug her pre-paid out of her purse and dialed. A woman's voice answered, sending her stomach bottoming out.

"Hello?"

She pressed her fingers into her palms and gathered her courage. "Mrs. Douglas? My name is Barbara. I'm calling from the Oak Hill High School Reunion Committee. I was hoping you could help us update our records for your son, John."

"Oh, uh...okay. You're calling from the Oak Hill High School committee?"

"Yes, ma'am. John Douglas is on our list as MIA. Anything you can do to put us in touch with him would be appreciated." Her tongue darted out to moisten her guilty lips.

"Well, he doesn't live in Indiana anymore. He moved to California. I can give you his phone number there if that will help."

"That would be very helpful. Thank you."

After ending the call, April stared at the paper in her hands. John Douglas's phone number. A connection to him.

She did an area code search and came up with a list of cities in Riverside County. Her heartbeat quickened. Could she really find him? And if she did, would he welcome her and their child into his life…or turn her away?

She had to find out. And she wasn't waiting around one more day just to let her nerves talk her out of it. She'd make the drive tonight, before she could change her mind, then find him tomorrow.

When Stacy left for her evening shift, April started gathering her things, packing up her car with as much of her stuff as she could fit. She scrawled a note to her one-time best friend, locked the apartment door, and slipped the key under the mat.

At the bottom of the stairs, she looked back over her shoulder one last time. "Goodbye, Stace."

April set out on the I-15 freeway, excitement and fear shuddering through her. She was betting it all. On a stranger. Though an intimate one.

The city gave way to desolation, craggy gray hills and dim tumbleweed bushes scattered along the sides of the road. The sun was gone, narrowing her view to only what landed in the line of her headlights. She went over her plan. Find a motel in the area to grab a few hours of sleep, shower and dress in her nicest outfit, do the reverse look-up, then knock on his door.

Had he thought of her again since that night? Was it crazy to think he could open his heart to her, see if they could have something together? For the sake of their child if for no other reason. A pair of strong arms holding her at night was something she barely had the courage to hope for. Yet she did.

The baby kicked and she rubbed circles on her belly. "He won't turn us away." Probably. Certainly not his flesh and blood. "Your dad is too good a guy."

At least that's what she kept telling herself as the miles ticked by out in the middle of nowhere.

On a long stretch of lonely highway, April's body broke into a cold sweat, and her stomach churned. She clenched her mouth shut. *Oh no, not now. Please.* She scanned for a turnout. Just as the acid began to burn the back of her throat, she pulled onto the shoulder, launched over the passenger seat, and thrust open the door.

A car whizzed by as she stumbled out and planted her hands on her knees. She choked and gagged, her belly tightening with every spasm. When her body finally relaxed, she leaned against the passenger side door and took in a few steadying breaths. Trembling and clammy, she crawled back inside and closed her eyes. When she opened them, the interior of the car dipped and spun and spots formed in her vision. She'd pushed herself too hard. She should've known better. "Okay, kid. I hear ya. We'll take a break." No more driving tonight. She wouldn't look up John until tomorrow anyway, and her body screamed for rest.

She pulled back onto the freeway just long enough to get to the next off-ramp somewhere in the Mojave Desert, then found a secluded spot to park. What was another night sleeping in her car? Though her stomach was unsettled, she forced down a granola bar and downed half a bottle of water before curling up in the backseat. But sleep came in shards, splintered by episodes of shivering and shaking.

She awoke with a full bladder and checked her phone. 2 a.m. Pulling on her coat, she grabbed her purse and headed for some tall grass down a small embankment. Desperate times and all that. On her way back uphill, April spotted two dark figures peering into her windows. One held what looked like a crowbar.

"Hey! Hold it! What are you doing?" She marched shakily toward them from across the road.

The skinnier one of the two glanced down the street, looking ready to bolt, but the other stood firm. His t-shirt sleeves were cut off and the muscles of his tattooed arms strained against the remaining fabric. He wore a backwards baseball cap that hid the color of his hair. But there was no mistaking the threat in his eyes. This guy meant business and April swallowed the anxiety in the back of her throat, unsure whether to keep walking toward her car, or turn around and run. But where to?

The menacing figure faced her full on, a creepy grin splitting his face. "Look at that. Didn't know the wheels came with a toy."

April shuddered, air refusing to flow into her lungs. She couldn't move.

"Come on, dude, let's get outta here." Her sight darted to her defender: dark-skinned, kinda short, wearing a dark jacket with a hood, the crowbar hanging at his side.

Please listen to him. Please.

232

The scary one gave her a sickening once-over. "What's the rush? She's harmless. We need a car, right?"

"Yeah we need a car. But…"

Her gaze darted from one man to the other. *Come on, say something. Convince him.*

"But nothing. We needed a car, and now we have one. Hey, Blondie, be a good girl and get yourself over here."

Just leave, she wanted to say. But she stood frozen. Silent.

"Come on now, do as you're told." He lifted his shirt, revealing a gun tucked into his pants.

She sucked in a quick breath, fighting panic and the adrenaline that told her to flee. Those instincts would earn her a bullet in the back. She commanded her legs to move closer, her eyes glued on him.

"That's a good girl."

"Okay, let's be quick about this then, dude. I don't want to hurt no lady. Let's just wire the car and go."

Yes, just hurry and go. She didn't care about the car anymore. And she just hoped that was still all they wanted.

"Hold up, man. I'm sure Blondie has the key." He scuttled toward her, his yellow grin just inches away. His breath gagged her. When she dropped her gaze he grabbed her face in his hand, forcing her to meet his evil eyes.

"You have the key, darlin'?"

She wanted to answer, to hand over the keys, her purse, everything—to make him leave her alone. But her throat closed and she couldn't find her voice. She stood there, blinking.

His eyes narrowed to angry slits. "Well?"

"Come on, man, leave her alone."

"She's gotta have it. Easier than wiring the thing."

Panting, April shot a pleading look to the other man, but he turned away. Her captor yanked her purse off her shoulder. "I'll find them myself." He dropped his hold on her and dumped the contents on the ground, then tossed the keys to his partner.

"Okay, we have them. Let's go."

The big guy waved him off. "Just give me a minute." A wolf-like smile crept into place and he brought a lock of April's hair to his face and inhaled deeply. Shuddering, she closed her eyes and turned away. He seized her jaw again, then ran his tongue along her cheek. She pushed down the bile in her throat.

He smirked. "Salty."

Her eyes filled, but she still couldn't move. She had a good idea what was coming. She'd lived and relived it a thousand times. It would be over soon.

"Come *on* man, let's *go*."

"Shut up! This won't take long. Go wait over there."

April's breath hitched as he wrapped his left hand around her neck, his thumb resting on her windpipe. He trailed the fingers of his right hand down her throat 'til they came to the collar of her jacket. She flinched when he yanked, popping open the snaps.

"You're very accommodating. I like that."

She squeezed her eyes shut as memories of Robert's boots and the pain of cracked ribs flashed to mind. *My baby, my baby…don't fight.*

His mouth traveled over her neck as she held back her tears, hoping it would be quick, looking for someplace to hide within herself.

When he stopped abruptly, April blinked her eyes open. The man curled his lip, then let out a frustrated grunt. He shoved her away and called his friend back. "Let's go."

"What happened?"

"She's *pregnant*," he spat. "And I'm not into that."

"What? She doesn't look pregnant."

"Yeah, I know." He swore. "Talk about false advertising."

They were in the car, turning the key, when April finally found her voice. "Wait—my blanket at least. Please!"

Her blanket and duffel bag landed on the street as they sped away, her clothes scattering across the road. She stared after them, watching her ever-faithful Corolla disappear down the desert highway.

When she could no longer hear the engine, she peered at the dark landscape surrounding her. An empty road. Distant hills. A big, black sky with mocking stars.

Reality crashed down like a ceiling caving in. Her knees wobbled under its weight. She'd thought she had nothing left to lose but she'd been so wrong. She was stranded. Vulnerable.

The familiar wave of nausea overtook her and she crumbled to her hands and knees. Afterwards, she pulled her knees to her chest and wrapped her arms around her legs. She stared out over the road, trying to numb herself to the fact she was probably the only soul around for miles.

Chapter Twenty-Three

John white-knuckled his steering wheel to hide the shaking of his hands. He glanced at Jenni in the seat beside him. She looked stunning tonight in her full-length, beige cocktail dress, hair pulled to one side, dangling earrings flirting with her neck. Her smile made his heart trip. He returned the grin and caught his left leg bouncing, again. If Jenni noticed anything off, the surprise would be ruined. And he wanted this to be a memorable evening. He tried to push away the thoughts of what was coming later, and focused on arriving on time for their dinner reservation. *Elliot's.* He thought it apropos. The location of their first date.

They were seated in a corner booth and the dim lighting hid the shaking of John's fingers as he reached for his water glass. He took several gulps but his throat remained dry. *Look at her. She's so beautiful.* His head swam. He'd be engaged by the end of the night, if all went well. Engaged to be married. And marriage meant a honeymoon and all that went with it, and God knew how ready he was to fulfill those duties. But this was about so much more than that.

He ran a finger under his collar and dragged in a calming breath, the aroma of filet mignon and roasted potatoes helping distract him from his train of thought. But his palms were sweating again, and his heart pounded against his rib cage through the entire meal. How he kept up their usual easy conversation, he had no idea.

When Jenni finished and pushed her plate away, John's pulse throbbed in his ears. He excused himself to the restroom, where he gripped the sink stared at his reflection. *Okay, John. You've thought this through and you're all prayed up. You want her, now go and get her.* He clapped his hands together then blew into his palms. It was go time.

John stopped their waiter on his way back and filled him in. The man looked at him with a gleam in his eye. "I know just what to do. Good luck, bro."

"Thanks."

John returned to the table and smiled at Jenni. She was so beautiful it almost hurt to look at her. Perched on her chair, sipping her strawberry lemonade. He reached across the table and wrapped his fingers around hers. "I'm the luckiest man on the face of the earth right now. I thank God for bringing you into my life."

She blushed but held his gaze. "No, John. *I'm* the lucky one. I can't imagine my life without you in it."

"I'm glad to hear that." He half-rose from his seat. "Come here." He leaned across the table and met her in the middle for a kiss, then settled himself back in his chair.

"Was that dessert?" She beamed, her thumb running along the back of his hand.

He breathed a laugh. "Just a start." He licked his dry lips and blew out a breath. "Jenni, you always point me to the truth, helping me be the best version of me. When we're apart, I feel like half my heart is missing. The past few months, you've been my shoulder to lean on, my best friend, and the love of my life. In my heart, you already feel like family."

Her eyes rounded, and John reached into his coat pocket and clutched velvet. "I want you to know I've prayed about this, about *us*, a lot, and..." He pulled out the box and watched Jenni's shimmering eyes dart to it, then back to his face. "I have something to ask you."

Her hand flew to her throat, then covered her mouth. Her shoulders pumped with her quickened breath. "Oh my gosh."

John pressed his lips together in a smile and took his time, savoring her reaction. Sliding out of his chair, he went down on one knee before her. She swiveled toward him in her seat, breathing fast and shaking all over.

He took her trembling hand. "You know the past I left behind and loved me anyway. If you'll have me, I want to give you my future." As he watched the myriad emotions playing across her face, his chest thumped.

"Jenni…" She gasped as he opened the box to reveal the ring. "Will you give me the honor of being your husband?"

She looked down and pressed her hand to her mouth, then bobbed her head.

John rubbed her arm and smiled. "Is that a yes?"

Lifting shining eyes to his, Jenni nodded and sucked in a staccato breath. "Yes. *Yes.*" Shoulders shaking, she held out her left hand, fingers splayed, and John slid the ring into place.

The restaurant erupted into applause. John stood and pulled Jenni to her feet. Someone whistled and glasses began to clink. John looked at his future bride and wiggled his eyebrows. He hoped she was ready because—

She kissed him. Deep and passionate and pure. Unashamed, barely restrained, hands cradling his neck, weaving through his hair, an I'm-all-in kind of kiss that knocked the wind out of him. He rocked back on his heels and blinked. The whistles and applause swelled to a crescendo. John looked down at this woman in his arms, utterly amazed. He gave her a slow half-smile. "And I thought *I* was in charge of surprises tonight."

She gave him a saucy smile he'd never seen from her before, then unclasped her hands from behind his neck. She swallowed, sobering. "John…" Her eyes warmed as they connected with his. "I'm so in love with you."

He kissed her again, briefly, then released her for them to retake their seats. Around the room, a few patrons stood smiling, and half the wait-staff had come out to watch the couple kissing in the middle of the restaurant. As if noticing them for the first time, Jenni blushed and gave John a shy look. But he'd seen the vixen she could be. And he'd be lying if he said that kiss hadn't sent his thoughts skating ahead to the honeymoon.

The manager appeared with some crème brûlée, on the house, and offered to take their picture. John hadn't thought of that but was glad the manager had. This was a monumental occasion, after all. Jenni bit her bottom lip, roses blooming in her cheeks, as he offered his congratulations and presented them with a generous gift card.

She admired her ring as they cracked into their creamy desserts, moving her hand from side to side and watching the light glint off the diamonds onto the ceiling. John didn't need to ask if she liked it, her face said it all.

He settled the bill, left a hearty tip, then guided his fiancée out to the car. As they drove, John reached for her hand and laced his fingers with hers, feeling the band of her ring when he did so. He looked down at it and smiled. "Hey, Jenni, I don't expect to get married right away. I know we should take our time, as hard as it is." He winked. "But I love having you wear this ring."

"I love *wearing* this ring! It's absolutely gorgeous, John. I've never seen a ring more beautiful."

"I thought you'd like it." He brought her hand to his lips, then turned it this way and that to admire the sparkling stones on her finger. "I need to make sure you understand I'm not trying to rush you into anything. I'd wait years." And he would if he had to, Lord help him. He kissed her hand again. "I just wanted the world to know you're mine."

Her lips pulled into a perfect curve, her eyes twinkling. "Yes. I *am* yours."

Back in her driveway, John reminded himself she wasn't fully his yet—no matter how tempting she looked in that dress, or what promises they'd made tonight. She drew close, circling her arms around his waist, molding her body to his and looking at him in a way that would have been dangerous had she lived alone.

"I love you." She made trails with her fingers on his back and lifted up on tiptoes.

"And I love you." He kissed her gently then held her tight to his chest, inhaling her scent and burying his hand in her hair, longing for the day he could express his love in full.

On his way home, he replayed the night in his head and smiled, pleased with himself. "It was perfect."

A perfect night.

Mojave Desert

At some point April got up, grabbed her stuff, and started walking. The road crunched beneath her shoes and her duffel bag swished against her thigh. She was numb. Panic wasn't an option. *Just keep walking.* Eventually there'd be a town, or a passerby would stop to help. The sun peeked above the horizon as April focused on putting one foot in front of the other. Just like she always did. She was strong, nothing would beat her.

She'd get them out of this mess somehow.

A gas station appeared half a mile up the road. Her pace quickened, renewed strength in her legs. Ten minutes later she was there, feet throbbing. A brown-haired woman with two small children in her car stood pumping gas. She looked sideways at April and diverted her gaze. As if she hadn't noticed her. But April needed to be noticed.

She licked her chapped lips. "Excuse me. Are you heading south by any chance?"

She nodded uneasily. "Yes."

"Could you help me out? I'm trying to get to Riverside, California and wondered if I could ride with you a ways." April shifted her weight and adjusted the bag on her shoulder, affecting a friendly smile.

The woman glanced at the two small faces watching through her car window then turned back to April with a shake of her head. "I'm sorry. I can't. But, here…" She pulled out her wallet. "For breakfast." She slid into her car and pulled away. April sighed and looked down at the ten dollar bill in her hand.

Shame washed over her. What must that woman have thought of her? But April didn't have time to care, so she sharpened her focus on what was important—get to civilization, find the father of her child, get *safe*.

She went inside the station and bought a pastry and water. Then she scuffed through the dirt and pebbles and slunk down onto the curb to wait for another car to come.

A pickup rumbled up to a pump then powered down, and April stood and smoothed her coat. She straightened her spine and put on her smile. The driver tilted his head as she approached, apprehension wrinkling his forehead. He looked pretty young, and didn't seem too eager to talk to her. She sized him up. Smooth face, open features. Instinct told her he was safe. And she didn't have the luxury of being too picky.

"Hey, um." She toed the ground then looked him straight in the eye. "Any chance I could get a ride?"

His gaze skittered around, like he didn't know how to answer that. April's little nugget kicked, and her hand instinctively moved to her stomach. The man looked down at her belly and back up at her, a conflicted expression on his face.

She turned her head and looked at him sideways while he seemed to weigh his answer. Then he nodded slowly. "All right." Was he speaking to her, or himself?

With a gulp, April climbed up into the truck and perched her duffel bag on her lap. She pursed her lips and blew out a slow breath as the man walked around to the driver's side. When he got in and shut his door, April jumped. She was about to get on a remote stretch of highway with a total stranger. How could she be sure he was as safe as he looked? She had little choice but to trust her instincts about this guy.

The engine turned over and April took a moment to study his face as he pulled away from the station. He had to be eighteen, maybe nineteen years old. Blond hair swept across his forehead. A few freckles scattered over the bridge of his nose. His black T-shirt was covered in some sort of scrolling design. April scanned the interior of the cab. Nothing that would hint at delinquent tendencies. A campus parking pass hung from his rearview. She tried to relax.

"So, what's your name?" he asked.

She hesitated, curled her fingers around her bag. "Tiffany."

"I'm Brandon." He held his hand out to her without taking his eyes off the road. She gave it a quick shake.

He passed the freeway onramp and panic pierced through her chest. She dug her fingers into the arm rest. "Where are you going?"

"Relax," he said. "I want to hit the drive-through real quick, okay?"

April's muscles remained tensed until he rolled up to a fast-food line and her heart rate settled back to normal. He ordered an egg muffin, hash browns, and orange juice. Sounded good. Her stomach twisted at the delicious smells coming from the bag. She unzipped the duffel and dug around hoping to find another granola bar.

"Here." He held the bag out to her with a smile. She raised an eyebrow. "I already ate," he said. "This was for you. Please, take it."

April blinked at him then slowly reached out to take the bag from his hand. "Thank you," she murmured.

"You're welcome."

April eyed him as she ate, senses on high alert for any threatening glance, any sign of danger. She found none. In all her observing she finally noticed that the scrolling designs on his T-shirt were crosses and hidden within the design was the word "mercy." A Christian logo graced the sleeve. A churchie, eh? No wonder he was such a Good Samaritan.

He didn't bother her with questions, just drove and let her eat. When she finished she released a sigh, happy the food was staying down.

"Feeling better?"

"Yeah. Thanks." They were on the freeway now, rolling along with little traffic for a Monday morning. He shot her a smile and refocused on the road.

She stared out the window, the speeding countryside hypnotizing her, making her drowsy. She blinked and rested her heavy eyelids. Just for a moment.

She awoke with the sensation she'd been asleep for quite awhile. They were still on the freeway.

"Oh good, you're awake," Brandon said.

"Sorry. I didn't realize how tired I was. Where are we?"

"Coming up on Barstow. Where did you say you were headed?"

"Riverside."

"Right. Well, I'm going to San Diego. Riverside is kinda on the way so I can take you all the way there if you want."

"Yeah, that'd be great. Thanks." She yawned and adjusted the seatbelt that had tightened uncomfortably under her belly.

"Well, we still have a good hour at least. You can go back to sleep if you want and I'll wake you when we approach town."

Too tired to argue, April simply nodded and closed her eyes again.

Brandon shook her shoulder gently. "Next exit is Riverside."

April inhaled through her nose and blinked to orient herself.

"So, where am I dropping you off? You got somewhere to go? Friend's place or something?"

"Uh...yeah." She ran her fingers through her untamed hair. "I have a friend here. I just have to find him. You can drop me here if you want, that's fine. And thanks for the ride, I really appreciate it. And for breakfast—you didn't have to do that." She suddenly found her throat constricting but she tightened her jaw.

He eased off the freeway and into a shopping center. He killed the engine and swiveled to face her. "Tiffany, are you going to be okay?" Concern creased his brow. "I mean, it's none of my business or anything, but...I'd feel a lot better if I knew you had somewhere to stay tonight."

"I'll be fine. Promise." She offered a smile, hoping to set his mind at ease. The last thing she wanted was for this guy to be burdened with worry over her. He didn't need that.

"Listen, I know it's not much, but take this." He pulled his wallet out of his jeans and pulled out twenty bucks.

April shook her head. "Oh, no. Really, you don't have to do that. I'm fine. It's all right."

"Please." He opened her hand and placed the money in it. "That baby needs to eat, right?" A soft smile appeared.

She glanced down at her protruding belly, which in her opinion wasn't protruding quite enough. She worried her lip. "Yeah. I guess you're right. Thanks...again." After slipping the money into her bag, she reached for the door handle.

He touched her shoulder. "Tiffany..."

April looked back at him over her shoulder and he fixed her with a penetrating gaze.

"You aren't alone. Ever." She inhaled and nodded. "I'll be praying for you."

She bit her lower lip and simply smiled. Then she pulled the handle, climbed out, and swung the door closed. She shaded her eyes and waved as he drove away.

A moment later she turned and surveyed her surroundings. This was Riverside. She'd made it.

She stood on the asphalt and surveyed the strip mall. Chiropractor, sushi bar, hardware store. She gripped the strap of her duffel bag and entered the Starbucks at the end of the row. After purchasing a Venti

Iced Tea, she threaded through pockets of early-morning customers to the seating area in the corner. She settled into a chair and pulled John's phone number out of her pocket, flattening it on the table. He was somewhere close. The hairs on her arms stood on end at the thought of that.

What was she going to say when she saw him? What if this number wasn't even right? The thought hadn't occurred to her. She pulled out her phone. The battery light flashed. She quickly punched in the number and hit Send. If he answered, she'd hang up. She was fairly certain she'd recognize his voice. She hadn't forgotten the way it had sounded alone in the darkness that night. Her phone gave a warning beep over the ringing. *Please don't die.* Not yet. Was her charger in the bag? She shouldered the phone and felt around in the duffel for the cord. She grabbed hold and yanked it out from under a pair of jeans just as John's voice filled the line. She stopped yanking. Her breath stuck in her throat. It was him. Well, a recording of him anyway. Her fingers tightened around the phone and she clicked it off.

She really had done it. She'd found him.

A business woman sat nearby with an open laptop. April smiled at her. "Excuse me. Any way you can help me MapQuest directions?"

Riverside, California

John awoke early Monday morning, too keyed up to focus on his Bible reading. The day before, he and Jenni had been like local celebrities at church, as women circled around Jenni to see her ring, and men clapped John on the back and pumped his hand. Pastor Dan had given him a hearty hug and congratulated them both. Jenni informed him they hoped he'd perform the ceremony, and Pastor Dan beamed and said he was looking forward to it.

Jenni signed them up for pre-marriage counseling and John fielded questions about when they expected to have the wedding. All of that was followed by an afternoon at Jenni's house with her family where there were hugs all around. The women wasted no time launching into talk of wedding planning and shopping trips. Christy seemed the most excited. And though Laura had been a bit more reserved in her congrats, she had produced a bottle of bubbly that John thought he was going to have to turn down. Until Jenni placed a hand on his arm and pointed out it was sparkling cider. He came home last night exhausted yet strangely energized.

Was he going to walk around with this level of anticipation for the time it took to get to the ceremony?

Maybe a visit to the gym would help work out some of the lingering nervous tension. He'd get in a good workout, take a cool shower, then he'd be ready for a day at the office.

He pounded the treadmill for forty-five minutes, a wave of excitement pumping through his system whenever he thought of Jenni. A hundred sit-ups clenched his abs as he envisioned her in a wedding dress. He flipped over, positioned his hands below his chest, crossed his feet behind him. Where should they take their honeymoon? Sweat dripped from his forehead as he pushed himself up, then lowered his body back down. His muscles burned by the end of the set, but not enough. He finished off with dumbbells, grunting through the last five curls as the extra energy finally drained enough for him to head home. John wiped his face on a towel and sucked down half a water bottle on the way out.

He'd have to hurry to give himself enough time for a shower before work.

He pulled the Camry into the carport and opened his door, whistling as he took the stairs two at a time. When he reached the landing he spotted a solitary figure huddled in the hallway not far from his door. Someone lost? Locked out? She'd slid down the wall to the floor. He pulled his brows together as he studied the woman. Filthy clothes and unwashed hair, blonde. She held her head in her hands and appeared to be crying. His heart squeezed. He took a few hesitant steps toward his door—closer to her. Clearly she was upset. His shoes scuffed the floor and the woman sniffed, wiped her palms over her damp cheeks, and scrambled to her feet.

She looked into his eyes and the floor tilted. His heart slammed to a stop.

April.

Chapter Twenty-Four

John stood in shocked silence. He couldn't breathe. April—the icon of his deepest shame—stood right in front of him, staring at him with wide, reddened eyes. The hairs on his neck pricked and his lungs went from frozen to hyper drive. Why was she here? Why now?

She tapped a balled fist against her thigh, hesitation clouding her eyes. "Hey, John," she said with a tremulous smile. "Long time no see, huh?"

He blinked. *How...?*

Her gaze skimmed over him. "You look good."

This could not be happening.

Glancing over his shoulder, he lowered his voice and stepped toward her. "What are you doing here?"

She shrank back, dropping her gaze to the floor. "Yeah, you probably didn't expect to ever see me again." She shifted her weight. "I didn't want to bother you. Really, I tried to take care of things myself..." Her voice pinched off. Suddenly, her hand zipped to her mouth and she whirled away, vomiting into a planter right there in the hall. She doubled over, hands holding her midsection.

And he saw.

Blood drained from his face as he took in the sight of her pregnant belly. Disconnected from reality, John watched April cough and sputter before him. Unable to speak, unable to move, he simply stared, mouth agape. Black spots danced on the edges of his vision and his own stomach soured.

She straightened and followed his line of sight to her rounded belly. "Crazy, right?" A dismal laugh. "John, I tried but...I can't do this alone. I have nowhere else to go. And I thought you'd want to know. It wasn't fair of me to keep you from knowing you had a ch—"

"Shh. Stop." Was she insane? Was she insinuating what he thought she was? "We can't talk about this out here." His gut tangled into knots as he fished out his keys and jiggled the lock. "Come in." *Oh, Lord God. What are you doing?*

April stepped passed him into his apartment and dropped a duffel bag and purse onto the couch. She pivoted toward him, hands outstretched. "John."

"Do you want some water or something?" John stepped around her into the kitchen. He reached into the fridge for a bottled water and uncapped it, downing half of it in one go.

"Yeah, sure."

He tossed one over the counter to her, then fell into the farthest kitchen chair. Questions poured through his mind as he watched her unscrew the cap and take a drink. Was this...some sort of scam? A ploy? Whatever it was, he had to convince her to leave.

The sound of his own shuddering breath filled his ears and he scrubbed a hand over his face. "Listen, I can see you're in a predicament here and I feel bad for you, I do. But I left Vegas, and *all* that, behind. I have a new life here. And I can't jeopardize that. Please, just move to the next...client...on your list. It's not me." It couldn't be.

But it could.

No. God wouldn't be so cruel.

Pain splashed across her face and John's heart cracked. He didn't mean to hurt her, but she had to go.

Her voice leveled. "There are no other clients, John. Just you." She moved toward him and took a nearby chair. "I wasn't a professional. Just desperate. I felt so guilty I was going to give the money back, but you were gone." She picked at her fingernail. "So I paid my rent. I found out later that I'd left that hotel with more than just your money."

John closed his eyes and pinched the bridge of his nose. He wasn't hearing this. She had to be lying. *But what if...?*

"It's the truth, John."

He wished she'd stop using his name. It felt too personal. Reminded him too much of just how personal their time together had been.

Tears gathered in her eyes and her straggly hair shook with her head. "I'd never done anything like that before. Or since." She wrapped her arms around herself. "I was desperate. About to lose my apartment. Terrified of being back on the street. You have no idea what it's like."

Her battered gaze locked on his, resurfacing a memory. Those blue eyes glistening with sympathy. A comforting hand on John's arm. She hadn't seemed like a prostitute then.

Or maybe she was just good at her job.

He clung to the thought. But as he studied her face, the truth bubbled up inside of him, pounding in his ears with every heartbeat—*the baby is mine, the baby is mine, the baby is mine.*

Oh, dear God…

"You believe me. Don't you?" She touched the back of his hand, but he flinched away.

John scraped his chair back and stood, turning from her. He raked his hands through his hair. What were people going to say? Derek, his mother. What about *Jenni?* Oh Lord, what would happen to Jenni? This would destroy her.

He planted his palms on the counter and dropped his head. The life he'd built here—the church, his friends, Jenni—he was going to lose it all.

"I know it's a lot to take in." April ran her hand up his arm to his shoulder and squeezed. "It will be okay though, right?" The hope in her voice twisted his heart. "John?"

"I can't do this."

"Sure you can." She began kneading his tense shoulder muscles. "You were a father once before. You have experience with this. You'll do just fine. *We'll* do fine, together."

"No." He shrugged out from under her hands. "I mean…" He waved his palms in front of him. "I can't do this."

"Wh…what?" She took a step back, looking like she'd been struck.

"You can't be here." John walked into the living room and stared out the window, emotions warring within him. Surely there was some way to…help…April and still hold onto his life. What was it? Where was the way out? Money?

"You ...you want me to leave?" Her voice came out small and defeated and John turned to look at her. She rubbed her belly and looked away. "I really thought you would help us. That you were such a decent guy, different, and..." Her face crumpled. "I don't know why I thought that. More desperate beliefs I guess."

His temples throbbed as he watched her move across the room. Pale and thin but for her belly, skin so clammy it shone. What had she risked to find him? What would happen to her if he turned her out? His conscience gored him as the voice of truth thundered in his ears.

God would never send this woman away. She was precious to Him. And that meant...

His eyes closed and he swallowed the panic surging through him. But way down deep in his gut, he found his anchor.

John dropped his shoulders. And surrendered.

"I should have gone through with the abortion." April hoisted her duffel bag and reached for the knob with a sniff. "Bye, John. Don't worry, you won't see me again."

"April, wait." He straightened his back and steadied his gaze. "Don't leave."

She stared at him warily, reading his expression. "Are you sure you mean that?"

"Yeah. We'll figure this out. Don't worry."

Relief washed over her face. "Thank you." Her shoulders quaked and she pressed the back of her hand under her nose. Instinctively, John approached to put his arms around her and she collapsed into him. "Thank you."

His eyes misted at the vulnerable pain shaking her. How could he have considered even for a moment sending the poor girl off alone? Even if he hadn't fathered her child? Yet, somehow, he knew he had. And he'd have to own that. Even if it cost him everything.

He held her while she cried, rubbing her back until the shuddering stopped.

She stepped back. "I'm sorry."

"It's okay."

"Your shirt's wet."

"Don't worry about it."

She wiped her hand over the tear-soaked blotch on his chest, eliciting memories he'd fought to leave in Vegas.

John pulled away and cleared his throat. "Why don't you have a seat." He ushered her to the sofa and she sank into it. The utter exhaustion in her eyes caught his notice then. No, it was more than exhaustion. She looked battle-worn. Clothing stained, a rip in her leggings at her thigh, swollen eyes. What horrors had she lived through on her way to him?

He took a seat on the ottoman across from her, resting his forearms on his knees. "You look the way I used to feel. Like you've been through the shredder. If you need to talk about it, you can."

Head coming to rest on the back of the couch, she peered down her nose at him and huffed. "We could be here till the baby comes."

John flinched at the reminder. April straightened and rubbed her lips together. "But I'll give you the highlights." She heaved a dismal sigh and started talking. About losing her job, having no money for a doctor, the pressure to abort.

When she finished, John pursed his lips and nodded. "So you haven't seen a doctor at all?"

"I went to a clinic at one point. But they strongly *counseled* me to terminate. *That* day. Seemed like they didn't want to let me leave. I felt like they were doing whatever they could to keep me from walking out, but that's exactly what I did and I never went back."

"Good," he whispered.

Yeah, she needed help. And it was clear the job fell to him. His head swam. She needed to apply for assistance, see a doctor, and who knew what else.

But first…he swallowed hard…he had to tell Jenni.

"Okay, I'll see you at the park in an hour." Jenni ended the call with John and tried to concentrate on finishing out her shift. But the ominous tone in his voice gnawed at her.

An hour later, she hiked over the hill toward their duck pond, where John already sat on the bench, waiting. His shoulders slumped and he looked…broken. Jenni's heart pounded, though she hardly knew why.

She placed a hand on his shoulder and he looked up at her with such swirling emotions in his eyes she couldn't breathe.

"Hey." She slid next to him and took his hands. That look on his face. He was scared, hurt. But why? And how could she help?

She ran her fingers through the hair at his temples. "Are you okay?"

"Jenni…" He pulled her hand to his lips then down to the bench and shook his head. "That's making this even harder."

"John… What's wrong?" She stared at him as trepidation skidded down her spine.

"I have something to tell you and you're not going to want to hear it."

"Whatever it is, you can tell me. I love you."

"You might change your mind."

She shook her head. "Never. What is it?"

The wind bit her cheeks as his chest expanded with a deep, sorrowful breath. "I haven't told you everything that happened after the fire, and I need to. For a long time I was really messed up—angry at God for letting it happen. I left home. Started drinking…" He looked out over the pond and cleared his throat, as if unable to speak.

"I know all this." Jenni rubbed circles in his back and shook her head. "It's all in the past. You're not the same man today."

"There's more." His eyes grabbed hers and what she saw in them rattled her to the core.

"John, wait. You don't have to relive every detail for my sake. Don't do this to yourself. Our engagement certainly doesn't mean we have to wade through every wrong choice we've ever made."

He was shaking his head, a pained expression on his face. "You need to know this," he insisted. "Please…just listen. And then…well, I hope you can still tell me it doesn't change anything." He drew in a deep breath, and pinched the bridge of his nose.

"In Las Vegas I spent most nights down in the bar and every day sleeping off a hangover and nursing my pain. I couldn't see anything beyond Hannah and Katy being gone. Over a year had gone by and the pain was worse than it had been the day they died. I'd have these nightmares where I saw them in the flames, calling me."

Jenni shut her eyes against the image. Why was he doing this?

"I'm telling you all this, not to make you feel sorry for me, but so maybe it will help you understand. I wanted to die. I'd decided to make that happen."

His matter-of-fact tone jolted her. He wasn't exaggerating. Her head throbbed as she stared at him, waiting.

"But instead…" His face contorted and his breaths came rapid fire. "I ended up in a woman's bed." The words were forced through clenched teeth, and Jenni's heart sank. This was the thing tormenting him? It was a shock to hear him say it, but she already knew he had experience she lacked in the bedroom. This was all before he'd come back to God. Before they'd met. It wasn't ideal, but…

She covered his hand with hers. "It's okay."

"It gets worse. So much worse." He hung his head.

What could be worse? He rubbed his hands over his face, then looked up at the sky and blew the air out from his lungs.

"Jenni…I paid her for it."

The words hit like a kick to the solar plexus. Jenni reeled. *"What?"* she whispered.

John? The man with the unwavering self-control? The one Jenni never feared would take advantage of her, even if given the opportunity? The man whose integrity she fell in love with more each day? She pressed her fingertips to her temples as he continued.

"I didn't know it at first, but by the time she…named her price…I didn't refuse. When I woke up with her it took me a minute to remember. I thought I'd awoken next to Hannah."

He drew his brows together and searched Jenni's face. Was he waiting for her to respond? What could she say to that? How could John be the kind of guy who would pay for sex? *No.* The thought repulsed her and she recoiled. She looked away out over the water, trying to calm her nerves.

"Jenni, there's more."

How could there be *more*? She blinked rapidly then turned back to him. The pain on his face undid her. His features distorted and twisted until he looked like a little boy. His shoulders heaved and he hunched over, looking at the ground. Jenni could do nothing more than breathe.

"She's pregnant, Jenni." His words sliced into her heart like razors, carving it into tiny, bleeding pieces. "And…she's here. She showed up today—tracked me down somehow, I don't know—but she's here. And she says I'm the father."

Jenni's stomach twisted into a sickening knot. "And…you believe her?"

He slowly nodded. "I think so. Enough to not turn her away. I've been sick over this all day, struggling with how to tell you." His throat bobbed. "I know I could lose you over this and it kills me, Jenni." He looked down at his hands. "It absolutely kills me. And the shame I'll endure at church is…"

Jenni felt a twinge of empathy but it didn't take root.

"But the bottom line is…" he looked her in the eye, "Jesus wouldn't send her away. So I can't, either."

Her mind rebelled against his words, screamed inside her head.

"She doesn't look well. I think she might be sick. And she's worried about the baby—"

Jenni's hand flew up to cut him off and she squeezed her eyes shut. "Please…don't. Don't say that word. I can't…"

"Sorry. I know." He twirled a lock of her hair softly around his finger. "I need to get her to a doctor, file Medi-Cal or something. I don't know." He withdrew his hand and pressed his fingers to his eyes.

Jenni's world was falling down around her, crushing her under the weight of it all. She couldn't think, could barely stay upright. "John, I can't listen to any more right now." She hadn't even shed a tear, just felt the strange rhythm of her breathing and heard her pulse whooshing in her ears. "I can't—"

"Process it all. I understand," he said quietly.

Jenni felt like she was watching the scene unfold as an observer rather than a participant. She was shivering the way she used to before a recital. "I—I need to go home now." She stood and John grabbed her hand and laced his fingers through hers.

He looked up at her with pleading eyes. "Jenni…I love you. I…" He scanned her face as if searching for words, but came up empty. Letting go of her, he dropped his head into his hands. "I'm so sorry."

His agony was so vivid, Jenni couldn't help but reach out and touch his shoulder. But she pulled back and left him there, sitting on the bleached park bench, head in his hands. Hurting. She massaged her throat.

"Will you call?"

Jenni stopped in her tracks, but didn't turn toward him. "I don't know."

John dug his fingers into the splintered arm rest of the bench, watching Jenni drive away, not knowing if she'd ever be back. With what he'd just dropped on her delicate shoulders, he wouldn't be surprised if it were too much to bear and she decided to cut her losses. He brought his knuckles up to his mouth. Lacerating Jenni's heart like that was the hardest thing he'd ever done. It had felt a bit like how John imagined Abraham felt when he put Isaac on the altar and raised a knife over him. Except John was the one at fault, and he hadn't been spared from plunging in the blade.

The cool breeze rolled over him as he pressed the heels of his hands to his eyes. He was emotionally drained. Spent. Chest aching, he dragged himself to his car. His focus was clear. He had to obey. Though it cost him everything in the world, he had to obey. For the first time in his life, he was learning what it meant to pick up his cross and follow Christ. To put himself last.

Climbing up to his apartment, his feet were like cinder blocks as he lifted them up each stair step. Before opening the door, he paused to regain his composure. For April's sake. He had to focus on her needs right now. Had to get past the shame and regret he felt every time he looked at her. Had to do whatever he could to help her and…his baby.

April lay asleep on the couch, right where he'd left her hours earlier. Her bag sat nearby, unzipped. John peered inside and saw some articles of clothing covered in dust and…gravel? He took them down to the laundry room and threw them in. She'd at least have something clean to wear in the morning.

Back upstairs, she shivered under the blanket and John put the back of his hand to her forehead. Hot, feverish. Remembering Hannah's pregnancy days, he knew she wouldn't be able to take the aspirin he had on hand. Tylenol only. He grabbed his keys and headed for the store.

John picked up a few other things she might need as well—shampoo, conditioner, soap that didn't smell like a man. When he got home she was still sleeping, and covered in sweat. Her hair was damp with it, dark blond strands stuck to her face. John frowned. Even asleep she appeared troubled.

"No," she mumbled. "No." Her head whipped side to side and her arms flailed as she struggled against an unseen assailant. A shudder ripped through him as he wondered again what horrific things she had suffered. Kneeling, John placed a hand on her shoulder. "Shh." He brushed the damp hair off her forehead. "Shh."

Her body relaxed and her face smoothed. John walked over to the window and gripped the back of his neck. This day had started out so different than how it ended. If only he could go back and undo that night.

But those thoughts would change nothing and only invite bitterness. He needed a cup of coffee to get him through the rest of this night. As he stirred his brew, April sat up and yawned.

"Hey. Have a good rest?"

She offered a tentative smile. "Yes, thank you. I haven't slept much lately. Guess I was pretty tired."

"I picked up some Tylenol. I think you're running a fever."

"I don't doubt it. Lots of stress, weakened immune system."

"Here you go." John handed her the medicine and some water. She popped the pills in her mouth and washed them down, then stood and arched her back.

The gesture reminded John so much of Hannah that his chest ached. She smiled at him again. She looked different in the light of day, and without all the sultry eye shadow or the low-cut dress. With her round belly and modest clothes, she resembled Hannah all the more. But that fact no longer stirred him the way it once would have. Not now that he had Jenni. If he still had Jenni.

An awkward silence stretched between them until John clapped his hands together and opened the fridge. "Think you could eat now?"

"Yeah, I hope so. I'm starving."

He peered inside. "I've got cold cuts, left over lasagna, probably a Hungry Man in the freezer. What sounds good?"

"Something safe, simple. Like scrambled eggs or something. If it's not too much trouble."

"Breakfast for dinner. Sure."

She gave John a soft smile, which he read as appreciation, and watched him get to work cracking eggs into a dish and whipping them with a fork. A thousand questions still needed answers but now wasn't the time. He dished up her scramble and set it at the table, then plated some for himself. The air was thick as they sat down to share the meal.

"These are delicious. What's your secret?"

"I use cream when I beat the eggs." Jenni had taught him that. He pulled in a deep breath. "We're going to have a lot to do this week. Especially finding you medical coverage. But I have to go to work tomorrow. Will you be okay here by yourself?"

Her eyes moved over him, shining, and she nodded. "I'll be fine. You go. I'll even try to clean up for you around here while you're gone."

An uneasy feeling turned over in his chest. "You don't have to do that. Just catch up on some rest." The last thing he wanted to do was play house with April. "I'll take the couch tonight. You can use the bedroom. Bathroom's down the hall to the left."

"Yeah, I found that earlier. Are you sure you want the couch?"

"Yes. It's no problem. I'd rather you get the bed."

She looked almost disappointed and the uneasy feeling returned. He pushed his chair back and carried their dishes to the sink. "You'd probably like a hot shower. I put fresh towels in there earlier."

"Yeah that sounds really good actually. If you don't mind."

He turned to face her and leaned back against the sink. "April, while you're staying here the house is yours. You can shower, rummage through the fridge, watch TV. You don't have to worry about whether or not I mind. It's fine."

Her head bobbed and she gave him another soft smile. "Okay. I'm going to grab that shower then."

"All right."

While she showered, John retrieved her laundry, folded it, and laid it out on the bed for her. It was all he knew to do. Hopefully she wasn't misconstruing his actions as anything more than kindness.

Later that night, April emerged from his room dressed in yoga pants and a T-shirt that clung more closely to her round belly than her sweatshirt had. She leaned a shoulder against the wall in the hallway and looked at him, hands rubbing her tummy.

"Everything okay?"

"Yeah. I used your toothpaste. Not your toothbrush though, don't worry." Her mouth tipped.

He shrugged and tossed a blanket onto the sofa. "Like I said, it's fine."

"Thank you, John." Her voice was a vulnerable whisper. She bit her lip and disappeared into his room, but not before he caught sight of the moisture in the corner of her eye.

John heaved a sigh and dropped onto the couch. He punched his pillow then brought an arm up under his head and stared at the ceiling. Just twenty feet away, a woman was in his bed. A woman who was pregnant with his child. But he had no idea where his *fiancée* was or what she was doing. His arms felt empty from wanting to hold her. Kiss her. He wished to God he could take her pain away. Make everything better, back the way they were yesterday. But he couldn't, and he went to sleep knowing she was hurting.

Because of him.

Chapter Twenty-Five

A thousand feelings pulled Jenni in so many directions she felt she'd be torn apart by them at any moment. She'd left the park and driven home in a daze, arriving at the house in shock. Her mother was out with work friends for the night. Her note said not to wait up.

The house looked different. Like a stage set. It didn't feel real, or familiar. She drifted to her room and quietly closed the door.

Then she surrendered to the storm.

Her stomach tightened and squeezed the air from her lungs. Her mouth opened but no sound came out. She doubled over, leaning on her thighs, trying to slow her spinning thoughts.

No. Impossible. John would never do something like this. How could he? *Why?*

She was supposed to be planning a wedding—not a delivery! Were all men prone to crush the lives they touched?

Her whole body quaked as she sank to the floor. She could hardly take in enough air between sobs. Her ribs ached and her chest burned for lack of oxygen.

God, this wasn't fair. I've done everything right! Was she now the one who had to take the high road, to show mercy as if she had no right to her pain? She'd done nothing to deserve this. She'd never done the things John had done. She hadn't gone to bed with a prostitute. John had. And he'd ruined everything. Everything. She'd risked her heart and now she wished she hadn't. If only she could just erase the last six months, erase John from her memory.

She pressed her cheek to the floor and grabbed fistfuls of carpet. How could such depth of agony be possible? She never knew she was capable of crying so hard for so long. Even when she ran out of tears, she continued sobbing. Her heart felt like it was bursting. Jenni was sure it had.

Oh God, why? Why did this have to happen? Did you give me all this just to take it away?

Jenni awoke on her floor, disoriented. But the memory quickly came to sharp focus. She squeezed her swollen eyes shut, then opened them and checked the time. 2:06 a.m. She'd never get back to sleep. Her ribs and stomach were sore, her puffy face hurt, her shoulders were stiff.

Heaving herself up, she rolled her shoulders then rubbed her hands over her face before opening her door. She crossed the hall to the bathroom and started the shower, avoiding the mirror.

Hot water pelted her neck and back, and she leaned her head into the stream, saturating her hair. The heat melted a measure of her physical tension, but not the dull ache in the pit of her stomach. It stirred again into a fresh wave of tears. *Oh, John…* Jenni flattened a palm against the tiled wall for support, the water and her tears both streaming down her face, until the tears gave way to sobs and she bent over at the waist.

Would the pain never end?

She missed John. Though it had only been hours since she saw him last, it felt like he was gone. Their love, their future, everything they had together, was just gone. She slid down to the tub floor and pulled her knees to her chest. Pain seared through her, and without thought, she seized the razor sitting on the ledge. She stared at it. Turned her arm over, exposing the fair skin there. In the heat of the shower she could still make out the faded scars. Her heart began to beat wildly.

It's no big deal if you want to.

Just to get a handle on the pain. Focus it where you want it.

She closed her eyes and remembered the way it felt at fourteen. The release. The rush. The control.

Nobody needs to know. There's nothing to worry about because you're in control.

When everything else was *out* of control. She swallowed. A *baby* was on the way.

If ever you had reason…

It's justified...

She clamped her teeth over her lip. *Stop worrying and just* do *what you have to. You'll feel better...*

Jenni touched the razor to the inside of her arm. Her hand shook but already her tears had stopped. Her breathing shallowed. Relief was so close...

John bolted awake with a sudden and overwhelming urge to pray for Jenni. The room was still covered in darkness. He sat up, gripped by fear and not knowing why. But something was wrong. John threw back his blanket and fell to his knees. He didn't know exactly what to pray for, only that Jenni was in trouble.

"God, please be with Jenni. I love her so much. Wrap Your arms around her, since I can't wrap her in mine. Lord I feel so powerless. Keep her safe. Protect her. Guard her."

His prayer continued, urgent, unlike any experience he'd ever known. He felt as if God were in the room with him, guiding him to pray. The spiritual connection was powerful, but left him nervous. What was going on with Jenni? Was she all right? He wanted to call and put his fears to rest, but knew he couldn't. He had to entrust her to the Lord for now. So he lay back down, unable to sleep, and prayed for the night to pass.

Pressing down, Jenni watched the skin whiten around the pressure of the blade, anticipation rising within her. All she had to do was slide it across. The razor was new. Sharp. She would bleed. There'd be relief.

She pushed harder and registered the faint sting. *Yes.* She closed her eyes to relish the moment.

Jenni.

She faltered at the unmistakable pleading in her spirit, then adjusted her fingers on the razor's handle. Angled the blade against her skin.

Let go.

"Why?" she whispered. Her heart thudded against her ribs. "Why should I?"

Old things are passed away.

She shook her head. "But this will help."

No.

"*Yes*, it will," she hissed. The internal pressure suffocating her was unbearable. She couldn't stand it another moment. "I..." she repositioned the blade, "I need this right now."

I AM all you need.

Her eyes squeezed shut, guilt constricting her windpipe, trapping her voice. But the ache was deep, throbbing, and nothing could make it go away. Nothing but this. With a quick sniff, she shook off the hesitation. "Forgive me. It just hurts too much," she scratched out, and pressed down, into the sting.

By My stripes you are healed.

Her body quaked, urging her to press harder, deeper, to slice herself open and drain the agony away. "Everything has fallen apart. My life doesn't make sense anymore."

I AM the master builder. Your life is hid in Me.

She dropped her head in shame. Because it wasn't enough; she was weak. "I...I just can't handle this without... It's just too much!"

Jenni...I will carry you.

The words cut through the fog of Jenni's mind. She blinked down at her hand, knuckles white, pressing the razor into her skin, still itching to finish what she'd started. She tried, but her fingers refused to release the blade, and fear gripped her. "I can't!"

Daughter, let go.

When the razor dropped to the floor, Jenni trembled and took a gasping breath. She examined her arm, the two red stripes a testament to the battle she'd just waged. The shallow cuts weren't bleeding, but her heart still was. But huddled there on the shower floor, she sensed the arms of her Comforter around her and knew she wasn't alone.

"Jesus," she whispered, "please help me."

Sunlight stretched through the room and woke John around seven a.m. Rubbing his stiff shoulders, he thought again of Jenni and could hold out no longer. Wrong or right, he grabbed his cell phone and punched in her number. After several rings, it went to voicemail. His heart cracked at the sound of Jenni's voice over the line.

He massaged the back of his neck. "Hey, Jenni. It's me. Just wanted to check on you, make sure you're all right and… Please call me soon… I love you so much." He tossed the phone onto the couch and raked his hands through his hair, thinking of all the other things he wanted to say to Jenni. *Do you still love me? What are you thinking? Can you ever forgive me?*

I love you didn't begin to cover it.

"Who were you talking to?" April's voice startled him.

He stiffened and shook his head. "Just leaving a message."

"Who's Jenni?" she asked softly.

Closing his eyes, John pulled in a deep breath, then looked over his shoulder. "My fiancée."

Her eyes rounded then she nodded, turned back toward the bedroom, and eased the door shut behind her.

Chapter Twenty-Six

"So this is a cash visit today then?"

"Yeah." John glanced back at April sitting in the waiting area. He had yet to begin filing for Medi-Cal. Hopefully, it wouldn't take too long to get set up, but they couldn't wait. This checkup had been put off long enough. He settled into the seat next to her and cracked his knuckles. The room was too cold for a November morning. John flipped open a magazine, then dropped it back on the table. He dodged knowing smiles from the other faces in the waiting room. Of course they all thought he and April were an ordinary, expectant couple. He slouched in his plastic chair, then exchanged an uncomfortable smile with April. All around were pregnant women, most with husbands in tow. Fathers and mothers beaming.

He unwrapped the peppermint he'd snagged from the reception desk and popped it into his mouth. One of the women seated across from him placed her husband's hand on her belly, and a smile lit the man's face.

John cast a glance at April beside him. She didn't glow or smile. She looked ashen, pale. Head bent over the clipboard and pen scratching out answers, she filled out her paperwork with businesslike concentration. Something inside of John wept. This wasn't how it was supposed to be. Bringing a new life into the world should be a time for bonding with family. Not straining the boundaries of responsibility.

"Does she know?" April spoke without looking up.

"Yes. She had a right to."

"I'm sorry." She shook her head. "I knew the baby would be a huge shock for you. But I had no idea... I hadn't considered that you might have someone." Her mouth twisted and her shoulders rounded with her exhale. "It was selfish to come."

Before he could respond, the door swung and a nurse stood with a manila folder, calling April's name. They signaled for John to come too, assuming they were together. And, he supposed, they were. If she'd told the truth, they'd created this child together, and that fact would forever connect them. The thought ran through him like a knife carving his insides. He'd never be free of his actions that night.

April looked pasty, and fidgeted as the nurse took her vitals and scribbled notes in a chart. John offered an encouraging grin but it felt fake. Then the doctor came in and glanced over the chart.

"April, hi. I'm Dr. Fuller. How are you?" He shook her hand, then turned to John. "And you must be Dad, yes?"

Dad. A hot coal seared his chest. He shook his hand.

The doctor turned back to April. "Well, I really wish you had come in sooner. Your chart says you've had no prenatal care, is this correct?"

April nodded, shame reddening her colorless cheeks.

"Well, you're going to need to take better care of yourself from now on, okay?" He sounded like a parent scolding a child. And April sat under his scrutiny looking the part. He went over diet and prenatal vitamins. Told John to pick up some vitamin B6 for her nausea. Like it was his job. Which it was, but not because she was his.

Dr. Fuller had April lay down while he felt her abdomen, measuring and making notes in her chart. Then he squeezed some gel onto her stomach and began running the Doppler over her belly. Moments later, the *swoosh-swoosh-swoosh* of a tiny, quick heartbeat filled the silence.

April's eyes rounded. "Is...that the heartbeat?"

Dr. Fuller nodded. "Yes, and the baby sounds strong and healthy."

A smiled stretched April's face and John felt her wonder becoming his own. A slight grin snuck up on him.

The sound stopped when the doctor pulled the device away and wiped off the gel with a paper towel. He helped April sit up then scribbled something at the counter.

"Here, I want you to take this lab sheet downstairs for a routine blood test. I'd like to get you feeling better. At this point in your pregnancy you should be much less sluggish. And I'm not happy with the paleness in your skin. You're probably anemic, but the blood test will confirm this. It would be best if you went downstairs and did this now so we can begin correcting it, okay?" He handed the lab sheet to April, who looked even whiter than usual. "Don't worry, anemia can be easily managed," he reassured her. "But we wouldn't want to wait on taking care of it. I'll call you when I have the results."

They stood to leave and Dr. Fuller patted John on the back. His muscles automatically tensed. "Congratulations."

John pasted on a smile.

"Oh—and you can schedule a sonogram appointment at the front desk on your way out."

Sonogram?

"And if you're interested, you're at the perfect gestation for a 3-D ultrasound."

John's eyebrows lifted as it hit him. His *baby* was actually growing inside April's womb. A child. And he was going to see it on a monitor. Not just hear that strange whooshing sound, but see a baby with fingers and toes wriggling around on a screen. In 3-D.

"Thanks, Doctor."

"You bet."

April spoke with the receptionist and made the appointment, while John got lost in his thoughts. And then they were out in the hall. April carried the lab sheet in her hands as John followed her toward the elevator. He stepped out of the building stunned with the realization…

Five days. In five days he would see his baby.

After work, John helped April file paperwork for Medi-Cal. She used his address as a residence for now, and John hoped it wouldn't widen the rift between him and Jenni. He prayed every day that she'd call, but so far nothing.

The house phone rang, filling one of the many awkward silences they shared. He put Dr. Fuller on speaker.

"April, your red blood cell count was low, as I suspected. You're anemic and will need to start on iron supplements." He paused for several heartbeats before going on. "Your white cell count was also a bit low. I'd…like you to come back for additional tests to determine the cause."

John's brows pulled together. What did that mean? April's face was expressionless, her eyes fixed on the phone. Neither responded.

"There's no need to panic. A low white count could be caused by a number of things—a recent infection, perhaps."

John cleared his throat. "She was running a bit of a fever a few days ago."

"Okay, good—that's a start. We'll look for the cause of the infection. I'll transfer you back over to the front desk to schedule an appointment."

April stared blankly.

John answered for her. "Thank you, Doctor."

"Mr. Douglas, would you take me off speaker for a moment please?"

John picked up the receiver and punched a button. "Yeah…I'm here."

"Listen, try not to let her worry. Stress isn't good for her. But…don't delay in bringing her in. We need to get a handle on this as soon as possible."

John slid a quick glance toward April, sitting on the couch now, her hands trembling as she pushed the hair back from her forehead. He swallowed hard. "Okay, Doc. Thank you."

Chapter Twenty-Seven

Work became John's refuge, a place where life felt closer to normal, where his thoughts weren't unceasingly pinned on April. Where he found distraction from worrying about Jenni.

He leaned back in his office chair, rubbed his temples, then dragged his palms down his face. It was almost time to go home. To the apartment he was no longer alone in. He'd considered putting April up in a motel, but decided to wait until they got the test results. After that, he'd figure out where else she could stay.

He grabbed a stress ball off his desk and plunged his fingers into it, staring at the calendar on the wall across the office. Thanksgiving was approaching fast and he'd assumed his reserved spot at the Dupont table had been rescinded. He was going to miss the family tradition Jenni had told him about, where each person took a corn kernel to drop into the ceramic gourd as it passed, declaring what they were thankful for that year. He'd been looking forward to sharing how grateful he was to have found family. He spun his chair a few degrees to the right and his thoughts slid back to his house guest.

How would this all play out? April had no job, no car, no resources whatsoever. That meant four to five months she'd need total financial support.

John squeezed the ball harder, faster, and tried to tell himself it wasn't his problem, or responsibility. She wasn't his wife. Never would be. But of course he'd never send her out onto the street. For the time being she was under his roof, so he *was* responsible for her. Long term arrangements would have to be figured out later.

"Ugh." A garbled groan fell from his mouth. He shook his head. *Long term arrangements?* As in, where will his baby go to live?

He opened a drawer and tossed the stress ball in with a thwump. This whole thing was a crazy, unfathomable mess. He was going to be a dad...again. But not the way he'd hoped. Not with Jenni a few years down the road. But with a stranger, and in a couple of months.

Assuming it really is mine.

He often clung to that sliver of doubt. But deep down he knew. God had already settled that question for him.

"John? You okay?" Gwen stuck her head into his office.

He gave her a fake smile. "Yeah, just tired." He straightened in his seat.

"You have the granite supplier holding on line two."

"Thanks." Pushing a button on his desk phone, John shifted back into work mode.

He kept his thoughts on business the rest of the afternoon, then reluctantly headed out of the building.

He climbed into his car and stuck the key in the ignition but didn't turn it. Expelling a weary breath, he stretched his neck and rested his head on the back of the seat. What was Jenni doing right now? Maybe walking Sadie or visiting with Aunt Mary and Christy. Or was she somewhere alone crying? Wishing she'd never met him?

She hadn't answered any of his calls but he had to try one more time. He punched in her number and counted the rings. It would go to voicemail after seven, he knew. At three rings, there was a click and John straightened in his seat.

Silence filled the line. "J-Jenni?"

A heavy pause. "I'm here, but I can't talk long."

Releasing his breath, John closed his eyes and concentrated on the sound of her voice.

"Listen, I don't want you to worry about me, but...I need more time."

"Wait. Please."

"John, I have to go."

"I love you, Jenni. This is killing me. I miss you so much it hurts."

He held his breath through the weighty silence.

"I miss you too. I've got to go."

Jenni ended the call, and the words she hadn't spoken left a lump in his throat and pressure behind his eyes. He started the car, but instead of heading for home, he called Derek.

"Dude, where've you been this week? You missed the Men's Study and Recovery. That's not like you."

"I know, I'm sorry. Derek, I need to talk to someone…and you're about the closest friend I've got. You busy?"

They made plans to meet at the coffee shop and John started going over what exactly he would say. How did you break news like this? With an overpowering cup of coffee, and a bagel he couldn't take a bite of, he sat at the round wooden table and waited. *God, get me through this.* Would Derek be the first of many to cut John out of his life, completely disgusted?

The glass door opened with Derek's arrival. He smiled and headed toward John. "Hey bro, what's up?"

"Hey." John gulped at his coffee so he wouldn't have to smile back. "I've got some really heavy stuff going on right now and I could use someone to talk me through it. Hope you can handle it."

Derek scraped a chair back and sat across from John. "Of course, man. What're friends for? You okay?"

"No." John rubbed his lips together then shook his head. "I don't know how to say this, where to even begin."

Derek leaned back and regarded him, concern etched on his dark brow.

Might as well get on with it. "Look, you know that I walked away from church and God for a long time after Hannah and Katy died, right?" He studied the coffee in his hands, his mouth going dry.

"It's okay. Whatever you need to say, I'm here to listen."

John looked out the window and nodded. "Yeah." Maybe it was like ripping off a Band-Aid. Do it fast and all at once. He drained his mug, then looked Derek in the eye. "My last night in Vegas, I went to bed with a stranger. She tracked me down somehow and showed up here a few days ago, six months pregnant. Says it's mine, and I think it's true. I told Jenni, and we haven't really spoken since." John worked a muscle in his jaw and braced for the fallout.

Derek nodded slowly, his expression grim. He was quiet for several moments. "That's…a lot to handle. I don't know what I can do to help, but…I'm here for you. What are you going to do?" He rested his elbows on the table and steepled his fingers.

John updated him on the recent blood tests, his last conversation with Jenni, how afraid he was to walk in the doors of the church on Sunday. Derek listened without judgment, and relief swelled in John's chest. Someone on his side.

"I'll save you a seat at church on Sunday. Don't you worry about that. You don't need to hide."

John nodded. Derek reached out and grabbed hold of John's shoulder, giving it a hearty squeeze. "I'm gonna pray for you before I go, okay?"

John exhaled and nodded. "Yeah." This kind of support was what had been missing all week and it renewed John's strength. Derek closed his prayer and stood to clap John on the back.

"Derek… Thank you."

"Any time."

They parted ways and John headed home. Where the mother of his child waited.

April brushed out her hair and slid on a headband. She hated looking so tired all the time. The circles under her eyes she'd have to live with but she could try to do something about her hair before John got home. She shuffled back to the sofa and eased down into it, shivering as she spread a blanket across her lap. The baby shifted and she rubbed her belly, smiling.

At least she could still smile about the baby. These days her smile was getting harder and harder to find. She hadn't known exactly what to expect when she found John, but a fiancée wasn't it. Crashing his wedding plans hadn't been part of her master plan. Yet he was still being so kind to her. So thoughtful. And even if the guilt constantly nibbled away at her soul, she wasn't going to reject his help. She wouldn't reject *him* at all. And even if all he could offer her was support through this pregnancy, she'd take it. Gladly.

She yawned and laid her head on the armrest, pulling the blanket up over her shoulders.

Of course, if this Jenni decided to leave the picture for good, who was to say what might happen. She and John were going to be a family of sorts either way, why couldn't something more blossom between them? Not that she would ever wish that kind of pain on him. He'd endured enough pain in his life already. He didn't deserve any more. Really he deserved some sort of award or something. Like Boy Scout of the Year, only for men who sacrificed everything to help practical strangers. She knew how it cost him. She saw the torment in his eyes and caught him dialing Jenni's number. By now he could've changed his mind, given April some cash and sent her away. Even that would be more than what Robert would have done.

Robert. How had that name popped up in her thoughts again?

Sleep pulled at her consciousness, dreams crowding out reality until the room faded away.

"I've got pizza."

April startled awake as John kicked the door closed with his foot and headed for the kitchen.

"Oh, sorry. Hope I didn't wake you."

He sure sounded in a better mood than the past couple days. April sat up and stretched as John brought her a slice of pizza on a paper plate.

She gave him a smile. "Thanks."

"Just cheese. I wasn't sure what you liked but I figured you'd want to avoid the spice of pepperoni or sausage."

"Good call." His thoughtfulness was unmatched. She took a cautious bite, testing her stomach, as John lowered himself into the armchair across from her.

He dug into his pizza but his gaze was on her, a question brewing in the blue depths of his eyes.

"April?" He wiped his mouth on a paper towel then cocked his head to the side. "How did you end up in Vegas?"

The question she'd hoped he'd never think to ask. She gazed out the window, her mind immediately tossing her back to the floor of her apartment in New Mexico, Robert's terrifying face above her. A shudder ran through her. "I was escaping a nightmare, like you."

He regarded her, gentle curiosity in his eyes. "I told you my nightmare. What was yours?"

She pulled in a slow breath and gave the simplest answer. "Robert." Some nightmares were not worth the telling, and she hoped he'd let it go. She took another tiny bite of her pizza.

"So…what about your family? Where do they live?"

Her temples pounded with her pulse. "I… I don't know where my mom ended up. Probably in some trailer park with one of her boyfriends. Or in jail. If she's still breathing. Mind if I get some water?"

He nodded and April went to the fridge for a water bottle, hoping the conversation would shift away from her past.

"And your dad? Do you talk to him?"

"My dad was never in the picture—and I didn't have any other family. No brothers or sisters. Just me, my mom, and whatever guy she was hooking up with." She returned to the couch and sank into the cushions. "Have you heard from Jenni?"

"No. Not for days now." The disappointment in his voice made her wish she hadn't asked. Her heart squeezed as he studied the fabric on his armchair. "She needs more time."

A dull ache filled her chest. "I'm sorry." She lifted her slice of pizza, looked at it, then set it back down.

"How are you feeling?"

"A little tired." Always tired. She stared at the plate in her lap, then turned her face away. All she wanted to do was forget everything bad that was happening and for once find hope that something good was possible.

"You have to at least try to eat. Please. Is it too greasy? If you don't want pizza I can fix you some eggs. Or a peanut butter sandwich."

His concern both touched and pained her. Everything she'd ever wanted was right in front of her, yet still out of her reach. But she indulged him with a smile, then lifted her slice in the air. "Yes, sir."

She tried for a playful smirk but when their eyes met, a deep longing arose and her throat tightened with emotion. Too late, she realized her expression hid nothing. She turned away but his face told her he'd seen it.

"April…" His low voice drew her gaze back to him, and she felt a drop of hope splash across her heart.

"That night," he eyed her belly, "should never have happened. It was wrong." His hand sliced the air, punctuating the word. "You know that."

Shame gripped her and she couldn't meet his eyes. "John, please. I know I shouldn't have taken advantage of you the way I did. I wasn't thinking straight, I thought it was my only option. But…" She had to lay it all out there. To make him understand. "…it wasn't all business. It meant something to me. I *wanted* to be with you." His face blurred behind the sheen of moisture welling in her eyes.

"I don't think I would've gone through with my plan if it hadn't been you I met that night. If I hadn't gotten to know you. As a man, not a mark. Your sensitivity, your devotion. Your pain. I was drawn to *you*, John, not your money."

She was drawn to him still, if only he'd give her a chance. "That connection we shared—and I know you felt it too—it was genuine. I didn't see things the way they really were…until after. I wasn't playing you, I swear. The worst part of all of this, is knowing what I made you see me as. I made what we shared into a transaction. Myself into…"

She couldn't speak it aloud in front of him. "If I could ask just one thing of you, it would be please…*please* don't think of me like that." Her eyes pooled, but she didn't care. She couldn't stand him thinking of her as…a woman of the night.

"April." John's voice was soft, and for one hopeful second April thought he might tell her that's not how he saw her at all. That their night together had meant something to him, too. But those were words that existed only in her dreams.

"That's not the only reason." His drew in a breath and gave her a pitying look. "It would have been wrong, regardless."

She winced then worked her throat. Scratched a piece of cheese off the edge of her plate. "So, why are you helping me?"

"Because…I care. And I think it was God who brought you here."

God? A sarcastic laugh spilled from her mouth and she shook her head. "Yeah, sure."

"God always has a plan. I don't know what that plan is, but I know that, just like me, He wants to free you."

"Oh, I'm free." She snorted. "I've got nothing holding me down anywhere. I'd rather be a little *less* free." To belong. Somewhere, with someone. To stop running, searching. "Jenni probably doesn't feel the same way about this, does she?"

A shadow passed over his features. "I don't know exactly what Jenni is thinking right now." His thumb tapped the side of his paper plate. "But I trust God to get Jenni through this, the same way I trust Him to get you and me through it."

You and me. Gooseflesh raised on her arms. She arched an eyebrow. "What's with all the God talk?"

"It's more than talk, April. I hope you'll come to see that." He took a bite of his pizza and April mirrored the action automatically.

Was that what had changed everything for him? Religion? She wouldn't have pegged him that way—not with the way he kissed. A burst of warmth radiated through her at the thought. But seeing him now, these last few days…it sort of suited him.

"How is it?" He jutted his chin toward her plate.

"Good." She nipped off another bite.

The conversation lightened as they finished the meal, and April was relieved. John took their plates to the trash and returned with a bowl of ice cream.

Her eyes rounded. "How did you know I liked Rocky Road?"

"Guess I was inspired." He grinned.

Her stomach twirled a little at the playful look in his eye. He pointed at the entertainment center. "I picked up a DVD, too. One of my favorites—*Groundhog Day.*"

"It's one of mine too." Something else in common.

If only *she* could have endless do-overs until she got things right.

The next couple of hours passed with Bill Murray distracting them both from their strange circumstances. Hanging out on the sofa watching movies and eating ice cream…this was something April could navigate. The laughter felt good, and John's laugh was rich and deep. So open. Unburdened. How she wanted what he had.

No. What you want is him.

The comedy also seemed to keep his focus off of Jenni, which was a good thing. Although once in awhile his expression went distant, and that could only mean he was thinking of her. She must be pretty special, but if she was on the fence….well, maybe something would tip in April's favor sometime soon.

Like seeing their baby on the ultrasound Monday.

The soft lilting melody of elevator music accompanied the tapping of April's foot. Nervous excitement hummed through her body. Why did they always make you wait so long? What was the purpose of an appointment time if they didn't stick to it? Beside her, John rifled through the stack of tattered magazines.

"Anything good?"

"*Woman's World* or *Parenting.* You interested?"

April shook her head and John dropped them back on the end table. The waiting room clock read 11:08 a.m. She shifted in her seat, crossing her legs, and John cracked his knuckles. "April?" A nurse stood at the door, smiling. "You can come on back."

John's brows lifted. "Time to roll."

They were led to a small, dimly lit room with green walls and a monitor mounted on one side. John took the chair and April climbed onto the patient table.

A young woman with auburn hair and kind eyes came in and sat on the stool beside her. "I'm Beth. How are you today?"

"Fine thanks."

"Good." Her voice held a nearly exaggerated enthusiasm. "You ready to see your baby?"

"I think so." April ran her tongue over her upper lip. Beth hiked April's shirt up and squirted gel over her belly. The imaging device pressed firmly into her abdomen, and April winced.

John's brows pinched. "You okay?"

"Yeah. I just really have to pee."

He chuckled.

"Shut up!" April giggled, then hissed again as the pressure in her bladder demanded her focus.

"There it is."

April and John turned their gazes to the monitor. The tech hit a button and froze the image at its clearest point and April found herself staring at a perfect little profile. She sucked in her breath and propped herself up on her elbows. "Oh my gosh, I can see it. John, can you see it?"

John turned to her and nodded. "Yeah," he spoke in a hushed tone and moved closer to the screen, "I see it."

April caught his eye and together they shared an awestruck laugh. Beth hit another button and the baby on the display moved. When she froze the image again, they saw a tiny foot. April's throat tightened and she caught a glimmer in John's eyes.

Was he as overwhelmed with the experience as she was? Did the realization hit him that he was seeing his own flesh and blood up there on the screen? Something he'd helped create, with her, one passion-filled night not too long ago?

She watched his Adam's apple bob and a smile tugged at her lips. Yes, he sensed it. He was just as moved as she was. They were connected.

The tech took measurements of the baby while April and John strained to make out what they were looking at.

"Do you want to know the sex?" Beth asked.

John raised his brows. "Do you?"

"I don't know." April chewed her lip. "It might be fun to keep it a surprise." Something to anticipate in the midst of the nightmare.

John nodded and his slow smile filled her with hope. "Okay, we'll wait."

"All right then." Beth grinned and continued with her work.

When the exam was finished, April and John walked out with a handful of pictures of their baby. She couldn't stop running her fingers along the images, nor could she keep her gaze from traveling back to John every few moments, astonished at his expression. Finally, someone to echo her wonderment. For the moment, it seemed they had risen beyond our circumstances. They were almost like any other proud parents, sharing a common joy.

John may not be offering a life together, but the fact he was interested, excited, about their baby was a sweet, sweet gift. And April wouldn't take that for granted.

The ultrasound appointment had been an emotionally charged experience for John. *He'd glimpsed his child.* Despite all the bad going on—and there was plenty of it—seeing his son or daughter waving its arms on the screen, scrunching up its face—for a moment, in 3D even—making all the expressions of a newborn... How could he not feel a swell of wonder? Even a measure of joy?

Sharing that joy with April was another strange thing altogether.

But now here they were in Dr. Fuller's exam room, and the good feelings from the ultrasound had evaporated into the uncertainty and fear of not knowing why April was feeling so poorly, or what her blood work meant to her health.

John stood in the corner, hands in pockets, and avoided looking at the large posters displaying the female reproductive system. The plastic model of a uterus sitting on the counter did nothing to make him more comfortable.

The doctor's smile didn't reach his eyes. "Hello again, April. John." After shaking both their hands, he sat in his swivel chair. He leaned toward them with his forearms on his knees. "April, I'm going to be referring you to a perinatologist. That's a maternal-fetal medicine specialist who is called in to work with higher-risk pregnancies. With unexpected test results like yours, it's always best to be careful."

Higher-risk. John's stomach dropped and he felt his eyes bulge. He looked to April, whose mouth was drawn into a tight line. Her color turned especially pallid—whether from the ultraviolet lights or the word "perinatologist" John didn't know. Adrenaline coursed through his veins.

Dr. Fuller stood in front of April and felt the lymph nodes in her neck. He lifted her arm, examining it on both sides. "How long have you had this rash on your arm?"

April blinked and drew her brows together. "What rash?" She looked down at her arm. "Huh. I hadn't noticed. Maybe John's detergent? But it doesn't bother me at all. Not itchy or anything."

John's gaze skated to the doctor.

Dr. Fuller's eyebrows puckered and his lips thinned. "April, we have to talk about the most recent blood work."

Chapter Twenty-Eight

Tori pulled Jenni's hair back behind her shoulders and ran a hand down its length. "How you holding up?"

Jenni pulled her legs up under her and took a deep, cleansing breath. "I miss him."

Tori nodded but didn't try to fill the void with words. Jenni pointed her face to the ceiling and silently prayed.

"It's been little more than a week, but it feels like an eternity. I don't know if I can do this."

Beloved, you can do all things through Me, she felt God's whisper in her soul.

She couldn't hide forever. She still loved him. "What am I supposed to do, Tori? Get over it?" *Offer to be stepmom to a hooker's baby?* She swallowed hard. "Should I break the engagement? Tell John I don't want to see him again?"

"Is that how you feel?" Tori's eyes were soft, her voice non-judgmental.

Jenni rubbed at the space between her eyebrows. "That's the trouble. It's *not* how I feel, no matter how hard I try to convince myself it is."

Her mother's voice carried from down the hall. "Jenni, I'm heading to the store. Need anything?"

Yeah. Her fiancé. She cleared her throat and answered loud enough for her mother to hear. "No, Mom. I'm fine." She stood and crossed the room

Was there ever a bigger lie? She could barely stand being away from John for a week. She positively *ached* for him. Even knowing he was spending time trying to help *that woman*, she longed to be with him. She wanted his arms around her, his lips soothing her. Tori's presence helped, but no arms other than John's could truly comfort her.

"I'll bring you back some mint hot cocoa."

Jenni captured her bottom lip between her teeth and looked at the strip of photo-booth images tucked into the edge of her dresser mirror. John and her. "Okay." Yeah, chocolate was a good idea.

"Tori, I've got you covered too."

"No thanks, Laura. I've got to get to work."

"Okay then. See you girls later." The front door opened then closed.

Tori came to stand beside Jenni, making eye contact in her dresser mirror. "How much does your mom know?"

"Just the main event. Not the details."

All her mother knew was that John was having a baby with someone else, someone from his past. Even without the shady details it was enough for her to conclude unequivocally what Jenni ought to do.

"Of course she thinks I should wash my hands of the whole, messy situation." *Kick the man to the curb, and find another.* She'd told Jenni that she didn't deserve this kind of pain; it didn't matter that the situation was created before they'd ever met and that John had been a rock of faithfulness since Jenni had known him.

"But it's not so simple, is it?"

"No." Jenni leaned her head onto Tori's shoulder and expelled a slow breath. "Tori, should I call him?"

Tori shook her head. "Only you can decide that."

"Thanks for coming by, checking up on me. Keep praying, okay?"

"Of course. You're my best friend, Jenni."

"I can say that I'm really learning to lean on God through this."

"Good." Tori embraced her then stood back and looked her in the eye. "Call me any time, you hear me?"

After saying goodbye, Tori left and Jenni was alone with nothing but her thoughts. Placing her palm on the leather cover of her Bible, she soaked up peace. Despite how bad she hurt, she sensed God's faithful presence with her, and strength was seeping back into her spirit. Enough strength, she hoped, to call and talk to John today. Gripping the phone, her hands shook too much to punch in the numbers. Maybe she wasn't strong enough after all. But she had to try.

Please God, get me through this.

With trembling fingers, she finally managed to dial and hit Send. It rang once. Twice. Heart tripping, she almost hung up in panic, but then John's voice came on the line, hopeful and heavy with emotion. "Jenni?"

Her heart cracked at the sound of her name on his lips. "Yes. It's me." What to say? She hadn't planned that out.

"How are you?"

"He's carrying me through." That was the truth, no matter how many nights she'd cried herself to sleep, how many meals she didn't eat, or how many temptations she'd faced down.

"Good." He let out a long, heavy sigh. Jenni felt the weight of it on her end of the line. "I miss you." His pinched voice undid her and she closed her eyes to soak it in.

"John…we need to talk."

"Just tell me where."

"The coffee shop?"

"I can be there in twenty minutes."

A sad smile curved her mouth. He was trying so hard, must hurt so bad. "Twenty minutes then…" She sucked in a breath. "John?"

"Yes?"

Her tongue froze and her shoulders drooped. "I… See you in twenty minutes." It wasn't what she wanted to say, but it was all she could get out.

Fifteen minutes later Jenni sat at the coffee shop with her hands wrapped around a hot cappuccino, trying in vain to steady her hands and heart. The door opened with a jangle, her head went up, and she saw him. Dressed in dark wash jeans and a brown cabled sweater, blowing into his hands as he scanned the room. Then he found her.

With a hesitant upward tip of his lips, he approached her little table and sat. "Hey."

"Hey."

He looked unsure what to do next, as if waiting for a cue from *her.* Unable to bear the chasm any longer, she reached for his hand. He drew in a deep breath and placed his other hand over top.

He inched forward. "How have you really been?" Worry etched his brow as he searched her soul—looking for the truth.

Jenni blinked, swallowing a gasp. Did he…*know*? "Been better." She pulled her left hand into her lap and ran her fingernail along the side of her thumb.

"Jenni?" He skimmed gentle fingers over her hand, plying for a fuller answer. "Please… I'm worried about you."

Somehow, he *did* know. She felt certain of it. "I'll be okay." She steadied herself with a fortifying breath. "John…" *God, give me the right words.* "John, it's been…hard. I can't make any promises right now. I'm…confused."

He looked stricken, but then his features smoothed to a calm acceptance. Closing his eyes, he nodded. "I understand."

Jenni slipped her hand from beneath his and touched her fingertips to his face. Ran her thumb across his cheek. "I'm not done. I'm confused…overwhelmed. But…I know that *I love you*. There's no confusion about that."

He met her gaze and held it, hope flickering in his eyes.

"That one fact has come into sharp focus this week. None of this changes how I feel about you. I…" She chewed her lip, wondering if what she wanted to say was more selfish than anything else. "I want to be there for you through this. I want to try. I just…can't give you any guarantees right now. So this might be unfair to do to you. But I want to try to be at your side through this."

He grasped both her hands in his and brought them to his lips. "I'll take it. I'll take you with or without guarantees."

He touched his forehead to her hands, and his shoulders rose and fell several times. When he lifted his gaze, his eyes were wet.

Jenni's heart twisted in her chest. "Oh, John," she whispered. She wanted to hold him, to reach for him, but was confined to the table. "Let's go somewhere else. A walk at the park or something."

They stood and went out the door hand in hand and nothing had felt so right since that woman showed up. They headed toward his car but before she could open her door, he slid his arm around her waist and pulled her close. Cradled her under his chin, cocooned her within his arms. Tension melted off her shoulders and evaporated with her sigh. It was the kind of embrace she never wanted to be free from.

She rested her cheek against his chest and wrapped her arms tight around his waist. His pulse throbbed against her throat. He pressed his face to the top of her head, his body surrounding her with warmth and strength. This was what she'd been aching for, what she needed, where she belonged.

She felt moisture on her lashes, the slight convulsion of her shoulders. There was tension in him as well, his muscles taut, his grip strong. His body quaked against hers, emotion to match her own, and she squeezed him tighter.

Stroking the back of her head, John buried his face in her hair close to her ear, and whispered, "Thank you, God."

Jenni moved her hands to his chest and raised her face to see him. His misty gaze bore into her as he ran his fingers through her hair and then framed her damp face with both of his hands. "Oh, Jenni." Warmth oozed through her veins as he breathed out her name. She covered his hand with hers, fingers tingling with the touch. His eyes were searching her, loving her. Healing her.

He swayed toward her and she held her breath as he brought his gentle lips to hers—soft, warm, and grateful. Her head spun. Emotions crashed over her. It was all too much. *I love you*, her soul cried out.

He feathered another kiss on her lips, drawing out a shuddering exhale. Her heart shifted rhythms, hammering against her ribs. This was John, the man who held every inch of her heart.

Need uncoiled deep within her middle and fanned out through her limbs. Her legs went weak, threatening to drop her, but John held on like he had no intention of ever letting her go. The tears slid from the corners of her eyes then, silently rolling down the sides of her upturned face.

He responded to her urgency, his gentleness giving way to burning intent. She felt the catch in her throat, the surprise as he dove into her, his kiss building, intensifying till she lost all ability to think. He held her with a hand at the small of her back, his palm braced against her spine, locking her in place. The other hand cradled the back of her head.

She sagged against him as his mouth claimed hers, bold and possessive. Stealing her breath. Stealing her heart. Again.

He loved her. She felt it in her bones.

He relaxed his grip and eased back from her, but she fought to hold on, afraid of releasing him.

Only when his voice hummed in her ear did the fog begin to clear. His breath tickled her ear as he whispered, "We *are* still in the parking lot you know."

Chest heaving, Jenni glanced around and saw two elderly women giving them looks as they shuffled into the coffee shop. She released uncurled her fingers from his sweater. "Oops." She slid a peek at John. His smile singed her belly.

"Yeah, oops." He breathed a laugh and touched his nose to hers.

Jenni's lips curved into a smile and she tamped down the ominous warning circling her heart. The one that told her it wasn't really going to be this easy.

They strolled through the park hand-in-hand, neither wanting to face the inevitable questions awaiting them. Jenni swallowed the tightness in her throat and looked up at John. "What's her name?"

A lengthy pause stretched between them before he answered. "April."

The name wrenched Jenni's heart. Personified her. And it was a beautiful name. Secretly she'd been hoping it was something ugly or plain.

A gust of wind rattled through the trees overhead. "So…what's happened this week?"

The heaviness in his sigh was palpable. He led her to a bench to sit. "Well…I took her to see a doctor. She hadn't been to see one at all."

Jenni shuddered. What kind of woman wouldn't get medical care during pregnancy?

As if sensing her thoughts, John shot her a glance "She couldn't afford one. Everyone around her was pushing her to get an abortion and the free clinic had done the same."

Her conscience pricked, and she resented it. She nodded and he continued.

"Her blood tests showed she's anemic, so they put her on iron. But…" He bit his lip and a twinge of jealousy stirred. Was he *worried* about her? "The doctor is concerned by her bloodwork. She has another appointment Friday."

Shame clawed its way through Jenni's chest. She had to do better than this, to melt some of her icy thoughts. She gripped his hand. "Is she really sick?"

"I don't know. Maybe the test results got screwed up or something. Nothing is certain right now."

Panic knotted her gut. "It's not...I mean, *you're* okay, right?"

The humiliation in his eyes made her want to cry. "It's nothing like that. I'm fine."

The lines on his face revealed the weight of the burden he was carrying. And though she couldn't help but feel some animosity toward this woman—*April*—Jenni had compassion for John. Of course this was hard for him. He felt responsible.

She stroked the back of his hand. "What can I do?"

"Just what you're doing now—listening and being here." He kissed her fingers.

"And the...pregnancy?"

"Amazingly, the baby looks healthy—strong as an ox." He smiled, and again the blade twisted in Jenni's heart.

Oh God, God—I don't think I can do this. It's too much! You ask too much.

Swallowing, she blinked away the tears before John could see them. She wanted only to ease his burden, not add to it.

A duck waddled toward them, a reminder of easier times, and her chest burned. No bread crumbs today.

He led her to stand and she watched her feet moving through the yellowing grass. "What time is the appointment Friday?"

"Early—eight-thirty. It should take about an hour. The doctor said that although the full results might take a couple of weeks, they should be able to tell us something immediately."

Jenni's gaze reached out toward the horizon. She dragged in a breath. "I'll pray."

John stopped and looked at her with rounded eyes, and nodded solemnly. Clearing her throat, Jenni gave him a tight-lipped grin. She couldn't tell him that her motives weren't all pure.

If April was sick, she'd need even more attention and care from John. If she was healthy, maybe their lives would be a little less complicated. Everyone wanted the same thing, and that was what was important, right?

Chapter Twenty-Nine

John pinned his eyes to the road ahead. Beside him, April shivered and rubbed her arms. "I didn't think it ever got cold in Southern California."

Her comment broke the silence permeating the car.

"Here." John flipped on the heater as they drove through the morning fog. He pulled onto the freeway, glad he'd accounted for rush hour, and found his thoughts returning again to Dr. Fuller's office.

April, we have to talk about the most recent blood work.

The scene had been replayed in John's mind over and over. The doctor had studied his chart, searching it, like he was looking for his next line in a medical drama. His focus had shifted again to April. "Your red cell and platelet counts are low, as well as your white cell count, and we've found some circulating lymphoblasts." He'd paused then, as if for effect.

John had swung his head toward April, whose eyes were glued to the doctor. His heart raced. What did that mean? Could the man just spit it out? In English?

Finally, Dr. Fuller had drawn a breath and laid it out there. "I'm referring you to a hematologist to rule out leukemia."

And with those words cycling through his thoughts, inspiring his prayers, John had been a bit dazed ever since. Seeing Jenni had bolstered his strength, but he hadn't told her the full details. He wasn't ready to lay that much on her, to send her running again. They'd know more soon. Very soon.

April sipped from her Styrofoam cup, set her decaf in the cup holder, then leaned her head against the back of the seat and let her eyes close. John fixed his on a gap in traffic and squeezed into the left lane.

The hematologist was on the other side of town and John had to refer to his printed MapQuest directions several times along the way. They pulled into the parking lot then John cut the engine and turned his attention to the passenger seat.

April's gaze was glued to her hands, clasped around her belly. "Thanks for doing this, John. It's more than I have a right to ask of you." Looking out her window, she exhaled, then reached for the door handle.

John unbuckled his seatbelt. "I wouldn't send you alone."

She hesitated before getting out. "I know."

They found their way to the right suite number and for once didn't have to wait before being called back. April sat like a statue on the exam table. She didn't look at John, she didn't look at anything...just stared ahead. Her eyes closed, and her breath shook, but then she became still and statuesque again.

John's nerves were shot too, but he tried to hide it. He offered a smile, hoping to dispel her fears.

The door hinges whined and the doctor entered—a man in his mid-fifties with gray hair, and a kind smile.

"Hello, I'm Dr. Corbin." He shook their hands, then tried to reassure them that the procedure was simple. He explained what a bone marrow exam was and talked them through both the aspiration and the biopsy.

John hoped April was getting more out of his pep talk than he was.

A crinkly paper sheet covered April as she lay on her side. She said nothing as the doctor prepared the anesthetic. Feeling useless, John backed into the corner of the room and stayed out of the way while the doctor administered several shots to numb the area. April closed her eyes tightly with each prick then opened them again, focusing on some unseen vision on the far wall of the room.

Dr. Corbin dropped the needle onto a metal tray. "I'll be back in a few minutes, once the anesthesia's had time to take effect. Sit tight."

Just the two of them now. John uncrossed his arms and pushed away from the wall he'd been leaning on. Doctor's offices had a way of making April appear especially pale. Had to be the fluorescent lights.

Was there something John was supposed to do? He caught her eye. "You doin' okay?"

"Yeah. I think so. So far so good." She offered a weak smile, which he reciprocated, glad that she seemed to be holding it together.

The doctor returned and tested the site with his finger. "Okay, looks like you're all numbed up." Good thing the doctor had a good-natured sense of humor because John was having trouble finding his.

A nurse joined them and stood beside a metal tray of instruments, kept discreetly out of April's view. The doctor made a small incision which April didn't seem to notice, and John tried not to. Then he handed the scalpel back to the nurse and held his hand out for the next instrument. April stared straight ahead, as if she were in a trance.

When the nurse extended the first needle to the doctor, April suddenly lost her composed veneer. Her wide, frightened blue eyes locked onto his. "John?" Shimmering tears ran across the bridge of her nose onto the table.

John's chest tightened. Intuitively, he moved closer and took her hand. Her hold was so strong it prickled. She squeezed her eyes, breathing too fast.

John leaned down near her ear and smoothed her hair. "Shh. Just relax. Breathe slowly…that's better."

Brown liquid traveled up a tube from April's hip to a syringe vial held by the doctor. Trying not to grimace, John focused on April's face. She was tense, braced.

Suddenly her tightly-closed eyes fluttered opened and she released a terrified gasp. "My leg!"

"I'm sorry, I know it feels strange. We're almost done with this part now, April," the doctor said. "Don't you worry."

Her grip tightened and her eyes shut tight as the long needle was slowly extracted from her hip bone. She exhaled loudly and John held back a shudder.

"All right, now—one down, one more to go. I'll try to be quick. You're doing great. You feeling okay?"

April looked at John with pleading eyes. Locking his gaze on hers, John gave a reassuring nod. "You're doing fine."

She nodded back, and blinked several times. Her tongue darted out across her lips. "Yeah. I'm okay." Her gaze remained fixed on him.

The next needle was more difficult to insert, and the doctor had to maneuver it this way and that to get it positioned properly. John looked away. Trained his eyes on April.

He brushed the hair from her forehead. "You're doing fine. It'll be over soon. Shh. Breathe."

She sucked in a breath as the needle was removed, and then her whole body wilted. She took several deep breaths before her grasp on John's hand loosened.

"That's some kung-fu grip you have there." He smiled.

She offered a weak laugh. "Sorry."

"Don't be."

The doctor spread a large bandage over the incision site and had April roll onto her back.

"All right, we're all done. You did marvelously. You'll need to lie down for about fifteen minutes or so to apply pressure to the biopsy site. I'm going to have a preliminary look at the marrow in the meantime."

"Thanks," John answered for her.

And again they were alone. April lay on her back staring at the ceiling tiles. Then she turned her head to look at John. "What if it's bad?"

His jaw muscles twitched. "We'll cross that bridge when we come to it."

She nodded and turned to stare at the ceiling again. A heavy silence filled the room.

"I'm scared."

"I know."

What else could he say? What was he supposed to say? "I'm sorry."

She took a deep breath and then blew it out. Time ticked slowly by, until Dr. Corbin reappeared. He helped April into a sitting position, and then took a seat in his swivel chair across from both of them.

He didn't scan his papers for the words he needed, he simply looked April in the eye and told the truth.

"April, I'm afraid the test has come back positive for acute leukemia."

No shock, no emotion. John felt nothing. His gaze traveled the room. Slowly. He turned over the pronouncement in his mind, tried to make sense of it, find a reaction. There was none.

But he watched the wind get knocked out of April, saw her struggle for air. And he watched the doctor help her to the sink just in time to vomit. John saw all this, but it wasn't real.

They moved back to their seats and he blinked. Tried to focus on what Dr. Corbin was saying.

"The chromosome studies will take several days to complete, and then we'll know better what we're dealing with. Acute Leukemia can take two forms and each has many stages. I'm sorry I don't have more details for you about that yet. But we'll need to start treatment right away."

April nodded but John wasn't sure she comprehended. For him, reality was settling over the room like a storm cloud.

April *was* sick. Very sick.

Though his head had caught up, his emotions lagged behind and he still did not have a proper reaction to display. He just nodded like a bobble-head doll as the doctor continued.

"As soon as we have the test results in hand, we'll want to admit you to the hospital and start you on chemotherapy."

The doctor rambled on, but April raised a hand to stop him. "What about the baby?"

She and John both stared at the doctor.

"Chemotherapy *is* very dangerous to a fetus in the *first* trimester, and we always recommend a termination in that case. However, in the second and third trimesters the risk is minimal. You should be able to continue your pregnancy." As if sensing April's trepidation and resistance, he took a detour. "Let's wait to get all the results in before exploring our options. We should have them within a couple of days."

April shook her head in protest but apparently found no words to her liking. Dr. Corbin looked at each of them in turn before standing. He squeezed first her shoulder, then John's, before heading to the door.

"We'll be in touch in a few days." He fixed his eyes on John. "Call if you have any questions or need anything at all." He held his gaze a moment before slipping out the door, leaving them alone.

Turning toward April, John expected tears. Outrage. She displayed neither. Merely shook her head and took a deep breath, her serene mask in place once more.

"I'd like to get dressed now. I'll meet you out there."

At a loss, John simply said, "Okay," and left her alone to change.

Throughout the ride home, April stared straight ahead and didn't speak a word. John stole glances now and then, but always she sat perfectly still, no emotion displayed on her face.

He couldn't begin to imagine what thoughts and feelings rolled through her right now. But he tried. "April? It'll be okay… You'll be okay." He turned his face toward her. "You won't be alone."

A slow nod of acknowledgment but she still didn't speak. She seemed completely lost in thought—and wasn't sharing those thoughts with John.

John unlocked the apartment door and swung it open for April. She set her purse down and turned blank eyes on John.

"I'm just gonna use the bathroom."

The first words he'd heard from her since they'd left the appointment. He affected a small smile. "Okay. I'll be here."

Then she moved, zombie-like, down the hall and through the door on the left. The lock clicked and John scrubbed his hands over his face, trying to shake off the tension knotting his shoulders. If she would just talk about it, maybe he could figure out what to do. But she needed time. He understood that. It hadn't sunk in.

He muddled about in the kitchen for something to do, finally making two mugs of hot chocolate. He added an extra scoop of cocoa to their mugs and swirled an extra mound of Redi-Whip on top. And then he sat at the table and waited.

Ten minutes later the whipped cream in April's mug had dissolved into the liquid, and she hadn't yet emerged. John frowned, pushing his empty mug away, then got up and headed down the hallway. He didn't want to intrude on her privacy, just wanted to make sure she was all right. He lifted his knuckles to tap on the bathroom door then froze, hand in mid-air. Muffled crying came from inside and his chest squeezed.

"April?"

No response.

He knocked on the door. "April, can I come in?" He tested the door handle. Locked. "Come on, let me in…please."

She didn't answer and John rubbed his mouth. Could he fault her for seeking out a bit of privacy while this news sank in?

He retreated from the hallway and waited in the living room. And he prayed.

Ten minutes, twenty-five minutes. Still she didn't come out, wouldn't answer him when he spoke to her through the door. Pacing the hallway, John raked his hands through his hair and prayed, wondering what on earth to do. How long should he leave her in there to grieve alone? Was this normal and healthy in light of the circumstances?

Please, God. What do I do?

Jenni's emotions were a big, tangly mess. She pressed the heels of her hands to her eyes, wishing she could just skip the day. The week. The nebulous future.

Giving up on the idea of breakfast, she picked up her plate of eggs and scraped them into Sadie's dish. The dog happily devoured them. "At least one of us still has an appetite."

Jenni went out back and sat on the swing. She'd promised John she would pray, and she had been, but it was a struggle. She *wanted* to get past her bitterness, but at the thought of some other woman in bed with John, touching him, joining to him, growing his baby in her belly, a sour taste coated her tongue.

She massaged her throat. *Oh God, please. Don't let April be sick on top of everything else. I just don't have that much compassion to give. Please Lord, don't ask it of me. Don't ask it of John.*

Hadn't they overcome enough? Proven their faith enough?

I am the Lord, who leaves the ninety-nine to go after the one.

The wind gusted as a sense of betrayal whipped through her spirit. It wasn't fair. Closing herself off, she sought solitude within the confines of her own thoughts, nursing her frustration.

What was she supposed to do?

Feed my sheep.

Words spoken to Peter after Christ's resurrection. After he'd denied Him.

Had *Jenni* denied Him? Was she doing it now? Her eyes burned and she squeezed them shut. She was so tired of crying. Surely she could have filled an ocean by now.

I have put your tears in My bottle; they are written in My book.

A sunbeam cut through the early November clouds and caressed her where she sat. Yes, God had seen every tear. And loved her through them. And He would always do so.

Feed my sheep.

But I am your sheep! And I feel so lost.

She is even more lost than you are. And I love her.

Her stomach clenched. *She doesn't deserve it.*

Neither do you.

Jenni's thoughts seized as truth pierced her heart. How could she argue? She didn't deserve the kind of love Christ had shown her, why should she expect Him to love April any less?

She pictured her then—a frightened, traumatized woman—and a speck of compassion stirred. But it died the moment Jenni's fiancé entered the scene and placed a hand on April's swollen belly. *God* may love her, but…

"But I'm not You," she whispered. Bits of Scripture floated through her memory. *Love covers over all wrongs… Love covers a multitude of sins… If anyone says, "I love God," yet hates his brother, he is a liar.*

Jenni rubbed her temples. She certainly didn't have that kind of love.

Let My love flow through you.

Her cell phone rang, making her jump. John's name flashed across the screen, and she moved swift fingers to answer.

"Jenni? Does that offer still stand?" His voice strained across the line.

Her lungs seized. "What offer?"

"To be there for me through all of this."

"Of course. What happened?"

John blew air into his hands as he glanced again at the locked bathroom door. Concern scraped through his gut. The woman had just found out she had leukemia and had locked herself in his bathroom for the last forty-five minutes. He hadn't known what else to do but call Jenni.

Fifteen minutes after making the call, he opened the front door to find her standing on his doorstep looking like a trapped animal. A beautiful, trapped animal. She shifted her weight, peering around him into the apartment.

John pleaded with his eyes for her to understand. To forgive him for calling her here. "She's still in there. Jenni, I don't know what to do."

Jenni rubbed her lips together, and stepped inside. She gazed down the hall, then back at John. One tentative step toward the bathroom, then another, then she quickly crossed the rest of the space.

She inclined her head close to the door. "April?" Her gaze flicked to his, then down to the knob. "April, can you hear me? What are you doing in there?"

John came and stood beside her. She cleared her throat. "April...this is Jenni."

"Jenni?"

At the sound of April's scratchy voice, they looked at each other, eyes wide, and John nodded encouragement.

Jenni rubbed her lips together again. "Yes. It's me. Are you ready to come out?"

"I...I don't think so."

"Well...how about if I came in there instead? It would be easier to talk without this door between us."

A shuffling sounded, then the click of the lock. Jenni turned the handle and cracked the door. For a flash, John saw April huddled in the bathtub, and then the door gently closed again.

There was nothing he could do but pray, and hope that God knew what He was doing. He stood in the hallway, alone, while Jenni and April talked on the other side of the door.

His fiancée and the mother of his unborn child.

Chapter Thirty

"Oh God, help." Jenni eased the door shut before shakily turning to face the room. The woman was huddled in the bathtub in a fetal position, head turned away toward the wall. Jenni took in the image of her thin arms wrapped around her legs and messy beach-blond hair spilling forward over her knees. She looked like a terrified child.

Yes, My child.

Heart thrashing, Jenni moistened her lips and inched toward her. She lowered herself onto the lid of the commode then managed a raspy whisper. "Hi."

"Hey." April's rounded back expanded with a tremulous breath, but she didn't look up.

Jenni's pulse was thready in her throat. Her hands had been pressed together between her knees, and now she rubbed them down the fabric on her thighs. "John told me about the appointment. Is there…anything I can do?"

A sniffle, then a soft, feminine, tear-soaked voice. "Why would you want to do anything for me? Haven't I ruined everything for you? Isn't that what you're really thinking?"

Heat crept into Jenni's cheeks. "I…" A thick swell of shame rolled over her. But she couldn't let that shame keep her from speaking now. "Yeah. I thought so at first." Any woman would have felt the same way. That didn't make it right though. "But…I've had time to think since then. I want to help. What can I do?"

April gave a bitter laugh. "Nobody can do anything. I just have to accept it and deal with it. On my own. Somehow."

"You're not on your own, April." The sincerity in Jenni's voice, in her *heart*, shocked her. As much as she still hurt, she couldn't stand to see this woman suffering without hope. Without God. Her throat constricted at the thought. "I'm here, and John is right outside that door. You can bet he's praying for you right now."

"Praying? That's not going to help anything. Besides...I know John wishes I wasn't here, that I'd never shown up. You both do. And I get it, believe me." Her voice pinched off and she took in another shuddering breath. "I wish I hadn't," she said in a hoarse whisper. "It would have been better if he'd never known."

No. Jenni shook her head and pulled in a shaky breath of her own. "That's not true and John had a right to know." Her throat ached from the effort to hold back tears. She forced her next words out. "Coming here was the right thing." She swallowed convulsively several times, trying to regain control of her roiling emotions. This was a conversation she never imagined having.

"Why are you really here, Jenni? Why would you possibly come?"

She blinked. "I...I want to help. John was worried and I..." What *was* she doing here? What were any of them doing here?

"You're here for him then." It was a statement, not a question. "You're here for John. John's here for the baby. Nobody is here for *me*."

Was that true? Was that Jenni's only reason for coming? She looked over April's suffering form again and felt her twisted heart untangle a little more.

No. It wasn't just for John. It was for her God, who was giving her an unnatural—*super*natural—tenderness toward this hurting woman. Jenni's pulse slowed to a normal rhythm for the first time since John had called her. She straightened and when she spoke there was a steadiness in her voice she hadn't expected to find. "I'm here partly for John, yes. Because I love him. But also because I *care*. I don't want to see you suffering alone. I've been praying for you, April. So has John. He'd feel a lot better if you'd come out. Please."

Silence hung in the air and Jenni held her breath. Then April finally turned her face toward Jenni. Mascara smudged beneath her lashes and ran in muddy trails down her fair cheeks. Her face was blotchy, eyes red and puffy, but Jenni could see that she was beautiful.

So this was her.

"You both must think I'm acting like a child having a tantrum, locking myself in here like this."

"No. I understand." *All too well.* Swallowing a jolt of jitters, Jenni held out her hand. "Come on."

April's wary eyes travelled between Jenni's face and the offered hand. She reached for it, curling her fingers around Jenni's, and allowed her to help her up. As she stepped out of the bathtub, Jenni caught her first sight of April's softly protruding belly. She felt the sharp intake of breath and gulped back her reaction. *Steady now.*

She forced a smile and looked April in the eye. "By the way, we haven't formally met. I'm Jenni."

"April." No smile. Suspicion still clouded her gaze, but she was talking and Jenni was getting her out of the bathroom, and that's all that mattered for now.

"Wait a sec." April turned on the tap and splashed her face, running fingers under her lashes. Her hair fell to her shoulders in a bright wave as she righted herself.

A strange pang shot through Jenni. *Blonde.* Was that what John preferred?

April patted her face dry and rehung the hand towel. "Okay." She exhaled through pursed lips and turned to Jenni. "I think I'm ready now."

"Good." Giving herself a mental shake, Jenni curved her lips upward and opened the door.

John's face was clouded with a mixture of relief and discomfort when Jenni and April stepped out of the bathroom together. Jenni gave him a smile to assure him she was okay. As for April, that remained to be seen.

"I put out some cheese and crackers." John gestured toward a plate of snacks on the table. "Come on, let's sit."

April's blue eyes met Jenni's as she took up a Ritz and stacked some Colby Jack on top. *Piercing, electric blue.* Jenni shifted her brown gaze and stood. "Thirsty?" Entering the kitchen, she shrugged off her instant, immature inclination to make a show of being comfortable navigating John's apartment. She poured a glass of milk and set it in front of April.

"Thank you." She remained quiet, stiff.

John filled the air with light conversation, and Jenni followed suit, until April dabbed a paper towel to the corners of her mouth. "If you two don't mind, I think I'm going to go lay down for awhile. I'm exhausted."

John nodded. "Yeah, of course."

April rose and carried her glass to the sink, absently rubbing a hand over her belly as she went. Jenni blinked away. Her stomach dipped as April disappeared into John's room—to sleep in his bed.

She closed her eyes and gave herself a mental shake. John was hers. And she sensed his longing, his desire, in every kiss. April didn't change that.

John stood and cleared the plate of crackers from the table, then Jenni scraped her own chair back and wrapped up the cheese and stuck it in the fridge, not knowing how to feel.

John came to stand in front of her and ran his hands up and down her arms. "Thanks for coming." Gripping her shoulders, he pulled her into a bear hug and rocked her back and forth.

"You're welcome." She held him tight. "I'm so sorry this is happening."

"Yeah, me too."

A quiet moment passed then John kissed her forehead, the touch of his lips a subtle torture. "I'll make us some coffee." He released her and went to his brewer. Jenni tried to shake off the sudden loneliness at his departure. This wasn't about her right now. She had to remember that.

"There's Vanilla-Caramel Creamer in the fridge for you."

One of her favorites. She smiled and retrieved the bottle. "And do you want the Hazelnut?"

"Of course." He ginned at her.

Moments later, they made their way to the living room with their mugs. Jenni blew across the top of her brew, then set it on the table to cool.

John moved a pillow out from behind him and settled deeper into the cushions, pushing up the sleeves of his dark blue, round-neck T. "We'll find out more about her leukemia in a few days. Then we'll discuss treatment. They'll want to start her on chemo right away."

"Did they give you any sort of clue as to how bad this is?" Jenni tucked a leg up under her and sat facing him. John's concern was written all over his face.

"They don't want to speculate, but the way her symptoms are progressing could mean it's bad. I haven't had a chance to search the Internet about it yet, and I don't want to do that with April around until we hear back from the doctor." He took a sip of coffee then placed it on the table and looked away. "He said chemo isn't very risky for a fetus in the third trimester, but…"

"But you aren't convinced."

He nodded. "Besides, until we know exactly what kind of leukemia it is, there's no way to know what the treatment will even be like."

Jenni's gaze traveled down the hallway to where April slept, the tightness in her chest returning. "So she's going to stay here with you then?"

John paused lifted his hands in the air. "I don't know." He sighed. "I don't know what I'm supposed to do, Jenni. She won't be able to care for herself. She has no money, obviously can't work right now. I just don't know. I think they're going to want to admit her to the hospital. So, yeah, I guess she'll be here until we hear back from the doctor again."

Jenni nodded and chewed her lip. John's shoulders were tense with stress, the muscles of his forearms stretched taut. "Are *you* doing all right?" She smoothed the hair on the side of his face and stroked his cheek.

He released a deep breath. "I guess so. I think I'm still in shock. This doesn't seem real. Everything was perfect, and now…" He shook his head and stared out into nothingness.

Jenni scooted closer, entwined her arm with his, and rested her head on his shoulder. He took her hand and rubbed the pad of his thumb across her fingers. If only she could say something to give him comfort. But all she could do was caress his hand, press her lips to his shoulder, and pray.

"I'm here," she whispered. "I'm not going anywhere." She'd tell him later about school. About dropping her classes for the semester.

She felt him nod against her head. "God won't leave us, John. We have to believe that."

"You're right. He won't." He shifted toward her and lifted her face in his hand. "But you could have. And you haven't." He smoothed a wayward strand of her hair. "You didn't deserve this, Jenni. And I'm more sorry than you'll ever know."

"I know." *Please, John. Just don't let me ever doubt your love.*

He touched his lips to each of her eyelids then placed a kiss at the corner of her mouth, eliciting a shiver. Jenni felt more connected to John than she'd ever felt with anybody. But she hadn't shared with him what he and April had. Her stomach fisted.

With April here, literally in his bed, how could he not have memories of their night? Of her body. Of the pleasure it gave him. The pleasure Jenni couldn't give. Not before they stood before a minister in the presence of God.

She gulped down the nauseating thoughts. *God, please…please, clear my mind.*

"What's wrong? What is it?" Concern creasing his brow, he slid his fingers up into her hair, massaging.

She pressed her trembling lips together. "Nothing, I just…" The thoughts running through her mind had to stay with her alone.

He touched another kiss to her temple. "Just what? You can tell me anything."

No, not this. He'd think her a fool and it would only add to his burden. She lifted her downcast gaze. "I…I just love you so much." She draped her arms around his neck and leaned into his solid chest.

"Oh, honey. You have no idea how much I love hearing that." He brushed the hair back off of her face and shoulders. "Or how much I love you. I'm so glad you're here right now. It means everything to me." He lifted her face and brushed his lips along her cheek, nuzzling her with gentle kisses. "Absolutely everything." He paused mere inches from her mouth, his breath mingling with hers, warming her lips, making the blood whoosh in her ears. He smelled like hazelnut and mocha and her future.

But he didn't kiss her. Instead, he rested his forehead against hers and stroked her back.

"How's your mom reacted to this?"

Jenni shook her head. Ever since Jenni had made the decision and called John, the chasm between them had widened. "Not good. But I don't want to talk about that right now."

"Fair enough."

He stood and pulled her up with him.

"It's getting close to three. Don't want you to be late for work because of me."

"Yeah." Would the world ever stop spinning? She ran a hand through her hair and grabbed her purse. "I should go. But I'll call tonight after my shift."

At the door, John took her left hand, turned it over, and placed a kiss on her palm, sending butterflies dancing through her veins. He traced his thumb over her engagement ring before releasing her hand.

"Thank you, Jenni," he whispered. "You're an amazing woman."

She cupped the side of his face and brought her lips to his. "Call me later."

Chapter Thirty-One

John nudged the bowl of popcorn over and propped his feet on the coffee table. April sat beside him on the couch, sullen and withdrawn, as if she'd lost that drive that had first sent her hitchhiking from Vegas to Riverside to find him. An hour after waking from her afternoon nap she already looked exhausted. Purplish shadows underscored her eyes, and her shoulders slumped. As if the diagnosis itself was making her deteriorate before his very eyes.

John massaged the back of his neck and tried to focus on the screen. But the movie wasn't proving the distraction he'd hoped it would. All the what-ifs hammered away in his brain and John admitted, if only to himself, that he was nervous about what might lay ahead. How much more so must April be? He looked over and caught her staring into space. This was pointless; neither of them was interested in the film.

"Want me to turn it off?"

She turned clouded eyes to him. "Sorry, I guess I'm too distracted for a movie."

"That's okay." He clicked off the screen and looked at her. "What are you thinking?"

She squirmed and tucked her legs up under herself. "This will sound odd but I was actually thinking about Jenni. About why she came over today." She scratched at the side of her thumb. "I figured she hated me and I didn't blame her. But she was so...*nice* to me." Her hair hid her face as she looked down at her lap. "I don't get it."

Interesting that the thing snagging her thoughts at the moment wasn't her illness or becoming a mother, it was the kindness she'd been shown. John propped an elbow on the back cushion and leaned against his hand. "Jenni was concerned and wanted to help. Nobody wants to see you hurt or upset."

"But she doesn't even know me. And I'm realizing…neither do you really. I may be having your baby, but we know nothing about each other. Yet here we are sitting on your sofa watching movies, having a heart to heart. I knew you were a good person, and might help with the baby, but there's more to take on than even I realized. Why do you care so much what happens to me? Don't get me wrong, I'm grateful. So grateful. But…why?"

"I need a reason?"

"You're doing more than anyone else would. Going above and beyond." She lifted her shoulders.

"I'm not a hero or anything."

"But you are." She blinked at him. "To me you are, John."

"A hero wouldn't have gotten you pregnant to begin with."

"Are you kidding? It happens all the time and the guy disappears. You didn't have to take me in, arrange medical care, *give up your bedroom*. And then your girlfriend is nice to me, too?"

"She *is* pretty special," he whispered.

"This isn't an episode of Full House. In real life, most people just don't care. Not this much." Her voice had dropped under the weight of her confusion.

John studied the hardened lines around her eyes. He started to reach for her hand but thought better of it. "God cares, April. He cares very much."

She huffed. "Oh, I'm *sure* He does."

"What do you mean?"

"Nothing. Look, it's been a rough day and I just want to sleep. I'm going to go back to bed if that's all right."

"Of course. Let me know if you need anything."

April pushed herself up and stepped toward the hall, supporting herself with one hand on the back of the couch. The day had sapped a lot out of all of them, and April most of all. After she disappeared behind his bedroom door, he bowed his head to spend some much-needed time in prayer.

Sobs broke the silence of the night, pulling John from sleep. He made out the time on his DVD player—3:28 a.m. The couch creaked as he rose and padded across the living room. How long had she been crying?

Flipping on the hall light, he closed one eye against the brightness and rapped his knuckles on the bedroom door. "April? Can I come in?"

"Okay." Her broken voice stirred his sympathy.

John eased open the door and peered into the darkness. April lay with her back to him, the bed shaking with her convulsions.

"I'm sorry. I d-didn't mean to wake you." Her voice was thick and raspy, as if she'd been crying for hours.

He crossed the room and sat beside her. "It's okay."

"John, I'm s-scared."

His chest tightened. "I know. It's okay to be scared. But we haven't even heard back from the doctor yet. Let's take one day at a time, okay?"

"It's bad. I know it's bad." Her shoulders jerked.

"Why do you say that? You shouldn't think that way."

"I just know. I feel it."

John stared at the back of her head, stomach churning. "People live with leukemia for years, and they recover."

April just shook her head.

"Why assume the worst?"

"Because. I… It's my p-punishment." A new gush of tears poured onto her pillow. She pressed her face into the crumpled sheets and stifled a wail.

Her words struck John hard and he felt the blow in his very spirit. "*What?*"

She fought for breath then answered, "After everything I've done…I deserve it."

"No, April," he rushed to correct her. "God loves you. This isn't a punishment."

"How do you explain it then?"

"I can't. I don't know why this is happening. But I know that God loves you."

"He loves *you* maybe. But he hates me. He wants me to suffer and maybe I deserve it. But…" Her voice squeaked. "But why the baby? Am

I so vile that God despises my offspring? It's just a baby, John. An innocent baby who didn't ask for me to be its mother."

John's heart skidded to a stop and dropped to the floor as he tried to calm the chaotic storm in his chest. April's whole body convulsed with sobs. He placed a hand on her back. "April...When Hannah and Katy died, I blamed God too. Hated Him for it. Until I was so messed up I had nowhere else to turn. I knew I didn't deserve forgiveness but I begged for it anyway. Though I didn't need to beg, because I came to see God had been waiting for me to come to Him all along. He's waiting for you too, April. Not to punish you, but to love you...*and* the baby."

"But why is this happening?"

"I don't know. We don't always get answers. But, do you think losing my family was my punishment? That it was my fault?"

"Of course I don't."

"Well, this isn't a punishment for you either. It's not your fault."

John rubbed her back as she stared ahead.

"But you're a much better person than I am. You haven't done the things I've done."

"Actually April...I have. In case you've forgotten."

She rolled over then and found his eyes. "No. I haven't forgotten."

John shifted uncomfortably. "April..."

She turned away from him again. "Lay down with me for a minute, John. Please. I...I don't want to be alone."

The anguish in her voice twisted his gut. John's mind raced for a moment, but his heart won out. He brought his legs up onto the bed, stretched out on top of the covers, and rested his head on the pillow.

April kept her back to him, shoulders still quaking with her shuddering breath. "Thank you," she whimpered.

He blew out a nervous breath toward the ceiling and folded his hands behind his head. "You're welcome."

She scooted herself backward, closer to him, until her shoulder butted up against his ribcage and she was nestled under his arm. His heart knocked around in his chest, second guessing the wisdom of being there. But her continued soft crying assured him that she just needed someone to be close.

"John?" she squeaked. "Will you...hold me?"

"No...I can't."

Stillness wrapped itself around the room. Eventually April's breathing evened out into a deep, slumbering rhythm.

John eased himself off the bed and crept out into the hall. A whispered groan sounded in his throat and he ran his hands over his face, feeling more unsure than ever about…everything.

Chapter Thirty-Two

April tip-toed through the hall, surprised by the silence of the house. John was usually up early, making breakfast or phone calls when she emerged from the bedroom. She adjusted the blanket around her shoulders and steadied herself against the wall, legs feeling a bit unreliable. Nothing a little protein in her system didn't usually cure.

The hallway opened up to John's modest living room. The kitchen and dinette to her left, the couch just ahead to the right. And that's where she saw him. He lay on his back asleep, his chest rising and falling in deep, peaceful measure, one arm draped across his firm abdomen, the other bent up under his head. The poor man was probably wiped out after she'd ruined his sleep last night.

He'd stayed with her. Not all night, but at least until she fell asleep. He didn't have to do that. He didn't have to do anything at all. He said he wasn't a hero, but he was wrong. He'd always be hers.

She watched him for a moment, then approached and straightened his blanket. He had to be the most decent human being she'd ever met in her life. She ran her hand over her belly then knelt on the floor in front of him, memorizing the planes of his exquisite face. The line of his jaw from ear to chin, the tiny scar hidden on his cheekbone, his full brows framing eyes that drew her even when closed. Would her baby have those eyes? Better yet, his kindness?

Thank you, John Douglas. She bent toward him for one quick, simple kiss of gratitude. Just there on the side of his face. But when her lips touched his unshaven jaw, she couldn't bring herself to break contact right away. She lingered there, breathing him in, cataloging the feel of the man. The father of her child. Wishing things could be different.

She moved to feather one last kiss on the hollow of his cheek. But he turned toward her and, to her shock, entangled his lips with hers. And suddenly they were kissing. She felt her sharp intake of breath as his hand came to cradle the back of her neck. Her eyes fluttered closed and she ran her hands over his chest, her heart soaring. Maybe God didn't hate her after all.

He broke away with a horrified gasp. "What are you doing?" He wriggled away, pushing himself up to a sitting position.

April dropped down on her haunches, realization painfully dawning. "You... thought I was Jenni." She stuffed down the hurt. The loss.

"Of course I did." He rubbed at his lips then raked his hands through his disheveled hair.

April pressed her hand to her mouth. That look on his face, like he'd been tricked. "John, I'm sorry...I didn't mean to...I wasn't trying to...When you turned, I thought..." She closed her eyes. "Oh, I'm so stupid."

How could she think for one second that he might want her, after everything? And she would've been so willing. But now...

Mentally cursing herself, she wrapped her arms around her middle and hung her head. She'd just confirmed everything she'd made herself out to be in Las Vegas. Everything she'd begged him not to believe about her.

He pinched the bridge of his nose. "It's not your fault, April." He exhaled through his nostrils. "It's mine. I kissed you." He pointed his face to the ceiling and shook his head. "I'm the one who needs to apologize. That shouldn't have happened. Forgive me."

What? She stared at him, more confused by the man than ever. "There's nothing for me to forgive, John. You...thought I was Jenni. It was an accident."

"Yes, it was. An accident that can *never* happen again."

She nodded. "I know. I'm sorry."

"No more of that, okay? No more apologies." Somehow, he managed to find a gentle smile for her, righting her world again.

"Okay."

He was right, it couldn't happen again. She knew that. But she couldn't deny that part of her was glad it had happened.

"Have a seat and I'll make us some breakfast." He held her hand and pulled her up from the floor, giving her the sofa. When he went to the kitchen and started pulling out pans, she snuggled down into the warmth of the blanket he'd been sleeping with and inhaled his scent.

No, part of her wasn't sorry at all.

Guilt and uncertainty needled him as John folded the blanket and draped it over the arm rest of the couch. He knew God had called him to help April, to not turn her away. But maybe he was going about it wrong. Things were taking an uncomfortable turn. First with him lying down beside her, and then with that kiss. It was an accident on his part, but it was clear to him that April hoped for more. She was lonely and scared and apparently saw him as some sort of knight in shining armor. It was more than simple gratitude. She was falling for him. And he wasn't sure what to do about it, other than stay the course. Keep being honest with her and pray, pray, pray.

A knock sounded as John tossed the last pillow onto the couch. When he opened the door, Jenni stepped inside and flashed that prized grin. His blood warmed, chasing off the cloud surrounding him. *This* was the woman he loved. And he'd protect her as much as he could. One side of his mouth inched upward. "Good morning, beautiful."

Her cheeks flushed, drawing the other corner of John's lips into a full smile.

"Morning? It's nearly noon." She glanced down the hall toward the bedroom. "How is she?"

John's smile slipped. "Napping. She was up half the night." His sigh erased the blush on Jenni's face. "She's really scared. She thinks this is a punishment from God."

"Well… Maybe it is." She dropped her gaze to the floor.

"What? How can you even think that? Leukemia used by God as punishment?"

"God sometimes uses disease and illness as a natural consequence of our sin. Is it so hard to believe?" She picked at her fingernails, not meeting John's gaze.

He lifted her chin and spoke gently. "She didn't get an STD, she has leukemia. And she believes it's because God hates her *and* her baby. Jenni…," He ran his thumb along the soft curve of her cheek, "you know that's not the way it works."

A shadow crossed Jenni's face and she hauled in an unsteady breath. "You're right. I'm sorry." Her golden brown eyes met his. "I've got to be honest with you, John. I…still struggle with anger sometimes. Confusion. This isn't easy."

He opened his arms and she fell into them, burying her face in his chest. "I get it. Believe me." Her long silky hair hid her like a blanket, and John stroked away her shield. He leaned back to see her. "Hey, how about some coffee? I picked up your other favorite, coconut creamer, just for you."

Her cheeks lifted. "Yum."

Jenni fidgeted in her kitchen chair. Was today the day she'd decide she couldn't do this? She'd been very careful not to make promises.

The precarious balance they were hanging onto drove John to prayer as he brewed her coffee. *If I lost her…* Straightening his spine, John forced himself to release her to God as he released the cup from his grasp to hers. The daily surrender.

"Thanks." She blew ripples into her drink, then tasted it. "Mmm. You make the best coffee." She took another sip. "So…how's work?"

"Going good actually. I'm overseeing my department, working with foreign suppliers. Moving up. I've had to take a few days off…" He coughed as she removed her gaze from his. "How about you?"

She gave a playful smirk and quirked an eyebrow. "Well, it's *Just Juice*, ya know? Not exactly a career path. But hey, the new Banana Rama Smoothie is delicious!" Her chuckle tickled John's ears and made him laugh with her.

"But I did drop my classes for the semester." She held up a hand before he could speak. "It's already done. There was no way I could keep up with school while all this is going on. And I… I don't want to be out of the loop on anything. It's hard enough knowing she's here with you. I'm sorry if that sounds immature or jealous, but it's the truth."

He sobered. He was going to have to tell her about that kiss with April, wasn't he?

"Jenni…"

"You don't have to constantly assure me. It's not like I don't trust you, it's just—"

A sudden *crash* and *thump* startled them and they both jumped to their feet. John reached the bedroom door first and found April on the floor beside the bed. Jenni rushed to her other side and together they helped her into a sitting position.

"Are you all right?" Jenni rubbed April's back, concern flashing in her wide eyes.

"I was going to go to the bathroom. I got a little lightheaded and…I just went down."

Jenni and John exchanged a look, then John's gaze travelled back to April. "Did you lose consciousness?"

"I…don't…think so?" Her brow furrowed and she looked back and forth between them. "No, I'm sure I didn't."

They each took one of April's arms and pulled her to her feet. She wobbled and dipped, threatening to collapse again. Her pale hand fluttered to her forehead as she swayed. "I don't know what's wrong with me."

John's stomach clenched. He'd never seen her like this. "You need to take your iron and get some food in you. Lie down and I'll get your pills." His gaze swung to Jenni. "Can you stay with her for a minute please?" He scanned her face, afraid of what he might see, but she nodded him toward the kitchen.

"Go. We'll be fine." Jenni slid an arm under April, who draped hers over Jenni's neck.

"I'm so sorry. I don't know what…I'm sorry."

"It's okay," Jenni answered.

Leaving them, John shot up a thank-you prayer for Jenni's strength. When he returned, April was back in bed, and Jenni stood at her side like a mother. He handed over the medicine and watched as April downed it, along with an entire glass of orange juice.

"Thanks. I should feel better in a minute. I just got up too fast."

A muscle in John's jaw twitched. "Yeah, I'm sure you're right. You haven't eaten in awhile. You want a sandwich or something?"

"Um. Sure. Thanks."

"I'll make it." Jenni took a quick step toward the door. "You stay here."

My sweet Jenni, how difficult is this for you?

John fluffed the pillows behind April, then creaked onto the edge of the bed. She leaned back and gave him a smile. "Thank you, John." Her eyes rounded. "Oh!" She laid a hand on her belly.

"You okay?" John's heart tripped, his voice cracking like an adolescent teen's. He cleared his throat.

"Yes, everything is wonderful." Her eyes sparkled. "I think our baby likes that juice."

He held his breath and lowered his gaze to the spot where April's hand rested. Her belly leapt beneath her fingers and a strange protectiveness rose up in his chest.

"Was that...?" He searched her face and found a broad grin.

She laughed. "Yes." Taking his hand, she placed it where hers had been. Nothing. "Just wait," she whispered, her countenance lit up from the inside.

A soft pressure against his hand yanked John's attention back to April's belly. He inhaled sharply, remembering the feeling well. A small foot was stretching out, demanding more room. For a moment he was pulled back through time and was sitting not with April, but Hannah, enjoying Katy's little flutters and kicks.

Swallowing against the tightness in his throat, he moved both hands to the place his child squirmed and rolled. It must be doing okay in there, this part of himself. He bent closer and raised his eyes to April. Shaking his head in wonder, he gently stroked his thumbs back and forth over her belly, coaxing another kick. His mouth curved and warmth spread through his chest.

A gasp sounded behind him, snapping his head back up. Jenni's lasered gaze was locked on their two sets of hands holding April's swollen belly. John yanked his away but not before Jenni paled and squeezed her eyes shut. She swayed and gripped the doorframe with one hand, the plate of food rattling in the other. John's stomach dipped, then twisted.

Their fragile balance had just taken a serious nosedive.

The dish in Jenni's hands clattered and she wanted to turn around and escape the room. John and April were huddled together, smiling down at their unborn child. Her stomach churned as their hurried response left her very aware she had intruded on their mother-father moment. That she was the outsider to this party. A shiver zapped her strength and she nearly lost her balance. She didn't want to open her eyes to the scene awaiting her, but she did. And somehow managed to walk to the bed and hand April her lunch, though April had to rescue the plate from Jenni's shaking hands.

Oh Lord, what am I doing here?

Love with all your heart, daughter. Love with My heart.

Jenni balled her hands together. "Here you go—I hope you like ham and cheese." The tremble in her voice surely gave away her struggle.

"Thank you." April's eyes held an apology that made Jenni feel worse—April shouldn't have to be sorry for feeling her baby kick.

Not trusting her voice, Jenni simply pressed her lips into a smile and nodded. John stood and took a few steps back, shoving his hands into his pockets.

April squirmed under the blankets. "John, can I talk to Jenni alone please?"

He shot Jenni an anxious smile. "Yeah, sure."

Jenni's heart galloped as he stepped out of the room, leaving her alone with April again.

"Jenni…" April's eyebrows almost touched in the middle and she looked nearly as nervous as Jenni felt.

"What is it?"

"Well…this is embarrassing." *Something embarrassing? Jesus, give me strength.* "I still need to use the bathroom. Can you help me get down the hall?"

Jenni's relief escaped in a bubble of laughter. "Of course. Don't be embarrassed."

"Thanks. I think I'd die if I had to ask John."

His name burned when she spoke it.

April needed little more than a firm hand on her elbow to potty-dance to the bathroom. Jenni waited in the hall and then helped her back to the bed. "So...you feeling cooped up in here yet?" She slid the armchair over to the bedside.

"A little. But it's okay. I found a TV channel with all the old classics and that keeps me entertained well enough." She bit into her sandwich. "What about you? What do you do?"

"Well..." She crossed one foot over the other and adjusted her long skirt around her ankles. "I'm preparing to work with special needs kids, and I have a very glamorous job making smoothies."

Jenni's nerves uncoiled as they chatted. Rather than the Jezebel of her imagination, she found April to be a normal, pleasant woman. Like anyone she might meet in one of her college classes. She even seemed a bit...sweet, taking interest in Jenni's love of ASL and their plans to start a music therapy program for the deaf.

"That's incredible." She smiled, then grew reflective. "You're so...*nice*, Jenni. I hate that I had to bust in and ruin your life."

"You can't ruin my life. I gave it to Jesus years ago."

April regarded her a moment, then looked around the room. "You know, John could really use a few more pictures on the walls."

Jenni swept an appraising gaze around the room as well, realizing she hadn't spent much time here before this. She and John seemed to have an unspoken understanding that this room be off-limits. "I agree... And everything he owns is blue!"

April chuckled and took another bite of her sandwich. "I did notice that. He needs to watch some HGTV."

"Believe it or not he *does* watch HGTV. He's quite knowledgeable about home improvement, just not decorating apparently." Jenni's smile was the first non-plastic one she'd mustered that day.

As they laughed together, Jenni forgot why each of them was here. Forgot that John was down the hall probably very nervous about the two of them talking alone. Forgot that April was sick and pregnant with her fiancé's child. Forgot that it hurt.

But as if someone flipped a switch and turned out the lights, the dark reality settled back over the room like a thick cloud, cutting off the air to Jenni's lungs and choking out her voice in one swift moment.

April seemed to feel it too, her smile fading away. She finished her food in silence, avoiding Jenni's gaze. When her eyelids drooped, Jenni stood, twisting her mouth to the side and looking down at April's weary body. "I'll let you get some rest."

April nodded, rolled to her side, and curled herself around her belly. "Maybe just a short one."

Jenni joined John in the living room, where he sat with his Bible and a fresh cup of coffee. "She's resting now."

"Good."

She joined him on the couch and studied the lines of fatigue on his face, wanting with everything in her to erase them.

Scooting up on her knees, she moved closer to him and massaged the kinks in his shoulders. Even now, her blood warmed at the feel of his solid muscles, and she remembered why they'd chosen to spend so little time alone here at his apartment.

John reached over his shoulder and clasped his hand around hers, then held it to his chest as he turned to her.

"Thank you." His eyes darkened as they whispered over her face, and her heart began beating in double-time. "Jenni... You know how much I love you, right?"

"Of course." He hadn't ever let her doubt, even when her heart was shattering. She splayed her fingers over his chest and stared at the spot between his collar bones.

"Good," he breathed. "I need to—"

She cut him off with a kiss. Slow and sweet. Hoping to express her heart, her trust in him. He responded in kind, gentle and soft, silently telling her that she was his world. The wordless conversation of their lips continued through a range of topics, each of them drawing her in deeper, and turning the slow and sweet into perilously hungry. Lost in the mind-numbing sensation of his kiss, Jenni lost track of all else.

She paused for breath and he stroked her cheek. "Jenni..."

"I don't *want* to stop..."

"Which is why we have to." His husky voice spun her head.

She nodded then leaned her forehead on his. With emotions running as high as they were, restraint was getting harder to hold onto. "I'll...check on April again," she scratched out.

He didn't release her hand until she'd taken two steps away from the couch. She looked back over her shoulder at him. It would be so easy to seek comfort from each other physically. But it wouldn't be worth the shame to follow, the damage to their relationship. With deep cleansing breaths, she shook off the electricity clinging to her and hurried down the hallway.

Jenni opened the bedroom door and moved to the side of the bed. Apprehension rose at the sight of April's cheeks, flushed crimson. Touching the back of her hand to April's forehead, she flinched, and a new kind of adrenaline shot through her body.

She flung back the blankets. "John, you better bring a washcloth and thermometer. She feels hot."

Cupboard doors opened and closed and moments later he was there, supplies in hand. Jenni's hands shook as she dampened the cloth in the bathroom sink. She returned to the room and John held up the digital thermometer display.

She swallowed as she read the number. "101.8. We'll have to wake her to take some Tylenol." Pressing the damp cloth to her cheeks, Jenni prayed it would both cool and revive her.

April scrunched her face and shrugged away. "I'm tired."

"Come on, April. Sit up," Jenni urged.

"No. Leave me alone."

Jenni patted the cold cloth to her forehead.

"Stop it. What are you doing?" April waved her hands to shoo them away. "Just let me sleep."

"You need medicine, April." John spoke with authority, and finally April roused enough to obey. She took the offered Tylenol and swallowed them down with some cold water, then lay back down and was asleep again in seconds.

Nervous energy still held on as Jenni ran the wet cloth across her forehead and cheeks, and placed another one on her neck. Then John slipped out the door and Jenni followed him into the kitchen.

"John, if her temperature doesn't come down I think you need to call the doctor—even if it is a Saturday. Take her to Emergency if we have to."

A slow nod but no words.

"I don't think we should wait more than an hour."

"Okay." His gaze bounced around the room as if not knowing where to land. Shock? Panic?

Reaching for his hand, Jenni led him back to the living room sofa and pulled him down beside her. There was only one thing to do. "We should pray."

John clutched her fingers as Jenni prayed for April. The words tumbled out—requests for wisdom, healing, peace. A love not her own poured into Jenni's heart until her greatest desire was for April to experience God's powerful love. That God would use John—and *her*—to show her that love.

"Amen."

Jenni looked up to see John's eyes swirling with emotion. A muscle in his jaw twitched, and his brows pulled together—a silent apology shadowing his expression. His mouth opened then closed. He looked away.

Jenni tilted her head, waiting for whatever he was working up to saying. When no words came, she placed her hand on his cheek and turned him to face her. How could she reassure him when she had no answers? Could make no promises? "God *is* in control. We have to hold onto that." She pulled him into an embrace, feeling the tension in his body. The load he bore. He always tried to be strong for her sake, but now she finally grasped how much he was dealing with. Not only April and the pregnancy, but *their* uncertain future. Jenni and her teaser-rate commitment. She hadn't understood before how much was on his broad shoulders.

She pressed her lips to his forehead, then stood. "You stay here. I'll go recheck her temperature."

She entered the room and approached the side of the bed, thermometer in hand. April's eyes opened a crack as she placed the thermometer in her ear, and she tracked Jenni's every move as she silently repositioned the washcloths and brushed the hair back from the side of her face.

"Thank you."

April's small voice startled her. "You're welcome."

"I'm glad you're here."

Strange emotions tumbled through her. She offered April a nod and a soft smile, words escaping her. April grasped Jenni's hand and locked onto her eyes. "My roommate wouldn't have done half of what you're doing for me. She...she'd probably say if I'd listened to her I wouldn't be in this mess. I wouldn't have lost my job, I'd have had insurance, I'd have realized sooner something besides morning sickness was going on and gotten a diagnosis right away. Treatment would have been easy."

Jenni's brow creased as April bit her quivering lip and shift her gaze to the ocean painting on the wall.

"She thought it was selfish to have a baby when I couldn't even take care of myself. Maybe she was right, but...I couldn't do it." Her voice squeaked on the last word. She cleared her throat and continued. "Even if I'm ruining your lives, everything in me screams to protect this baby. No matter what happens to me. Stacy couldn't understand that." Her hopeful gaze swung back to Jenni. "Can you?"

Clutching April's hand with both of hers, Jenni leaned forward until their faces were inches apart. "Yes, of course. Selfish would've been to throw away the baby's life in order to make your own easier. You're acting as a *good mother*." Jenni meant every word, surprising herself. Heartsick, she shook her head. "I'm sorry your friend wasn't there for you."

Chin quivering, April raised Jenni's hand and pressed it to her cheek, closing her eyes. When she opened them, the gratitude Jenni saw staring back at her was so pure that it robbed her of breath. "Thank you."

Her lungs dragged in air. "Are you hungry?"

"Not really."

"Can you try to eat something for the baby's sake?"

She gave a grateful smile. "I'll try."

"Okay, I'll be right back." With a squeeze of April's hand, Jenni stood and left the room.

She found John at the kitchen table, hunched over his laptop. "April's awake enough to try and eat. And her temperature has come down to 100.5." She grinned as she gave him that news. He attempted a half-smile of his own but she could see the weariness in his shoulders, the worry in his expression. "Find something online?" Her stomach rolled and she wished she could take back the question.

He nodded. "First let's feed April though. You hungry too?"

"No." His body language made her too nervous to eat.

John fixed up some scrambled eggs for April. She nibbled her way through half the plate, then gave up finishing. They let her go back to sleep again.

John closed the bedroom door and led Jenni to the kitchen table where he had his laptop with several web pages open. He stood and pointed at the screen. "Most of the websites say the chemotherapy is not a danger to the fetus after the first trimester. So there's that."

"Really?"

"That's what they say. But I did read that there was increased risk of...," he bent down and read from one of the screens, "...'intrauterine growth retardation, premature labor, and spontaneous abortion.'" His expression said he didn't like the sound of what he read.

"Yikes. What percent chance of those risks does it give?"

"Very small," he admitted.

"Well, that's something to hold onto." She pushed through the foreboding rising in her chest and asked the next question. "What did you find out about delaying treatment?"

He dropped into a kitchen chair. Jenni lowered herself into the one next to him and watched as he massaged his temples, shielding his eyes with his hand. "Three months." His voice was low. "Without treatment she might only have three months."

Jenni's heart rattled around inside her chest, then settled like a rock in the pit of her stomach. *Three months?*

Her hand moved from her mouth to her chest. "The doctor didn't talk to you guys about...time frames?"

He shook his head. "I think he wanted to let us process the diagnosis before weighing us down with facts and figures. He only told us the chemo wouldn't hurt the baby and that they'd start it right away."

"So...*with* treatment? What did you find?"

His Adam's apple rose then plummeted. "In children, eighty percent are cured. In adults...it's thirty to forty percent."

That's all? Jenni's breaths shallowed. The numbers didn't get through to her brain. With chemo and all the advancements in treating cancer today, people got cured.

Right?

Jenni shoved an arm through the sleeve of her favorite cardigan. "I'm heading out, Mom."

"Heading to John's again?" The low register of her voice made it sound like an accusation.

Jenni held onto the strap of her purse hanging on the coat rack, feeling weighed down on every side. "I'm going to church first, but I'll probably go over there afterward."

"Okay. See you whenever." Her false disinterest only highlighted her negative opinion of Jenni's choice to stand by John. She stood from her spot at the kitchen table and picked up her empty oatmeal bowl. "I'll let Mary and Christy know you won't be joining us this evening."

"They're coming over?"

"Just pizza and board games. Nothing as important as your current situation." Her tone didn't match her words and Jenni felt saddened by the rift in their relationship.

"Sorry to have to miss it." She picked up her Bible and gave her mother a contrite smile. "Tell them I'll be here in spirit. Love you, Mom."

"Your family loves you too, Jenni. Remember that when you're there with John's other girl."

"Her name is April. And *I'm* John's only girl."

She headed down the steps of her porch to her car, praying for her family to try and understand. Jenni couldn't walk away, didn't want to. She was in it now, even if they thought she was nuts.

She started the engine, whose rumble seemed to flood her bones with questions she wanted to avoid.

How would it all turn out? Would she and *John* be all right? What of their future? They'd had such beautiful plans—a ministry to the deaf community, a wedding, a family someday—and in a single gut-wrenching moment, it had all been replaced with a future so nebulous she often felt paralyzed by the thought of it.

"God, I'm scared." She admitted aloud as she pulled into the church lot. "I'm doing my best, but...this is so far beyond my strength."

She entered the sanctuary and greeted the worship team backstage. Then she put on a brave face as they filed on stage to begin the set.

John had stayed home from service this morning to tend to April, and Jenni felt his absence as she stood on stage signing the worship. But even without him there, holding her hand through the sermon, she drew strength. Peace. Felt the reassurance in her soul that she was in the center of God's plan for her, and that He would, as always, carry her through it.

After the closing song, she made her way out to the foyer and found Derek and Tori both waiting for her.

"Hey, have you guys met?" She asked.

"Yeah, we sort of figured out who we were." Derek jerked his chin up at Tori. "What's up?"

Tori rolled her eyes. "I don't know about you, but I already knew who I was."

With a squint, Derek clucked his tongue. "You knew what I meant." He looked back to Jenni. "Anyway, I guess we're both wanting to ask you how things are going."

These two people in front of her were the only ones in the congregation who knew the situation. As they stood there in silence, waiting, Jenni couldn't find words. She drew her mouth into a tight line and shook her head. "Not great. But better than yesterday, according to my last text update."

Derek looked at her through narrowed eyes. "*You* okay?"

"Hanging in there."

"You're in my prayers… All of you." Tori pulled her into a hug.

"Yeah. Me too," Derek added.

"Thanks, you guys. We need it. Badly." She pulled in a strengthening breath and lifted her chin. "I should head over to John's apartment now. Pick him up some lunch since he probably hasn't eaten real food today."

"I know he's grateful to have you around. That boy was a mess without you."

"I can believe that," Tori agreed.

Jenni looked at each of them. "Hey, why not come with me, eat lunch with us? Derek, maybe get John downstairs for a little basketball. He could use the distraction and male company, I'm sure." She looked to Tori. "And I could use the support."

Derek nodded. "Sure, I can do that."

"Me too. I'm dying to meet this woman anyway."

"She's actually…pretty normal. Which makes it easier."

Tori lifted her eyebrows. "And harder?"

A wave of emotion washed over her. "Yeah…and harder." Tori knew her well. "Well, it's settled then. You can follow me over."

Chapter Thirty-Three

April stood and stretched her back, twisting just in time to see John emerge from the bathroom with a head full of wet hair. A shame he always wore a shirt. She sighed, then shook the thought away as he entered the living room.

"Jenni messaged me just now. She's on her way over and she's bringing a couple friends."

Friends? How many people knew what she'd done? "Oh, I uh…"

A knock sounded and John moved to answer it. "Don't worry, they're great people."

He opened the door to reveal Jenni, bags of fast food in her hand, and two others behind her.

Jenni pecked John's cheek and stepped inside. "April, I brought a couple people for you to meet."

"Hi, I'm Tori." A woman with curly auburn hair and an olive complexion extended her hand.

She shook it, mustering up the friendly smile she used to use as a waitress at Jake's. "April."

"Hey, I'm Derek." He offered a large, dark-skinned hand.

"Hello."

Jenni smiled at everyone, then settled her gaze on April. "Looks like you're feeling better than yesterday. Why don't we eat outside?"

All four of them looked at her, and John slid his arm around Jenni. "You up for it, April?"

"Um, sure. I guess." She hadn't seen the sun in days. And the protein shake she'd had earlier had really made a difference in her energy.

A few minutes later the women were sitting at a patio table in the apartment complex's courtyard with sourdough burgers and eggrolls. A few feet away, John and Derek dribbled a basketball.

Jenni cupped a hand around her mouth. "Come on, honey! Don't let him get that shot!"

"Yeah…wipe the floor with him!" Tori shouted.

Derek turned to them and stretched out his arms. "Hey, how come I don't get no love? What's everyone ganging up on me for?"

Tori made a face. "Quit whining, or go home, big guy."

"You know I love you, Derek."

"Jenni, I don't blame you for rooting for your man, but your friend there… she's just cold." He swiveled toward John who was setting up a shot, and smacked the ball from him like it was nothing.

John growled and went after him.

"I don't know, Jenni," Tori pulled a curly fry from the bag. "I think Derek's gonna whoop him. Just don't tell him I said that."

April smiled as she watched everybody. She liked Tori's bold teasing and Jenni's soft-hearted answers. She liked seeing John move down the court with Derek. She liked that she was included in this group.

"So, hey…" She stood and looked at the guys. "Can I try?"

"Good idea." Tori wiped salt off her hands. "Girls against guys."

"You have an extra player."

"What, you don't think you two big strong men can take on three quiet little darlings like us?"

Derek slanted his eyes at Tori. "You scare me, you know that?"

"Just pass her the ball. It'll all be okay."

Laughter tickled April's throat for the first time in ages. Her new friend bounced the ball her way and she got hold of it then dribbled it between her feet.

Jenni guarded John, shuffling in front of him with her arms outstretched, clearing a path for April. John poked her ribs and made her laugh, looking more interested in her nearness than in the effectiveness of her defense.

Tori did the same with Derek, except that Derek did not look amused. He looked like he wanted to flick her away from him like a gnat.

April took a few steps closer to the basket, moving slowly, the men closing in on her despite their guards. Derek made a swipe but she spun with a little squeal and retreated.

"That's traveling."

"Shut up, it's fine."

The girls held the boys back, and April could tell they were all going easy on her, trying to give her the shot. She wasn't offended. She felt...accepted.

Derek growled as Tori caught her eye. "Go on, girl. Take the shot. You got this."

April smiled back, planted her feet, and threw the ball. It bounced off the rim and she jogged toward it. "That was awful! I stink!" She laughed then felt her legs start to wobble beneath her.

Her laughter died on her lips as she realized what was about to happen. Before she could react, the world dimmed, sound fled, and she crumpled helplessly to the asphalt.

Blurry faces surrounded her. Strong arms slipped under knees and shoulders.

"I got her. I got her."

Her head landed heavily against a firm chest. "John?"

"It's Derek, baby girl. And you're gonna be fine. Talk about leaving it all on the court, huh?"

"Will you just get her inside?"

"What do you think I'm doing?" he huffed.

April's lip twitched in amusement even as the voices faded and darkness shrouded her.

April opened her eyes, then closed them again. The last thing she remembered was a game of basketball but it seemed so long ago.

"April, time to wake up." John's muffled voice seemed to come from far away. "Come on, giddyup." His strong hand shook her shoulder. "We have that appointment with Dr. Corbin. Gotta get moving."

Appointment? Was it Monday already?

She sat up and tried to make the fog in her brain burn off so she could think. That's right, she'd fainted during the game. Everyone had fussed over her, prayed over her, sat with her until she felt normal again.

"Okay, okay. I'm awake." She yawned as John handed her a plate of eggs she had no appetite for. But she scooped up a forkful and forced it down.

"Is Jenni coming, too?" Strange that April hoped she was.

"Yes, she's already here."

"Knock-knock." Jenni poked her head in then entered. "Did I hear my name?"

April smiled. "Hey." Being around Jenni should have felt awful, but April liked her more and more each time she saw her. Jenni was the kind of woman John deserved.

"So, how are you feeling after yesterday?" Jenni sat on the bed beside her.

"Oh, you know…not ready to run any marathons, but I'll manage."

John cleared his throat. "You're sure?"

"Yes." Her nose tingled as she looked at the two faces in front of her, felt their concern. "I'm sure."

They left her to get ready, and when she emerged, Jenni handed her a cup of coffee.

"It's decaf. Vanilla creamer, I hope that's okay."

"That's perfect, thanks."

"It's about time to hit the road." John stuffed his wallet into his back pocket, and April sat in the recliner and reached down for the shoes she'd left there last night.

"Oh. Here, let me." Jenni grabbed the pair of black flats. "So you don't get dizzy bending over." She knelt on the floor in front of April and helped her slip her foot into her shoe.

April blinked. "You didn't have to do that."

"It's no big deal."

A strange lump formed in her throat as April stared at Jenni's brown head, bowed over her feet. How could anyone be so kind?

"All set, let's go." Jenni offered April her hand and helped her up.

"Thank you," she said quietly, then followed the couple out the door.

Today was the day she'd find out how bad this thing was, and how it would affect her future. Dread squeezed her chest as she buckled up. She wrapped her hands around her decaf and pulled her gaze from the window to John and Jenni's clasped hands on the console in front of her. He probably held her hand often. Robert had never been a hand-holder, even when things were good.

Half hour later, they pulled into the hospital parking lot and John rolled toward the front entrance. Pressing her fingernails into her palms, April looked out her back seat window, sized up the building, and wondered why hospitals always looked like they were out to get you.

John let the car idle while Jenni and April hopped out at the front entrance. Then he went to find a parking space.

"Does he always do stuff like that?"

Jenni's mouth curved in a half-smile. "Always."

John rejoined them a moment later and the large glass doors parted for them. The scent of antiseptic and air freshener set off nervous butterflies in April's stomach. This was real, this was happening. She placed a hand over her belly as if the baby were the one needing to be calmed.

"I'll check in at the desk." John strode off toward the counter and April felt the gratitude and longing swelling within her.

"He takes good care of you, doesn't he?"

Jenni looked at her and nodded. "He does. I'm lucky to have him."

"So am I." April rattled her head. "I just mean, he's done a lot for me."

"I know." Jenni reassured her with a smile as John waved them over.

April didn't need a wheelchair, but the staff said it was policy and made her sit in one. She chewed her lip as she put her feet up on the foot rests. It made her feel too much like a patient, like she was sick. And she preferred not to be reminded.

"Hi April, how are you feeling today?" April started at Dr. Corbin's greeting. He approached with a friendly smile and she tossed him one back.

"Not too bad. A little tired."

"Glad to hear it. And how about you, John?" He shook John's hand, then turned to Jenni. "Hi, I'm Dr. Corbin. Are you a friend of April's?"

April's breath caught. How would anyone describe what they were?

"Yes, a friend." Jenni placed a hand on April's shoulder and squeezed, and the warmth of it snaked its way to April's heart.

She rubbed the sting out of her nose and tried to pay attention. John was wheeling her past a bank of elevators, a nurse's station, down a long hall, and past several doors as he followed behind Dr. Corbin. Finally the doctor paused and opened a door, and everyone filed into his personal office.

The doctor straightened his coat and looked down at her. "April, I need your permission to discuss this in front of your friends. If you'd rather, I can have them wait outside so we can speak alone."

"No, I—I want them both to stay. Please."

"All right then." He squeaked into his leather chair, and John and Jenni took up spots on either side of her. "As you know, we diagnosed you with an acute form of leukemia called Acute Lymphoblastic Leukemia, or ALL, and unfortunately it is an aggressive form. So we're going to begin treatment today." He paused.

Was it her turn to say something? Her mouth wasn't working. Instead she got lost in the beige carpet under his feet. Her head felt like it was lifting right off her body. April's gaze traveled from the rich mahogany desk to the walls covered with family photos and plaques. How could such warm décor leave her so cold? *And what about...?*

She gripped the arms of the wheelchair, panting, as the fearful question worked its way around her mind. Only then did she realize the doctor was still talking, had been for who knew how long. "What about my baby? You can't give me chemo now." She dragged her gaze to his eyes and her hands went protectively around her middle. "I won't terminate, I don't care what happens to me."

Two firm hands squeezed her shoulders and she looked up to see John and Jenni standing on either side of her, exuding quiet strength. As she swung her head back to the doctor she realized her face was wet, though she couldn't remember starting to cry. Dr. Corbin held her gaze with compassionate eyes.

"The chemotherapy is not dangerous to your baby, April." He glanced at John then back to her.

Not dangerous? Could she believe him?

"We *can't* delay your treatment. There isn't time. But it's not a danger to the fetus."

Wait. She shook her head, trying to grasp what he'd said. The baby was due in less than three months, what did he mean there wasn't time? Fear choked her. She stared at him, unable to form the question. She was going to die, wasn't she? Mary Tyler Moore was wrong. She wasn't gonna make it after all. She'd never have that fresh start. The office job, the loving husband, the house with a yard and a swing-set. She'd never even be a mother.

John and Jenni had sunk into chairs on either side of her. They nodded at the doctor with straight lips and furrowed brows. April slumped further into her chair and stared down at her belly, stroking her baby. She tried to focus.

"Today will begin an induction phase of chemotherapy which will last thirty days. The goal during this phase is to destroy ninety-nine percent of the leukemia cells. If successful, we'll move onto the second phase—consolidation therapy. This phase will last anywhere from four to eight months."

April blinked, hoping someone was writing this down because it wasn't getting through to her clouded mind.

"Dr. Corbin, excuse me." John held up a hand, voice tinged with concern. "I know you said the treatment won't hurt the baby, but you *will* monitor her, right?"

"Yes, of course. We'll be monitoring the pregnancy very closely. As soon as the baby is ready we'll deliver April by Caesarean section." He must've caught the confusion in April's eyes and explained. "You won't have the stamina for a natural childbirth, so a planned C-section is best for everyone. Best for the baby."

Closing her eyes, April pressed her fingers to her forehead, reeling. "C-sections," "chemotherapy," "T-cells," "no time"…His words swirled around in her head over and over and over and she couldn't make sense of any of them. She only understood one thing.

She was being punished.

John and Jenni could try to convince her all day long, but she knew the truth. God was angry with her.

She was being admitted for the next thirty days, for constant fetal monitoring over the course of treatment. April was brought to her assigned room, and finally allowed out of the wheelchair. But it was only minutes later that they came to prep her for chemotherapy.

Jenni's face was painted with concern. "Are you nervous?"

April forced her lips into a phony smile. "Hey, people do this every day, right?"

Her heart rate was high, the blood pounding in her brain. She felt like she was at the top of a roller coaster with no way of getting off the ride.

The looks on their faces confirmed they weren't fooled. Jenni eased down onto the edge of the bed, John by her side. He rested one hand on Jenni's upper back and stuffed the other in his pocket. "April... Is it all right if we pray with you?"

Pray *with* her?

April looked back at each of them. They could send positive thoughts her way, or pray *for* her, but pray *with* her? Would they expect her to—?

John caught her eye. "You don't have to pray out loud or anything. But we would very much like the chance to pray over you before your treatment—for you and the baby."

April bit the inside of her cheek. The idea of talking to the Almighty scared her as much as the chemo she was about to receive. Maybe more. But could it possibly earn her some favor? Wasn't it worth trying, for her baby's sake?

She nodded. "Sure. I guess that's okay."

Jenni took one of April's hands in hers and bowed her head. John rested a hand on April's shoulder and closed his eyes. April followed suit.

A hush settled over them, then John began. "Father, please be with April right now. Make the treatment effective, and use it to rid her body of this disease. Give wisdom to the doctors. As Your Word promises, You are the Great Physician, and we ask for healing."

The Great Physician?

"We pray that she won't experience the side-effects so common with chemotherapy. And we ask that you would protect the baby. Make this child grow strong and healthy."

April's lashes dampened, and she nodded. Pleading whispers came from Jenni too. April sniffed, unsure why the room felt different. Holy.

"Lord, You have created this tiny person and we ask that You hold it in Your hands, and in Your perfect time bring this baby into the world to live a long and healthy life."

Oh, please. April fought the jerk of her shoulders.

After a pause, Jenni filled the silence with a prayer of her own. "Father God, wrap loving arms around April and her baby. Help her feel You—her Comforter, her Deliverer. Fill her with peace. Your Word says that You bind up the brokenhearted and bring freedom to the captive."

It does? That didn't sound like her image of God. That sounded...nice. Kind of wonderful. She blinked her eyes open after the amen.

Comfort, deliverance, mercy, love, the Great Physician...*peace*. April did feel *something* settling over her. But was it supernatural or simple gratitude for the compassion that John and Jenni had shown?

Whatever it was made her throat burn. "Thank you."

"You're welcome." Jenni leaned over and actually hugged her— *hugged her!* April's shivers settled. Her pulse slowed. Their concern must have been what touched her—she'd never felt so smothered in kindness—but whatever the source, April felt better.

And she would try to hold onto this sense of calm as long as she possibly could.

Chapter Thirty-Four

Jenni rounded the corner of the paint aisle and snaked through the kitchen cabinet displays on her way to John's back office. A dark-haired man in a suit shirt looked up and smiled at her. "Hi, Jenni. Go on in, he's expecting you."

"Thanks, Conrad."

She found John at a desk with a phone to his ear, tapping a pen against a yellow legal pad. She smiled as she watched him, looking so professional and handsome.

He hung up and she approached, setting a paper bag on the desk in front of him. "Hey, handsome. Brought you lunch."

John stood with a smile and pulled her into his arms, planting a warm kiss on her mouth. "Mmm...You're wonderful, you know that?"

"You haven't even seen what I brought yet."

He peered into the bag and removed a sandwich and a piece of pie. "Ooh." His eyebrows shot up. "Looks like I'm being spoiled today."

"Enjoy it, that's the last of the leftover turkey." She smiled and sat in the chair across from him. "I'm thinking of going to the hospital after this."

It'd been three weeks since April began treatment. Too soon to know if it was working, but she seemed to be handling it well.

John settled his gaze on her. "Your visits mean a lot to her. And me."

An uncanny realization dawned on her. "Me, too." The more time Jenni spent with her, the easier she found it to care for April. The baby bump could still be hard to look at sometimes, but the two had become something like friends. With tensions so high at the Dupont home, Jenni and John had even spent most of their Thanksgiving in April's hospital room.

But April wouldn't be in the hospital forever. And then where would she go, back to John's?

"I keep praying she'll turn to God."

Jenni nodded. "She asks for prayer, but I can sense there's a concrete wall around her heart."

"Maybe one of these days it will come down." He polished off his sandwich then dug in to his pie. "This is delicious, thank you."

"You're welcome. I know how much you like dessert." She smiled. "Even if my mom does mourn the loss of that last piece of pumpkin pie."

"Great, now she'll be gunning for me even more."

"Eh, I'll protect you." She sighed. "That's another wall I hope will come down."

The set of John's mouth as he nodded conveyed his agreement.

The phone on his desk rang and Jenni stood to go. "I better scoot and let you get back to work." She leaned over the desk for a kiss then headed out.

Jenni parked in the hospital's lot and cut the engine. Snatching the canvas tote and plastic bag from the passenger seat, she got out of her car and set the alarm. The path to the main hospital doors was familiar. Three weeks of chemo…and several chances to pray with April. She had asked for prayer before every treatment, saying it calmed her. But often, Jenni still felt a restlessness deep in her bones.

She pulled her sweater sleeves down over her hands and hooked them over her thumbs, preparing for the frigid blast of air she knew would hit when the glass doors slid apart. Why the hospital thought it needed arctic leaf blowers at the entrance in December was beyond her comprehension.

The elevator let her out in front of the nurse's station on April's floor. Jenni grinned at the familiar faces and moved down the hall to her room. With a light rap, she opened the door and went in.

"Hey." April smiled at her and rubbed the sleep from her eyes.

"Hi. I brought you a few books...and this." Jenni pulled out a plastic bowl of Rocky Road ice cream. "Thought it might brighten your day."

"*Yes*...mmm, thank you. So, *so* glad my nausea is gone."

"No problem. I'm not working today, so I thought, if you weren't busy, I'd hang out with you this afternoon."

"Well, I *had* planned to do some body boarding and hit the gym today, but...I guess I can do that tomorrow." She snickered and Jenni matched it, but the joke landed in her gut with a thud.

"So is it cold outside?"

"Yeah, and wet. It's not raining anymore though."

"Hmm." She turned her face toward the window. "I miss weather."

"That's got to be tough." Jenni dragged the visitor's chair closer to the bed. "Getting cabin fever?"

"A little." She spooned another bite and closed her eyes as she slid it into her mouth. "I admit sometimes it gets a little lonely."

Speak.

The command resounded deep within her. An urgency she couldn't define built within her and Jenni tried to still the rumbling storm in her chest.

"April...you're not alone."

"Oh, I know that." Her eyes went soft. "I'm beyond thankful for you and John." She set aside her empty bowl then picked the lint off her blankets. "You're the only ones who've ever actually cared."

"No, we're not. God cares—"

"Jenni." April cut her off, adjusted her position in the bed to face her. "You know nothing about my life. Nothing from before..." she looked down at her belly, "*this*, do you?"

Jenni looked into blue eyes that reflected a lifetime of pain, and shook her head. "No."

"Then you wouldn't know how alone I've always been." Blonde hair fell in wavy tendrils around the pale face of a lost little girl.

In the next breath, her eyes hardened. "The overview is, my mom never cared about me and I never knew my dad. I doubt my mother even knew who he was. She'd hide me when she brought men home because 'men don't stick around when there's a kid involved.' Didn't matter how hungry I was or how much I had to use the bathroom…only the creaking sounds coming from the other side of the wall meant it was safe to come out of my room. Back then I used to think that if she got married, I wouldn't have to hide anymore." Her throat bobbed. "That I'd have a regular family, someone to call daddy. But they never stuck around long enough."

Jenni's insides flinched, and thoughts of her own father came to mind. It had hurt when he walked out. It hurt still to remember. "That's awful, April. Must've been really painful."

A sardonic smile tipped her mouth. "Those were the good days, Jenni. I was about ten the first time I saw a man hit her. I tried to talk to her, but she denied it. Cursed me out and made up some lame excuse for the bruises. And he was just the first in a string of horrible men."

April shook her head in disgust. "She was stupid, pathetic. So I just stayed away from home, avoiding her drama and the abuse. Then as soon as I had a car, I was out of there."

Jenni's throat burned as April's gaze travelled past the bed rail, past the IV bag, out toward the window where gray clouds blocked the sun. "I never saw my mom again. She never came looking for me." She sniffed. "She didn't even call any of my friends."

Had no one shown this girl she mattered? Jenni handed her a tissue, trying to fathom what that must've been like for her, how it would shape her. "You didn't deserve that, April."

She shrugged. "I found my feet. I moved on. Got a job, worked hard. I learned one thing from my mother—what *not* to be. A victim. I was careful. I guess in the process I isolated myself. So maybe it's my own fault that I've always been alone. But now…" she met Jenni's eyes. "Now I suddenly have two of the best friends in the world. I don't know how that happened."

How could she not see? Jenni leaned forward and laid a hand on April's knee. "Well, it wasn't luck. It was God. He's always been there, April. Even if you didn't recognize it."

She smoothed the sheets over her legs then swiped the tissue under her nose. "Look, I admit there's something comforting about your religion. But that's because of you guys, not me. You two love your God, and He seems to love you back. I'm lucky to be around for a bit of spillover. But it is *not* me He's taking care of. Never has. He wasn't around when I was stuck under my mother's roof."

"Yes, He was. Don't you see? He protected you. Do you know how many children are hospitalized or killed every year because of domestic violence? But not you. How many things could have gone even worse over those years? You were left home alone to fend for yourself at a young age, yet you made it through. You watched your mother get beaten time and time again. You were surrounded by drunk and violent men. But you 'managed' to avoid the violence that went on in your own home for years. That wasn't luck…God held you in the palm of His hand."

Her gaze held doubt. Fear. She searched Jenni's face, saying nothing. The silence stretched, broken by the occasional beep of a monitor. Jenni's heart pounded. Was she getting through?

April twisted the tissue in her hands over and over, wringing it till it began to shred. "God didn't protect me from Robert." Her voice was a near whisper, but there was unspoken challenge in the tilt of her chin.

Who was Robert? A knot formed in the pit of Jenni's stomach as she looked into April's steely eyes. "I can't explain why certain things happen to us. But sometimes God doesn't stop the storm—he carries us through it instead. I know it sounds like a cliché but it's something I've found to be profoundly true in my own life."

The tissue had disintegrated into a pile of fuzzy white bits. "April…" Jenni handed her a new one. "Do you want to talk about Robert?"

A weighty silence ensued as April began wrapping the tissue around her finger again. "I wouldn't even be in this mess if it weren't for Robert," she whispered. "I thought he was a good man. Not perfect, but who is? But after we got engaged he changed. Started drinking more and more, staying out late. We fought about it constantly."

Jenni held her breath and waited for her to continue.

"Reminded me of one of my mom's boyfriends but I told myself that was crazy. I only wanted him to cut back, I wasn't trying to control him. I cared about him, and he was developing a real problem."

She worked her throat as she stared straight ahead, unblinking. "Then one night he…snapped. He was drunk and I was angry. Hurt. I said something I shouldn't have…" Her eyes flicked to Jenni before she pointed her face away, and the rhythm of her breathing filled Jenni with dread.

"It started with a slap." She brought her fingers to her cheek. "Then before I knew it, I was on the ground..."

Her chest rose and plummeted, and the beeping monitors increased in tempo.

"I couldn't breathe...I was bleeding. He—he was on top of me. And then he...he..." Her shoulders shook and she squeezed her eyes shut.

Jenni's stomach soured and her own pulse roared. "April..." She whispered and gently reached for her hand. "Did he...rape...you?"

Chapter Thirty-Five

Eyes still shut tight, April clutched Jenni's fingers and bobbed her head, moisture silently rolling down the bridge of her nose.

"This is the first time you've told anybody, isn't it?"

She bobbed her head again, covered her face, and moaned through her tears.

Lord, why? To think of the pain, the secret this woman had been carrying alone all this time… Jenni's heart ripped in two. "I'm so sorry, April." What else could Jenni say? "No one should have to carry that burden alone."

A long moment later, April sniffed and pulled her face out of her hands, achieving a measure of composure. Jenni handed her the whole box of tissues, pulling one out for herself. After blowing her nose and wiping her eyes, April turned back to Jenni, her voice faltering. "I never saw it coming. But if you're right, God *did*. And He didn't stop it. So tell me…" hurt and anger built in her voice, "where was God then? Why would He let this happen to me?"

Jenni just shook her head. "I don't know."

How was she supposed to give answers when she had the same questions? Why did God allow women to be hurt this way by the men they loved? Her chest ached. "We don't always get to know why. But God *was* there. And I can promise you that every time you were hurt and crying, God was hurting with you. He's kept all your tears in a bottle— that's what the Bible says. That's how much He loves you. And even now, He is right here. And He wants to comfort you…if you'll let Him."

The last traces of April's hardened mask fell away. Her gaze locked onto Jenni's as she tried to form words but failed. She chewed her lip, a war waging in her eyes.

"April…" Jenni gentled her tone, and shot up a desperate prayer. "The peace you feel when John and I pray with you…it doesn't come from some magic words. It doesn't come from *us*. We're just people. It comes from a living God who loves you and wants to give you that same peace deep inside. Do you want that?"

Please let her hear the truth. Several beats ticked by as Jenni held her breath and prayed for April harder than she ever had.

"Jenni, it sounds wonderful when I listen to you talk. It does. I mean, who wouldn't want that? But I…" She shook her head and looked down at her hands and gave a dismal laugh. "I just. Don't. Deserve it."

"Nobody does, but—"

"No. You don't know what I've done. Not all of it." She paused and ran her fingers back and forth across her forehead. "Yeah, I've had bad stuff done to me. But I've done some really bad things too."

Jenni's eyes moved to April's round belly and her breath caught in the back of her throat. Oh, she knew. All too well. And she didn't want to relive it. But April needed this soul purging, so Jenni swallowed down her own anxiety.

"That night…that night that I was so desperate to keep off the street that I went looking for some schmuck who might pay me to…"

April covered her mouth and shook her head. Took a breath. "I didn't want to think about it that night, but I've thought about it a lot since. I knew how drunk John was—I *knew*. And from the first words out of his mouth I knew that I looked like his dead wife. He was in so much pain. I told myself I was comforting him. But really, I was taking advantage of him in the worst possible way. Oh, God—I even let him call me Hannah!" She dropped her face back into her hands.

Her confession cut off Jenni's air. But the truth of the events that night somehow crumbled the wall of bitterness around Jenni's heart. Moving closer, Jenni wrapped her arms around April and cried with her.

Cleansing grace washed over and through Jenni with those tears. More grace than she'd ever experienced before. Finding her voice, she whispered in April's ear. "None of us deserve it… None. But God loves us anyway."

Jenni stroked April's hair as she continued to cry, leaning her cheek against Jenni's chest like a child. "Jesus paid for your sin, April. He wants a relationship with you. All you have to do is believe and say yes to Him."

Jenni waited, hoping. "Do you believe what I just told you?"

"I want to," she whispered.

"What's holding you back?"

"I don't know. It's just…I need to think about it some more. Is that all right?" Worry lines etched her forehead.

"Of course. Ask God to show Himself to you. And you can call me any time, day or night, if you want to talk about this. Okay?"

"Okay." She offered a weak smile. "But Jenni?" April looked at her, agony behind her red-rimmed eyes. "There's one more thing that's been eating me alive. And I just can't keep lying to you."

"Lying to me?"

She nodded. "It's about John…I've had feelings for him since I got here. And I…I kissed him. I didn't plan it but—"

Jenni smiled. "Shh. I already know. John told me."

Her brow furrowed. "He did?"

Jenni nodded. "Yes, weeks ago. I know it *was* an accident. And I understand how you'd have feelings for John. And I forgave you."

April shook her head. "Jenni, I don't know how you do it. I really don't. But thank you for being my friend—my best friend." Her eyes pooled.

Jenni squeezed her hand. "I'm *happy* to be your friend." Through God's grace, she meant it.

April's face lit up suddenly. She placed Jenni's hand on her belly and Jenni felt the small but strong kicks and squirms of the baby in her womb. A smile formed on her lips without hesitation. For the first time, the thought of this baby didn't wrench her heart in two—it brought an unearthly excitement.

Jenni headed back out to her car with a bounce in her step. Unable to keep her joy from bubbling over, she sang and signed worship songs as she drove home. More than one driver on the road shot her strange looks as her hands worked to form wordless praise at every traffic light.

Her cell phone rang just as she pulled into the driveway, and Christy's name flash across the screen. "Hey Christy, what's up?"

"Um… Well, I was just wondering if I could go to church with you again this week."

Jenni beamed. "Absolutely."

"Okay. I'll see you then."

"See you then."

First April, and now Christy. The Lord was moving in lives all around her. And she had the privilege of being a part of it.

As she sashayed into the house and hung her purse on the rack by the door, her mom's hardened eyes reminded Jenni there was one life she was still waiting to see transformed.

Chapter Thirty-Six

John stepped into the doorway of April's hospital room, a checkerboard tucked under his arm. Two vases of fragrant flowers perfumed the air, and late-afternoon light streamed through the open blinds. April's nose was in a book so John knocked on the open door, announcing his arrival.

She looked up and grinned, her expression bright despite the washed-out skin and the dark circles beneath her eyes. "John! Hey, how are you?"

"Doin' good." He closed the distance between the door and bedside chair. "What are you reading?"

"Oh, baby development." She turned the book toward him. "Did you know our little bean can *see* now? And probably recognizes our voices? It's amazing."

"It is," John responded, smiling.

April gestured toward the game board. "Whatcha got there?"

"Checkers. It's got to get boring in here after awhile, right?"

"Uh yeah it does." She sat up straighter and adjusted the incline on her bed.

John spread the game out on the rolling tray and set up the board. April seemed in good spirits, her energy level up from a few short weeks ago.

A nurse knocked and let herself in. "April, we're going to be prepping you for a transfusion in about half an hour, okay?"

"Okay. Thanks, Nora."

John nodded toward the door as she left. "I see you're making friends here. She seems nice."

"Yeah, everyone's been great."

"Glad to hear that. So, when's the next ultrasound?"

April moved her game piece. "Two days, and I can't wait. It's my favorite thing in the world right now."

Images of his child filtered through his imagination, and John smiled as he took his turn. "Just think. Soon it will be time to shop for baby clothes, diapers, the whole shebang."

"Yeah…" April's face went serious. " So much to think about." She moved her checker piece then caught his eye. "I don't even know where I'm going to live, let alone how I'll take care of a baby. What if I'm an awful mother?"

"You won't be. You already have strong maternal instincts. And you won't be raising our child alone."

"I'll certainly be glad for your experience." Her eyes went wide. "I'm sorry. I didn't mean to bring up…"

He waved a hand at her. "It's okay. I'm not going to pretend Hannah and Katy never existed. They did, and I loved them. I didn't get a chance to be a father to Katy for very long, but I know she's with the ultimate Father now." He jumped her checker piece and placed it aside.

"Wow," she shook her head, "When I first met you, you could barely speak their names aloud."

He shrugged his brows. "When I first met you, I was nursing my anger and grief. Resisting God, and the healing He wanted to give me."

"And now…" She searched his eyes, questions in her own. "You're different."

"I sure hope so." He smiled. "Your turn."

April double-jumped him, tying up the game. "How?"

"How what?"

"How did that change happen?"

"Well…it was a process. I had to learn some things about myself first. For a long time, I blamed God for what'd happened. Hated Him for taking my family."

Sympathy radiated from April's eyes the same way they had in that Vegas bar, and John shot up a quick prayer that the tenderness of her heart would give ears to her soul. "I'd always thought that since I was a Christian, God wouldn't let anything real bad happen to me. When it did, I totally lost it. I got mad."

"That's understandable."

"No." John shook his head, checker game forgotten. "No, that was wrong. See, I didn't realize it at the time but I'd been going to church and 'being' a Christian for all the wrong reasons. I believed, but it was more of a strategy for life than a real faith. I thought if I did all the right things, I'd get blessings. So as soon as something bad happened, I tossed my faith out the window, deciding I had wasted my time on God."

He pushed the tray out of the way and continued. "But all that got me was loneliness, depression, rage, and a bad drinking habit to boot. But somehow, God has a way of turning the bad stuff into something He can use for good. He doesn't waste any of our pain."

As if orchestrated by heaven, sunlight poured in from the window at that moment. "After our night together, I woke up—in more ways than one—and saw what I had become, how far I had fallen."

April's eyes darkened with remorse. "John, I'll never stop being sorry. I'm so ashamed of what I did. I had no idea how bad it would turn out." Tears accumulated at the base of her eyelids, but John took her hand and gripped it tight.

"I'm not finished. This is the part I want you to hear. I needed to see myself for what I was so that I would admit that I needed God. Not to make this life easy, but to make my soul clean. I prayed to Him—and *He heard me.*"

John searched her eyes. "And since that day, whenever I start to feel guilty or ashamed, God's voice has been there to comfort me. And, April…He wants to do the same thing for you."

Deep longing filtered behind her eyes and her breath quickened.

Silence hovered until Nora knocked and entered the room, shuttering the windows to April's soul. "All righty, April, it's time."

She blinked at him and nodded. "Thank you."

Leaving her room, John greeted Dr. Corbin as he came down the hall toward him.

"Doc, hi. They just took her for a transfusion."

Dr. Corbin's gray hair was neatly combed as always, his glasses framing his kind eyes. "I know. I was actually hoping I might have a word with you."

John nodded. "Yes, of course."

The doctor led him to his office and closed the heavy door behind him. He sat at his desk and motioned John into the seat across from him. "We're almost finished with this first phase of treatment. Tomorrow is April's last round of chemo and soon we'll know how successful it was."

A sigh of relief left John's lungs. "Yeah, that's great." He raked a hand through his hair. "Thank you, doctor."

"My pleasure." He smiled. "I just want to make sure that you prepare for whatever the results might be. So that she has a strong wall of support.

"Okay, yeah. Of course."

"The next thing in front of us is the baby." He held up a steady hand. "Everything looks great, the baby has remained right on target in its development. So now it's a matter of deciding how long we're going to wait to deliver."

He leaned back in his chair, ankle resting confidently on his knee, and spread his hands. "We of course want to balance the needs of the mother and of the baby, and I don't make these decisions lightly. That being said, April is just over thirty-one weeks along now, and I'd like her to deliver within a week."

John's back straightened. "A *week*? That's too early. That's like, two *months* early."

"Don't worry. The steroid shots we administered have helped the lungs develop. The baby should be fine, just a little small."

John ran his fingers over his mouth as the facts settled. "You're sure?"

Dr. Corbin uncrossed his legs and leaned forward, steepling his fingers. "I can't eliminate a hundred percent of the risk, no. But you have to understand, that baby needs to be delivered before April can begin the second phase of her treatment. It's her best chance—no, her *only* chance—at beating this." His gaze firmly held John's. "The baby will be fine, John, but April might resist, to the detriment of her own health. You, and Jenni, can help reassure her."

John wiped his palms on his jeans. How could he do that when he was so anxious himself?

The doctor studied him, then leaned forward, compassion in his eyes. "John… I can promise you that if it were my family on the line, this is the course of action I would take—with confidence and no hesitation."

John nodded, processing the news. They were out of time. The future was here, chemo was almost done—and within a week John would be a father…again.

Chapter Thirty-Seven

April strained to open her eyelids, knowing she'd slept a long time already. The drawn shades of the windows kept the hospital room dim. What time was it? She searched the wall for the clock and squinted to bring it into focus: four o'clock. Afternoon or morning?

Blinking, she struggled not to let her eyes close again. A shiver raised goose bumps on her arms and she pulled the blankets closer, tightening her curled position.

Helpful hands appeared and tucked the blankets around her, then brushed across her forehead.

"Hey...how are you?" Jenni's voice brought a smile to April's face.

"How long have you been here?"

"A couple hours. John was here too, but I made him go home and rest. He said he'd be back by six. Are you thirsty? The nurse brought in some juice earlier." Without waiting for an answer, Jenni brought a straw to April's lips and she drank.

She felt herself waking up more, her head clearing. "I'm sorry I slept through your visit."

"Don't be silly. I know the chemo takes a lot out of you. You must be so excited to have the last treatment behind you."

"Yeah, but I'm too tired to show it." Truth was, she was beyond ready for this all to be over. Thirty days in a hospital bed, repeatedly sickened by drugs she willingly allowed into her body. In the hopes it *might* cure her.

"I know." Jenni smoothed April's hair back. "But it will pass. It'll all be behind you soon."

"I hope so," she managed through a wave of nausea.

A Bible lay open on one of the chairs. Jenni must have been reading while April slept. April's head buzzed with questions she was too afraid to ask. Squirming under her covers, she fixed her gaze on the flowers nearby—a gift from Tori. Everyone was excited that this induction phase of her chemo treatment was finished. So was she, but…the future scared her.

What if the baby wasn't doing as well as they said? What if the treatment had hurt it? What if the chemo hadn't even worked? How would she get through the next phase—three months of different, but still intense, chemotherapy treatments—while caring for a newborn?

The biggest fear of all wound around her heart and held fast.

Being a mother.

Very soon, she'd be responsible for a tiny new person. A thrilling, terrifying thought on its own. But while battling leukemia?

Her stomach lurched and she reached for the bedpan on the tray beside her. Jenni rubbed her back as she coughed and spewed what little contents were in her stomach. When the retching stopped, she spit and lowered the pan to her lap.

"I'll call a nurse. Get you some more anti-nausea meds."

April nodded, tears pooling in her eyes, as Jenni stepped out.

Some days, like today, she found fear everywhere she turned. Some days, even John and Jenni's friendship couldn't touch the loneliness deep inside. And as much as she found it hard to believe in a God who cared about her, the idea of it kept circling her mind.

What if He was real? What if He loved her?

"Okay, they're going to send someone in." Jenni returned, and April looked up at her face, noting the peace shining in her eyes.

"Thank you."

Jenni took the pan away and carried it to the bathroom. When she returned, she looked at April and cocked her head. "Are you all right?"

"I…" April's eyes skidded to the Bible, as her heart skidded to a stop. "What's the catch?"

"What do you mean?"

She dragged her gaze to Jenni's face. "It can't be so simple, there's got to be more to it. Something I have to do…some sort of trade-off…"

The Bible drew her gaze again. She didn't have much to lose. Even if it wasn't everything John and Jenni made it out to be, if their faith could help even a little...

Jenni followed April's sightline and a soft smile touched her lips. "The trade-off is...you give Him your brokenness, and in exchange He gives you peace, forgiveness, strength, love."

April's brows pinched as Jenni settled into the bedside chair and leaned close. "You'd be trading the life you have now for a new one only He can give. Because He *is* all those things. He is life."

April's pulse kicked up a notch. "That doesn't sound right. It sounds too easy."

"It isn't complicated, but it isn't always easy. Sometimes we hold onto things that bring us pain. Because it's familiar, it's what we know. But what God gives us in exchange is *so much better*. Because He gives us Himself, and everything He is."

Could that be true? Oh, if only...! She stared into Jenni's passionate eyes, so full of conviction, and bees buzzed in her belly.

"April..." Jenni placed her hand over April's. "Do you want Jesus?"

She scraped her teeth over her lip. "I do...but I don't have your faith. I still have doubts. Questions. Could God still want me if I have doubts about Him?"

Jenni's smile was gentle. "He wants you, April. Just the way you are, questions and baggage and all. He's big enough to handle your doubts. Even your faith will come from Him."

April's heart thudded wildly in her chest. Like she was standing at the edge of a cliff, about to leap into something that could change her life forever.

Jenni seemed to read her mind. She squeezed April's hand. "If you want Him , all you have to do is tell Him."

April hesitated. "I don't know how to tell Him. He's *God*."

"I'll help you if you want, but there is no magic formula or anything. Just a conversation you're having with Him...saying that you need Him, His forgiveness. And that you're inviting Him into your heart to give you a new life."

Her stomach knotted, but she coaxed out her voice. "Help...would be great."

Jenni's smile widened as she held April's hands. They bowed their heads, then Jenni led her in a prayer which, though the words were not her own, came from the very core of her being. Because she did want God to change her, to give her peace, love, joy. And to never, ever leave her.

Yes. She meant every word.

Chapter Thirty-Eight

John stepped off the elevator, his face sore from smiling. Jenni's message about April was just about the best news he could imagine. When he entered April's room, she was standing beside her portable IV, Jenni supporting her by the elbow, and John just grinned and wrapped her in a hug.

"Is it too soon to say I feel different?" she asked when he released her.

"Not at all."

"It's...strange. Something definitely happened when I prayed. I feel...lighter inside. Like I'd been carrying around something heavy without realizing it."

Jenni slipped her hand into John's. "You were. And now it's gone. I can't wait to see what God does in your life now, April."

"Me either." April lowered herself back onto the bed and looked up at them. "So, what now? Am I supposed to do something else?"

John smiled at her eager new faith. "Just get to know Him."

Jenni left his side and sat beside April. "And the best way to do that is through reading His Word, the Bible."

"I don't even have one."

"Here, you can borrow mine for now." Jenni reached for her faux-leather Bible and handed it to April. "I have another one at home."

"Thanks, Jenni. I'll be careful with it." April ran reverent fingers over the scrolling design etched into the soft teal cover.

Jenni beamed. "Don't worry too much, it's well-worn already."

"Okay." April cut her gaze to John. "But, um. This is kinda huge." She thumbed through the pages, eyes wide.

John took the Book in his hands and flipped the pages. "Start small. Gospel of John, book of Romans—Psalms would be good right now. Lots of encouragement there. I'll bookmark those places so they'll be easy to find."

"Okay. Thanks."

He handed back the Bible and April hugged it to her chest. "Oh you guys...thank you so much. For everything." Her eyes misted as she looked between the two of them.

Dr. Corbin strode in. "Hey there, young lady, how are you feeling? I'm actually surprised you're awake, you're usually pretty exhausted the day of a chemo treatment."

April's lips inched upward. "My body is tired, but I think my spirit just woke up."

The doctor's forehead wrinkled but he said nothing. April laughed. John's cheek twitched with a smile. The sparkle in her eyes was evident despite the deep dark circles around them. "I gave my life to Jesus today."

"Oh. Well, congratulations then. Anything that brings a patient hope is good in my book." He turned his attention to her chart. "The chemotherapy will continue working in your system for about a week, but I'd say within forty-eight hours we can test you and get a pretty accurate picture overall of how the leukemia has responded. Everything in your chart looks good though."

"And the baby?" Jenni asked.

John's eyes moved over the small roundness of April's belly, knowing her pregnancy days were few, but hoping that news could wait another day.

"We looked at the baby again today and everything looks really good."

"Well that's great news." Jenni smiled at April, who returned it.

The doctor hung her chart back up then nodded. "Okay. You hang in there and we'll see where things stand in a couple of days."

"Thank you, Dr. Corbin." John turned toward April. "We're gonna let you get some sleep now. See you tomorrow, okay? I'll be here right after work."

Jenni bent to hug April. "Welcome to the family." Her eyes shimmered as she stood and slid an arm around John's waist.

"Bye, you guys. See you tomorrow." She hugged the Bible and grinned.

John carried their coffees to the table and handed Jenni her peppermint mocha. Soft, lilting music filtered through the air as he slid into his seat in front of the gas fireplace.

"I'm still smiling about April." John pulled in a swig of hot Irish cream. "And that it was you God chose to use."

She shook her head. "I have to admit, it's pretty humbling to be in that place. Thinking back to the many times I wanted to harden my heart, but God was faithful to help me."

My sweet Jenni. "I know it's not easy. That caring about April, watching her come to the Lord…it doesn't make the situation a cake walk. But I'm so grateful that you've stuck it out with me. I don't know how I could live without you."

"Me either." Jenni smiled as she sipped her latte and licked a bit of whipped cream from her upper lip. "And you're right. It's not easy." She ran her thumb along the top of her mug before turning sober eyes on him. "I've been thinking about what's going to happen…after."

"Well, if she has the stamina to work, Chris Bowen from church has offered to give her a part time data entry position at his investment firm. Help her get on her feet."

"Yeah, and that's great. But I meant after all that, after she has the baby and therapy is entirely over… What does life look like at that point, do you think?" She broke eye contact and toyed with her paper napkin.

"Well… Honestly I haven't thought that far ahead." Maybe he should.

She slowly nodded, rubbed her lips together. "Do you think she'll stay in Riverside permanently?"

"Oh…" John had assumed April and the baby would stay close enough for him to be an involved father. Now his gut was knotting. He looked into her eyes. "Would that bother you?"

Jenni lowered her gaze and spoke into her mug. "No. I mean, I'm not sure." She took a pull of her mocha. "Don't misunderstand. I love April. I don't want her *gone*. And I want you to have full access to your child." Her throat worked. "But...I don't want to live like I'm in a bad episode of Reba. April popping over for coffee every morning or something. Waving over the fence between our side-by-side houses? I'd need a certain amount of space...if we're going to build a life of our own."

Trepidation crawled up his neck. "How much space?" He'd lost one child already. He didn't want to let this one go.

"I don't know, John. But it's something we need to talk about. I don't want to feel like the fifth wheel as you two raise your child. I know there are no feelings there, on your part at least, but you two will be connected. Forever." She lifted her eyes to his. "I admit, that scares me. I wish it didn't but it does."

John reached across the table and took her hand. With a deep breath, he prayed for the right words to ease her fears. "Jenni, you have never been, and will never be, a fifth wheel. I love you with everything I am." He pressed a kiss to her knuckles. "I will do what's right by my son or daughter, and April, but my heart is yours. No matter what our location, my relationship with you will always be a higher priority than my relationship with April. And my love for my child will never be a competition for you."

He rubbed his thumb along the back of her hand. "I know it won't be easy, but I'll always work hard at being a good husband to you, if you'll still have me."

"Of course I'll still have you. I love you. It's just that...God has strengthened me in all of this, but my heart isn't made of steel. Part of me is still terrified of facing this baby—and of living in its shadow."

"Then we'll pray, and agree to always talk about our feelings in this, and promise to listen to each other. Besides..." He lifted one corner of his mouth. "I expect we'll be making babies of our own before too long."

Red crept up her neck and stained her cheeks.

"I believe you're blushing, Miss Dupont." He wiggled his eyebrows until she laughed. But John knew the subject would still be on her mind, and could be yet another minefield to navigate.

As John entered an order for a Levadia granite countertop, his cell phone rang. He pushed back in his chair, stretching his legs beneath the desk, and checked the caller ID: Dr. Corbin.

"Hello?"

"Hello, John."

John's stomach immediately curdled at the sound of his voice. "Hey, Doc."

"I'm calling to tell you that April has developed a mild fever."

Blood pounded in John's ears. "W-what does that mean?"

"Now don't panic. We're working diligently to find the source and bringing her temperature down. But I did want to make sure you were kept aware of the situation. Can you come in after work so we can go over everything?"

Fear coiled itself in his gut. April's immune system was fragile. Vulnerable. "Yes, of course. Thank you." His voice sounded airy.

He clicked off the phone without saying goodbye, then leaned back in his chair. *What do I do?*

Prayers poured from his mind steadily over the next two hours while he finished working. He prayed more fervently as he drove down to the hospital, and he was still praying when he cornered the doctor for an update.

"The fever hasn't broken but is still low-grade. So for the moment she is okay. But we need to find the infection and bring it under control quickly. John…" He placed a firm hand on John's shoulder and looked him in the eye. "It's time. I know we'd planned on doing this later in the week, but we'll have a better chance at treating her if we deliver the baby immediately. I've already talked to her about this. She knows it's necessary. Now that you're here, we're going to start prepping her for the C-section."

John's legs went weak. *What? Now?*

He nodded as his shock dropped into his stomach and back up again. Just a couple months ago he didn't even know about this baby, and now in a matter of hours he'd be meeting it. He wasn't ready. And would April be all right?

He rubbed a fist in his palm. What was he supposed to be doing right now? He had to call Jenni.

His lungs burned as he dialed and waited for her to pick up. Oh man, this was really happening. He heard the line click on.

"Jenni? I'm at the hospital. They're prepping April for an emergency C-section."

"What? Right now? Was this planned?"

"I knew they wanted to deliver the baby soon, but it wasn't scheduled yet. It wasn't supposed to happen till then end of the week." He rubbed his temples. "But she's got a slight fever. They can treat her easier if they deliver the baby."

A soft gasp carried over the line. "Oh, no."

John closed his eyes against the fear that came with it. Everything was going to be fine. It had to be. "Can you come?"

"Of course. I'll come right down, okay?"

"Thank you. See you soon." Ending the call, John headed for April's room. She was probably wild-eyed with panic. Her door was ajar. He poked his head in and blinked. She wasn't hyperventilating or wringing the hospital sheets. Instead, April was blanketed in calm.

John approached her. "How are you?"

"I'm about to be a mother." She smiled. "I'm excited. I mean yeah, I'm nervous too. But I've been praying all day today and I can tell God is with me. I feel it somehow."

John's heart pulsed with joy. April finally knew that God was with her, not trying to punish her. He wrapped his fingers around hers. "Jenni's on her way."

"Good." She squeezed his hand, then let go. "I'd like to see her."

"So…are you ready for this?" he asked.

"Ready or not, it's time." Her brows came together. "But strangely, I do feel ready—or at least at peace with it."

A nurse entered to take April into the delivery room, and April was loaded onto a gurney for the ride down the hallway. John walked alongside as far as he was allowed, then watched her disappear behind the heavy door, fingers raised toward him in a farewell.

"I'll see you soon," He called out.

Was this really happening? It hardly felt real. Another nurse escorted John's disembodied self down another hallway and gave him some surgical scrubs so he could be in the room for the delivery. When he came out from putting them on, Jenni was there, talking with Dr. Corbin.

"John." She turned her attention to him as he joined her.

"Hey." He moved away her silky brown hair and gave her neck a squeeze. "You got here fast." Relief flooding his chest, he kissed her cheek then rubbed his hands up and down her arms. "I'm so glad you're here."

She pointed round, luminous eyes toward him. "Can you believe this? You're going to be a dad again!" Her cheerful response made him love her even more. "How is April?"

"She told me she's been praying and she can tell God is with her." He rubbed Jenni's shoulders. "She was hoping you'd make it, she wants to talk to you."

"Me? Right now?"

"Yeah. Before the delivery."

Jenni received scrubs and a mask and entered the room where April was. After a look back at him, she held the mask over her mouth and nose, and headed toward April's bedside. John watched the two of them for a moment, as if recording a movie in his mind, until the door closed on the scene.

Chapter Thirty-Nine

Jenni was shaking as she walked toward the surgical bed. Doctors and nurses were busy prepping instruments, and the metal trays and monitors confirmed the looming event. April was covered in blue hospital sheets. Her hair was tucked into a plastic cap, and tubes and wires stretched from the bed to their various sources.

Flat on her back, April pushed her chin to her chest to see Jenni as she approached. She gave a tremulous smile. "Oh, I'm so glad you're here, Jenni. I wanted to talk to you."

"What is it?" Jenni searched her face.

"Well, I…" Nervous laughter spilled out of her. "It felt important, but now I feel kind of silly."

"Don't. What did you want to talk about?" Jenni's heart drummed against her ribs as she laid a hand on the railing. The sterile, papery smell of the surgical mask filled her senses.

April's pale eyes peered up at her. "When I came here, I never expected to find… What I mean to say is, I don't think I could've gotten through all of this without you."

Jenni smiled at her.

"I don't know anyone else like you, and there's something I hope you'll be willing to do…" She paused and again lifted her gaze to Jenni's.

"Tell me." Jenni leaned closer, curiosity piquing. A nurse approached and placed an oxygen cannula in April's nose, then stepped away.

"It's about this little bean here." April's rubbed her tummy. "I know how...*difficult*...it is, me having John's baby. But I have to ask this anyway."

A shiver shot down Jenni's arms as she waited silently.

April rubbed her lips together. "If anything should go wrong...or I guess, even if it doesn't...I'd like to know you'd care for my baby. Like a godmother. Can you do that?" Her pleading eyes bore into Jenni.

Jenni's mouth opened and then closed. She blinked. Her conversation with John the previous night replayed in her mind. What had she required? *Distance.* A life of their own. Yet here was April, who had suffered so much. And John. How deeply Jenni loved him. But would Jenni be strong enough to look at this child every day and not grow bitter?

You can do all things through Christ who strengthens you.

Lord, are You telling me to say yes?

April was still waiting. Jenni smiled. "Yes. I can do that." *Oh dear God, I hope that's not a lie.* "But, you're going to be fine. You've got this."

April released the breath she'd been holding and relaxed into her pillow. "Thanks, Jenni." She reached out her hand.

Jenni took it, careful of her IV line. "You're welcome. Now, I know John is out there dying to come in and not miss anything. Should I send him in?"

"Yeah, good idea." April looked at Jenni, exchanging a thousand unspoken words.

"We're ready to begin," A nurse said.

Jenni squeezed her fingers. "Good luck."

"I don't need luck." April beamed. "I have God."

Jenni's chest warmed as she smiled and crossed the room.

John hopped to his feet. "How is she?"

"She's fine. I think they're ready for you in there now."

"Right now?" His eyes darted around the room, and a muscle in his cheek twitched. Jenni pressed her lips together to smother a chuckle.

The doctor rounded the corner and gave a terse nod. "We're ready to start, John."

Jenni took his face in her hands, holding his gaze. "Go get your baby. I'll be waiting right here."

John swallowed and nodded, then dropped a quick kiss on Jenni's lips. He tied on his surgical mask and vanished into the delivery room, leaving her alone in the hallway.

Her body pulsed with adrenaline. She was excited, nervous, amazed at the hand of God. And yet, in a small corner of her heart was the familiar sting. This was it. A few minutes and John and April would be parents. They were in there together, while Jenni waited out here alone.

Lord, help me

She wandered to the nearby waiting room and lowered herself into a hard plastic chair. She crossed her legs. Strummed the armrest. Snatched a magazine from the stack nearby, set it back down.

Studying the tiled floor, she listened to the buzz of hospital machinery coming from every direction. Her leg bounced. She crossed her arms over her chest, then ran her fingers back and forth across her bottom lip. How long did they say it would take? She paced down the hall toward April's room. Had they started yet? Shivering, Jenni pulled her sleeves down over her hands, tucking them under her arms, then returned to her seat. How much time had gone by? She checked the clock. Not even five minutes? It felt much longer.

She was going to explode.

A baby's weak cry rose above the sound of Jenni's hammering heart. She stopped breathing. Easing out of her chair onto trembling legs, she smoothed the wrinkles from her shirt. Took a timid step toward the door.

Everything was different now.

A tiny new person would call the man she loved 'Dad.' Any second, John would bust through the door with a goofy grin on his face, parental joy supplied by another woman's womb. Rubbing her forehead, she swallowed the rock in her throat.

The door swung open and jerked her attention. Jenni held her breath as John emerged, eyes gleaming. His gaze landed on her and he trotted over.

Oh, be still my beating heart. "Well?"

"It's a boy! He's beautiful, Jenni. He's perfect!"

A boy. A miniature John. Jenni's wobbly smile found its footing. "Of course he is." Somehow her voice didn't even crack. "I'm sure he's the most handsome little man this maternity ward has ever seen. He has you for a father." She winked and kept on grinning. "So...how much does he weigh? Does he have hair? I need details."

John gestured as he spoke and Jenni noted the new hospital band around his wrist. It was official, all right.

"He's tiny, but perfect—three pounds and thirteen ounces, sixteen and a quarter inches. And a full head of light hair."

Jenni's lower lip found its way to between her teeth and she wrapped her arms around John's neck. "I guess all I can say is, congratulations...Dad."

But what did that make Jenni?

"Thanks!" He beamed.

"How's April?"

"She's good, she did great. But she's pretty wiped out. They're stitching her up now but she insisted I come out here to give you the news. Jenni, it was amazing. One minute we're anxiously holding our breath, and the next minute here's my son. It's incredible."

Bittersweet feelings swirled within her. She needed boxes to sort all her emotions. "I'm so glad it all went well. You better get back in there with her until they're done. I can wait."

"Yeah, okay. But hey..." His gaze penetrated straight into her heart. "I love you."

A tight band cinched around her throat. "I love you too." She swallowed, the weight of the words heavy on her tongue.

Yes, she loved this man, this new father, and always would. No matter what happened in the past, or what lay ahead—she would love him until the day she died. She was sure of it.

And she was equally sure that the road ahead was paved in thorns.

Once April was settled into her private room, Jenni and John went in to ooh and ahh over the baby pictures John had snapped on his phone in the delivery room.

Despite her marbled emotions, Jenni couldn't help but smile. The baby lacked the chubby arms and legs of most newborns, but he was perfectly formed—ten cute fingers and ten cute toes, and plenty of hair. Jenni even recognized his daddy's forehead. Though they'd put him in the neonatal intensive care unit where his temperature could be regulated, he was breathing on his own. A major victory.

"Ready?" Nora scuttled in with a big smile, pushing a wheelchair. "I'm here to take you down to see your son."

"Oh, yes." April smiled and accepted help getting into the chair. "I want them to come, too."

"Of course."

Jenni's stomach was in her throat as she followed next to John behind the nurse as she wheeled April to the NICU.

The wheels of the portable IV rattled, and Nurse Nora's shoes squealed across the linoleum. But the racket was soon drowned out by the pounding in Jenni's head, growing louder with every step. Was she ready to see this child?

Her breaths came faster and she curled and uncurled her fingers until John took her hand. His warmth seeped into her and Jenni laced her fingers through his, sending him a wordless thank you. He lifted her hand to his lips. Could he possibly know how in love with him she was?

They arrived at their destination and John and Jenni waited outside the NICU doors while April had some time alone with her newborn. Shifting her weight from one foot to the other, Jenni pressed her fingers to her temples. Her stomach, heart, and head seemed to conspire together, all going haywire at the same time. The nurse reappeared, gave them surgical masks, and invited them in. Jenni almost declined.

John took the lead and together they drifted toward April, who sat holding a doll. At least that's what he looked like. All he wore was a diaper and hospital tags—both of which swam on him. The feeding tube in his tiny nose made him seem even more fragile. Jenni just blinked down at him. How could any baby be this small?

John stared at his son with a look of pride and wonderment. And, Jenni thought, a little bit of concern.

April smiled up at John. "Do you want to hold him?" Though her voice carried a joyful lilt, she appeared shockingly pale and feeble. The worry began dancing through Jenni's belly again.

John hesitated. "Is it all right?"

"They say it's actually good for him." April dipped her head toward the chair beside her. "Here, sit down."

John settled into the chair and April passed the baby to him like she was afraid he'd break. "The nurse says that he'll get strong faster the more he's held and has skin-to-skin contact."

John reached for the infant, and transformed right before Jenni's eyes. In that moment, he became a daddy.

April looked on as he cradled the baby against his chest, supporting the tiny head in the palm of his large hand. He sat rocking and cooing at his son, and Jenni watched with fascination. And a little bit of heartache.

She should have been the one bringing him this miracle.

She shoved away the thought. Replaying what might, or should, have been would only get her pain.

When her turn came to hold the child, she feared her wobbly arms would drop the precious cargo. But she didn't refuse the opportunity. She accepted the bundle and was stunned at how light he felt. She could barely feel him in her stiff arms at all.

"Hi, baby. I'm...Jenni." Her chest squeezed painfully. Was that all she'd be known as?

He slept on, his little eyelashes fanned out beneath his lids. The tubing taped to his cheek didn't seem to disturb his slumber in the least. His small chest rose and fell rapidly with each breath. Jenni dared to touch the tip of her finger to his velvet cheek. So soft she almost couldn't feel it.

Before long, it was time to leave him in the care of the nursing staff and get April back up to her room. To Jenni's eyes, she looked almost as small and frail as her newborn. And once she was settled into her hospital bed, April's eyes quickly drooped.

"Good night, April." John brushed her bangs off her face and pressed a kiss to the top of her head. "You were awesome today."

She gave a sleepy smile. "Thank you, John."

Jenni shifted her gaze away and forced a smile. "Good night. I'll come by tomorrow, okay?"

April blinked in response, clearly exhausted.

Out in the hall, Jenni tried to chase the chill away by rubbing her arms.

"You cold?" John wrapped an arm around her and tucked her in to his side.

"Thanks." She leaned in to him as they walked silently through the hospital and stepped out into the parking lot. She dragged in a lungful of the December night air. "What a day, huh?"

"Incredible. I'm glad you were here to share it with me."

"Of course." Jenni reached up to squeeze the hand he rested on her shoulder.

He stopped in the middle of the lot, pulled her into an embrace and placed a gentle kiss on her lips, unraveling the emotions bound inside. "I'll call you tomorrow," he whispered, locking his arms behind her back.

She nodded. "Okay. It's been a long day. I'm going to go home and get some sleep."

"Me too. Drive safe." He tapped her nose, then released her waist.

Making her way to her car, Jenni tried to bring order to the swirling mess inside her. Was it really the Lord's strength carrying her, or was she in shock and denial? Maybe staying in the thick of things—staying *busy*—was just a way to avoid processing it all. What if this was going to break her?

Exhaustion overwhelmed her as she walked through her front door. She couldn't think any more. But her mom was there on the couch waiting for her, the question in her eyes. They were still barely speaking, but Jenni wasn't up for a fight tonight. She couldn't talk to her mom, and defend John, and her decision to be with him, when she wasn't sure herself how they were going to get through this.

Her mother's eyebrows rose. "Well?"

Drawing in a breath, Jenni dug down deep and gathered all her strength to meet her gaze. "The baby was born today." She tried to put happy in her voice. *Nope, no drama here.*

Her mother's expression told her she wasn't fooled.

Jenni braced for the 'I told you so.' But instead, her mother opened her arms, and Jenni fell into them and cried like a little girl. She knew her mom would have plenty to say in the coming days, but for tonight Jenni was grateful that she held her tongue and simply stroked Jenni's hair while she sobbed into her shoulder.

Chapter Forty

Jenni's cell phone rattled her from sleep. Eyes closed, she reached out and felt around for it on her nightstand, then pushed the button to answer. "Hello?"

"Good morning." John's voice eased her awake. "Hope I didn't wake you."

Her legs stretched out under her cotton sheets and she rubbed her eyes. "That's okay," she yawned. Shaking the sleep from her head, she checked the time. Ten o'clock. "Sorry... Oh, I can't believe it's so late."

"Yeah...big day yesterday. Anyway, I'm heading down to the hospital. Just got off the phone with the doctor and wanted to give you the update."

Her ears perked. She swung her legs over the side of the bed and sat up.

"April's fever is still low-grade but they haven't been able to knock it out. Dr. Corbin wants to talk about what they're going to do next for treatment."

Would the roller coaster never end? "What can I do?" She closed her eyes.

"Pray. We've come too far—*she's* come too far—for things to go downhill now."

The slight tremble in his voice gave away his fear. Did he feel like Alice falling down the rabbit hole, like Jenni did?

"Of course—I'll put her on the church prayer chain. Call me after you talk to the doctor."

"I will. I love you. We'll get through this, Jenni. Together."

She hoped so. She wished she could put *that* on the prayer chain. Please pray that John and Jenni make it.

She sighed. "Love you too." The call ended and she wished she could lie back down, pull the covers over her head, and sleep through the coming storm. Instead, she pulled on her robe and trudged to the kitchen where she poured an extra-large cup of coffee. Then she returned to lock herself in her room and pray. Plead. Beg.

Surrender.

Two cups of java later, her phone buzzed again. She inhaled and opened her eyes, digging around in her robe pocket for her cell. John.

"News?"

"Hey, hon, I'm here. They started April on full-spectrum antibiotics and are running more tests. As soon as they knock out the fever, she'll begin the next phase of treatment."

His voice was strong, like he'd settled down to business.

"How's she holding up?"

"Resting now, but I'd like to be here when she wakes up so I'm going to stick around. If you want, you can come and sit with me in the NICU."

She'd sit with him anywhere. "Yeah, of course. I'll leave now."

After sliding into a pair of jeans and yanking a pink cotton turtleneck over her head, she grabbed her peacoat and stepped past Sadie on her way to the front door. Poor thing probably wouldn't get her walk again today.

John greeted her with a kiss in the hospital lobby. Jenni smiled, warmed by his nearness, then looked around. She'd stood here countless times over the past weeks, but the place felt different now.

Today there wasn't a pregnancy…there was a baby.

As if he sensed her thoughts, John pulled her into an embrace and rested his chin on the top of her head. She breathed in his scent, holding on to the comfort. The familiar.

His hold loosened. "Ready?"

"Yeah."

At the NICU, they went through the prerequisite wash-up before being led inside. Rows of incubators lined the wall and the cold, sterile scent of rubbing alcohol hung in the air. Medical equipment seemed to be everywhere. NICU was quieter than Jenni expected. The babies weren't crying like in the nursery upstairs. These babies lay silently in their isolettes attached to feeding tubes, some on breathing machines. The only real sound came from the beeping of monitors. Jenni's heart stirred with sadness over the uncertain future of the little ones surrounding her.

"Is it always this quiet?" She asked the nurse in a near-whisper.

"It doesn't get real loud in here, but it isn't always this quiet. The babies do cry sometimes, and it's a good thing when they do. Here he is."

The clear box stood before them. John's son on display. Bees buzzed in Jenni's stomach.

"Hey, little man." John reached in and stroked a tiny arm through one of the holes in the incubator. The baby squirmed and grimaced before settling back into sleep.

"It's time for his feeding, would you like to try?" The nurse gave John a bright smile. "He's still struggling a little with his ability to suck but he's really coming along. We hope he won't need that feeding tube for long. Maybe even by tomorrow."

"Yeah, okay." John settled into a chair and the nurse instructed him on how to hold the bottle and the baby. A lump lodged in Jenni's throat. She watched the scene as if she were standing on the other side of the glass window looking in. She wasn't part of this magic, but it was a beautiful thing to watch. She took the chair beside John's and clasped her hands in her lap.

John took the little one and nestled him into the crook of his arm, then held the bottle to his lips, twisting it back and forth to encourage the little guy to suck. John looked like a natural. The baby made a couple half-hearted attempts to drink, each time losing suction after a second or two. Formula trickled from around the bottle nipple, down the sides of his mouth.

"Keep at it," the nurse said. "Even if most of it spills, let him practice. I'll be back in a minute."

John shifted as the nurse walked away, leaving him on his own. More milk rolled down the baby's chin. With John's hands full and nobody else there but Jenni, she reached for the cloth and bent to dab the baby's little face clean. The action drew a response from the infant and he took a couple of good long sucks from the bottle, with much less spilling out his mouth. Jenni sat transfixed. The little cheeks, the little nose. He was so amazing to watch.

Clearing her throat, she turned aside to swipe at a stray tear that had appeared on her cheek, then let herself get lost in the sight unfolding before her. .

She looked up to find John watching her. A corner of his mouth tipped. "Do you want to try?" He nodded toward the baby. Her stomach leaped. Before she knew it, she was being handed a tiny person to feed.

The feel of him in her arms stirred embers in her that she never knew burned. A rush of other-worldly warmth swept through her chest.

This is surreal. Is this normal? My fiancé's newborn child… Lord, how am I supposed to feel?

"Come on, little guy, time to eat." Jenni spoke softly, parting his lips with the bottle. He wiggled and blinked, opening his eyes and fixing them on her. His mouth opened and took the bottle, then closed around it, and still he watched her. She stared back into his eyes—John's eyes—in awe. What did he see when he looked at her? His little eyelids shut again as his mouth worked the bottle. Light and warmth and sweetness swirled together inside her.

As he fed, Jenni stroked his tiny leg with her thumb. She drew in a soul-deep breath and whispered to him. "You are so precious."

The nurse returned, crossed her arms over her chest, and smiled. "You did good."

Jenni lifted her head to see both John and the nurse watching her with grins on their faces.

"It's time to get him back under the bili-lights."

"Okay." Jenni set the bottle down and John dabbed his mouth. The incredible moment came to an end as the nurse took him, leaving Jenni's arms feeling strangely empty.

When they reached April's room, she was just waking up.

"Morning." She sounded weak, but greeted them with a smile.

She waved them into the chairs near her bed. "Oh you guys…I had the most amazing dream. Jesus was in the room with me, watching me sleep. Then in my dream I woke up and He talked to me. He told me not to be afraid because He was with me and wouldn't leave me." Her eyes shone. "I never knew the love I was missing out on. All this time I didn't even think He was real, let alone that I could have a relationship with Him. So many wasted years." She shook her head. "I don't want to waste one more minute."

John and Jenni shared a smile, energized by her excitement. Jenni reached for the Bible on the table beside her. "Let's dive in, then."

April grinned and gingerly straightened herself in the bed.

John read aloud from the Bible, pausing so they could talk about passages they found especially moving. And then they prayed together.

A rap at the door drew their collective gaze to where the nurse was ushering herself in. "Do you feel up to holding the baby awhile? Now would be a good time on his schedule, unless you'd rather we wait."

April's eyes glowed. "Yes. I'm aching to see him."

The walk down to NICU didn't feel as treacherous to Jenni as yesterday. Inside the unit, April's face lit up when she saw her baby, and Jenni's cheeks lifted in a smile. How could she not feel her joy? They approached his isolette, and April trailed her fingers gently over the glass before the nurse opened it and scooped up the infant. Once April had pillows tucked all around her and the baby safely snuggled in her arms, the nurse stepped away.

Jenni leaned down and ran the back of her finger down his tiny arm. "He's beautiful, April. You did good."

"Thanks." Her eyes crinkled with her smile. "He is adorable, isn't he?" A tear slipped down her cheek and she wiped it away, laughing. "Look at me," she said, "I'm crying just thinking about how amazing he is."

"He still needs a name," John said.

"I was thinking Joshua. Do you like it?"

"Joshua…" John drew his lips together and looked toward the ceiling. "Good name. I like it."

April pressed her lips to Joshua's forehead. Starting at his head, she ran her hand over his body, caressing his tummy, his fingers, as if reveling in the feel of him. Mother and child were bonding in such a beautiful way, completely enthralled with each other. April let out a soft laugh, then smiled at Jenni, her eyes glistening. Jenni blinked back at her, nothing but happiness in her heart. April bit her lip, shook her head, and returned her gaze to her son.

When April's energy was spent, they escorted the worn-out mommy to her room so she could rest.

"I wish I didn't have to leave him down there," April said.

"Yes, I know it's tough. But we're taking good care of him." The nurse put the foot rests down on the wheelchair and supported April under her arms as she moved back to the bed. "There you are. You need your rest just like your boy."

"Thank you." April gave the nurse a soft, heavy-lidded smile. The nurse patted her hand then wheeled the chair out the door.

The moment she was gone, Dr. Corbin stepped into the room. His shoulders seemed a bit more rounded, his steps slow, and Jenni found her mouth suddenly going dry. Holding his clipboard, the doctor took up a chair near the bed then cleared his throat. "I'm afraid I have some news you won't like to hear."

Corbin was always a straight-shooter. But now he looked down and tapped a pen against the chart he held. Jenni's skin itched. She slid her hand into John's and tried to swallow.

The doctor pressed his lips together and gave a slight shake of his head. The wrinkles etched around his mouth seemed to deepen as he raised his eyes to April's. "The progress we'd made with your treatment…well, we've lost some ground. Your blood counts are off, quite significantly."

The air was sucked out of the room. Jenni tried to fill her lungs, her mind snagged on the words *lost some ground* and *significantly.*

Dr. Corbin cut his eyes to John, and then spoke again directly to April. His tone was not unkind, but businesslike. "We'll keep working to fight whatever infection is causing your fever, but we can't start you on your next phase of chemotherapy until we get that under control."

Reality blurred and the floor seemed to be dropping out from beneath her. Releasing John's hand, Jenni felt behind her for a chair, gripped the armrest, and sank down.

Oh, Jesus…

John ran his hands through his hair then over his mouth. Jenni watched him trudge over to the window and lean against his forearm, his free hand planted on his waist. His expression was unreadable, his thoughts far away.

April stared blankly at the doctor and then nodded. None of them, it seemed, had words.

Dr. Corbin reached out with a large, age-spotted hand, and squeezed April's shoulder. "I'll be back later to talk more."

And then he was gone.

Yea though I walk through the valley of the shadow of death, I will fear no evil...

John pushed off from the wall and grasped Jenni's hand. "Let's pray."

Nodding, Jenni rose and wiped her sweaty palms on her legs. She and John stood on either side of April's bed and they all joined hands, forming a circle. John led them in prayer, and with all the confidence she could round up, Jenni stroked April's hand, trying to infuse her with peace.

"Don't worry, God is in control." Platitudes. But they were all she had at the moment.

"Thanks so much, you guys." April smiled, forced or not, Jenni couldn't tell. "I'm really tired; I think I'm going to sleep."

"Okay," John answered. "We'll check in on you later."

Jenni and John eased down the halls toward the hospital exit in silence. A biting wind swirled around them as they walked through the lot. Jenni shivered and wrapped her fingers around his arm. They stopped in front of his Camry and he pushed the button on his key to unlock the door.

"I'm parked farther down that way." Jenni pointed to her right.

"Want me to give you a lift?"

She nodded and climbed into his car. John started the engine but didn't shift into gear. He gripped the steering wheel hard and stared out the windshield. The muscles of his jaw contracted. He was turning in on himself. He looked just like he had the night he'd rear-ended Jenni's car. Scared, guilty. His eyes skittered across the dashboard.

Jenni touched his shoulder. "John?"

"Yeah."

"You've been lost in thought since Dr. Corbin's visit. More so than usual. What were you thinking up in April's room just now, when you were staring out the window?"

He turned his gaze to her, then looked away. "I'd rather not say."

"Why?" Jenni ran her fingers through the sandy blond hair at his temples.

His chest expanded, then released. His eyes met hers. "I was thinking…" He jetted a breath through his nose. "I needed a drink." He shook his head. "The thought just popped into my head, and it scared me." His eyes darkened with sadness. "I'm an alcoholic, Jenni. I'll probably always struggle with the pull when things get hard. I thought it was behind me, a season of recklessness that I came out from months ago. But now, I don't think I'll ever be safe from it." He turned from her, jaw tensed as he stared ahead.

Jenni reached over and turned his face back toward her. "Then it will keep you dependent on Jesus. Which will make you an even better husband."

He closed his eyes. "It's a label I never wanted, never thought I'd own."

"Labels shmabels. Have you forgotten we all struggle with sin and temptation?" Her thoughts flitted to her own struggles, and she ran her fingers over the scruff on his cheeks. "Don't let Satan paralyze you with shame. That's what will make you want to pull away. From God and from me. So dust yourself off and accept the fact that you're surrounded with love and support. The only label you need to care about is *child of God*." She smiled. "*Jenni's fiancé* isn't a bad one either."

He smiled back. "I do like that one." His eyes dimmed and he combed his fingers through her hair. "I just wanted to be a better man for you."

"John…there *is* no better man for me." She leaned forward and drew him into a languid kiss.

Nope. No better man existed.

Chapter Forty-One

Jenni rubbed her eyes and squinted to make out the time. The display screen on her phone sharpened into focus. Two a.m. and John's name was flashing across the screen.

Her heart flew to her throat and adrenaline jolted her fully awake. "Hello?"

"Jenni, the hospital just called." Panic laced his voice, and the blood drained from Jenni's face. "The fever spiked. They said it's not looking good," his voice cracked, "and to get down there right away. She's asking for both of us."

Feeling instantly sick, Jenni sucked in one breath, then another. Her head swam. She closed her eyes and gulped air as a deep foreboding rattled in her spirit. *Oh, Jesus, give me strength. Please, give me strength.*

"I'm getting dressed now." She threw the covers off her legs and jumped up.

"I'm on my way to pick you up."

"I'll be ready."

Silence filled the car on the way to the hospital. Jenni stared out the passenger window and ran her fingers along her bottom lip. John pulled into a parking space, cut the engine, and paused, looking out over the steering wheel. When he reached for the door handle, Jenni placed her hand on his arm. She looked into his eyes, not knowing what to say but hoping he understood. He worked his jaw, then opened the door.

Clutching sweaty hands, they arrived at April's room. Several hospital staff buzzed around her bed, checking monitors and working with her IV drip. Jenni's stomach clenched. April looked tiny, her complexion pallid, as she caught sight of them and smiled. The nurses saw them too. They nodded and left the room.

"Hey guys," April's voice was so small. Thready.

"Hey yourself," John answered.

Jenni bent and wrapped her arms around April's slight shoulders. Holding on for several heartbeats, Jenni tried to tame the emotions stampeding through her heart.

April rubbed her back. "Hey now, it's okay," she whispered. "It'll be all right."

Releasing April from her embrace, Jenni looked into her eyes and saw no ounce of fear. She swallowed against the ache in her throat. "How are you feeling?"

"I'm fine, really." She gave a weak smile. "God is here with me. I can feel Him so strongly—right now, in this room with us." Her eyes roamed the room then settled back on Jenni.

Jenni pressed her lips together and nodded.

"Jenni, I'm not afraid. I have peace because I know that Joshua is okay, and that I'll be going to meet Jesus. I know what lies ahead, where I'm going, and all I can do is thank God He sent you two into my life when He did. You've done so much for me." Her eyes darted between the two of them. "But…I do have more to ask of you both."

She slid a thin stack of envelopes out from her Bible and held them with both hands. "I've written a couple letters. Just some things I needed to say. There's one for my old roommate, Stacy, and for Robert, and one for my mom. If anyone can find her. And there's one for Joshua."

Jenni's legs were shaking. She wanted to cut April off and tell her to stop talking like this, but everyone in that room knew it was time.

"John." April pinned him with her eyes and he moved closer. "Raise him right. Be there for him. Protect him. Tell him every day that you love him. Teach him about Jesus."

"I will," John croaked. He cleared his throat and blinked rapidly.

"Tell him about me. Tell him I loved him very much." Tears fell from her lashes and rolled down her cheeks. Her face contorted as she struggled to finish. "Tell him I'm s-sorry I had to leave him. Make sure he knows that someday I'll hold him again. Let him know th-that it's okay if he feels mad at me sometimes—I think God understands, and so do I."

She ran trembling fingertips under her eyes. "John, don't let him *ever* feel like a mistake. Tell him…he is the greatest thing his mother ever did. And tell him God used h-him to bring me to Jesus."

John nodded, and pressed a knuckle to each of his eyes.

"Jenni," April took her hand and squeezed it tight, her gaze slicing into Jenni's soul, "I know this is hard, but please… *Please* love my son." She pulled in a labored breath. "Raise him as your own. He needs a mother and I…can't be there. Please be his mama. I need to know you'll hold him when he cries at night, kiss his elbow when he falls, read him bedtime stories. I'm begging you…take him into your heart and give him all the love I won't be here to give."

The band around Jenni's sternum was unbearably tight as April took John's hand too, the three of them now connected in profound ways far beyond the touch of their fingers. "Be a family, you guys. Give Joshua that. Give *me* that before we say goodbye."

The weight of her words hung heavy in Jenni's heart. Raise her child? Be a family? The reality of April's condition was barely beginning to sink in, and now a new burden was placed on top of Jenni's weary spirit. Could she do it? She knew the 'Christian' thing to do was to shout, 'Of course!' But the reality wouldn't be so easy. Yet she knew, despite her fears, that she could do nothing else.

Jenni busied herself with a tissue, dabbing her eyes, while John made his promises to do all that April asked and then some. He hugged her and pressed a kiss to her temple.

April looked back at her again, waiting. Jenni pasted on a smile and nodded, too shell-shocked to speak.

A weary, yet satisfied smile stretched across April's ashy features as she sank back on her pillow. Her eyes closed. "Thank you," she whispered. She was asleep within seconds, her breathing shallow but even. Who knew how much longer she had? The staff filtered back in to do whatever it was they had to, and John and Jenni ambled toward the door.

Out in the hall, John pulled Jenni to his chest. He wrapped his powerful arms around her shoulders and pressed his cheek to the top of her head. Through the mournful silence, Jenni listened to his pounding heart and fought for balance. This couldn't be real. It didn't seem right. After everything…

John stroked her hair and pressed his lips to her forehead. "Let's go see Joshua." His voice broke on a whisper.

Jenni let him lead the way, his fingers laced through hers, as she continued blinking and sniffing. Her lungs were opening easier by the time they approached the NICU and Jenni pulled John to a stop. "John, wait. It's the middle of the night. I can't go in, I don't have twenty-four hour privileges." She touched the hospital band on John's wrist. "I'm not a parent."

John's brow creased as he weighed her words. His gaze traveled to the NICU doors.

Jenni's heart clenched, her throat tightening again. "It's all right. You go in and I'll wait here."

"That won't be necessary." One of the night nurses approached and ushered both of them toward the scrub station. "April explained the situation earlier. And there's nobody else in there visiting right now. It's fine."

John thanked the nurse and pumped antibacterial soap into his hands. Jenni pulled up her sleeves and started scrubbing up to her elbows. A moment later, they entered and Jenni followed John toward the bank of isolettes, to Joshua's designated area.

The moment she saw him asleep in his incubator, that strange, warm sensation spread through her chest. Joshua's eyes were covered with a miniature sleep mask, shielding him from the bili-lights shining overhead. A tiny knit cap covered his head. His fragile, bare chest rose and fell in steady rhythm. Jenni stared at his tiny form, studying every detail of him.

Mother, behold your son.

She sucked in her breath and blinked. *Lord...?*

Bending toward the infant before her, she took in his delicate features. She reached inside and stroked his cheek with the tips of her fingers.

Mother, behold your son!

She gasped and straightened. The shout in Jenni's spirit felt so loud she cast a look around her, surprised the whole room wasn't echoing with the sound of it. The message beat hard on the carefully-constructed walls of her heart until they came crashing down in a thunderous rush.

Blood whooshed in her ears. Her hand flew to her mouth. The other gripped her middle. From the corner of her eye, she saw John watching her. He cocked his head and pulled his brows together while she swallowed back a sob.

"Jenni? What is it?" John drew closer and rubbed her back.

"John..." She locked onto his eyes. "That's my son!"

John's brow smoothed and he pulled Jenni to his chest. He rested his cheek against the crown of her head and spoke in a choked whisper. "That's *our* son."

Jenni shoulders jerked. They clung to each other, then turned to gaze at the tiny, sleeping baby before them.

They stayed a while longer with Joshua then returned to April's floor. The elevator doors opened and Jenni took a fortifying breath as they made their way down the hall back to her room.

The doctor met them at the door. "John. Jenni." He looked them in the eyes and shook his head. "There's nothing more we can do for her. I'm afraid this is the end." His ever-calm eyes were now red and held...grief. "It's time to say goodbye."

Right now? So quickly? Fear snaked down Jenni's spine.

"Thank you, doctor," John managed.

"You know, I've never seen anything quite like what I've witnessed between you three. April told me...that it was all God's doing. I have to say I think she's right." He nodded. "Let me know if you need anything. Good night."

Jenni banished the ice coursing through her veins as they entered the room. A nurse was turning off one of the monitors but ducked out as John and Jenni pulled their chairs up to the side of April's bed. Jenni's brows knit together as she watched her shallow breathing. She leaned close and brushed the hair back from April's face. She really was beautiful.

April lifted her hand several inches off the bed, and John took hold of it. "We're here, April. We're both right here."

"That's right." Jenni stroked April's fingers and tried not to cry. Not in front of her. "We won't leave."

"Thank...you."

Minutes passed. Jenni bowed her head to hide her emotions. Oh, Lord, why? Why? Her heart felt like it would burst.

"John..." April turned her head toward them, fixing her eyes on him.

He sniffed and met her gaze. "Yes?"

"I...love you."

Jenni's belly twisted, but she couldn't feel mad. John pressed a kiss to April's hand.

"You too...Jenni."

Jenni's heart cracked wide open and tears fell from her lashes. "I love you, April. Don't be afraid."

"Not...afraid." She turned her face back toward the ceiling and closed her eyes, the trace of a smile on her lips. "Have Jesus."

"And He has you." Jenni caressed the back of April's hand, a mixture of sorrow and joy washing over her.

She and John stayed at April's bedside as she slipped into Heaven. The room fell silent. At last they released April's hands and gingerly laid them at her sides. They both shed tears. The empty ache in Jenni's heart was matched by a fullness she couldn't describe. For a very long time, neither of them spoke. There was nothing to say.

Finally, they stood. John wrapped an arm around Jenni's shoulder as she trailed her fingers over the back of April's hand one more time. "Goodbye, April."

They returned to the NICU. Jenni's nose was sore and her eyes puffy, but her tears were dry for now. Pulling the baby close, she kissed his head and breathed in his scent. "Hi, sweetheart...I'm going to be your mama."

John slid his hand under Jenni's hair and massaged her neck as he looked on. He'd have to wait his turn, Jenni wasn't through snuggling her boy.

"I love you." She rocked little Joshua, soaking her heart in the feel of him. Jenni had experienced more in the last eight months than she'd ever imagined she would in a lifetime.

A dream for her future was replaced by an inconceivable new reality. She'd fallen in love, had her heart torn in two, faced old demons, and wrestled with the Lord. But God had not forsaken her. He knew what blessings He had in store from the beginning. The grace in the flames. Now she sat holding a soft, warm baby—her son—while her husband-to-be looked on. Though still reeling, Jenni could clearly see the hand of God working throughout everything, and she rejoiced at the way He had given joy through the sorrow.

Epilogue

Fifteen months later

John plated some beans and rice then went in search of Jenni. He found her pushing her way through their guests, wide-eyed, and carrying the cutest little boy on the planet.

"Honey, he walked!" She laughed. "All the way across the lawn! He let go of Christy's fingers and just...wobbled his way toward me. He did it—isn't it amazing?"

John released his breath in a chuckle then raked a hand through his hair. "Yeah, that's incredible!" He traded the plate for the child and tossed him above his head. "I can't believe it—you're growing up so fast."

"Yeah, our baby is becoming such a big boy. Aren't you?" Jenni scooped a bean and a few grains of rice onto her forefinger and fed it to Joshua. After shooting a quick glance around them, she lowered her voice. "Should we do it soon?"

John gave a conspiratorial nod.

"Okay. I haven't said hi to Natalie yet. I'll meet you up front." Squeezing his arm, she glided away toward her friend to play hostess.

John nibbled on Joshua's fingers, then planted a big, loud kiss into his neck, eliciting a giggle. Though small, Joshua was healthy and suffered no major complications due to his premature birth or mother's chemo. When adjusted for gestational age, he was hitting all his milestones right on target, to the delight of his doctors and his parents.

Sadie trotted from one person to the next, tongue lolling from her happy muzzle. As Christy bent to scratch Sadie's ears, John approached his cousin-to-be with a smile. "Christy, can you take him for a minute?"

"Of course." Christy reached for Joshua and hoisted him onto her hip, giving his chin a tickle. "Who's your favorite auntie?"

Joshua smiled and shoved his fingers in his mouth, sending a wave of tender warmth washing over John.

Across the Dupont's yard, a cluster of church friends stood near the Taco Man's cart, laughing and chatting. Derek handed a glass to Tori, and John smirked. Those two both seemed clueless about how good they were for each other. But John had watched them interact over the months and knew it was only a matter of time before they figured it out.

Stepping onto the makeshift stage—a quickly assembled collection of plywood planks and hinges—John lifted a glass and tapped a spoon against the edge until he had everyone's attention. "Thank you all for being here today. It means a great deal to Jenni and me."

Sidling up beside him, Jenni slid her hand into his and squeezed.

"I'm especially happy that my mom could be here, flying in all the way from Indiana. Love you, Mom." He nodded her direction, his gaze taking in her form—hands clasped under her chin, blonde hair neatly tucked behind her ears, eyes glowing. Her mouth moved in silent prayer, but this time, John knew it was a prayer of gratitude.

Beside her, Laura and Mary wore expectant smiles and John shot up his own prayer of thanks that God had softened Laura's heart enough to accept him. Christy shifted Joshua to the other side as he made a grab for her cheek.

"You must have all been confused why we planned this dinner, nearly a month out from the wedding. Well, it's because this actually has nothing to do with the wedding. Jenni, do you want to tell them?"

"Yes." She let go of his hand and took a step away. "We're very excited." Her hands signed along with her spoken words. "Watching me use ASL is a familiar sight to everyone in this room. Most of you know that I've had a dream to work with the deaf community through music. John came along and put feet to that dream. John…" She turned to him, eyes sparkling, and John tried to focus on her hands as much as her voice as she addressed him directly. "Thank you. If it weren't for you and Hannah's Harmonies, we wouldn't be here today, about to make this announcement. I love you more than words—or hands—could say."

John answered in silent ASL, *I love you too.*

Jenni turned back toward the rest of the room. "So here is the big news. As of yesterday, our organization, Feel the Music—Therapeutic Music for the Deaf, is an officially recognized non-profit service and set to begin working with its first clients on Monday!"

As the room erupted in applause, Jenni covered her smile with both hands and doubled over in laughter. John bit back his smile as he watched the pure joy on her face.

He held up his hands. "This woman right here, that light in her eyes…she loves people. I've never met a woman with a greater capacity to reach beyond herself and love others."

He coughed against the sudden constriction of his throat as April's face came to mind. "And for some insane reason, she's chosen to love me. No clue why." She leaned into him and playfully slugged his arm. "But I know this program is more a ministry than a job or anything else, and with Jenni's heart leading the way, it's going to do a lot of good for a lot of people. And I also know…" His gaze paused on his mother's then travelled to Jenni's, "I know that Hannah would be very pleased."

Jenni's lips curved slowly and she reached a hand behind his neck, bringing his mouth to hers. Her softness, her goodness, the headiness of the moment, worked exquisite magic over his lips and through his body and soul. God, he loved this woman.

"Woo!" Tori's voice broke through the haze, followed by someone's slow clap.

"Nice, bro!" Isaiah yelled then cat-called. The rest of the guests began laughing and Derek's loud whistle pierced the air.

"How many weeks till the honeymoon?" someone shouted. He scanned until he found the source: Laura.

John smiled. Two weeks, six days, and twenty hours. But who was counting?

AUTHOR'S NOTE

Dear Reader,

Thank you for taking this journey with me through the lives of John, Jenni, and April. Their story has been with me for many years, and I am grateful for the chance to now share it with you. I pray that something in these pages spoke to your heart as deeply as it did to mine.

When I first "met" these characters, I was struck by the idea of how difficult and refining it would be to love someone through such a deeply traumatic situation as theirs. What would that be like? If God asked it of me, could I respond the way Jenni did? Probably not, but she inspires me to dig down deep and let God have his way with me.

Writing this story challenged me to answer tough questions about my own faith. How do I respond when life gets hard? Do I become resentful and pull away from God, or do I surrender to His will? I pray to have a heart like Job's that answers "the Lord gave and the Lord has taken away. Blessed be the name of the Lord," rather than the heart of the prodigal who fled from his father's shelter and provision.

It's so easy to sing "I Surrender All" until you're asked to surrender what's most precious. As I wove the details of this story together, God revealed my own weaknesses and areas I struggle to surrender to Him. I'll be honest, I still struggle. But I cling to God's promise that "He who began a good work in me will be faithful to complete it." Sometimes we are very slow to learn, but God is so patient! And *Grace in the Flames* has reminded me of our Father's perfect love, and ability to take us through any storm in life if only we will cling to Him.

Let that truth take root in your heart today as well.

~ Michelle

READING GROUP GUIDE

1. Were the characters convincing? Believable? Compelling? Which one do you identify with most, and why?

2. Have you ever been guilty of believing something good in your life was due to your own moral superiority?

3. John feels pressured to respond a certain way as a Christian, compelling him to hide his deep struggles and questions in the wake of losing his family. Do you believe this to be a common and accurate experience within the church? Have you ever walked through a difficult time where you felt you could not expose how you really felt to your Christian friends? Did it make you feel alone?

4. The Israelites set up "stones of remembrance" after crossing the Jordan, as a testament to God's faithfulness to them during their wilderness wandering. (Joshua 3 and 4) The stones served as both a personal reminder and a testimony to others. Jenni's bracelet fills the same role, reminding her of what God had saved her from and enabling her to share that message with John and Christy. Have you set up any "stones of remembrance" for yourself? Some tangible thing that helps you recall intimate moments with the Lord?

5. Does your faith suffer in difficult times? How do you deal with that? Did John's story resonate with you regarding the idea of surrender?

6. Has God ever called you to love someone that you didn't think you ever could?

7. April believes that God couldn't possibly care about her, other than to punish her. Why do you think we have such a hard time believing God loves us? How can we help one another overcome this lie?

8. Jenni struggled with the temptation to self-harm. This is an epidemic in our society, even within the church. Why do you think there is a pull toward this, and how can we help those suffering with this?

9. John numbed his pain with alcohol and still finds himself lured to it in times of great turmoil. Why do you think that Christians are drawn to their vices even after coming to faith? Did you find encouragement in these pages regarding your own weaknesses and the way they can cause you to depend more fully on God?

10. What passage from the book stood out to you?

11. Have you had a life changing revelation from this text?

ACKNOWLEDGMENTS

This book would never have seen the light of day had I been alone in the task. My deepest gratitude goes out to everyone who had a hand in it. After eight years, there are a lot of you.

To my husband, Mike, for your encouragement from day one, for listening to me talk endlessly about plot and character arcs, for cheering my milestones and comforting me in my setbacks; for using your mad skillz to create imaginary book covers, magazine headlines, and book trailers, all of which show me how much you care, it is a great honor to be your wife. I love you.

To Brandon, Kaitlyn, Amy, and Trevor—you've pretty much grown up watching me write this story. Thank you for being so patient with me. I'm happy I get to show you what a realized dream looks like.

To my mom, Shawn, for being my biggest fan and staunchest supporter. Thank you for believing in this story and having just as much passion for it as I do. And to Kris, you're a rock for our family.

To my critique partners, April Gardner and Jessica Patch, I am so fantastically blessed to have each of you in my life. You've stuck with me through more drafts than anyone has a right to, knocked me upside the head when I wanted to throw in the towel, and are never afraid to say "you can do better." I don't know what I'd do without you!

To Tracy Baber, one of the first readers outside my family to read that early draft chapter by chapter, and come running to me every church service begging for more. Your enthusiasm truly propelled me, and to this day is a highlight of my journey.

To Delia Latham, Cathy Bryant, Carol Moncado, Jessica Keller, Joanna Politano, Jacki Newbery, thanks for always cheering me on from the earliest days and right up to the finish line.

To my beta readers, friends, and street team, for being my guinea pigs and helping me launch this book.

Nikki Grimes, Karen Ball, and Tammy Barley—thank you for the wisdom you poured into me.

And finally, to Jesus, who, for reasons unknown, rejoices over me with singing. Thank you for weaving the story of my life into something beautiful.

ABOUT THE AUTHOR

MICHELLE MASSARO writes contemporary fiction soaked in grace. She makes her home in Southern California with her husband of over two decades and their four children. She's dabbled in homeschooling, teaching Creation Science, Jr. High Bible studies, and leading worship. She has a wide range of tastes and among her favorite stories are C.S. Lewis' The Chronicles of Narnia, and Francine Rivers' The Mark of the Lion series. When she isn't tinkering with words, she enjoys old Rogers and Hammerstein movies, making kefir, and Sudoku. A new lipstick and a good French roast always make her happy.

BETTER THAN FICTION
Coming April 2016

Romance novelist Meghan Townsend's marriage is slipping, and no amount of prayer seems to help. She aims to recapture her husband's waning attention by getting in shape and finds escape by crafting her own fictional love story. Taking inspiration for the hero from a new friend—the attractive, spiritual, and attentive Curtis Jameson—she pours her yearnings onto the page, and craves the kind of pulse-pounding romance found in her book, *Racing Hearts*…

In 1916 Corona, California, motorcars are all the rage, and racing them is what Meghan's hero, Russell Keegan, does best. But when his competition vandalizes his car, the only mechanic available is a greasy woman in a man's overalls.

After a racing accident claimed her father's life, Winifred became the sole breadwinner for her family. She is disdained as a female mechanic, but her daddy's trade is all she has left. Can she swallow her hatred of the races and take up Russell's offer of big bucks to fix his car, or will she lose everything to mounting debt?

Under Meghan's skillful pen, these two embark on a thrilling, adventurous romance. But she finds that writing those loves scenes with Curtis's face in mind takes her heart places it shouldn't go. Will she realize in time that real life can be better than fiction?

PREVIEW CHAPTER ON NEXT PAGE

Chapter One

Corona, CA, Present Day

Meghan laced her fingers in front of her face and listened to the ceiling fan whir. Looking past the dancing dust particles, she stared through the window behind her computer screen, vaguely aware of the hum of little-girl voices and the thump-thump-thump of the clothes dryer down the hall. Biting the inside of her cheek, she nested her chin atop her hands and closed her eyes.

The scene rolled behind her closed lids, like a movie. The camera of her mind panned across the 1916 Stutz Bearcat—the shiny red paint, the long steering column, the red wheel spokes. She focused on the hero until she saw the flecks of green in his eyes and the smudge of grease on his shirt. Watched him check the street sign as he walked down the sidewalk, searching for something. Desperate.

Determination shot through her own veins . . .

Okay, good. She felt it. Time to make her readers feel it too. She opened her eyes and positioned her fingers . . .

        Walked. Strutted. Plodded—

"Mommy!" The little voice came from behind. "Faith pinched me and called me a jerk."

        Stomped.   Russell   stomped   down   the
        street . . .

Ooh, wait! Meghan backspaced one more time.

        Slapped the pavement . . .

"Mom, are you listening? Tell her to stop being mean to me."

"Yeah, sweetie, give me a minute. I have to finish this line." Meghan tossed the words over her shoulder, keeping her eyes on the monitor. The perfect phrasing eluded her, like a needle in a . . . forget the cliché. She'd get the rough sketch down first, then go back and dress it up. Her eighty-word-per-minute fingers flew across the keyboard.

`Russell Keegan's loafers slapped the pavement. The only sound on that empty street. The town was dead by six p.m.`

"Nobody ever listens to me! You don't even care!" Zoey's voice broke, and a whimper-and-sniff drifted to Meghan's ears.

"I do too care. Be patient." She raised her voice. "Faith, quit picking on your sister."

From the end of the hall, Faith wailed. "But that's not f-a-i-r! She's the one being mean to *me*. She took my fuzzy pencil that she *knows* I didn't want her to touch, and she didn't even ask."

Though tempted to charge to the bedroom and bust some heads, Meghan remained in her seat. She swiveled her chair and tightened her lips into a thin line. "You two better knock it off before I lose my patience! I'm trying to focus here."

"You always say that."

"I always mean it." Meghan tried to read the line she'd been working on a moment ago, before she lost her place in the haystack. The dryer buzzed. She blocked it out.

"I'm hungry."

"It's only four thirty." Meghan kept typing.

`Dead like his chances of winning the Corona Road Race . . . unless he could find a mechanic.`

As if burdened by the falling economy, a mortgage, and two car payments, Zoey dragged herself over to her mother's side. "I'm b-o-o-o-r-e-d." The whine curled like barbed tendrils around Meghan's eardrums.

Her shoulders and neck tightened, and a twitch threatened her left eyelid. She pinched the bridge of her nose. This child was going to be the death of her. Or at least the death of her novel.

Drawing in a slow, deliberate breath, Meghan looked her youngest daughter in the eye. "If you promise to be a good girl, I'll let you turn on the TV and watch two episodes of *Veggie Tales*. Then I'll start dinner, okay?"

Zoey's blue eyes brightened as she bobbed her little blonde head. "Okay, I promise."

With her five-year-old settled into the beanbag in the family room, giggling at Larry the Cucumber, Meghan plopped back into her office-in-the-dining-room chair, cracked her knuckles, and somehow found her way back into *Racing Hearts*. . .

STAY IN THE KNOW WITH MICHELLE'S NEWSLETTER

Opt in at: **http://eepurl.com/bPQL0T**

You'll receive behind-the-scenes news on covers, new releases, contests, FREE books, and information on how you can be part of Michelle's next Launch Team!

<u>Connect on social media</u>:

<u>Facebook</u>:   MichelleMassaroBooks

<u>Twitter</u>:   @MLMassaro

<u>Instagram</u>:   Michelle Massaro Books

Made in the USA
Columbia, SC
13 February 2022